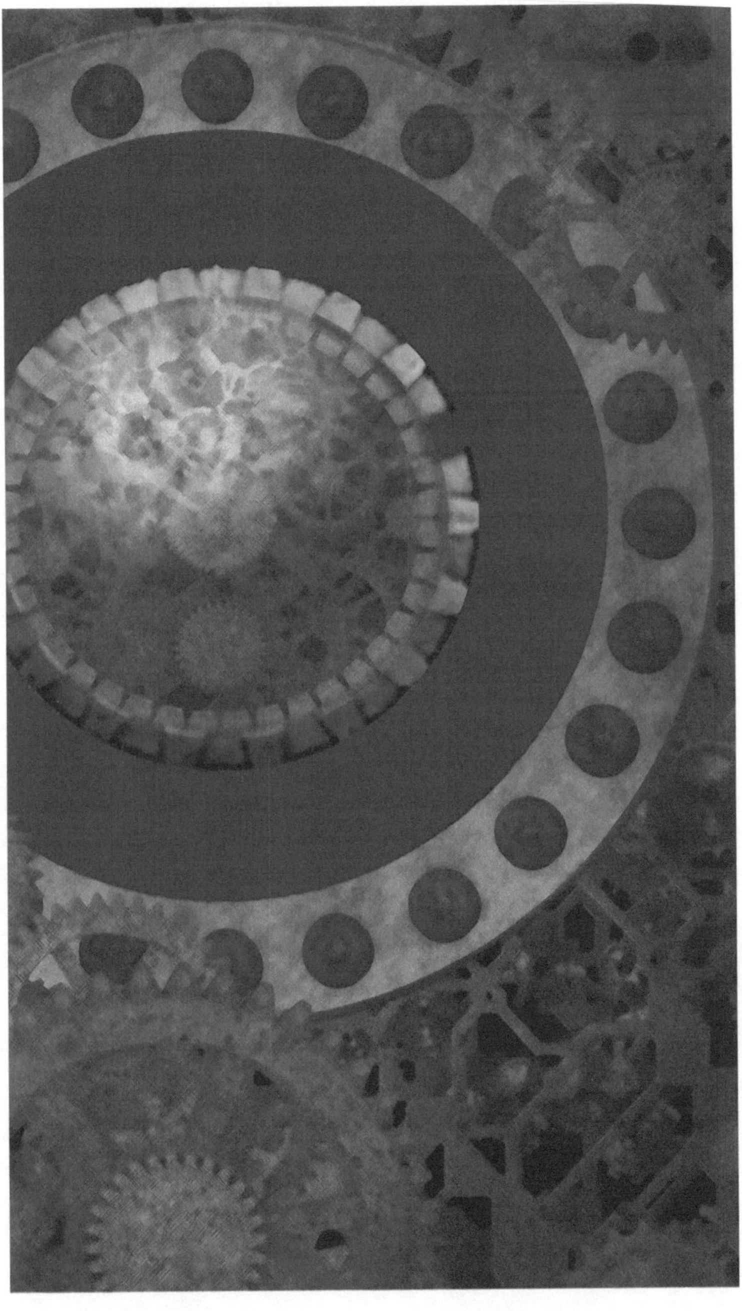

THE MAYHEM OF MERMAIDS
The Adventures of Smith and Jones, Book 2
Copyright © 2020 by Marie Andreas
ISBN 978-1-951506-00-1

Printed in the USA.
Cover art: Deranged Doctor Designs

Interior Format
© THE KILLION GROUP INC.

The Mayhem of Mermaids

The Adventures of Smith and Jones

Book 2

MARIE ANDREAS

BOOKS BY MARIE ANDREAS

THE LOST ANCIENTS SERIES
Book One: The Glass Gargoyle
Book Two: The Obsidian Chimera
Book Three: The Emerald Dragon
Book Four: The Sapphire Manticore
Book Five: The Golden Basilisk
Book Six: The Diamond Sphinx

THE ASARLAÍ WARS TRILOGY
Book One: Warrior Wench
Book Two: Victorious Dead
Book Three: Defiant Ruin

THE ADVENTURES OF SMITH AND JONES
Book One: A Curious Invasion
Book Two: The Mayhem of Mermaids

BROKEN VEIL TRILOGY
Book One: The Girl with the Iron Wing

ACKNOWLEDGEMENTS

Writing is a wonderful journey that takes a lot of support from folks around you. Thank you to everyone who has helped me, bought my books, let me cry on their shoulder, or helped in any way.

Extra thanks to editor extraordinaire- Janet Tait for her insight and wisdom. Sharon Rivest for picking out many mistakes and Ilana Schoonover for trying to keep me out of too much trouble. Any errors or mistakes are completely mine. Thanks also to Lynne Mayfield for helping create the Mudger.

And thank you to Deranged Doctor Designs for a lovely cover and The Killion Group for the formatting.

CHAPTER ONE

NETTIE JONES' HAND SHOOK AS she slowly closed the tweezers on the tiny barb. Considering that she normally had nerves of steel, this was extremely uncommon. Moreover, extremely dangerous. The barb she was inspecting, and trying to move to a slide for further examination, was a modified weapon. In truth, it was a sea urchin barb. However, one that had been specially created to have enough poison in its tip to kill an elephant on contact. At least that had been the report from the agents in Bath. They had been able to tell it was deadly after two fishermen had been found dead with the sea urchin barbs sticking out of them. What they needed from Nettie and Gaston was to find out what, exactly, the sea urchin was. Something changed this creature, and actions would be modified dependent on if it was a natural change or not.

The assumed strength of the poison was strictly theoretical—neither Nettie, nor any of her fellow members of the Society for the Exploration of the Unexplainable would risk an animal to test it. Even before these two deaths there had been rising chatter among the agents that the Society was now focusing on the sea. Yet the information behind it was restricted to the highest levels in Edinburgh and London, and no one seemed to know precisely what had led to this change in focus.

The barb before her clearly gave a partial answer; deadly sea urchins, that were never previously deadly, would need thorough investigation. But so far, the only difference she could tell was an odd slight yellow coloring.

Nettie let out her breath as she safely placed the barb on its specially designed slide. Her hands steadied as she placed two drops of the solution sent down from Edinburgh on it. She sat back on her stool to wait the required ten minutes for it to work.

It had just been two months since they'd fought back the alien menace that had launched an invasion against Earth from the skies. At least an invasion of Britain. A vampire hive had also been defeated, and while Nettie was proud that her theory of Master vampires ruling the undead had been verified, she was still trying to mentally suppress the events that led to that validation. Going from being a half-vampire by birth to a full vampire by blood, through the control of a Master vampire, was horrific to say the least. At this point, she wasn't completely sure what she was. Neither was Gaston, but her superior was loathe to admit it.

She shook her head at her own drifting thoughts and turned back to the sea urchin. Slipping on lead lined gloves, heavy enough that most dockworkers couldn't move them easily, she trundled the rest of the sea urchin into its lead lined box and secured it. This specimen had been carried, at great risk, from the waters near Bath to Gaston's home and agent headquarters in London. Taking over an entire train for a single agent and a lead lined box had been difficult to hide from the public—even for the Society. Yet, as always, they persevered. Or Caden did.

Another annoyingly disturbing thought. Her feelings for that insufferable man. Unfortunately, he was proving to be an asset to the Society, so avoiding him would be problematic. They'd worked closely together during the alien battle, and both appeared to have developed feelings for the other.

Nettie was strong, smart, and could grasp most topics immediately—however, she'd never really dealt with romantic feelings. Growing up being passed around like a plate of winter gruel between distant family members and total, but well-meaning, strangers, she'd never had a chance to build real friendships, let alone any romantic entanglements. Having one dropped on her doorstep in the form of a handsome, but sometimes difficult, American man was confusing.

He'd been moved to the Bath office almost immediately after the alien and vampire battle, so she could delay her feelings—such as her reaction to the kiss they'd shared in the dirigible after defeating the aliens. However, he was the agent who escorted the tiny urchin weapon back to London—charming and sneaking his way back into the city without causing a stir last night.

Except to Nettie.

She'd done the only logical thing at his arrival. Nodded a brief hello, taken the sea urchin box, and secured herself in the Dungeon. She could hear Rebecca's voice in her head now. She would be chastising her soundly for her behavior.

Her best friend and confidant had also been stationed away from London immediately after the battle. She was from a small town in northern Wales, and whilst there was no official SEU station there, the coastal town of Llandudno was becoming a center for sea-based mysteries as of late. No deadly sea urchins that they'd heard of, but odd, bipedal creatures had been reported near the shores late at night for the past few months. However, no one had been able to get a clear description of them, and most of the agents believed it was simply small town tales and too many late nights at the pub.

Gaston thought differently and sent Rebecca and Lisselle, an older agent with witchy abilities and now also a very dear friend of Nettie's, north a month ago under cover of being a rich widow and her youthful travelling companion. Nettie missed them both.

She checked the timer for the solution the sea urchin was in, still two minutes and thirty seconds remaining. That was another bone of contention of which Gaston was winning by simply refusing to discuss. The fact that all of the participants in the battle against the aliens had been re-assigned to new and exciting locales, while she remained here.

It wasn't false pride that made her think she was an asset to the organization. And no one had implied anything of the opposite—at least not within her hearing. The acclamations she'd received after the battle were heady to say the least. The only deduction she made, which she agreed with somewhere deep inside, was that her transformation to a full vampire, even briefly, had made other agents concerned. Gaston assured her that her blood had returned to its half-vampire status after the event. Yet, she was still here doing laboratory work in London while other agents were in the field.

Nettie sighed and leaned backwards on her stool. Just in time to almost fall off as the timer went off.

Swearing at herself under her breath, a sad side effect from evenings spent in the company of Gaston and Homer, a retired airship captain of a rather salty background, she resumed her seat and tightened the focus on the scope.

The bloom of bright magenta that engulfed the barb tip was exciting even if it wasn't what was expected. The chemical sent from Edinburgh was designed to determine if a component was man-made—a dark blue reaction— or of nature—a bright orange reaction. Magenta was not brought up.

The transformation of color began to fade after a few moments, so Nettie quickly jotted notes as the structure's colors changed and eventually vanished. The barb remained, but looked withered and brittle.

"Is it done?"

Nettie jumped, screamed, and spun all in less time than a normal person would have taken to adjust their seat.

"Damn you, Caden! Don't sneak up on people!" Nettie stepped back to her stool when she realized that her hand had still been raised to hit him.

"It's good to see you too." If he was disturbed by her almost attacking him, he gave no sign. Tall, handsome, American men with soft, dark brown hair that perpetually falls down over their foreheads should not sneak up on people.

Nettie narrowed her eyes and scowled. If she was honest with herself, the scowl was more aimed at herself for her reaction to him than at him directly. "What do you want?"

He shrugged and pulled over the other stool. "I figured that since I risked my life to bring that thing in, I should get to see the results. Manmade or natural?"

She couldn't be annoyed at scientific inquiry, so she dropped the scowl. "Neither. That was why I reacted in such an abrupt manner to your sneaking. The barb is not reading on either of the two parameters. It was magenta."

He leaned over the scope. "Nothing there now."

"The effect was short lived, but I took excellent notes. Bright deep pink. I've never heard of such a reaction."

"May I?" He held out his hand toward her notes.

At least he didn't just take them. Nettie handed them over.

"How deep was the color?" He didn't look up as he was still reading.

"Very." Nettie went to the mountain of resource books that Gaston kept in the Dungeon. One was a color wheel book created by the Society. She had questioned its inclusion until he pointed out that many times knowing the precise color of an item could help identify it. She flipped through and found the exact color.

"It started as this, then drifted into this."

"Found anything of interest?" Gaston's appearance wasn't unexpected, this was his home after all.

"The barb's color faded quickly," Nettie said. "I took as many notes as possible, but it was a short-lived reaction. This color was created because whatever that sea urchin is made of is both created and natural."

"I can't say that I've ever heard of that kind of reaction." Gaston nodded. "But Edinburgh will look into it."

"But we have to—" Nettie's comment was cut off as an explosion rocked the room. Nettie didn't fall but she did stumble forward.

Caden and Gaston quickly recovered and both fled out of the Dungeon with her not far behind. Had it only been Caden, Nettie might have passed him, but it would be bad form to pass her superior.

The hall was tumbled about, with items spilled off tables. Gaston's manservant, Damon, came running out from the kitchen, with Cook not far behind.

"Whatever it was, it came from the front yard," Caden said. He clearly had no concerns of passing his superior and ran out the front door first.

Nettie nodded to Gaston, who was already slowing down, and ran out behind Caden.

The driveway around the entrance to the mansion was crumbling. Nettie brought herself up and grabbed Caden's collar before he could fall into the abyss that formed directly in front of them.

Abyss was a bit extreme, but the five-foot-wide gash was extremely deep.

Even Gaston's normally self-absorbed neighbors couldn't have missed this, and servants from the houses around them came out. The ground had stopped moving but there was still no sign of the cause.

Nettie released Caden's jacket and they both crept forward. At first, it appeared that the explosion had come from the ground level, but further examination indicated the gap was wider at the bottom. Whatever happened, it came from underground.

"There's a device of some sort down there." Ignoring the looks from the surrounding neighboring servants, Nettie went to her knees and crawled forward on her hands. Caden dropped next to her.

"I can't see anything."

Nettie turned to him and tilted her head. Along with superior strength, she also had better eyesight than normal humans.

"Ah, never mind. I almost forgot your special abilities." He glanced around but no one aside from Gaston and Damon were near enough to hear them. Cook had stomped back into the mansion at the first opportunity. He lowered his voice. "What do you see?"

Nettie peered closer. The shape hadn't been discernable at first, but now looked like a small torpedo. How or why such a thing would be buried that far underground was a mystery. "A small metal cylinder? It looks like it might have come from further down. Or from the side." She held up her hand and pointed down toward the street. "That way." There were many things in the direction she pointed, but none of them should be sending off missiles underground.

"Move along now, nothing to see here." The London police usually avoided things having to do with the mansion, but three were now working their way up the other side of the driveway. Looking up, Nettie also noticed that the path of the missile was in evidence on the surface of the ground. Nothing as large as the fissure before her, but a small rise in the ground went down toward the street. It had definitely come from the direction she'd indicated.

Servants from the neighboring houses all scurried back with what information they'd gathered. Gaston walked around to meet the police.

Nettie started to rise, then movement from the rift caught her attention. "There's something else down there." She dropped her voice as she didn't want the nosy police to hear.

"I still can't see anything," Caden said, also with a voice barely above a whisper. "What is it?"

"Something…shiny. And wriggling. Okay, not moving, but there is something around the object." She pulled back in shock. "It's covered in sea life. It came from the Thames."

CHAPTER TWO

———◆———

"WHAT? THAT'S NOWHERE NEAR HERE."

"It's got sea life and water on it. The Thames is in the direction it appears to have come from; what else matches that?" Nettie tried to get a bit lower, but unless she wanted to take a chance of falling in, she was as close as she could get.

Gaston came back as the police left. No one looked happy. "Mon Dieu, I have convinced the constables to leave for the moment, but they will be sending more. We have to get whatever it is out of there, and come up with a plausible explanation before they come back in greater force."

Damon followed Gaston to Nettie and Caden.

All four looked down in the rift. It was easily two stories deep.

"If I climb down there, I am afraid the neighbors will notice." Nettie had been gauging the distance down to the object and the number of handholds in the jagged rock that lead down to it.

Gaston shook his head, then finally shrugged. "We can block this from being seen. Damon, get a standing screen, no three of them, from the Dungeon." Granted, they would be noticeable, but the screens would cause less talk than Nettie climbing in and out of the crevasse.

Caden joined him and they jogged back inside.

"Are you certain you can safely do this? Homer will be back in an hour or so. We could use his airship to haul it out," Gaston said.

Nettie rocked back on her heels. "That would be extremely noticeable. I think I can do it quickly." She looked down at her dusty skirts. "I would like to change however." At Gaston's nod she ran back to the mansion. She'd been wearing split skirts whenever possible for months, but Lisselle had some actual ladies' long pants made for her before she left for the north.

It only took her moments to run into her room, change, and come back. Damon and Caden might not have the supernatural speed she did but they'd still moved fast enough to get the screens out front and in place by the time she'd returned. The screens wouldn't block a determined investigator, but they would stop casual passersby from seeing anything untoward.

Nettie ran to the rift, but stopped when Caden stuck out his hand with a rope in it. "I've tied this end to that statue, I'll let you tie it around your waist."

She started to shake him off, but Gaston looked like he agreed with Caden. "Fine. But I will secure it around the item when I get down there."

Caden handed her the rope. "Am I the only one who thinks that moving a missile type object might be a bad idea?"

"Yes." Nettie didn't even look up as she tied the end around her waist. Homer had been teaching her rope tying these past few weeks and she was becoming quite proficient at it.

"Non," Gaston said. "I believe this is a risky thing. Mais, I also believe we don't have much choice. The police will be back, and in greater numbers; the ones who were here did not seem to care as to the status I wield."

The local law enforcement were vaguely aware that Gaston consulted with the queen and her people, and that usually offered them some room to be left alone. It appeared that this event was simply too blatant for such willful ignorance.

Nettie nodded and started lowering herself in. The rope was actually a good idea as the rocks she'd thought to use to help her descent were not as helpful as she'd originally believed.

The walls of the gap were rough and smelled of sulfur. Something she hadn't noticed from the top and shouldn't have been in the ground here. She quickly dropped to the object, it was definitely a missile of some kind, but smaller than she'd originally believed, not more than two feet long with perhaps a ten inch circumference. It was also damp and had wires protruding from a damaged side panel. Considering that, based on its trajectory, it would have continued right under or into the mansion, she was extremely grateful for the damage that must have shorted it out.

Still, she was cautious as she placed one hand on the casing. She held her breath as she tried to feel, hear, or sense any movement. After two minutes, she removed the rope from her waist and wrapped it around the missile. She pulled on the rope and looked up. "It should be secure enough to lift."

Caden had been watching her with Gaston peering over his shoulder. He moved out of view and the missile started inching up. Nettie steadied it as far as she could, cushioning it from the sides until it was out of reach. It crept along until it vanished over the edge.

She started slowly making her way up the rocks when the smell of sulfur suddenly grew stronger. She glanced down. At first there was nothing odd, then she heard a crackle and saw a thin glowing line appear where the missile had been. It looked as if someone had transported a bit of magma up. How exactly that would have occurred was something for later study.

"I might need that rope after all." She tried to climb faster but the rocks continued to fail in their assist. Hydrogen sulfide could explain the foul smell; although what it was doing here she had no idea. But the growing crackling line in the stone where the missile had come to rest wasn't as explainable. Nor did she want to take time to examine it further. It was rare that fear outweighed scientific inquiry for her.

The rope dropped down and she quickly looped it around herself and used it to help herself climb up. More crackling and popping made her increase her speed.

She quickly reached the top.

"Everyone should probably get down." She ran away from the crevasse and dropped low.

The following explosion knocked everyone who didn't heed her warning to the ground and a burst of flame shot out of the crevasse.

Fortunately, the flame was short lived and immediately shrank back into the ground and extinguished. Unfortunately, the police had come back and at least eight of them were now picking themselves off the ground.

The missile was missing and so was Damon. She glanced over to Caden but he came over and gave a quick shake of his head. Hopefully Damon had gotten the missile inside and secure before the police showed up.

"Now see here Master Gaston, you are given some leeway with your behavior, but this destruction of yours goes all the way to the Thames. That cannot be born."

The police officer who was speaking had the most ridiculous mustache Nettie had seen outside of a work of theater, but he appeared to be extremely proud of it.

"You cannot believe that I did this? My boarders and I are victims! Attacks against the intellectuals. It could even be culprits trying to discover things about the queen." Gaston had a way of dropping his voice when he was trying to be dramatic. Like the mustache on the officer, it was over played, but got the point across.

Gaston's mansion was known to be a boarding house of bookish intellectuals and artists. Most of the agents living there were able to keep the ruse up.

The query was dropped as a horse and rider came running up. "Officer Tryol! I've been sent to send you back. There's a ship under the water in the Thames!" The rider was little more than a boy and must have been running before he started riding, he looked ready to fall over.

Officer Tryol first looked like he was going to ignore the boy and continue his investigation of Gaston. But with a shake of his head he backed off. "I regret the imposition. We will be back for further questioning if needed."

"Most likely that ship is who shot at us!"

"From the water? Under all of this land?" Tryol was already taking his men and moving down the drive.

"It could be the Americans. They have that ability you know. And they are always after our secrets." Gaston had a well-known dislike of Americans. Or he did. Working with Caden so closely had broken him of the habit. Nettie could tell he was playing that former bias for effect.

Tryol rolled his mustache and shook his head. "We will be in contact."

Most of the crowd, which had re-formed while she had been down below, scattered.

"It's inside, I presume?" Nettie said as she walked back to the crevasse. The sides were black from the flame, but there was no crackling and no smell. She would have to make detailed notes of her observations when she got back to the lab.

"Yes, but barely." Caden gave the gap a worried glance. "What caused that, and should we really be standing here?" Caden was an excellent spy and fighter, and actually quite smart. But he hated things he couldn't fight back against.

Nettie rubbed her arms as a chill overtook her. She had no delusion as to what would have happened to her had she been caught in that flame. Even a full vampire wouldn't have survived that. "I will make notes of what I saw down there, but it made no scientific sense." That was an understatement—nothing in the last hour made sense in the scientific world.

Another horse rode up the street, but this was a welcome addition. Homer never looked completely at ease on horses; he was a big man who looked happier on the deck of one of his airships. Technically retired from her majesty's air service, he still did work for the crown along with the SEU.

"I see my return is in good time." He rode past the screens and peered down at the fissure as he passed. "Doing some digging, are we?"

"Excellent timing, my friend." Gaston waited until Homer got off his horse, then dragged him back to the hole. "We need this covered in such a way that it will not cause notice, but that we might still be able to get into it should we need to investigate further."

Homer nodded and pulled on his thick gray beard. "That might be something my crew could do. I was about to meet them at the Cloak and Dagger when I saw there was a situation going on down this street." He looked around. "I made a guess it was here."

"Come inside and we'll explain briefly while Nettie writes up her notes." Gaston led his friend into the mansion with Nettie and Caden following behind. Damon passed them going the other direction and took up a watchful stance near the crevasse. Although under Gaston's employ as his manservant and general butler, Damon had been privy to more state secrets than some agents. Nettie had never been able to find out much about his private life, but Rebecca had been quite taken with him before she was carted off to the north.

Nettie waited until they were all in the drawing room and armed with tea before she made her assessment. "I believe that the mansion was targeted from a ship lurking in the Thames. The missile was not only explosive, but it had some other material on it which caused the fire bomb." She pulled out a pad of paper from the desk next to her and began making notes.

Homer's eyes went wide but then he glanced at the others' expressions. "A fire bomb?"

"Oui. Nettie almost failed to make it out of the fissure in time. Flames shot directly up, then vanished." Gaston added a little bit of something stronger to his tea. He handed the bottle to Homer as well.

"And where is this missile?"

"Gaston had Damon secure it in the Dungeon. It appears to be disabled, but after what happened with that flame spout, we didn't think we should take chances," Caden said. He waved off the offer of alcohol for his tea. Although he still occasionally put milk in it, he'd become quite a tea drinker in his months here in England.

"Gaston nodded. "Excellent job getting it out, Nettie. I hate to think what would have happened had that flame gone off with the missile in that crevasse."

Nettie nodded as she kept writing. She had a remarkable memory, but always felt better if she jotted notes on any major event. She would go back later and incorporate them into a full report.

"But how do you know it came from the Thames?" Homer was still trying to catch up, being as he'd missed the actual excitement.

Gaston filled him in on the events, including the police dealing with an underwater ship in the Thames.

Homer shook his head. "But how could this missile go through all of that ground? It's one thing to pass through air or water but solid rock and dirt?"

Nettie looked up from her notes as a thought hit her. "What if the missile's design included a way to melt a passage through rock and dirt with heat or a corrosive solution? In effect, creating its own tunnel as it went toward its target?" She put down her pen. "In fact, that was an oddity that I failed to notice until now. The trajectory tunnel left by the missile, coming from the Thames, was closing in on itself. Had the missile not shorted out, it would have travelled under the mansion, exploded, and the path it made would have returned to normal quickly. It would have been impossible to tell where it came from. I'd venture that the other ground damage mentioned by the police is gone or vanishing now as the area under the surface is returning to normal." She was rethinking her choice not to put anything stronger in her tea as the reality of it hit her. "I have no idea how it was done, nor what would be used to do it. Whoever was behind this is far more advanced than we are." She looked around. "And by we, I mean the entire Society."

The parlor went silent.

Gaston rose to his feet. "There must be some scientific research that could lead us to how it was done. And I also mean the Society as a whole." His face didn't match the confidence of his words. "We need to contact Edinburgh immediately."

All four went down to the Dungeon, however, Gaston paused at the entrance and turned to Nettie. "I don't suppose that you were able to gather much information on the magma-type substance left in the ground? Do you suppose that was the fuse element?"

"I believe that was what triggered the explosion of fire and also helped the missile travel so well underground. But, sadly, I couldn't gather any of it. It appeared quickly and was concerning enough that I felt continuing out of there was the best course of action." Nettie regretted it, but the more time she spent with the Society, the more she realized that self-preservation sometimes beat scientific inquiry. It had been a difficult lesson to learn. "However, I did smell sulfur. And there was something else…almost like an electrical charge." She hadn't paid attention to it at the time, but it had been there.

"You will need to speak to Edinburgh directly once we get the Mudger up." Gaston continued into the Dungeon and quickly began setting it up.

The Mudger was a secret of the Society's that enabled agents in the main hubs to speak to each other over long distances in a secure fashion. It also transferred their images, albeit they were grainy, as well. Nettie had gotten more acclimated to the technology, but it still gave her a shiver of excitement each time they used it. She did regret not being able to fully draft her notes on the subject prior to this conversation however.

Even Homer hovered close when Gaston got the Mudger running. He normally was more of a hands on agent, more brute force and battle strategy than scientific inquiry.

"Hello Gaston, and the rest of you," the woman on the other end smiled as she nodded to each. "What has happened?" She was polite but to the point; if an agent was calling on the Mudger, it wasn't simply to chat.

"We've had an incident. A missile was aimed at the mansion—from underground. We believe it came from an underwater vessel currently being taken by the local constables."

"I am glad that they missed the mansion." She continued to smile. Calling in a failed attempt at destruction wasn't worthy of the Mudger either. A Runner could have been called and a message dispatched.

Gaston stepped back and motioned for Nettie to move forward. "Good day Agent Hemles. Gaston wanted me to speak to someone up there about what I observed. The missile had some way of cutting through the rock underground. A way that led to a fireball and would have trigged the weapon had I not already removed it. Aside from a damaged panel on the side, there was no damage to the missile even though it travelled quite a distance underground. Then the ground closed up behind the passage. Whatever chemical or element that was used to make it cut through like that is one I've not heard of before."

Agent Hemles dropped her smile. "That is serious. Not that an attempt on all of you isn't, but this has long reaching ramifications. You are one of our up and coming leaders in science. If you are concerned by it...let me get Agent Ramsey." She left the screen.

Agent Ramsey was the second in command to the mysterious Agent Zero.

Nettie wiped her palms on her pants. Not that she would be shaking his hand or anything, but it was still a bit unnerving speaking to him directly. She'd only spoken to Agent Ramsey three times in her career with the Society.

"Agent Jones! Glad you were at home when this happened," Agent Ramsey said as he settled in in front of the Mudger. He was a large man who always managed to make the speaker on the Mudger rattle when he spoke. Nettie was almost afraid to meet him in person. "I have our best scientists up here standing by to take notes. Start when you first saw the object and the ...explosive ooze?"

"That's as good of a word as any, sir." Nettie went through everything she could recall from the smell, the crackling noise, and the damage to the missile.

Agent Ramsey nodded and said a few well-placed 'ah's' but she knew most of the information was being jotted down out of sight of the Mudger.

"Now what of the missile itself?" Agent Ramsey leaned forward.

"I haven't had a chance to examine it, sir. These events happened a short while ago."

"That was my call," Gaston said as he moved in closer. "The information provided on what had been in the crevasse before the explosion caused some concern on my part. I felt its uniqueness warranted a call up before we moved forward."

"Understood, Gaston, and agreed, this call was warranted. Didn't mean to imply you were shirking your duties. When you find out more, please contact us immediately. I am also sending a Runner down to you to wait on call."

"Thank you," Gaston said. "Oh, one other issue. The police were far nosier than usual. Would it be possible to have some pressure applied to back them off? This was an unfortunately noticeable incident, but it would be better if they left us alone."

"I think we can take care of that. Ramsey out." He tapped a button on the Mudger on his end and it went blank.

"Well, having a Runner on hand will be useful. Will he let it stay stationed here for a while, do you think?" Nettie hadn't originally been sure what to think of the mysterious men called Runners—beyond the fact they were impolite to say the least. That was until she found out they weren't men at all but the semi-mechanical alien survivors of a long ago vanished civilization that had come to Earth seeking help centuries ago.

A soft popping sound came, then one of the Runners stood before them. Garbed in black from head to toe, the beings moved outside of normal time and space. The Society used them as messengers and stealth weapons when there were no other options. They in turn had a place to stay away from prying eyes. Their technology was so far beyond modern man they might as well have been living among cave dwellers.

"Thank you," Gaston said as he pointed to a chair in the

corner. "If you could wait there?"

The Runner gave a nod then went and stood in the corner. Nettie didn't think she'd ever seen them sit.

That settled, Gaston led the way to the large examination table with Nettie and Caden following.

Homer stood in front of the Runner for a bit, then shook his head. "I'm still unnerved by you. No offense."

"None taken." The Runner's voice was monotone, but that little bit of social interaction was an improvement. Nettie had sent a strongly worded letter to Edinburgh that teaching the Runners common responses, beyond "What do you need", would go far in integrating them into the Society and this world. It was satisfying to see they might have made progress.

Homer gave it a nod, and then turned back to the others. "I'm more concerned with what sent that missile and less what is inside of it. Although, I would enjoy a read of the breakdown of whatever explosives they have inside of it. I'll be down at the Thames, hopefully most of the constables have moved on by now."

Caden was already helping Gaston secure the missile, but looked up. "I'll come find you in a bit then."

Homer left and Nettie turned to Gaston. "How will we get the underwater ship back from the police if they managed to retrieve it?" She brought out a set of clock working tools. She'd found they worked superbly for finer detail work.

"Homer will find out what they know," Gaston said. "It would be better that they had not found it, however, since they have, we must proceed with caution. The stronger we react, the more they will take notice."

The inside of the missile wasn't nearly as exotic as Nettie had been expecting. Instead of gears and tiny workings, there were pieces of metal, all encased in dying sea life. She used tweezers to pull at a strand. Correction, dead sea life.

The like she'd never seen. It looked to have a familiar light yellow tinge, and the hairs on her arms stood on end.

"What is it?" Caden looked closer.

"Stand back." She spun and grabbed the remainder of the chemical that Edinburgh had sent down for the sea urchin. Once satisfied that both Gaston and Caden had moved away from the table, she threw it at the interior of the missile.

The reaction was far faster this time, but it was also a much larger sample. The flare of magenta started where the chemical hit, then spread to everything nonmetal in the canister. Then a crackling sound came.

The small sea urchin hadn't done anything to indicate it was explosive, that didn't appear to be true for whatever was in the missile. "Get behind the shield!" Nettie stopped short of picking up both men and dragging them, but at least they moved quickly and without question at her yell.

The shield was a bit small, so all three had to crouch closely.

There was an explosion, but in Nettie's mind it was very unsatisfactory, even if it had been unexpected. "Is that all?" She peered up and looked at the ruins of the canister.

"Had you not warned us that would have been enough to kill Caden and me, possibly even you." Gaston shook his head as he looked at the results of the explosion. Metal had gone through a few items but luckily appeared to have missed the major equipment.

Caden donned heavy gloves and was already poking about. "This turned the same color as the sea urchin, but that wasn't explosive."

Nettie also got some gloves. "Yes, I will have to look further as to what it is, but I think we can assume that whoever sent this has found a way to weaponize sea life."

CHAPTER THREE

—◆—

"THAT'S IMPOSSIBLE," CADEN SAID, THEN raised his hands in surrender. "Forgive me, I forgot where I was. That's highly improbable. Couldn't there be a chemical put on the sea life?"

Nettie was already gathering the slides and containment units she would need. "There could be, however the evidence doesn't support that. Both showed magenta. Obviously, I can't operate on either assumption but will need to do a thorough examination." She put on protective goggles then turned back to both men. "Well?"

Gaston laughed. "I believe that is our cue to leave, my lad. This is thoroughly her domain now, I don't see any explosives that you or I would recognize, and yet whoever sent it was intending it to do us damage. I think we best leave her to her studies. Let's see what we can discern elsewhere."

Nettie was grateful. She understood that Gaston was possibly as scientifically curious as she, but the fact was when she was looking at something intently, it was better not to have other people in the room. Her senses were acute enough that it was impossible to ignore too many distractions. Not to mention being close to Caden was starting to fracture her composure. *That* situation would need to be dealt with soon.

There were samples of the element all over the lab, unfortunately, but she needed clean ones. Once the mess was removed, the canister itself still had enough left in it for study. At first it looked as if the material was the same as the sea urchin Caden had brought back, but a few more rounds through the spectroscope revealed it was more advanced. She quickly flipped through her notes to make certain, but yes. The explosive nature hinted at in the sea urchin was completely developed in whatever had been put in the missile—this sea life was designed to explode rather than poison.

More disturbing, the evidence fully supported this being part of the sea animal itself, not a component added upon it. Had the creatures of the sea risen up and begun fighting back against humankind's cruel treatment of their domain?

Then she looked over to the missile canister. Not that sea life wasn't intelligent enough to have designed such a thing, she personally believed there was evidence that porpoises and whales were far more intelligent than humans were, but they lacked the opposable digits and hands to build an item such as that missile.

She swore as she pricked a finger on a piece of dead sea life. A drop of red appeared on the surface of her skin, then turned bright pink. She grabbed iodine and poured it over her finger, but she felt a strange tingle, as if something was crawling up her arm through the small cut.

She forced herself to get angry; not at anything particular. She hadn't shared this with Gaston as she was still experimenting, but she'd found that her half-vampire blood could be called up if she became angry enough. When called up it raised a heat throughout her entire body. Which seemed counter intuitive since pure vampires had colder blood, not warmer. That dilemma was part of why she hadn't mentioned it yet.

Right now there seemed to be a battle going on in her hand and arm. She poured more iodine on the wound, and her blood became hotter. After a few tense moments, the tingling stopped.

"I do hope that means whatever it is has been defeated and not that it's coursing around on its own in my blood." She peered at the pinprick-sized wound for signs of infection, but aside from a now red drop of blood that came out, there was nothing to see.

"What do you need?"

Nettie jumped. She'd completely forgotten the Runner. Even her senses couldn't pick them up and she *had* been concentrating on a disturbing event.

"Nothing, I was simply…" She studied the Runner. No one knew how they did what they did, but there might be more things they could do. "Can you scan a person?"

"I am able to see you with my scan, yes."

That wasn't what she'd asked, but maybe it gave her the answer. The Runners had no eyes that could be seen. Their faces were black cloth in a vaguely human head alignment. They scanned their surroundings.

Nettie excitedly held up her injured finger and arm. "Can you scan this?"

"It is a human arm. Belonging to Agent Nettie Jones."

"Yes, yes. But is there anything that is not normal, not matching a standard scan?"

The Runner tilted its head and a slight whirling emanated from it. "Foreign elements detected. Entrance was wound on finger. Breaking down now. No remaining threat."

"You broke down whatever was in there?"

"Negative. Body is destroying invading substance. All threat removed."

Nettie stepped forward. This was almost more interesting than the sea life weapon. Primarily the Runners used their abilities to transport information and items for the Society. Based on this information, they might be able to do so much more.

"So there was a threat?" Judging by her own body's reaction there had been, but since she'd never had venomous, explosive sea life try to enter her bloodstream before, she would like verification.

"Less than point-o-two chance of infiltration given updated parameters of Agent Jones."

She tapped her lip in thought. "Had I not been enhanced?"

"Greater than fifty percent chance of damage or infiltration of the human organism."

Nettie rocked back. That was far too high to be chance. The missile would have exploded under the mansion, destroying a good portion of it based on the flame spout that had come out of the crevasse outside. Then the attacking shards of modified sea life would have decimated any survivors.

She quickly placed the remains of the missile, and the refuse from the explosion, into a lead box. Then, after some searching, found yet another lead box to place the first one in. Had she thought there might be another larger box, she would have probably done that as well.

This was not only a concentrated attack on the mansion; it was one far beyond their current knowledge. Edinburgh was going to have to be involved. She knew she had skills, but this was beyond her.

"I'm going to need you to travel to Edinburgh, but first let me check with Gaston." She added the last bit as the Runner appeared to get ready to leave.

"I await your direction." This Runner was almost becoming polite, quite a nice change if she said so herself.

She went into the house, unsure where to find Gaston since she took over his Dungeon. He wasn't in any of the common living areas, and she was about to go into the men's wing of bedrooms to hunt him down when she heard singing. Odd, discordant singing, but there was a level of happiness behind it that compensated for the lack of ability.

It was coming from the back gardens, but she didn't see anyone as she stepped outside. Usually these gardens were used by Homer for airship repairs that he didn't want to do at the landing field, but Cook sometimes planted vegetables out here.

She rounded a high wall and found Gaston. Planting flowers. And singing.

"How long have you done this?" She'd been living here for months and she'd never seen him in the yard, let alone gardening.

He jumped. "What?" He looked extremely out of place with a long rooted bulb dangling from his hand. "Oh, this…my doctor suggested it, helps me think." He slumped forward with a sigh. "He has mentioned that my blood pressure is a bit high and a soothing hobby would help."

"We are secret agents after all, I would expect that most people in the Society have high blood pressure of some sort."

"Yes, yes. But I am getting older. He's got me watching what I eat, sticking plants in the ground, and all sorts of strange things. It's this new thinking. Can't be healthy."

Nettie laughed. Gaston might be an amazing agent for new and unexplored things for the Society, but when it came to introducing something new to his own life he was more stubborn than a herd of goats. "You sounded happy to me." She smiled and moved on to her intended topic as a blush creeped up his cheeks. "I wanted to get your approval to send the Runner and the bulk of the missile samples to Edinburgh immediately." She quickly filled him in on her findings.

"This is disturbing news. We must assume these components came from Bath. Edinburgh is going to have to send more agents down there immediately. Elfthrith Allsmythe is good, but she doesn't have enough support down there."

"They might not have come from Bath, though." Nettie raised her hand as the thought struck her—they'd made assumptions. "I agree, our major coastal towns need to be watched, however we can't focus on the entire coastline at once. But I've discovered that the Runners have advanced scanning and might be able to narrow our search in this case. If they can determine what waters the sea life came from, we will have a better chance of finding who is behind this. At least where to aim our focus." She wasn't sure if the Runner could discern that information, but always good to give it a try.

"Excellent thinking," Gaston said. "Let me change out of these dirty clothes and I'll join you. I might have a few things to share with Edinburgh as well."

Nettie left him to finish picking up his flowers. She was annoyed at herself for not thinking of it earlier, but the waters around the British kingdom had subtle differences. Contaminants from specific areas and such. The assumption would be Bath, since that was already documented as a problem spot of these deadly sea life. However, she would be remiss in letting that assumption stand without validation of some sort.

The Runner was exactly where she'd left it. She quickly unlocked the lead boxes and extracted a good-sized sample. "Can you determine where in the ocean this came from?"

"Yes, Irish Sea."

That narrowed it down and moved Bath out of the running. "Can you tell where in the Irish Sea?" The Irish Sea was smaller than simply saying the Atlantic Ocean, but still large.

"No."

Nettie waited a moment to see if anything else would be forthcoming, and then sighed. She put the sample she'd shown the Runner in a smaller series of lead boxes—she'd keep that one for them. The rest would go to Edinburgh.

"Any luck?" Gaston bustled in with a packet in his hand.

"The Irish sea, nothing narrower than that." She tapped the larger lead boxes. "These can go." When she re-boxed the bulk of the samples, she'd added detailed notes to the Edinburgh crew. Someday she dearly wished she could be part of the massive lab up north. But for now, she was happy to be a field agent. Providing she was allowed back in the field at some point.

Gaston handed his packet to the Runner. "Please take this and the lead box to Edinburgh. Only to Agent Zero or Agent Ramsey."

The Runner nodded once then took the box and vanished. It said a lot that, even with her own advanced speed and abilities, Nettie still couldn't see them when they moved like that.

"Do you think we are under attack?" Nettie waved her hand around. "Not us specifically, although, clearly we are, but the country? Does the Queen need to be advised?" This had been the biggest thing to happen since the issue with the vampires and aliens. If the Queen needed to be notified, Nettie wanted to be involved.

Her interactions with the Queen had been few, but they'd been warm. Although Queen Victoria had willingly, in a fit of panic, gone to be made into an immortal vampire, she hadn't realized the turn it would take. She was grateful to the Society at large, and Nettie in particular, for rectifying that situation. She confided to Nettie once that she still had nightmares sometimes.

Nettie had been grateful that her odd blood had been able to pull back both the Queen and herself from vampiric status. Queen Victoria had returned to normal, and Nettie had returned to her previous half-vampire self. Although she told no one, she too had nightmares about her brief time as a full vampire.

"I intend to make a report to the Queen's man, but I want to hear back from Homer and Caden first." He had already turned away and was pulling out another project he'd been working on.

Nettie sighed. There was nothing she needed to do on the urchin file until they heard back from Edinburgh, and that could take days. Any of her other projects could be addressed in her own private lab. "I will be off then."

Gaston nodded. He was already deep in whatever he was studying. The doctor might have prescribed gardening to relax him, but Gaston practically oozed happiness when he was deep in an investigation.

CHAPTER FOUR

Nettie was lost in thought as she drifted upstairs from the Dungeon. She paused in front of her own smaller lab, but there was much to be deliberated and the enclosed area wasn't always the place for it. Perhaps it was finding Gaston there, but she found herself heading toward the back gardens.

They really were quite charming, tended, but not overly so, with elements of wildness still upon them. She was getting used to the idea that strolling about might have some health benefits for herself as well, when a shout came from above her.

"Ahoy! Is this the home of Gaston?" The woman peering out from the deck of the airship hovering above her waved.

"Aye! The house is his," Nettie shielded her eyes to see the ship and pilot better. Homer might be able to tell the airships apart, but beyond differentiating between an airship and a war zeppelin, they all looked the same to Nettie.

"I've come from Llandudno, and Edinburgh before that." There was enough emphasis on both cities' names to let Nettie know she was of the Society as well. "I need to speak to him immediately. Can we drop anchor here for the moment?"

Nettie really couldn't say yes or no, since it wasn't her house. However, she doubted that someone out to attack them would have asked so politely. "There's a dock and landing back behind that wall." She pointed to where

Homer brought down his ship when he needed to bring it to the mansion. It was a good thing that Gaston held rights to a sizeable portion of land.

She was torn as to whether she should leave this woman and her small crew, three others were visible as the ship lowered, to get Gaston, or keep an eye on them. Her dilemma was resolved when Damon appeared a few feet behind her.

"Do you need anything, miss?" He was always impeccably polite and acted far older than he appeared. And he had exceptional timing.

"Yes, thank you. Could you notify Gaston that we have an airship visitor from Edinburgh?" She kept her eyes on the ship. If something went wrong, she would be better equipped to handle it than Damon.

"Immediately." He was gone a moment later.

It took a few minutes for the captain to settle her airship down, it wasn't a large one, but it looked new and the balloon was a sleek, narrow design. The landing was finished before Gaston appeared.

The captain marched forward, leaving the final tie downs to her crew. "I'm Bethlyn, also known as Captain Ragthin, or Agent Ragthin. I presume that you are Nettie? Agent Jones?" She was a large woman, probably close to Homer in size. And her handshake was reminiscent of him as well. Had Nettie not been half-vampire she might have found herself flung about from the handshake alone.

"I am. Good to meet another agent, and a captain as well. Homer will be happy to have someone to talk ships with."

Bethlyn's laugh was shocking in that it was delicate and soft. "My cousin and I usually agree to disagree. He takes the south, I take the north. But it will be good to see him again. Is he up on an adventure somewhere?" She hooked a thumb over her shoulder and up to indicate the sky.

"He is out and about, but I don't think he's taken his ship

up. He normally keeps it at the yard."

"Agent Ragthin!" Gaston's voice boomed out from behind them. "Good to see you." He strode forward and shook her hand, then nodded to the crew finishing up the tying down of the airship. "Here for a social call?" His smile was broad enough that Nettie knew one of their more nosy neighbors was most likely in hearing range—or at least Gaston assumed so.

"Aye, a short one, thought to drop in on Homer." Bethlyn waved to her crew, and a man and woman came forward to join them. The last man stayed next to the airship. Subtle, but it supported that whatever they were here for, it was more serious than visiting a cousin.

"Please follow me; we can conduct introductions and re-acquaintances in a more civilized fashion." He led the way back into the house and down toward the parlor.

"How do you like living here?" Bethlyn asked Nettie as they made their way through the house. "It certainly is impressive. Not sure if I could handle walls around me all the time however. There are quite a few, aren't there?"

Nettie laughed. "I never thought of it that way, but there are. It was an adjustment, but I had been living in a boarding house with a disagreeable landlady. Gaston is a step or two above that."

"I do hear you," Gaston said. "As you can see, I get little respect."

Damon wasn't in sight, but the way the parlor was set up with tea and biscuits showed he'd been through the parlor.

"Please sit. If Gaston doesn't object, I will pour." Nettie began setting up the tea while their guests sat. Bethlyn introduced her two crew, and they all accepted tea and biscuits but waved off Gaston's additive. Nettie had a feeling they weren't staying long.

Bethlyn sipped her tea with a smile. "Thank you. I'll be blunt, how quickly can you relocate to northern Wales?"

It was a good thing that Nettie hadn't handed Gaston his cup and saucer yet; he visibly started at her words. "What now? I can't pick up my entire household…the idea is preposterous…why wouldn't Edinburgh have notified me directly? We just spoke to them."

If Gaston had been a bird his feathers would have been ruffled high over the top of his head by now. Most agents moved around, but he'd been *the* London base for far longer than Nettie had been alive. Setting up his mansion as more of an agent home and place of work was his idea as he really believed, where possible, stationary agents worked better.

"It's only temporary and I am simply the messenger." Bethlyn took a long sip of her tea and sighed. "Well… and partial transport. Homer will have to take the rest; my Bessie is designed for speed, not people carrying capacity."

"When?" Gaston first waved off the offer of tea, then changed his mind, took it, and added some alcohol in his cup. He was starting to look a bit wild around the eyes.

"They said no more than two days. Agent Ramsey suggested that you might yell less if a charming lass presented it to you in person first." Her smile was charming, but Nettie doubted that anyone had called her a charming lass since she was about five. Like her cousin, Homer, she was large and strong looking.

"Damn him. Did he say why? Who all must go? Where we will stay? Northern Wales is a far cry from London and civilization, but that is a rather large area."

"He will tell you the why himself once you've settled down. His words, not mine. It's urgent, but not so that you and your people can't be allowed to settle things here. Nettie and Caden Smith will need to go; Perlia and Rostenburg will be down from Edinburgh to make sure nothing happens to the mansion while you are gone. The rest of the London agents will help as well, and make sure it appears well lived in."

"This is not acceptable. I need to stay here, there are things afoot that require my attendance." Gaston perked up. "We are in the middle of a very important discovery concerning the weaponization of sea life. Something is afoot near the Irish Sea. There is simply no way we can travel at this point."

Bethlyn hid her smile behind another sip of tea. "I believe that is what is behind the move. As for the location, I believe they are finding accommodations for you in a small resort town, Llandudno; it does face the Irish Sea after all."

Nettie drank her own tea as she watched Gaston. His face reflected as his mind whirled trying to find a way out. Unfortunately, he'd overplayed his hand by mentioning the sea life and the Irish Sea.

His shoulders slumped. "It seems we have no choice. Might I bring my household staff? It is only two, but I would be lost without them."

"As long as Homer can fit them, aye." She sat down her cup and nodded to her two crew. "Would it be possible to leave Bessie here whilst we wait? I'd rather not go through proper logging in at the yard."

Gaston was already wandering in thought as the idea of having to relocate, even for a short duration, was working its way through his mind. Bethlyn had to repeat herself twice.

"What?" He looked around at everyone watching him. "Yes, yes, of course. We can put up you and your crew, if you'd like, as well. I do wish Ramsey had made mention of it earlier. When did he send you down?"

Nettie was wondering about that as well. Bethlyn's ship looked fast, but still there was no way she could have come down from Edinburgh in the two hours since they'd con- tacted them. Clearly, this move was planned long before they'd contacted Edinburgh.

"Thank you for the offer; my crew and I have things to do in London, so we'll be out and about. I welcome the offer of berthing and beds. I gather from the damage visible out front that you've had shenanigans happening. Agent Zero decided to relocate your team completely two days ago. Originally he was planning on sending you all to Bath, but there were some new instances in Llandudno, or at least stronger rumors. Part of your team is already there, and I believe Agent Lisselle suggested that you lot might do some good."

"What is that wild witch setting us up for now?" Homer spoke before he entered the room, but his face lit up when he saw his cousin. "Now, if you're in cahoots with Lisselle we are all in trouble." He strode forward to engulf her in a hug, and then stopped and looked down at himself. He wasn't dripping, but his clothes, and he, had obviously been in water. Dirty water. "I think everything can wait for a bit. I'll be back."

He bumped into an annoyed, and equally soggy and disheveled, Caden. Homer moved around him, but didn't meet his eyes.

Caden took a step into the parlor. "I'll be back down after a quick shower and change. The good news is we got the submersible boat back. The bad news is this happened because Homer doesn't listen." With a tip of his head to their guests, he stalked off.

"Oh, he is a charmer, even filthy and annoyed," Bethlyn said. "We've all heard of Caden Smith. Must be quite a lady killer, eh?" She nodded to Nettie.

Nettie wasn't encouraging that at all. "I wouldn't really know, I was very busy when he first arrived, and he was deported to Bath soon after our events with the vampires and the Queen." She tried to keep her annoyance out of her voice. The look on both Gaston and Bethlyn's face said she failed.

Bethlyn's crew members nodded to their captain, then rose. "Thank you for the refreshments, but we have other appointments." The man, Joseph, said.

"And thank you for the offer of the rooms. At least for tonight, we won't be able to take you up on it. We'll be back in the morning." The woman pilot, Ivy, smiled to them and then they both showed themselves out before Gaston could recover enough to rise to his feet.

"Sorry for that, but they have a number of things to investigate before we depart," Bethlyn said. "I take it that Homer and Caden were in the Thames? An underwater boat?"

Gaston was muttering to himself and making notes to prepare for their departure, so, after a distracted wave from him, Nettie filled Bethlyn in on the missile and the boat.

"And I will never trust Homer on a water ship again— ever." Caden came in with his hair still wet from his brief shower.

Nettie focused on being a good hostess and pouring him some tea, and not on the fact that he was disturbingly attractive damp. "Biscuit?" She would also ignore the way her voice went up just now.

"Two, if you please, and two lumps of sugar. That was a distressing event." He took his cup and saucer and stepped back out of the way.

Gaston pulled himself out of his distraction and nodded to Bethlyn. "Agent Bethlyn Ragthin, might I formally present Agent Caden Smith? Bethlyn has come to whisk us all away to the heathen north of Wales."

"Very pleased to meet you Agent Ragthin. Please call me Caden."

"Likewise Caden. Please call me Bethlyn."

Caden took his seat, then turned back to Gaston. "I thought you were raised in Wales?"

Gaston was French by heritage, but when he was still a boy, his family relocated to Wales. It made for an odd accent when he was fatigued or drunk.

"Cardiff, my man. I was raised in Cardiff. Not London, obviously, but still civilized. The land is wild in northern Wales."

"Lisselle says it is lovely," Nettie said. "So does Rebecca, but she was raised there. I am looking forward to an adventure." To be honest, going anywhere at this point would have made her happy. She loved London, but she wanted to see more as an agent.

"It is quite nice up there, a bit more rugged, but lovely," Bethlyn said.

Homer came in and settled in with a cup of tea. "So what is my headstrong cousin doing now?"

"Coming to bring you all to Wales." A brief catching up took place.

Homer took the news much better than Gaston, who was still muttering and writing lists in the corner. "Aye, my crew and I can bring up the rest of the group. Are they relocating me as well?"

Bethlyn nodded. "They've reassigned me and mine to watch the south once things are settled up north. Agent Ramsey feels that having fresh blood up there might be useful. Now why did you dump this fine young man into a filthy cesspool?"

Caden smiled over his tea, but said nothing.

"It wasn't my fault—" Homer cut himself off as Caden set down his cup. "All right, it might have been partially my fault. I'm not a sea-going captain, after all. The police had been unable to get the vessel out. However it got there, it had begun to sink not long after our explosion here. The water is so murky they couldn't see it anymore, so went back to the station. I calculated that it had kept moving somewhat and found where it had gone. Very small pod really. A single person was probably working it. They got out before we found it."

"He thought we could take a boat over to it and haul it up." Caden ran his fingers through his drying hair. Judging by his face, most of his annoyance was for show at this point and after a few well-placed pints from Homer they'd be fine again. "Your cousin is strong, Bethlyn, he is not always bright about balance. He dumped us into the Thames. Luckily we weren't near anything else and we were able to drag the empty submersible out."

CHAPTER FIVE

⬥

THE REST OF THE CONVERSATION drifted into a few more details about what had been in the missile and then what to do with the submersible.

"There was no way for Caden and me to haul it back here, at least not during daylight," Homer said as he defended his actions. "My crew has to come by later with supplies to fix that hole, so we hid the pod and they'll bring it here then."

Gaston finally stopped reviewing his pages of lists; assumedly they were what he wanted to get done before they left. "You *hid* a top secret boat? Where?"

Caden laughed and shook his head. "At The Crown pub. He has a friend there, and there's a lovely, and very hidden, storage area out back. For a nice fee, it's safe."

"Have you been smuggling again?" Bethlyn laughed.

"It's a handy place for items that you don't want to be found. In this case, it worked out quite well. Caden and I will meet my crew at the pub before supper, then we load the boat with their repair equipment and tuck it back to the mansion neat as you please."

Bethlyn rose to her feet. "I'd love to go with you and watch this operation, but I'm going to secure Bessie and relieve Thomas. He and I also have some errands, but will be back to take the offer of your rooms, Gaston."

Gaston made it to his feet before she left, a bit after Caden and Homer, but he made it. He stayed standing. "I will be in my room, organizing things. There will be a serious conversation with Edinburgh on this relocation, mark my words. There are so many issues to address." He waved his papers over his head and marched down the hall toward the private rooms.

"I believe that Caden and I should be off also. I'm sure you have much to get together as well?" Homer nodded to Nettie as he and Caden stayed standing after Bethlyn's departure.

"Actually, I believe I will join you two," Nettie said as she too rose to her feet. That hadn't been her initial plan, as she did have things to settle, but she had lived in London most of her life and yet never frequented one of the seedier pubs. She knew that after this Welsh adventure, they most likely would be back here; but it seemed a shame not to go this time—and she was curious about the smuggling location as well.

"I don't know that The Crown is a place for a lady," Caden said it but Homer's face echoed it.

"First off, I ain't no one's lady," Nettie dropped into a rougher accent and scowled at both of them. "Secondly, I think I can hold my own." Now that she had decided to go, the idea was growing on her. She was an excellent mimic although there had been little to no need to use that particular talent since she'd joined the Society. Growing up as a lonely child with an inquisitive mind gave her a number of skills that she was looking forward to using. She folded her arms and dared either man to comment against her.

Caden opened his mouth, then shook his head and stayed silent.

"Wise man," Homer said. "Nettie, we would be honored to escort you to the pub." He held out his arm.

Nettie almost took it, then realized that she was still wearing women's pants. She knew someday seeing women in actual pants wouldn't cause a stir, but she knew it wasn't now. And a place like the pub would be surprised enough at her arriving, there was no reason to give them more to chew on. "If you will both excuse me, I think I will change into something a bit less comfortable. It won't be but a moment."

She darted down the hall. Mostly to remind them that, unlike some women, she could change quickly. She had no doubt they would wait for her, and if they didn't, she was perfectly capable of finding the pub on her own. Her excitement grew. She honestly had no idea why she'd never thought to visit one before.

Both men were about where she'd left them, but they dropped their conversation as she came down the hall. Homer smiled.

Caden looked her up and down and tilted his head. "It's not that rough of an area."

She'd changed her appearance by wearing her oldest clothes and hat. Sadly, she only had her old reticule, not the Jeanized one. A year ago, Gaston had made her one with almost magical properties, it was far larger on the inside. Alas, it had gotten lost during the battle with the master vampire and Gaston said he didn't have the resources to create another. The limitations as to what one could fit in the regular ones was annoying.

"I think I look fine. I'd rather not stand out like a dandy." She gave Caden back his look. Yes, as a man he would be less noticeable, but he was a bit of a clotheshorse.

"I believe you look charming." Homer got his arm out in front of her before Caden could respond. "Let's depart. The dandy can walk behind."

The Crown pub wasn't that far from Gaston's home, but she rarely travelled through that neighborhood so had never seen it before.

Old wooden beams that looked like they'd been assembled when the Romans first created Londinium managed to form a large, rambling building. It was early in the evening, but there were plenty of people already inside.

Nettie's stomach gave a grumble. "They do have food here, yes?"

"Actually, they have extremely good food. Far better than many of the places in the nicer parts of town." Homer quickly scanned the room, then led them toward a table in the back. A slender blond man sat eyeing the crowd with a scowl. "My man Potts. Don't let the look fool you, he's got his pub face on."

Once Potts noticed them bearing down on him, his face lit up and he pulled out a chair for Nettie. "Good evening. I believe I have seen you at the mansion, but don't think we've met?"

Before Caden or Homer could do the proper thing and formally introduce them, Nettie stuck out her hand to shake his. "Aye, you work with Homer. I'm Nettie." She'd already noticed curious looks as they made their way to the table. She quickly sat to avoid the awkward social issue of gentlemen standing.

"Potts," he said, and shook her hand. He was shorter than her, and slight. Possibly the reason for what Homer called his pub face. A smaller man in a rough pub might be constantly proving himself. "I've been flying with this one longer than anyone else. I could tell stories that would raise the dead!"

Homer clapped him on the shoulder and sat them both down. "Which is why I keep you in my employ, lad. Keep you quiet." He nodded to Caden and he sat as well. But all three men were watching the pub more thoroughly than Nettie would have expected.

She looked around as best she could, the seat she'd been presented with had its back to most of the pub. "I say, Master Potts, might we swap seats? I have never been here, and would relish a chance to see everything." She gave him her most winsome smile.

He might be an air rat, but somewhere there was some training in social niceties as well. Potts immediately rose to his feet. "Of course!" They swapped seats under Homer and Caden's scowls.

That sealed it. This might or might not have been planned as a standard 'pick up the crew' run, but something was afoot now.

Nettie scanned the crowd as Homer and Potts made small talk of airship updates. Most of the men were working class, start early in the morning and be off by now. But a few appeared dangerous. And injured—old injuries. Living was rough for most people, and injuries occurred on farms and in the city. But the types of injuries before her were more likely the result of multiple fights. And fighting far from proper medical facilities, if she had her guess.

One of the men in question moved across the pub and she verified her guess. He walked with a distinctive swagger, one found on people who spent more time on water than on land or in the air. Pirates.

Now, they could be honest seafarers, but that walk, combined with the injuries and general snarly appearance, indicated sea pirates. Two more of Homer's men came to the table and nodded. But they were watching the crowd as well. Most likely the ones she had picked out as pirates. She had nothing personally against them and, had there not been a growing tension in the air, she would have been intrigued by the chance to study them. But the crowd noises were slowly dying, and more and more silent touching of various weapons was occurring.

"Lass, I know you wanted an experience, but this might be one we want to stay out of. Caden can escort you home." Homer didn't even look at her as he kept watching the crowd.

Nettie snorted. "I am probably the most qualified to be

here, as I have my weapons ready all the time," she kept her voice low and also kept watching the crowd. She didn't extend her fangs, but she tapped on a tooth to remind him. She was far stronger than any human. The crowd slowly diminished as others realized that something was wrong. "I assume our pirate friends are not normal customers?"

"Agreed on you defending yourself, forgot who I was dealing with. And no, I've never seen them here before." Homer kept his eyes on the room as he spoke.

Caden started swearing under his breath. "I have. When we were fishing that damn boat out. The big one that just walked in was coming down the road as we left. Hard to miss him, doesn't look human."

Nettie waited a few seconds, then glanced where Caden was looking. A massive, squatty man, with a too broad mouth in a round face strode in. The hairs on the back of her neck rose. "He might not be." Before any of her companions could object, she got to her feet and stumbled her way over. After watching enough drunks, mimicking their walk wasn't difficult.

She heard rustling behind her but knew Caden and Homer wouldn't risk trying to grab her. Vampires, and even the odd half-vampire like Nettie, had a strong sense of smell. Over the years Nettie had trained herself to block scents out. Now she was focusing on them.

A salty brine filled the air, not too surprising given the pirates, but it was odd—like the sea, but something else. She aimed her stumbling toward the newcomer and the sense of *something else* grew stronger.

He grabbed her arm as she passed and tried to pull her to him. Nettie pulled back but had to use far more force than she would have needed against a human male. He looked as surprised as she felt. He wasn't fully human, and now he knew she wasn't either.

They glared at each other and the pub went silent. So

much for trying to find out who these pirates were without causing a stir.

"'ey! Get your hands off me!" She took a step back and rubbed her arm. He hadn't hurt her, just startled her. He might have guessed she wasn't human, but there was no reason for the entire pub to know.

"What game are you playing at?" He stepped into the space she left. He was a full head shorter than her, but when he spoke, a flash of teeth made an appearance. Very sharp, tiny teeth, and too many for any human mouth. Were his people some sort of shark-humans?

"No game. Let me go back to me friends." Nettie wasn't afraid, and if he attacked her, she would fight back. But starting a pub brawl wasn't something an agent of the Society did lightly.

"You ain't going nowhere." He reached forward to grab both her arms this time and a scuffling came from behind her. A lot of scuffling.

She twisted out of his hands and spun one of his arms around behind his back. It wasn't easy, he was almost as strong as she, and his arms were oddly short. But while he might have realized something was off when he first grabbed her, he had been surprised by the move. "I think you should leave now," she hissed in his ear, then made sure he could see a bit of fang as she dropped them then pulled them back.

"Undead scum!" he didn't get a full yell out as Nettie took that moment to deliver a solid punch to his gut.

Yells and the clang of steel behind her told her that all bets were off. Her accoster noticed it as well.

His back swelled up until it ripped his coat and he pushed her hand to let go of his arm. He was still winded from her punch, but those teeth came into full exposure as his gums pulled back. Two full rows of those tiny sharp teeth.

Nettie dropped her fangs completely. She had no idea

what he was, but when a pair of sucker covered tentacles started coming out from the mound on his back, she punched him in the face. Hard enough to send him slamming into the wall. Yes, she had fangs, but there was no way she was going to use them.

She turned and shoved off one of his pirate friends who was trying to bash her with a chair. He didn't look completely human either; but so far nothing had burst out of him and his teeth looked normal. At least from what she could tell as she used his chair to send him across the room. Homer, Caden, Potts, and the rest of Homer's crew fought the pirates. A few noncombatants were huddling along the edge of the wall, trying to get to the door. A pub brawl was one thing, non-human creatures were something else. She retracted her fangs and darted to the door. Someone wanted this fight to happen. Where it had been freely swinging before, the door was now stuck closed. She lifted the door off its hinges, then let it fall. "Run! They broke the hinges!" She didn't know how much it mattered, but she'd keep her ruse up of being a normal woman as long as she could. Her removal of the door was subtle enough that hopefully they didn't see it.

Five men ran out as the man with the tentacles got to his feet and charged her. He hit her with enough force to carry them both across the room and pin her to a table.

"Nettie!" Caden's yell came from somewhere to the left. Then he came into sight as she pounded on the man attacking her. Caden swung a chair at the man's head. It got the creature's attention enough to turn him from her, so Nettie grabbed his head and twisted.

She'd received extensive hand to hand combat techniques from the Society when she started. This move should have snapped the man's neck.

It didn't.

CHAPTER SIX

HIS NECK WAS SO THICK that, not only did it not snap, he was turning back to face her.

She got her feet under him and pushed as hard as she could and grabbed a sharp hook-like blade embedded on the table behind her from one of the other fighters. He slammed backwards but one of his tentacles wrapped around her arm. The suckers burned as they dug into her.

Except during the battle with the Master Vampire back in Bath, Nettie had always had complete control over her vampiric tendencies. The layer of red now covering her vision told her that was over. That creature was trying to kill her, this was a battle to the death. She allowed the tentacle to pull her toward him, then yelled to Caden as he rushed forward. "Stay back! All of you!" There was still some fighting, but most of the pirates were down.

The tentacle pulled her close and she lunged for his throat. He went to block her fangs and she swung her arm up and stabbed him in the heart with the hook blade.

The grip on her arm gave a spasm and then released as he fell back.

The pub was silent but there was a group of constables lingering directly outside of the door.

"Stand back! Let the Yard through!" An older man, one Nettie knew as Agent Smythe from Edinburgh, forced his way through the crowd. He had two men and a woman with him. Nettie didn't recognize them, but she was fairly certain they were agents as well. Even if they were also claiming to be Scotland Yard. Or maybe they were both Yard and SEU. Gaston wouldn't clarify that when she asked about agents in the Yard.

"What has happened?" Agent Smythe puffed out his barrel chest even more than it already was.

"These scallywags attacked us for no reason," Homer said as he quickly stepped forward. Caden was right behind him, and both were trying to block Nettie from the crowd. She put her hand to her mouth, her fangs were still receding. A moment later they were gone. Caden and Homer were also trying to block Nettie's attacker. Luckily, most of him had fallen behind a table when he fell backwards in death. Nettie kicked a stray tentacle under the table for good measure.

There were a few people left inside the pub, and more were crowding outside the door. Smythe nodded and his people escorted the pub people outside to interview them and push back the onlookers.

He looked down at one of the dead pirates, then peered closer. "Is that sea foam?" Unlike the one who had attacked Nettie, this one still looked mostly human.

"Possibly. There are also markings of scales, but they are extremely difficult to make out." Nettie leaned forward to point out the slight marks on his neck. And the odd liquid dribbling from his mouth did look like sea foam.

She went to another. "This one also has the foam, but no scales…wait, there they are." The faint outline of scales began to appear on his neck as she watched. But these were of a slightly different shape. Like the first, they didn't come into full appearance, but the outline was clear.

"They appear to be fishmen of some sort. Different breeds perhaps." She stepped over to a third. This one had still different scales, and one outthrust hand had webbing between the fingers. "I'd say they were all some sort of fishmen."

Agent Smythe pulled back from his investigation of the pirates. "You have seen these before?"

"Never." Nettie grinned. "Isn't it fascinating?"

"She has a different sense of fascinating than most people," Caden said as he gathered the weapons from the dead pirates and put them on the table closest to Smythe. "Do you need us to help, or do you have more people coming?"

"Thank you, Agent Smith, we have more coming. And thank you as well, Agent Jones, for the insight to the fishmen. I saw the end of your battle. You accounted for yourself well against a dangerous foe."

As much as Nettie would have loved to stay and examine the fishmen and the tentacled pirate, that was clearly a dismissal. Smythe appreciated what they'd done, but this was his area now. She would have to wait until she could read the reports. She would have pressed harder to be involved, but by now all of the higher level agents in London would have been notified that Gaston and his people would be leaving for Wales in short order.

Not to mention both Homer and Caden were already heading toward the back and what Nettie assumed was the storage place of the mysterious underwater boat.

"Thank you. And thank you for your timely arrival." A few more agents made their way in. Two stayed to block the wide open doorway, the other five moved toward Smythe.

Nettie caught up to Homer and Caden. "So these creatures were after our underwater boat? Where did the rest of your men go, by the way?" She'd seen Homer's men during the fight, but they'd vanished quickly once the agents appeared.

"Not all of them feel comfortable around the Yard, and I needed them to bring the wagon around to the back alley—we need to release the locks from inside here, but the boat will be loaded from outside."

Nettie's adrenalin had been fired up by the fight, and she

was extremely excited to see this underwater boat. The marvels it held would be stupendous. She'd have to get right on it to have decent time to examine it and still prepare for the trip.

She followed Homer, with Caden behind them, through the back storeroom of the pub. There was a wide shelf along the outer wall and, with moves that spoke of a lot of experience, Homer popped a few hidden locks. The panels dropped down and, judging by the dim light now coming through, they were coming down on the other side as well.

The boat was little more than a six foot long tube, wide enough for two people—possibly—if they were fine with being that close. No markings. Nothing external that she could see. "That's it?" Nettie was extremely underwhelmed. Hopefully there was more inside of it.

The face of one of Homer's men appeared on the other side, gave a nod, then a dozen hands rolled the boat out into the alley. Homer waited until it was clear of the hiding spot, then closed things back up.

"How could they see anything? And how could it move?" Nettie got her questions out before they got out of the back room, but didn't get any answers. With nods to Smythe and the rest of his team, Nettie, Homer, and Caden went out the front door.

The crowd had broken up, most likely due to strong looks and encouragement from the Yard and assorted constables hanging around the perimeter.

Caden still kept his voice low. "There was a long stalk that had been extended when we first found it. It had retracted by the time we got it out of the water. Not sure on the movement, but there were small holes in the back that closed up at the same time the stalk vanished."

Nettie still wasn't certain that the underwater boat was of more interest than the fishmen, but she didn't have a choice in the matter.

Once Homer had verified that his men had successfully loaded the boat onto their wagon, and hidden it under repair materials, Homer, Nettie, and Caden made their way back.

"That was an extremely interesting night at the pub," Nettie said. "And is anyone else concerned that we had pirates over thirty-five miles from the ocean? I do believe a pirate ship would be noticeable traveling up the Thames." She wouldn't discuss the fact that they were fishmen until safely back in the confines of the mansion. Ears were everywhere.

"Our friends were after what we have, whether it was theirs to begin with or they knew of it the same way we did," Caden said. "Which would be another issue entirely."

Homer's men and wagon were already at the mansion when they walked up. Some of the repair supplies were on the ground. The crevasse, while smaller than it had been, was still noticeable.

"Any chance it will go away on its own?" Caden peered down into the hole.

"No worries, lad, I've got enough men, you don't have to worry about damaging those pretty hands." Homer looked down as well.

"I think it's closed in as far as it will, Captain." One of Homer's men, a thin, almost impossibly tall man said. "It had still been marginally decreasing when we arrived. It's stopped now."

They couldn't have beat them by much time, but he sounded like he'd been analyzing the crevasse for days. Yes, Nettie and the others were on foot, but the wagon had been heavily loaded. She studied the man for a moment. "You're Reaves, aren't you?" He was from Bath, had been with Homer for years, was whip smart and an intuitive. He felt things that others didn't. Gaston had been trying to get him into the Society for as long as Nettie had been a member. He kept refusing.

"That I am," Reaves said as he bowed. "And you are the estimable Doctor Agent Jones. I am pleased to finally meet you. The Captain here is a bit stingy with his groups meeting each other." His grin was wide.

"Please, call me Nettie. Will you be joining us on our adventure north?" She didn't know if the people relocating them would stay up there once the trip was finished or not. Bethlyn's people would be coming back to London, which would indicate that Homer's would not.

"Aye, at least for a bit. I'd love to talk about some theories I have, if you wouldn't mind."

"Reaves, you made yourself target number one," Caden said. "Dr. Jones loves to discuss theories." He patted Reaves on the back and went into the mansion muttering about tools they would need.

"He can be a most insufferable man at times." She watched Caden walk off and then turned up her smile. "However, I do look forward to spending time conversing with a civilized man."

"Now, where is this thing?" Gaston looked to have come from dinner, or a nap. Knowing him when left to his own devices, he had dinner in the dungeon. The nap might have been unintentional.

Homer pulled back the tarp.

"Is it just me, or is it not very impressive?" Nettie was disappointed, it looked even less impressive now than when it was in the secret storage wall. "I would have expected more…" She wiggled her fingers.

"Doodads?" Reaves asked as he helped remove the cover completely from the underwater boat. "I do agree, it is rather unremarkable."

"Aside from what it did." Homer, Reaves, and two more of his men grabbed the boat. "It did fire a missile underground and almost destroyed this place. It might be plain, but I'll wager there are plenty of doodads, as you called them, inside."

The boat was clearly far heavier than it looked, as the men were struggling. Nettie didn't want to step on their fragile egos, but the fact that none of them thought of asking her, even though she knew they were aware of what she was, was a bit silly.

"Would you like some assistance? Dropping that might be problematic if it still is armed."

All four men looked up, and even Gaston, who was directing, not lifting, looked embarrassed.

"I still forget about you sometimes, lass," Homer said and motioned with his elbow. "Step right in."

Nettie stepped forward, adjusted the weight, it *was* significantly heavier than it appeared based on size alone. "I have it now."

"By yourself?" Gaston came forward. "Don't strain yourself."

She shifted and waved the men off. "I might need Homer to stay on the end for balance."

The other men stood back slowly. It rocked a bit, but she was carrying most of the weight. Homer kept the tail from rising or dipping and they made their way into the mansion.

Gaston was right behind them. "I never did run those tests on your abilities. I believe we might want to add it to the agenda for the north. Aside from looking for sea monsters, there won't be much to do anyway."

Nettie grunted in agreement. This was pushing it even for her, but it was easier to strain a bit than having to lift it with three others. They made their way into the dungeon. Caden was in there rummaging through tools but jumped forward when they came in.

"I know you're strong, but you'll hurt yourself." He continued closer to help, but Nettie shook him off.

"Can you clear that table?" There were a number of tables in the Dungeon, but the one in the center was a massive cinderblock.

Caden swore and moved the items.

"I think we can safely state that my limit is whatever this thing weighs." Nettie sat it down as gently as she could, then shook out her arms.

The rest of Homer's men halted right outside of the Dungeon door, but Reaves followed inside. "Captain? Mind if I stay for a bit and observe? I'll still get out there for the repair work."

Reaves was busy staring at the equipment, so he didn't see the look Gaston and Homer shared, but Nettie did. She also knew that had she not been interested in the Society the moment she heard about it, things like this room would have swayed her to join.

Homer clapped him on the back. "By all means, lad." The rest of you, let's go get things ready." Unlike Reaves, the rest of Homer's men looked happy to leave.

Once Homer and his crew left, Nettie started going through cabinets. "We should probably don protective materials—gloves, aprons, and goggles. We have no idea what we will be exposed to." As she spoke, Nettie handed out supplies.

 "Do you really think these will be necessary?" Reaves put them on slowly.

He wasn't a member of the Society, but he was one who helped it and knew of it—at least the basics. Nettie wasn't sure how much he could be told. And if strange yellowish sea life exploded out of that canister, she thought it best he be prepared.

Gaston came to his side, the eagerness in his face clearly pointing out that he'd found a possible way to convert Reaves to the Society—always a feather in one's cap when people in Edinburgh had been trying for years to do so.

"That is one of the wonders down here, we never know what we'll be up against." He grinned like a madman and donned his protective gear. Which succeeded in making him appear more like a madman.

Satisfied that everyone was covered, Nettie approached the boat. She took out a sounding scope and listened to various areas first. Had it been rigged to explode, or had a bomb been inside, the amount of jostling it had gone through would have probably triggered it. But it never hurt to be cautious.

Finally she took a step back.

"Anything?" Caden might be a man of action, but he was also very curious.

"A slight whirling, sounding like perhaps a motor, approximately here." She pointed to the nose. "I suppose you are ready to try and open it?"

Caden smiled and patted the table next to him, he'd collected everything of size that could open stubborn metal. "Unless you or Gaston would prefer?"

Nettie shook her head, she was more interested in what lie inside rather than what it was surrounded in. Gaston gave a slight bow and waved Caden forward.

Caden cracked his knuckles and took up a small saw. He appeared to be going for the more delicate options first, something which surprised Nettie. She was impressed with his restraint to not grab the largest item and just start tearing things apart.

Unfortunately, the small saw did nothing but make small scratch marks on the side of the boat. When Caden stepped back, Nettie came forward to inspect the marks and listen again. The marks were simply scraping of paint, the dull metal showed under the murky white paint job, and the whirling she heard before appeared undiminished.

"I'll keep working my way up." Caden stepped forward with the next largest saw.

Five saws later, and still nothing beyond scratched paint, Reaves stepped forward. "There has to be a way in, this wasn't created as a single piece." He looked up. "Might I?" At their nods, he walked around the boat, tapping it from time to time. One spot he went back to twice. The spot looked like the rest of the boat, but something caught his attention. "Try here, right along this line." He held up a hand as Caden came forward with the largest saw. "I'd say with a small one."

"Would you like the honors?" Caden handed him the saw.

Reaves' eyes lit up. "I would be honored." He delicately pressed it to the section he'd pointed to and pressed the gears into action. At first it looked like the same results would be coming, then the sound changed and it was clear something was being cut through. Working in a pattern only he could see, Reaves continued until a small square was completed.

Nettie rushed forward with a plunging device to suction the piece off so it didn't fall back into the boat. Like the gear-saw, she handed it to Reaves. There was no way he would balk at joining the Society after this.

The square revealed nothing at first and all of them crowded forward. Then a blast of jet black fluid shot out at them.

CHAPTER SEVEN

—◆—

REAVES, CADEN, AND GASTON ALL spread themselves out in an attempt to block Nettie from the spray. A sweet, if incredibly misguided, gesture. The spray only lasted a few moments and, judging by the tube that was visible through the forest of male arms, was simply the result of Reaves cutting through it, not a defensive mechanism. The spray also didn't go much further than the sides of the ship.

"I appreciate such valiant defenders, but, again, might I remind you all that my physiology is far hardier than yours? Had that been an attacking chemical, moving everyone behind me might have been the better option."

Reaves shrugged, Caden looked embarrassed, but Gaston shook his finger at her.

"True, you are tougher than us mere humans, but you are not invincible. You need to not rely on your strength and physiology to save you. You have met things you couldn't win against." His look softened at the last bit.

Nettie nodded. "You're right, but so was I. Even mere human females are stronger than men give credit for. Or would any of you like to go up against Lisselle?" Excluding the fact that her tiny friend was a witch, she was also one of the best fighters Nettie had ever seen.

"Noted," Gaston said. "However, I believe we can debate women's rights after we finish our investigation, yes?"

Nettie turned away before her cheeks could betray her. Women's rights were near and dear to her heart, but they shouldn't distract from scientific inquiry. Reaves stepped back so she could see inside, but it was more respect for her knowledge than her being a woman. Or so she told herself for now.

The boat, such as it was, looked like a larger version of the missile which had attacked them. The inside was more spacious than appeared however, and aside from a thin row of cables and circuits that seemed to encompass the interior of the entire thing, didn't have much in the way of moving parts. And no windows. "The mechanics appear to be around the space for the pilot, but look awkwardly put together." She tapped a small odd-looking tube near the edge they'd cut in at. It brightened briefly, revealing an animal inside. An eel. But there were no life signs, simply a reaction to her contact. She wondered if it had been alive and died when the ship was brought out of the water.

"I could crawl inside," Reaves had stayed back behind Gaston and Caden. "I am thin, and fit in places easily."

Nettie looked at the inside. There was little that frightened her. Actually, only two things came to mind—being taken over by a Master vampire, and small spaces. It might have been because of the feeling of being trapped in her own body when the Master vampire had taken her over, but the claustrophobia had gotten worse in the past few months.

She stepped back with a smile. "That would be lovely." She pointed to her dress. "I'm not dressed appropriately for such an adventure myself."

Since Reaves was narrower than both Caden and Gaston, they waved him on as well.

The size of the small vessel was even more noticeable once he settled in. He touched the electric eel lamp and it flared again, then dimmed. "There are four of those down on the other side. I don't know how the pilot could see… oh."

Nettie was going to climb in after all if he held that pause much longer. "What?" She finally broke down.

"I am sorry, they have a sensor. A man-made device to see the world without seeing it. Like the fish in the deep. My Da told me about them."

Nettie was intrigued by many things, but odd sea life had never been an interest. Clearly, that would have to change.

"It's dying now, everything in here is. I don't think it was ever alive per se, but it was charged. Even the eel was dead while the ship was running, they were using it to run a current through." He taped a small screen in front of him. Then a few more times when it didn't do anything. If Nettie hadn't been staring directly at it when the flare happened, she wouldn't have seen it. The screen burst to life with lines and markers. Then died. No amount of taping brought it back.

"I wasn't able to make that out, but I think it does what I said." Reaves moved on to tapping other items, but nothing lit up or moved. "It's advanced equipment, but badly used. As if the users weren't the ones who invented it." His scowl deepened and he looked like he wanted to say more, but shook his head instead.

"I saw it." Nettie backed out of the space and found a paper and fountain pen. She quickly drew the markings from the brief flash on a bit of paper. She had an impressive memory, but even it needed help. She held it out, then turned it around a few times to see if it made sense in a different direction. Nope. She was secure that she copied what she saw correctly, she simply wasn't certain that she had a clue as to what it was.

Reaves and Caden stayed looking inside the ship, but Gaston peered at her sketch.

"Does it look like anything to you?" Even holding it at a distance, it meant nothing to her.

"Not really. Although," he pointed to a solid wall. "It was

in this direction when you copied it, yes? With this here?" At her nod he pointed from the map to the wall in front of them.

"Ah! Then this spot is this table and the equipment is here." Nettie quickly applied labels to the parts. "That is impressive."

Gaston's smile turned to a scowl. "And also far beyond anything we have. Caden? Your people experimented with submersibles, how do they see where they are going?"

Caden had been almost crawling into the boat to see something Reaves was talking about, but looked up at Gaston's statement. "Periscope while near the surface. A small screen of triple strength glass when in the water. They don't have great visibility from what I understand." He tapped the boat. "They are also larger than this. Making something this small, with the capabilities it has, would be extremely difficult."

"We need to take this up to Edinburgh," Gaston said.

Reaves climbed out of the ship. "Begging your pardon, but this would be difficult to get on an airship and Homer would probably end up dumping it overboard in frustration." He grinned. "I have been flying with him since right after his Royal air army days, he's touchy about his airships."

"I was thinking of more direct transportation." Gaston held up a summoning envelope. Runners could be called by contacting Edinburgh directly or by summoning them. Nettie had tried taking apart one of the envelopes once, but there was nothing inside, and she couldn't tell what was unique enough about the envelope to call one of the runners.

Gaston tore it open, and by the time Nettie counted to eight, the black clad Runner stood before them.

"Cor! Never seen one of them before." Reaves went up to it and walked around it slowly. "You are impressive."

"Thank you." The Runner's intonation was still flat, but Nettie was pleased that it gave an appropriate response.

Reaves jumped almost a foot in the air. "And polite!"

"What is your need?"

Back to basics. Nettie still had hope for a stronger socialization program for the mechanical men. She might need to wait a bit longer.

"I need this to be taken to Edinburgh at all urgency. Give to Agent Ramsey."

"Please." Nettie added, then shrugged at Gaston's odd look. "If we want them to be socialized, it needs to start with us. They learn from our behavior."

"Did I say I wanted them socialized?" He held up his hand, then turned to the Runner. "Please."

The Runner walked over to the boat and tilted his head. A moment later a second Runner appeared. "We will take." They each grabbed an end and left. Again, so quickly that it appeared they vanished.

"Now they *are* impressive." Reaves rubbed his chin and looked around the Dungeon. "If I were to join the Society, could I be working somewhere like here?"

Gaston swallowed the massive grin that burst out. "Of course you could. There are also field jobs, scientific outposts, many options."

"I think I'd like to learn more."

Caden smiled. "I believe we need a nightcap, join me in the parlor? I was an agent in the States, but I am still a recent addition to the Society over here. I can give you a fresh view."

Nettie thought about joining them, then realized Caden might be a better choice alone. Gaston appeared to come to the same conclusion.

"Very well, go about your drinking. I need to talk to Edinburgh and get things closed up here before our move." He waved to them, then started to uncover the Mudger.

Nettie figured he not only wanted to tell them about the boat and their findings, but to brag that he had Reaves on the hook.

"I should be sorting my own notes and projects, make sure that I have everything ready for our trip." They weren't supposed to leave until the day after next, but one should be ready for anything with the Society. Not to mention she had no idea what relocating them all, even temporarily, would entail.

Gaston nodded but was focusing on the Mudger.

Nettie had her own smaller laboratory next to the dungeon. She quickly packed up her investigative supplies, not that she felt there wouldn't be any up north, but the move did seem to be rather sudden and they might not be properly prepared. She glanced over her ongoing experiments, but aside from shutting them down and insuring that nothing would be left to blow up the mansion, there really was little to do for them. Until the arrival of Caden and the sea urchin, there really had been little excitement as of late. She scooped up her notebooks to take with her; like personal diaries, they contained far more information than she would want to be left behind.

Clutching her supplies and notebooks, she started to go toward the parlor for her evening tea, when a burst of raucous male laughter reminded her of their guest. Actually, the house had been quiet the past month since the others left, so it was nice hearing Caden laugh as well.

She was turning away when she heard her name.

"Now, not to talk out of turn, but what of Miss Nettie? She is one of a kind."

"That she is," Caden said. "Did I tell you how she almost left me for dead when she picked up my attacker at the train station instead of me? True! I'd managed to overcome him in a fight on the train, stashed him in plain sight in the station while I went to clean up before I met her. Next thing I know she's wheeling him out of the station!"

Nettie scowled at the wall, or rather, that difficult man on the other side of the wall. Her behavior was perfectly to be expected. She started to march in there and defend herself when he continued.

"Of course, then she did save my life. More than once, to be honest. She's a good person."

"And attractive."

"Reaves, I thought you said you had a mistress you were quite happy with seeing every few months? I don't know if chasing this one would be your sort of thing."

Reaves laughed. "No, Missy and I have a perfect arrangement. But it doesn't mean Nettie isn't lovely."

Caden was silent for a bit, and this time Nettie wanted to walk away before someone noticed her.

"Honestly? She is gorgeous. And terrifying. And charming. And so smart she makes my head hurt."

"And you have no idea what to do." Reaves laughed, but it was a comment not a question.

"Not a damn thing," Caden said. "I almost welcomed being transferred to Bath these past two months. I've never been this confused about a woman."

Their discussion changed quickly to Homer's airship and various things about its speeds and whatnot. Judging by the relief in Caden's tone at the change, Reaves did it for him.

Nettie took that as the time to go to her room. After picking up a small pot of tea and biscuits from the kitchen anyway. Cook didn't like people in the main kitchen after he'd gone to bed, so he always left a small self-service section near the front for evening refreshments of the non-alcoholic kind.

Normally after events such as the past day, including that insightful bit of accidental eavesdropping, Nettie would be writing letters to Rebecca and Lisselle. It seemed a bit silly to do so, however, when she herself would be on the same dirigible that would have carried her letters to them. Which left her mind with plenty to ponder as she packed up her private things.

When she re-folded the same skirt five times, she sat it and herself down. It wasn't the attack on the mansion, the missile, the tracking of the boat, or even the battle with the fishmen that was rattling her. It was those words of Caden's. She hadn't been sure how she felt about him, and a big part of that was because she was definitely not sure how he felt about her. Knowing that he didn't know either made her perversely happy. She didn't like feeling like she was at a disadvantage in anything, and romantic entanglements were very much a new topic for her. Caden's romantic exploits—just the official ones, conducted in the line of duty, mind you—were part of his official portfolio when he came over. That someone with his background and experience was as befuddled by her as she was by him was extremely satisfying.

With a contented sigh that she and he were back on equal footing, she got up and finished her packing. A few notes to herself in her diary, finishing up the tea, and she went to bed.

CHAPTER EIGHT

———◆———

THE MANSION WAS BLISSFULLY QUIET when Nettie first awoke. She had enjoyed her mornings of solitude since the rest of the mansion's occupants had been relocated. Not at the same value as her missing of them, but it had been a nice time to gather her thoughts.

The silence was broken moments later by an explosion. One strong enough to rattle her collection of exotic tea cups that she kept on her wall.

Nettie leapt out of bed and quickly donned her clothing. Another smaller explosion made her slow down a bit. She was becoming an expert on odd explosions, and the first was louder in part because it had been so sudden. The second was almost mild. She polished off her dressing at a more respectable speed, then ventured down the hall.

A third, much softer, explosion helped her figure out where they were coming from. Outside, in the rear yard. It was still early enough that she was certain their neighbors were not going to be pleased, but they were probably not under attack.

Gaston, Damon, and Cook were all standing just outside the wide glass doors to the garden. None looked concerned beyond a general annoyance. Caden and Reaves were fussing with something on Homer's ship. Bethlyn hadn't come back yet, but her ship was docked in such a way that Homer's fit as well. Nettie didn't see Homer, but Caden and Reaves looked like kids with a new toy. Nettie stepped out the door and watched alongside Gaston.

"One more?" Caden was far too excited for that to be anything good.

Homer was on the ship, but in the pilot's box, judging by the location of his head when it popped out. "No, I think we've done enough testing. We don't want to disrupt Gaston's neighbors."

Gaston stepped forward while shaking his head. "Too late for that, my friend. Care to share with us what you hooligans are doing?"

How all three of them managed not to realize Gaston and the rest were watching, Nettie had no idea. It seemed to her that Caden turned a slight shade of pink when he realized she was watching, but her awareness of his situation concerning her might have been modifying her own perceptions.

"Sorry, Gaston," Reaves jumped down off the ship platform and bent to retrieve some odd square devices. They'd fallen with such force that they'd half embedded themselves in the ground. Caden jumped down as well, and the two of them removed them all.

"Reaves and I realized that if we are dealing with fishmen, and they are underwater, we needed something that could cut through that. He had some amazing ideas as to how water can impact explosions; we built off of that." He held up the block he had freed. There were a number of wires attached.

Nettie and Gaston moved closer to examine the devices, Cook and Damon went back inside the mansion once it was clear they weren't under attack.

"The wires here will show us what would happen had the device been dropped over differing levels of water, with standard exploding jelly added to it." Caden definitely blushed when Nettie brushed him to get a closer look.

"How are you going to fully measure the impact?" It

sounded intriguing, but looked extremely crude at this point. Of course, it was created by two men staying up all night drinking. She hadn't missed that both of them were wearing the same clothes as yesterday.

"We're still working on that part," Reaves said. "We'd been hoping you could help once we're in Llandudno." He couldn't be more than a few years older than Caden, but he definitely had a matchmaker look about him.

Nettie shrugged. "Of course I'll help. And hopefully, we'll have more room and won't be so close to neighbors." She nudged Gaston who'd been looking at the items. People were peering from both sides. They couldn't see much, Gaston's property was extremely wide in the back, but it would be better not to take the chance.

"I believe we should move this inside. The two docked airships are enough gossip fodder for our nosy neighbors," Gaston said. "And you two should shower, change, and pack. I think our leaving might be moved up if our two captains agree. There's been another attack, or rather, sighting. And that should be discussed inside as well." He nodded to everyone and stomped back into the mansion.

Nettie handed the block back to Caden. "It is a marvelous idea, we will have to completely rethink how we will fight fishmen and whoever is working with them."

He paused to see if she was being sarcastic, then smiled. "Thank you." He watched for a few more moments, then shook his head. "I'd better go follow Gaston's orders. I'll see you at breakfast."

Nettie nodded, then backed away and moved inside before she said something stupid. Perhaps knowing what she did was only going to make things more awkward.

"Why such a sigh?" Gaston had been packing some things from the hall as she passed through.

"I really miss my women friends. Not that it hasn't been grand puttering about with the men, but there are things that are best discussed with one's own sex." She tilted her head at what he was packing. "You think they really won't have brass candlestick holders that have never been used? Are you afraid there won't be enough clutter?"

Gaston looked at the candlestick holder he was about to wrap up. "You never know what will be needed." But he put it back on the small hall table.

Nettie smiled and went on to the dining room. Some cooks might have waited on breakfast for those who had been outside and needed to freshen up. Knowing Cook, he probably expedited the food because he was annoyed at their shenanigans. A full breakfast was in place in the dining room in warming trays.

She served herself tea, and helped herself to eggs, bangers, potatoes, grilled mushrooms, and slices of thick toast.

Gaston gave up his packing of the entire hallway and joined her. He settled in at the head of the table with enough food for two people. He looked over at her. "You don't know, this may be a very long day. Travel always messes with dining times."

Homer came in, followed by Caden and Reaves.

Gaston waited until all three had gathered their food and sat. "Very good. Bethlyn and her crew will be joining us later, but I can fill you in on the latest from the north."

"Anything about the boat?" Reaves hadn't officially accepted joining the Society, but he was already fitting in.

"Nothing as of yet, I'm afraid." Gaston said. "But there was another sighting in Wales. This time whatever it was went into the estuary and accessed the River Conwy. Unlike prior times, the creature didn't accost people, last early evening it simply climbed one of the guard towers in Conwy castle. And stayed there until dark completely fell. As far as the team out there can tell, it did nothing but make sure it was seen."

"What did it look like? I notice you are using *it*, not he, so it wasn't one of our fishmen?" Nettie was becoming even more intrigued. What would a monster from the sea want with a thirteenth century castle that was little more than outer walls?

"Yes, I meant *it*. The description was specific in that no one seemed to agree what they were seeing, other than it didn't look like what you described of those fishmen. It was described as large, vaguely human shaped, with a larger rounded head, and appeared to be covered in sea kelp. That was about it."

"And for that we're moving up our timeline?" Homer said. "I have no problem, as most of my things are already on the ship. But that could be a time issue for the rest of you. Not to mention Bethlyn's agenda."

"What about my agenda?" Bethlyn said as she came into the dining room. The rest of her crew trailed in behind her.

"Well met!" Homer waved them toward the food. "The timeline has been moved up, or will be if you and I agree. Edinburgh must only be suggesting the time change, not demanding it?" He looked toward Gaston.

"That was the way it was presented. A strong suggestion, but not an order. I believe this incident pointed out to them that they needed more agents set up in the area quickly. Conwy and Llandudno are quite close to each other, but that is still a wide range to cover in terms of water access to land."

Bethlyn gathered her food and sat. "But there have been no real attacks yet? Just a few odd interactions with drunks coming out of pubs in Llandudno and now an even odder sighting? Nothing aggressive?"

"Maybe not there, but we had an encounter, and they were plenty aggressive," Reaves said, then nodded to Homer to continue the story.

It only took a few minutes to tell of the attack of the fishmen, and the belief that they were after the boat as well. It had felt much longer at the time, but looking back, Nettie realized the entire event had taken less than ten minutes.

Bethlyn pounded Homer on the back. "I leave you for a short while and you go out picking fights with fishpeople! Does sound exciting, but with Nettie on your side I'm sure it was no problem."

Nettie felt a twinge. She understood what Gaston had said about her not counting on her abilities in every situation; over-confidence could kill an agent. But the same needed to be addressed with the people she worked with. "Actually, I almost couldn't keep their leader at bay. If Homer, Caden, Reaves, and the others hadn't done so well, he would have beat me." The shudder she gave wasn't faked. "He was as strong as me, and those tentacles were terrifying."

"Tentacles?" Bethlyn glared at Homer. "For a sky pirate you are a horrible story teller. You didn't even mention that."

Homer shrugged. "Things were moving fast, but yes, the one Nettie fought had them—seemed to be the only one."

"I think they were different types of fishmen," Caden said. "The markings that appeared were different on each one I saw. Have we heard from the Yard?"

"Nothing as of yet, but Smythe contacted me via a messenger early this morning to say he understood we would be relocating soon and he would send updates north."

Bethlyn's crew settled in to eat and the discussion turned to the trip. Between the two airships, getting them relocated wouldn't be a problem. The airship crew finished quickly and went on a supply run for their ship.

After they left, the discussion returned to packing—there would be enough room, providing that Gaston didn't bring the entire household. Or at least the entire Dungeon.

"They will have equipment up there for you," Homer

said for the third time. "Lisselle has a fully functioning laboratory up there. And it's closer to Edinburgh than we currently are, so they can get whatever you feel is missing down there quickly."

"But our studies—"

"Need to take place up there." Nettie would normally never cut him off, but round four of this debate was quickly going to descend into round fifteen and she really had had enough. "Think about it, Gaston. Theses fishmen have abilities we have never seen. No one in the agency has seen, that we know of," she added. "This is a chance for true exploration of the complete unknown! How can you not be excited?"

Gaston frowned for a bit. He really preferred the excitement to come to him for the most part. Here in his comfortable, safe, well stocked mansion. He couldn't admit that, obviously, but it was clear on his face. "What do you mean; that we know of? Are you implying someone in the agency has had some sort of contact or knows something they aren't telling us?"

Nettie smiled at his change of subject. "There might have been something. Remember when Agent McGrady went missing? His tracker was found in the ocean."

Caden nodded. "But he wasn't. He almost killed me."

"Oui, and we never found his tracker, nor why it was showing live in the ocean. I believe Edinburgh continued searching but nothing was ever shared." Gaston helped himself to some more tea, but he was clearly pondering that dropped thread. "Yes, this might tie in with our other mysteries."

Trackers were placed in every agent to help identify them should they go missing. Nettie didn't find out she'd been given one until Caden had arrived and had his almost removed by an attacker. Caden had come to London to replace Agent McGrady, who was supposed to go abroad.

He instead betrayed the Society by destroying two airships and killing over thirty people. Then he went vampire and had to be taken down. Yet, for a while after his confirmed death, his tracker showed him alive in the waters off Bath.

"Well then, nothing to be done for it. So we'll be off today?" Reaves had polished off enough food for five men and finally looked content. The mystery of the tracker wasn't as exciting as a chance for adventure.

Gaston looked up and waved them on. "Yes, yes. My things are mostly done, since I can't take everything I would like." He shot a glare to Homer, then got to his feet. "I do believe that I will be giving a quick call to Edinburgh, just to check on the state of things." He nodded to Nettie. "If you will excuse me." He left the room muttering to himself.

Caden rose as well. "Since we were up most of the night working on our depth bombs—which are still not completely done—I believe I will go gather my things, as well." He also nodded toward Nettie and left,

Nettie finished her tea and shook her head.

"What's so amusing, lass?" Homer was still finishing up, but he and Reaves looked like neither were in a rush.

"It has struck me a few times recently that it will be nice to be in the company of women on a regular basis again. I'm getting tired of being the only woman." It wasn't that Gaston or Caden were usually rude when there were others, but their behavior appeared far more deliberate since it had only been her. Had Bethlyn and her crew still been in the dining room, they would have nodded and excused themselves to them as well, however this more formal excusing to Nettie was getting old.

Homer laughed. "It must be difficult. I don't know how I would do if the roles were reversed."

Nettie finished her tea and took her leave. They had plans to make, and she wanted to make one final check that all was ready on her end. Gaston hadn't mentioned what time they would leave, but she had a feeling that might change after he spoke to Edinburgh.

Damon was having the same thoughts, as he was outside his room arranging boxes. Gaston had tried to convert him to an official agent years ago, but Damon had been happy as things were. And he was always on top of things inside the mansion.

Except now.

He would bring a valise out into the hall from his chambers, to join one already there, then take it back. The hall was long, but he'd still managed to complete that action three times since Nettie started walking toward him.

As she passed his room he was inside, so she stuck her head in. "I'm sure whatever you have in there will be fine."

Damon jumped. That was another first. He rarely was startled. He was a young man, somewhere around Caden's age but he had the soul of a wise old man.

"Oh! Miss Nettie, very good to see you. Yes, I…well, you are the soul of discretion, are you not? I can tell you." He stood there in silence for a few moments, then finally shook himself. "Yes well, please don't tell anyone. But I am hoping to begin courting Rebecca. Officially. At some point when we are in the North." He looked so earnest that Nettie had to reduce her estimate of his age by quite a bit.

She smiled. "That is wonderful. Just remember, she will care for *you*, not whatever you bring with you. Have you heard from her?"

Again the earnest nod. "Yes, only a few times, but it has given me hope." His face dropped. "But there is the class situation."

"That you are a servant in technicality?" Nettie knew what it was like to be on the other side. Spending most of her life growing up being passed from family to family left her very unclassified. Which meant she was considered lower class.

"Yes. I know most agents within the Society are fully dismissive of class boundaries, but it is outside of it that I fear. And what will her family think?"

"The easiest way, which still would not be easy by any means, would be to apply to join the Society. I believe you are right, in that the majority of agents, at least the good ones, don't hold by those antiquated ideas of class level. Sadly, most of polite society does." She stepped forward when his head went down. "Don't join only to make things easier in your relationship. If you feel it fits you, talk to Gaston to start the process. If you don't, know that many of us are outside of what is approved by society in terms of class structure, and we fare fine." She gave him a smile that he finally returned.

"You are always kind and extremely right. I have many things to think about." He picked up the valise he'd been bringing back and forth and brought it to the hall. "Do you think I might make a good agent? If I decide that is the best direction?"

"I think you would make a superior agent, Damon. You are exceptional at everything you do." With a nod, she continued on to her own room. Damon and Rebecca were in a sticky situation, she hadn't mentioned it, but Rebecca's letters had been becoming more maudlin about missing Damon. They'd only had a short time together as Rebecca went from new agent to vampire victim to relocated to the north in a fairly short time. But they'd both fallen for each other.

She'd restacked her boxes near the door, after checking each one five times, when Caden appeared in her doorway.

"We have a lift off time, two hours. He won't share what they said, but Edinburgh got Gaston moving quickly." He looked around the room. "Looks like you're ready?"

"Yes, although I did debate on the guns." She was issued two Society gear pistols. Even regular guns were rarely used outside of anyone in the Society or in military service. These were special inventions of the Society. She couldn't decide if one or both should go with her.

"I would take them. We don't know what we're up against. It's better to have them and not need them than the other way around." He nodded to her boxes. "Might I assist you in relocating your collection to the backyard, Agent Jones?"

Nettie smiled. Normally she would have said no, she could do it herself. But she knew he was aware of that. She also had that snippet of his conversation last night with Reaves floating around in her head.

"That would be lovely, thank you, Agent Smith." She selected a relatively light one and he grabbed one of the heavier ones. That it would have been easier for her to take most of them in one swoop was known, and ignored, by both. The small talk about the trip, the north, and some-how the garden, as they carried her boxes out, was relaxing and insightful.

She knew Caden was charismatic, but she had never been certain how much was real. She could tell he was trying to be charming, and it worked. But there was a genuine appeal there as well.

"Ah, there you are!" Gaston came out of his hallway carrying a small box. "I might need some more help with my things." Trailing down the hall were Homer, Damon, Reaves, and even Cook. Nettie was going to chastise Gaston, but he was looking too pale. She took the box from him. It was surprisingly heavy for the size. Most likely books.

She leaned forward and whispered quickly into his ear. "You need to sit. I am the only doctor here right now and if you don't sit while we move things, I will tell the others of your doctor's statement."

He narrowed his eyes, then gave a short nod. "Ah, thank you, Nettie," Gaston said loudly, and then rubbed his back. "I believe I slept wrong and activated that old gunshot injury." He sat down on a nearby bench.

Nettie narrowed her eyes back at him, a silent glare to keep him in place. "You must be careful. We will move your things to the airship—you stay here. Doctor's orders."

"You deal with the dead." Gaston argued even though his color was returning as he sat.

"Yes, and you don't want to join them, do you?" With a huff, Nettie turned and led the line out to the ships.

They were stacking the boxes between the two airships and letting Bethlyn's crew load up first.

Within a half hour, everyone's belongings were stowed, even though Nettie did have to make Gaston leave some more obscure books behind.

Bethlyn's hold was filled and then Homer's. His airship was the larger of the two, they still almost managed to fill it completely.

"You really need all of these things?" He scowled into the hold. A heavier airship would move slower and lower, neither of which made a captain happy.

Gaston had come outside and was sitting on one of the garden benches as the final items were brought out. He stood, but a quick glare from Nettie got him sitting again. "Since Edinburgh will give no indication as to how long we will be relocated? Yes." He folded his arms.

"So be it then. Okay, I can take Nettie and Caden. Bethlyn will take Gaston and Damon. Cook is staying here. It will only take about ten to twelve hours." Homer was clearly proud of the time, as well he should be. Even though Homer's was older, both airships had been upgraded with secret technology from the Society to such a degree that they were far faster than any standard airship, or even a war zeppelin.

Gaston didn't see it the same way. "Twelve hours? On that? No offense Captain Bethlyn, but I simply cannot be floating about for that long. If you give me my small travel case back, I will make arrangements for a train and join you there."

He was higher ranking than any of them, but Nettie wasn't sure she trusted him alone. "For continued safety, I believe someone should ride with him." She tried to keep her voice light, but at the same time remind Gaston what she would tell the others if he refused.

Damon nodded. "I will get our travel cases and set up the train." He might have been trying to delay his meeting with Rebecca, he clearly had been afraid of what she would say. But he was also the best person to stay with Gaston.

"I can take care of a train by myself." The argument was simply for appearances, Gaston knew he wasn't going to win the fight, and Damon simply nodded and moved their smaller bags back into the mansion.

The only change in plans after deciding that Gaston and Damon would take the train, was that Bethlyn would go straight to Llandudno. "Very well, then I think we are ready to depart." Homer nodded to Nettie and Caden to board.

CHAPTER NINE

—◆—

NETTIE HAD RIDDEN IN AN airship, this one in fact, to Edinburgh a few months ago whilst they were trying to save Queen Victoria. That had been her first trip and she'd been too concerned about the actions of the queen, aliens, and vampires and had not paid attention to the trip itself.

This time she paid attention. And loved the views for the first two hours. Then she started pawing through Gaston's boxes to get out something to read. She would have been more comfortable in the cabin, but being on deck was far more exciting. In theory at any rate.

"Bored already?" Reaves said as he came beside her. He was still part of Homer's crew, so had jobs to do on their trip, but he didn't look like that was why he was coming by.

Nettie shut her borrowed book, The Theoretical Transmogrification of Sheep into Monsters —a hypothetical book based on a Society agent who spent too much time alone on a sheep farm—and smiled. "Not so much bored, but, well, the scenery becomes a bit the same once you get out into the countryside. At least from this height."

"Which sounds like bored." He grinned.

"I was trying to be polite?" She laughed. "Yes, a bit bored. What do you and the rest of the crew do while on longer trips?"

"Mostly read, think, in some cases, write." The pause at the last word caught Nettie's attention.

"Write? Do tell." There was an almost guilty look on his lean face that definitely caught her attention.

"You mustn't tell anyone, but…well, if I do join the Society, I suppose it will come out. I am Miss Pelock."

He dropped his voice so low she almost didn't hear him. "Wait, the swooning female who writes those sensational short romances? The ones that usually end up near a beach of some sort?" She laughed, but kept her voice down. "The ones the upper classes devour, then deny having heard of them?" She herself hadn't read one, but she had been meaning to just for scientific inquiry. They caused quite a ruckus in the upper tiers of society as people kept trying to guess who the author really was.

"Yes. My publisher is even more embarrassed that I'm the one writing them than I am, so they work extremely hard to keep my identity a secret. I did the first as a lark on a dare. After a lot of drinking." He shrugged. "It was a huge success, and oddly fun to write, and they paid me to do more."

"I will keep your secret; however, you will need to tell the Society if you apply."

"I figured you would. As for the Society, they might work even harder than my publisher to keep my identity a secret. And it might work in their favor if a way of coding information could be worked into the books." He looked thoughtful.

"You know, you're right. Especially for the agents with higher tier profiles. Thank you for sharing your secret with me."

"It's nice to know that someone else knows." He nodded to Homer. "He doesn't even know, and it was his drunken dare that launched it. If he ever reads the first one, I'm doomed, as it is basically the premise I came up with while drinking with him."

Nettie watched Homer striding across the deck booming orders to his people. "I think you're safe on that."

Reaves nodded and got to his feet. "So, if you get too bored, that's always an option." He raised his hand as Homer spotted him. "Bethlyn's veering toward Wales and I'm about to fix that line, Captain, never you fear."

Homer stopped before he got his yell out, nodded, and strode off to the other end of the deck.

Caden was helping the ship hands where he could; he seemed far more excited than one would deem normal, to be honest. The Theoretical Transmogrification of Sheep into Monsters held little sway now, and she sat the book down next to her. Nettie watched Caden carefully. He'd discarded his overcoat and loosened his collar. He'd also rolled up the sleeves of his shirt in a becoming, yet inappropriate, manner. From a scientific aspect, he was an extremely fit male specimen. And if she admired the way his muscles bunched as he helped Reaves pull in a line, then that was strictly scientific observation.

The laughter in her head sounded clearly like a combination of Rebecca and Lisselle's. She let out a sigh. She'd made it this far in life without any serious romantic entanglements, she didn't see why she couldn't make it out of her twenties without the drama of one. She also wished it hadn't been someone she had to work around all the time. It wasn't unheard of for agents to fall in love—no one else but another agent knew what they went through on a regular basis. Although they never confirmed it, she was fairly certain that Homer and Lisselle had a relationship of the romantic type long before Nettie joined the Society.

But there were so many variables to consider. How did one know for certain the other person liked them at the same level? She had an advantage in overhearing the conversation, but Caden had admitted he had no idea what to do about her.

That feeling was definitely mutual. She watched the crew

for a while more, then found some other books to read for a bit before heading to the cots inside and some sleep.

It was quite a bit later when a yell from the deck jolted her awake. She quickly adjusted her clothing and ran up on deck.

The crew were all there, most making sure they secured their lines which held them on the ship. A caution used when on the deck of an airship. The dangers of falling off were far more permanent than being swept off a sea going ship.

"Ahoy, Captain! There's a war zeppelin bearing down on us! She's moving fast, but I can't see her colors!" The crow's nest was in a different position on an airship than it would have been on a sea going vessel, but the job for the barrelman was the same. British war zeppelins worked for the crown, one would never be without the Union Jack. Nettie secured her own line that tethered her to the deck.

The ship went silent as all hands waited to hear what the barrelman in the nest would say. Nettie had exceptional vision, but had yet to see any ship in the air anywhere around them.

A shot of a cannon cracked the airspace off the port bow. Immediately, Homer started yelling orders and Caden and Reaves went below deck to man one of the cannons. Two more of Homer's people went down to man the second. Homer had retrieved his own spyglass and was watching the clouds where the shot had come from. Eventually, a war zeppelin came into view above them.

Had Nettie been of the swearing type, the air around her would have been blue. As the barrelman, and everyone else on the ship, could now see, the Union Jack was displayed. But the white lines looked wrong—it was upside down. Either a desecration of the flag and country—or that war zeppelin was in extreme distress. Judging by the movements she could make out, Nettie would bet the later.

"Make way! We have lost control!" The voice shouting from the war zeppelin was even louder than Homer could be. A moment later a body, clad in the uniform of the royal British air army, fell not ten feet past the balloon onto Homer's ship and silently vanished below them.

The ship above them was silent for almost a minute then a second body jumped off, they pushed themselves away from the zeppelin but Homer was ready and he and five of his people had a pair of giant hooks with heavy netting swung out away from the side of the airship. The person hit the net and stayed in.

Nettie stumbled a bit, but then ran over to where they were pulling the nets in. They might have saved the solider from falling, but they hadn't saved him from his death. He had many wounds, including some tentacle marks, most of which were bleeding profusely.

Nettie moved closer to offer what comfort she could before he passed on.

"Good catch, Captain," the man got out the words with difficulty. "Hoped you would. Ship over Irish Sea, they snuck onboard. Not human. Fish-like." He handed Homer a crumbled paper. "Going to crash into London shipyard."

Homer rocked back and Nettie held both of the man's hands. It was clear Homer knew him, might have even been with Homer when he was part of the Royal Air Army. The man had hoped Homer could get him so he could pass on the information. A fully armed war zeppelin could wipe out all of the grounded airships in the royal yard if it crashed at the right angle.

"Move forward and up, we're taking that thing down!" As he yelled, Nettie noticed that the barrelman was sending a code, most likely to Bethlyn's ship. She would be too far away to help in time, but if something happened, at least someone would know about the zeppelin.

The war zeppelin rocked as a small explosion hit from

within. It took Nettie a moment to realize that it wasn't Homer, someone on the war zeppelin was trying to bring it down.

"Captain, destroy them. Please." The dying man's last words came out in a wheeze. Nettie gently closed his eyes and turned to relay his words, the grim look in Homer's eyes told her he'd heard them.

The war zeppelin was trying to stay above them but Homer's ship managed to come up level with them and Homer yelled, "Fire!" The airship rocked as the cannons fired and the zeppelin took two hits, one in its balloon.

Two more shots, and the war zeppelin started to spin. Nettie looked down and noted the large lake below them. "Is that the Threipmuir Reservoir?" The new reservoirs were the only bodies of water she could think of in their location.

"Aye," Homer said as he too peered down. "Probably not going to make too many people happy, but there's naught to be done about it now." He took a sheet and covered the dead solider. "We'll leave him at Edinburgh. Our stop there will be brief, we need to drop off what we brought them from London, and tell them about this attack and what happened to the zeppelin. I don't know that the attack on the zeppelin had anything to do with our current issue, but we can't ignore that it might."

"Those were fishmen on that zeppelin."

Homer turned back to Nettie. "Your eyesight is that good?"

She turned back the edge of the sheet to show the dead man's arm. "No, it's not. But he has many tentacle marks." The ugly red welts looked painful, and having had a brief encounter with them, she could image how horrific the pain had been.

"There's nothing to be done then." He called up more details to the barrelman to send to Bethlyn.

Caden came up at that moment and looked at the somber faces around him and the sheet covered form. "One of ours?"

Homer shook his head. "A solider from the zeppelin, he managed to get to us to tell us the fishmen took over their ship before he died. We need to find out where that ship had been stationed. He mentioned the Irish Sea, but they had to have been set down somewhere—I don't think the fishmen can fly."

"Don't even suggest that," Nettie said with a shudder.

The rest of the crew began to prepare the ship, Edinburgh would be upon them soon. They needed to check in and Gaston had sent a box of samples to drop off, plus some mail from other southern stationed agents. But they would make it a quick stop.

"Are you okay?" Caden had stayed next to her. He looked genuinely concerned.

"I will be." She rubbed her arms. "What kind of beings can take over a war ship? This poor man had tentacle marks up and down his body."

"Did they leave anything behind? Anything of the suckers that might help you figure out what they are?

Nettie's eyes widened. "You amazing, wonderful man! I could kiss you. But, propriety dictates that I do not." She dropped down next to the body. She had two sample vials in her pockets. Gently she pulled back the sheet and turned the arm closest to her. Yes, there were pieces of something where the creature had dug in. "I need—"

A pair of gloves appeared near her head. "Gloves? Someone taught me I should always carry them."

Nettie was embarrassed she didn't have any, but she was glad that he'd listened to her. Gloves on, she carefully removed the small bits and put them in her vials. Caden dropped down to his knees and handed her two more empty vials. "Trade?"

"Thank you." She searched for more particles and stoppered the final two vials. "And thank you again for thinking of it."

"I've had a great teacher."

They both rose to their feet and he handed her back the first two vials once she removed the gloves.

Edinburgh was coming into view, Nettie waved to the increased activity on the deck. "Go play with the others, I want to secure everything I took out on our trip."

Caden gave her a speculative look and a small smile, then went off to help bring the ship in.

Their arrival in Edinburgh was anticlimactic compared to the recent attack. The ground crews came out and helped lower the airship without any issues.

Homer was almost ready to jump off before the gang plank even got lowered. "Reaves, make sure everything is secure and let no one on this vessel unless it's one of us. Nettie and Caden, let's go drop our mail, boxes, and information. Kipen, Rhys, Stan, and Franks, take our departed with us to headquarters. He might not have been of the Society, but we all serve the crown."

Homer and Caden grabbed the boxes and mail and Nettie kept her vials close. She wouldn't hide them from the agents in Edinburgh, but she wanted to make certain that she had something to study as well.

There was really no main headquarters for the Society in the south, only small, organized clusters of agents, such as at Gaston's mansion. Edinburgh definitely was a headquarters. Providing one knew where to look for it.

The entrance was hidden behind a ramshackle building a bit off of the Royal Mile and down a very unassuming alley. Going down the alley was what allowed one entrance, if the person was a member, or simply a view of a dead-end if one was not.

The small door to the left at the end wasn't designed for

entrance, but for communication. It slid to the side, revealing only darkness, no clues as to what was there.

"Agents Homer Tremain, Nettie Jones, and Caden Smith. Plus crew members bearing a fallen royal airman. Requesting entrance." Homer's voice was somber and he rose to his full height.

A creaking sound was heard and two panels high above them slid open. Two crossbows came out and pointed directly at them. A bit old fashioned, but Nettie wasn't sure even she could beat a bolt at this close range.

CHAPTER TEN

◆

AFTER A FEW TENSE MOMENTS, the crossbows vanished, a door to the right of the panel slid open, and two agents came forward. "Sorry for that, there have been strange happenings of late. You have all been confirmed. A dead royal airman you say? I'm not sure why he would be brought here." But they motioned for everyone to come inside.

Homer waited until the door shut behind them. "He was serving on a Royal war zeppelin that was overcome by fishpeople. It crashed into the Threipmuir Reservoir."

The first agent, the one who had spoken, raised an eyebrow. A look of extreme surprise for an established agent.

"Fishpeople?"

"It's long and complicated," Nettie said. "And he should probably be examined before turning him over to the Royal air army." She wasn't going to go about telling them their business—unless of course they weren't doing it.

"Good idea, Agent Jones," The booming voice behind her could only belong to Agent Ramsey. His massive form blocked out most of the hallway behind him. "Take our unexpected guest to the morgue. I will bring our living guests inside. He shook everyone's hands and offered nods to Homer's men before turning and leading them down a long hallway.

The chamber they were brought to was very neat, clean, and looked like a formal guest meeting room—not somewhere that agents would be taken. Nettie wasn't the only one to think of it.

Homer sat down the boxes he'd been carrying, folded his arms, and glared. "What are we being questioned for? And what was that business at the door? Weapons?"

Nettie stood at the ready and was pleased to note Caden had set down his parcels and taken the same stance as well. She certainly didn't know enough about headquarters to know what or what was not normal. However, a senior agent like Homer would, and he didn't look happy.

"Easy there, lad," Agent Ramsey pulled out a tea cart from behind a wall. "We heard of the fallen war zeppelin, but the noise was that it fell under attack of a rogue airship. I assume that was you. Considering that no single airship that I know of, even yours, could take down a war zeppelin under normal circumstances, I had my doubts of the story."

"Then why are we in this room?" Nettie could tell Homer was still not appeased.

"Always questioning, aren't you, Jones? One of the things that will make you one of our best one day, if it doesn't kill you. There is a Royal envoy here taking up the lounge, and we thought it best to keep the groups separate until we figured out what happened." He nodded for Nettie to sit. "Tea and a debriefing of the attack, nothing more." He grimaced. "Well, and the war zeppelin destroyed Agent Hudges favorite fishing boat when it crashed."

Nettie glanced to Homer and when he nodded and laughed, she took her seat. "That's the real reason we've been banished." His smile dropped. "No one was hurt, were they?"

"Nay, the ship was in dock. The war zeppelin sank immediately and we had a thought to leave it since there would have been no survivors at the depth it went in. But if what you said is correct, and these are the same type of fishpeople Gaston notified us of, I think we can't let things go unwatched." He nodded to Nettie and Caden. "Please make yourselves comfortable. I need to go pass this along to Agent Zero." He was gone before they could respond.

Agent Zero was the mysterious head of the Society, but few beyond Agent Ramsey had ever seen him. He was supposed to be wise and aged beyond any human—but no one would admit to what he was.

Nettie went over to the tea cart. It was generously stocked with biscuits, scones, and finger sandwiches. They might be in a room not to Homer's liking, but it was stocked well.

"I could pour," Caden said.

Nettie tilted her head. She had no problem with men taking care of domestic duties such as serving tea, in fact, she encouraged it. But it was uncommon for Caden. He also wasn't very good at it.

"Thank you, but I shall serve this time." She started setting up the cups and saucers.

"I hate to be blunt about it, my boy, but you are not good at serving hot beverages." Homer came and took a seat.

Once they'd filled their plates and settled around the tea cart, Nettie started examining the room they were in. "I would call this a sterile room, but I'm not sure as to why us being here upset you so." When she'd been here before they only made it into the hall before the information came that the queen was heading south again.

"That's why. It's sterile. They put us in a safe room." Caden sat back with his tea and took a healthy bite of his second sandwich.

"Aye. This place is huge, and most agents are brought further inside. That they only brought us to this place, a room more often used for formal information gathering from non-agent contacts, instead of further in, raised my hackles. Even more than having crossbows drawn on us."

"But that it was done to avoid the Royal representative makes it acceptable? We do need to tell them about their people." Nettie was still missing some dynamic here, but she had a feeling it might be a personal animosity between Homer and the Royal representative rather than a professional issue. She enjoyed Homer's company quite a bit, but it did seem that like the way many people reacted to Gaston, there were many folks who didn't feel the same.

Homer sighed. "Yes, my parting with the Royal air service was understood by some and not by others. I gather whomever is here is one of the ones who felt I was betraying the Royal Air Service. Ramsey can get their man back to them after the Society people have examined him. Clark was a good man. We were only on the same zeppelin a short time, but he was a good soldier."

"What was on the paper he gave you? Things happened quickly and I forgot to ask." Nettie decided that while she might not like the décor, there was a quietness to this room she very much enjoyed. Particularly after ten hours on an airship manned by a chatty crew of men.

"I forgot as well!" Homer reached first in one pocket, then the next before pulling it out. The paper was torn on one edge, possibly from a book. As he held it up, a map was clear on the back side.

"He must have already been in bad shape when he wrote it, just grabbed a page out of a book, and wrote 'beware the red sea and the orb'." He flipped over the page, then back again. "That was it."

Nettie sat down her tea. "Might I look at it?"

Homer shrugged and handed it to her.

She looked at the map side first, she didn't believe Clark just grabbed this page. He knew he was dying, they were under attack, and he had enough foresight to scribble a note before he threw himself off the zeppelin in the hopes that Homer could bring him on board his ship. This page would have been deliberate. She'd hoped to see a map location of where they'd gone to land and had been boarded.

Instead it appeared to be the coasts of Northern Ireland and Wales. Namely the large section of water between them. The page appeared to be from a map book, but the side he wrote on was blank before he made his warning.

She flipped back and forth a few more times before a cough from Homer brought her back. "I do apologize, I was trying to see the connection between his words and the map."

"There might not be one, lass. He was dying."

"He had time to talk to us, briefly. Yet, he said nothing of this, but gave it to you. And since he did say they had been in the Irish Sea, and this is a map of a section of it, I think the two are related." She waved the paper around.

"Might I?" Caden hovered on the edge of grabbing it, but he refrained from doing so.

Nettie handed it to him. "Is there anything in the area of water between the two lands?"

"That they could land a zeppelin on?" Homer asked. "No. There would need to be a station of some sort for them to go down with any hope of rising again."

"There has to be a connection of some sort." Nettie polished off her plate of food while trying to figure out what she was missing.

"I agree with both of you," Caden said as he scowled at the page. "He was deliberate in his actions and might have picked this page for the map. Or since he had limited time and knew he was dying, grabbed the first blank page out of any book he could find." He pointed to the side with words. "It is odd though, that he wrote so little, but clearly left room for more."

"They found him before he could finish?" Nettie said. But the writing, while not great in penmanship, didn't appear rushed. She'd love to have more time to look over it herself, but a junior agent shouldn't be taking liberties with things in the Society's Headquarters. Ignoring the vials she had hidden in her pockets. If asked, she would hand them over, she just wasn't going to offer them.

Homer held out his hand for the page and quietly folded it up and put it back in his pocket. "Somethings might do best when looked at slowly."

Caden shrugged and Nettie nodded. While she wouldn't *suggest* hiding it, Homer was a senior agent, and his action worked for her. If they found anything of importance, she knew Edinburgh would be told.

The door cracked open at that moment and Agent Ramsey came in. "We have a team going out to the reservoir, they can't dive as deep as the wreckage, but all will be armed as well. Thank you for the warning about the fishmen? That is the term you used, aye?"

"It does seem to fit, although the one with tentacles wasn't a fish, so maybe mermaids? Now, we've only seen men, granted, but the myths of mermaids could have some validity. Merpeople?" Nettie had never thought of naming new creatures, or people in this case. They must have something they called themselves.

"Sounds good to me, and if there are men, there are most likely women as well." Caden added.

Ramsey laughed. "Aye, I've read your docket, lad. If there are women, we'll send you in to seduce them and solve this without a fight."

Caden smiled, but looked decidedly uncomfortable as he quickly glanced to Nettie. "I'm sure those days are behind me, but we should assume these merpeople are both genders."

"They could be oddities, a group of men who somehow transmogrified into sea creature hybrids. They might not be a separate species at all." Nettie watched Caden and she noticed that she wasn't the only one, Homer had his eye on him too.

"Now, don't sell yourself short, lad. I won't go into details since there's a lady present, but you have a way with the ladies that is legend. More female enemy spies fell due to Caden Smith than any other source." Ramsey was clueless as to Caden's reaction, but Caden's face was getting redder.

Nettie was now also becoming uncomfortable. How could she think about romantic entanglements with someone with his history? Would she ever be sure he wasn't just building his skills?

"Now, I think Caden is retired from that aspect of his career," Homer said with a speculative look at both Caden and Nettie. "He's other skills that we need more. We'll get these merpeople, never you fear."

Now Nettie had another thing to worry about. Homer might suspect something was going on between her and Caden and was stepping in to smooth things through. She didn't know what was going on with she and Caden, it was going to be annoying if others were speculating on it as well.

"I'm sure whatever Caden's skills are they will all be well used. These merpeople have already shown to be a danger." Nettie set down her teacup and plate. She really thought they'd have left by now, she was anxious to see Lisselle and Rebecca.

Ramsey grew serious. "Aye, they have. They tried to destroy Gaston's mansion, and there was a crew of twenty-eight men and women on the war zeppelin. The merpeople might have only been walking about in Wales, but they're killing now. And if they had succeeded in crashing that war zeppelin into the London zeppelin yard, there would have been dozens, perhaps hundreds more lost." He handed a folder to Homer. "Here's the information on the sightings in Llandudno and Conwy, I would have given it to Gaston, but I've heard he's taking a train in a day or two?"

"Day or two?" Nettie wasn't happy about that. "He said

he'd be right behind us. Someone might need to nudge him, he really doesn't want to come north."

"Well, he'll have to if he wants his things, a goodly portion of his worldly belongings and equipment is still on mine and Bethlyn's ships."

"I'll have Smythe check on him to make sure he's still moving. Now, on another topic, there was a mention by Gaston that your man Reaves might actually be warming to joining us? He would be a good fit, smart, book educated, and clever about inventions." Ramsey stopped before he rubbed his hands in glee, but it was implied.

The conversation went into the benefits of encouraging Reaves in joining the Society. Nettie almost brought up Damon's interest as well, but stayed silent. He was still trying to work things out, and while she did think he would make a great agent, she didn't think that would be the case if he only joined to win over Rebecca. Or to make things easier in terms of class levels.

Conversations about the Society always seemed to digress into long drawn out things; particularly when in a secure place where discussion could be open. It was a full hour later that Ramsey finally got up and made his goodbyes. Nettie knew Homer hadn't planned on being there that long, but there had been many things to discuss about the attack on the mansion as well as the fight at the pub. The basic information had been passed along before, but there were always little details missed during the first telling.

"I have some items for Lisselle, she asked for some more scientific supplies," Ramsey said with a nod to Nettie. "I think she's setting up your lab. She and Rebecca are doing some studies, but for the most part they've been investigating. Having you all up here will give us a bigger force." He came back and handed them three large boxes. "There will be more coming, since the relocation was rather last minute there wasn't time to gather everything. Nettie and

Caden will be stationed with Lisselle in Llandudno, she has cover stories for you. Homer, you'll be officially staying with Gaston in a small house in Conwy—per Gaston's choice—but you'll all have covers that build in together. They are basic and not deep, we want people there to mostly ignore you lot." He nodded to the boxes and he herded them toward the door. "The cover stories are all in there, but Lisselle also has them since she made most of them up."

Nettie stopped him when she was almost out the door. "Will you pass along anything important about how Clark died? The airman."

Ramsey nodded. "Of course." He smiled, but obviously something else had come up and he needed them to move on.

There was no fanfare as they left. Homer looked around once they were in the alley. "Shall we shop for supplies here in Edinburgh?"

"No," Nettie said, then smiled to take the sting out, she had been rather abrupt. "I'm sorry, but we still have a ways to go before we hit Wales, I'd really like to get there sooner rather than later." Part of it was seeing Rebecca and Lisselle, the other part was that she was really not a big travel fan. She'd thought she'd like it, but she apparently was mistaken.

"I agree." Caden adjusted the box he had. It was clearly heavy, but Nettie refrained from offering to trade. "I would like to get a base set up quickly. Just because these merpeople," he dropped his voice at the word since they were back in public, "haven't attacked anyone in Wales, that we know of, doesn't mean that they won't."

Homer held up his hand. "I'm fine with that as well. Let's get back and head south again. It will be interesting to see what Gaston has selected for our lodgings."

The airship was prepped and ready. Reaves was standing

at the top of the loading plank glaring at anyone who got too close. It looked as if the rest of the crew had come directly back onboard after dropping off Clark's body.

"I wonder why you and he aren't staying with the rest of us? Or at least in the same town?" Nettie had done careful study of the area and knew Conwy was close to Llandudno, but they were still a bit of a ride apart. And if Gaston was unhappy about leaving his beloved and extremely hectic London, going to a tiny fishing village like Conwy was an odd choice. Llandudno wasn't large at all, but it was bigger than Conwy.

"That is a good question, and when that wily Frenchman gets up here, we can all ask him." Homer stored the new boxes in the hold, then motioned for his crew to bring up the plank and prepare to leave.

Caden went back to helping the crew. Nettie would say he was bored, but he genuinely looked interested, and was actually good at it.

Nettie took a few extra items below decks. The crew and guest cots chained to the beams below looked more inviting than they had last night. It would be late afternoon by the time they arrived, and whilst she normally wasn't one for too much napping during the day, this time it felt warranted; she was exhausted.

She'd only meant to rest her eyes for a quick nap, but judging by the amount of scurrying and yelling above her, she'd been out longer than that. Or they were under attack again.

She got to her feet and ran up the stairs to the deck. No attack that she could see, just the crew preparing for landing. She'd been asleep for that long? She did feel much better, but that was odd enough that if it happened to someone else, she'd recommend they go see a doctor.

"There you are, I told my crew to let you sleep, and you were out hard. Are you all right?" Homer handed her some water.

"I am surprised. I didn't sleep well last night, but this is odd. More than odd, it's disturbing." She finished the water and suddenly a burst of itchiness hit her left arm. Scratching wasn't done in polite company, but Nettie didn't really care at this point.

"Lass?" Homer took back the empty cup from her and she unbuttoned and rolled up her sleeve. An odd rash was spreading on the inside of her arm, starting at her elbow and traveling toward her hand. It was almost as unattractive as it was uncomfortable.

"I wouldn't be scratching that," Reaves said. "It looks like an allergic reaction; used to happen back home sometimes. Something got you." He looked around. "Do we have any salt water?"

Nettie tried to not scratch, but the urge was overwhelming.

Caden darted down into the hold, then came back with a bucket of water. "We do now. Sorry, dumped your salt supply in here."

"That should work. It sounds odd, but put your arm in the bucket." Reaves gave her an encouraging nod.

As if she needed encouraging. If they said hanging upside down from the crow's nest and singing God Save the Queen would stop this, she'd do it. She pushed her sleeve up as far as it would go, although a wet sleeve was nothing if it would make this stop. The itching was becoming stinging, and was getting worse.

CHAPTER ELEVEN

SHE GAVE A SIGH OF relief as soon as she managed to cram her entire arm in the bucket. "What was that?" She peered at her arm. The red splotches appeared to be dying down, but she'd keep her arm in there as long as needed. "And how did you know?"

Reaves peered in the bucket as well and shrugged. "It looks like an advanced case of octopus sting rash. At least that's what we called it growing up in Bath. Surprised it didn't get you sooner since that merman you killed had his tentacles on you. Impressive that the damage went through your sleeve though. Back home it only happened on exposed skin."

"This is from two days ago?" That was definitely a long delayed reaction, but she agreed about the impressive feature of going through fabric. She would have noticed if he had torn her sleeve.

"Have Lisselle look it over, and if you need, we've some more medical support not far from town." Homer also looked into the bucket.

"Do you want to look as well? My spotted arm is a thing of beauty." She held the bucket toward Caden which did cause the other two men to back down. "By the way, thank you for the quick thinking on making salt water."

He waved her off. "I'm fine without seeing it, it did look…uncomfortable before you put it in the bucket though." The pause said he'd been about to say something else.

"Ugly. It looked ugly. You can say it." She started to lift her arm out of the water, but the stinging and itching came back immediately. "I might need something larger if this is going to carry on for a bit."

"I'm sure Lisselle will fix you up." Homer gave one final nod then went back to landing the airship.

Nettie took her bucket with her and went to watch.

Great Ormes Head was a very large hill overlooking Llandudno that functioned well as an airship docking and landing port. It did get some heavy winds at times, at least according to the reports Nettie had read, but the airship captains swore it was one of their favorite places to dock, when it wasn't unapproachable. It wasn't a large landing area, there wasn't a lot of air traffic that came over this way—most vacationing travelers took the train instead. Even the very wealthy.

As lovely as the Great Ormes Head was, the view of the town of Llandudno was gorgeous. It looked like the perfect classic seaside location, with blocks of brightly painted row homes facing the water and a pier that jutted out into the Ormes Bay. A good sized hotel was being built near the pier, which, along with the improved train routes, would only lead to more visits from the rest of Britain.

She tilted her head at the new building and other nearby construction. "How long has work being going on at that hotel?"

One of Homer's men turned where she pointed. "Aye, The Grand Hotel, they started a few months ago, maybe six?" When she nodded in thanks, he went back to his business.

Nettie chewed her lip as she stood there with her arm in the bucket, and squinted in thought toward the hotel. "What if all if this construction bothered the merpeople? This area wasn't really even settled until not that long ago, and these are gorgeous beaches. Maybe this was their land home." Nettie found herself feeling almost sorry for the merpeople, then she thought of Clark and the rest of the souls lost on the war zeppelin. "Or perhaps they are just evil." She hadn't thought of anyone hearing her, she was simply thinking out loud. But a cough behind her told her someone had heard.

"They could be both, you know." Caden had stepped beside her at some point and was fixing his shirt sleeves to a more respectable status. "You might be on to something as to when the visits started and when this mass of construction started. And having seen their work a few times now, I have to say they are probably evil."

"Perhaps Lisselle and Rebecca have more information about our visitors." Nettie nodded as she looked out at the area before them. "There they are!" She got so excited about seeing her friends that she let go of the bucket to wave. Caden made grab for it, but managed to take him, her, and the bucket to the deck. And left them both soggy.

Caden rolled to his feet, then reached down and helped her up. "Sorry about that, but your arm seems to look better?"

Nettie wrung out the worst of the water from her skirts and then looked at her bare arm. "It does look better, and not as itchy-stinging anymore." She peered closer at her skin and frowned. "But the bumps are still there. Bother." The airship was almost to the landing platform, so she finished buttoning her sleeve.

"Nettie!" It was a good thing that this wasn't a call for decorous behavior, Rebecca was bouncing up and down like a small school child who'd gotten into the sweets. Lisselle was smiling and wearing all black, in widow's weeds she was trying to stay more composed.

Nettie waved back. It had been far too long to be separated from her friends. Logically, she knew, since they all were agents, they could and would be stationed where the

Society felt best. Emotionally, she didn't agree.

The airship landed and Nettie was the first to get off. She'd debated jumping, she was certain she could handle it, but it wouldn't be good for people watching them.

She did run to hug first Rebecca and then Lisselle as soon as she disembarked. She always felt to be towering over them both. Both tiny, Rebecca had black hair and bright blue eyes, and with her size and features, people were always thinking she was much younger than she was. Lisselle was an older agent with short grey-black hair that often was spiky in appearance and wide grey eyes. She usually had a slightly wild, devil may care appearance, but playing the role of a rich widow with her travelling companion left her in all black. Her normally sharp face was practically gaunt with all the black around her.

Lisselle returned the hug. "It is so good to see you! I must say that, while I do love a trip to the country now and then, the last few weeks have been a challenge. That one has been chomping at the bit, and she's from here." She nodded to Rebecca who was now saying her hellos to Caden and Homer. She was also peering around the crew coming off. "Oh dear, I'm not sure how that is going to go. Rebecca was extremely happy about seeing you again, but very mixed about Damon."

"What? Why? Her letters have been filled with how much she missed him! How can she be confused?" Nettie watched her friend. "Gaston decided to go by train and Damon went with him to make sure it happened. They took their time and will be here in a few days."

"That Gaston, he really is fighting coming up here." Lisselle shook her head. "As for Rebecca, it's the fear that what she thought was there wasn't really there. With little time actually together, she started questioning if it wasn't all made up in her head."

Nettie watched as Rebecca turned to greet Caden and

Homer. Caden lowered his head to say something in a whisper and Rebecca blushed but nodded. Most likely he realized who she was looking for.

"Where's the Bessie? Bethlyn's airship should have arrived yesterday, if not sooner." Nettie wasn't great at telling apart airships, but there was only one other one docked besides Homer's, and it was a massive thing twice the size of Bethlyn's ship.

Lisselle had been clucking over Rebecca's quandary, but her look turned serious at Nettie's words. "There was another airship sent from London that came directly here? The port director told us both airships were going to Edinburgh together, then were coming down here."

"That's bad—they had a lead on us because once Gaston took himself off the airship, Bethlyn decided there was no reason for them to go to Edinburgh." Nettie called over Homer. "Bethlyn never made it."

"They told us she was flying with you the entire way," Lisselle said. "Damn it. How can an airship go missing?"

Nettie and Homer shared a look as the same thought hit them. There was a much more powerful war zeppelin lying in the Threipmuir Reservoir that said how they could go missing.

"Let me confirm with the dock master what he heard and when. We'll start sending the belongings that we have to your home. It is good to see you, though." Homer's grin flashed through his beard as he went off to find the dock master.

Caden and Rebecca walked over. "I heard the other ship didn't get here?" Caden kept his voice low, even though no one was standing nearby.

"That is correct." Lisselle took his arm as she scanned the crowd and raised her voice. "It is so lovely to have my nephew and his fiancée here in this trying time. Come now, you may drive the carriage to our borrowed home."

Caden looked over to Nettie but she shrugged. She hadn't seen anything about her being anyone's fiancé. But the dossier she'd read hadn't been written by Lisselle either, regardless of what Agent Ramsey had said. Being his fiancé up here could be very good or very bad for their budding relationship. If it would ever get around to budding.

There was no reason for a carriage other than Lisselle was playing a part, they only rode for five minutes. The place Lisselle had picked out was large and Nettie was again surprised that Gaston had chosen not to stay there. While not as massive as his mansion, there was enough room for probably all of the agents, as well as Homer's crew if they so wished. It was set a bit back from the promenade and the bay, but still, any room facing the water would have lovely views.

Caden handed off the horse and carriage to Lisselle's stableman, most likely an agent, even though Nettie didn't recognize him, and then Lisselle escorted them inside.

Lisselle held up her hands. "Before anything, I need to change. This is simply the most annoying and uncomfortable outfit ever imagined." She didn't wait for a response but went up the stairs.

Rebecca laughed. "She does that every time we go out officially. When we are sneaking she wears more comfortable things. She built up that her persona was a bit of a recluse so people wouldn't be shocked at not seeing her much." She led them into the parlor. "We do have a cook, but she is off visiting her cousin for a day. Can I get you some tea before supper?" At their nods, she scurried toward the back of the house.

"Fiancée?" Caden got it out first, but looked as unsure as Nettie felt.

"I know that wasn't in the dossier that I read, and I think I would have noticed had you proposed. I was supposed to be here as a distant family relation to help around the house. A poor distant relation, if I recall."

"I was supposed to be Gaston's traveling companion."

"That was before he went and rented a place all the way in Conwy," Lisselle said as she came down the stairs. "He fuddled things up badly. I am still holding the rented lease on the house next door if he changes his mind." She looked far more comfortable in her loose light sweater and women's trousers. "I felt the nephew, fiancé bit might allow for less notice."

"Why is Gaston picking a smaller town, I thought he disliked small towns in general?"

"He does, and who knows. I didn't find out he was taking the train until now. Clearly, he's not going to let us in on anything." She waved her hands at the annoyance that was Gaston. "Bigger issues, tell us about the attack."

By the time Homer and his crew had made it down with their things, Lisselle and Rebecca had been filled in on the war zeppelin attack.

Homer's people moved everything into a back room, some of it was Gaston's, then most of his crew left. Reaves stayed with Homer after a few words with the other crew members. Rebecca poured tea for Homer and Reaves, and Lisselle even waited until they'd had their first sips before launching.

"First off, welcome aboard, even if unofficially, Reaves. Secondly, what happened to the other airship from London?"

"It's too dark for an official search, it could have gone down anywhere between here and where we separated. The dock master states he received notice from the air station in London that both airships would be going to Edinburgh first."

"What? We didn't go through London air station, how would they know?" Nettie knew the airships that worked for the Society had to file something of their comings and goings officially, but that change would have been made by Gaston, or remotely by Edinburgh.

Homer leaned forward to pull forward the curtain. Night was falling early. "I know that. You all know that. The dock master wouldn't know that. So no one was looking for Bethlyn's ship."

"Do we think they fell afoul of the same fate as you almost did? Could there have been another war zeppelin compromised?" Rebecca's face was pale.

Nettie knew that she was concerned for the people on the airship even if she'd never met them. But it was also that, even if Rebecca knew Damon wasn't on that airship, he should have been.

"We've no idea. I telegraphed Edinburgh immediately from the air station, they hadn't heard of any other missing ships. Nor any sightings of an airship crashing. They had the information of our battle with the war zeppelin and its crash into the reservoir before we got there ourselves."

"I'm sure you brought your maps, so let's take over the dining room and see if anything stands out as a place they might have been attacked." Lisselle was on her feet and halfway into the next room before anyone even rose.

"So, the assumption is that she was attacked, not accidently crashed somewhere?" Caden asked.

"No idea, but we have to look at all options. We'll take my airship up tomorrow and see what we can. I'll contact Edinburgh to see what airships they can send down to help search as well." He gave an odd noise. "Maybe Gaston does have a sixth sense, something more than just not wanting to be up here that made him refuse taking that airship."

"Thank goodness," Nettie said as she looked over the maps. "I do wish he were here though."

The maps showed the regular routes and the not so regular routes followed by airships. While it appeared they could go anywhere they wanted, and they actually could, certain areas were more dangerous than others. Weather, not only around them but coming off higher elevations, could cause a crash. And following established routes made it easier to do what they were going to have to do tomorrow—find a missing one.

They mapped out first the route Homer had taken, then added where the war zeppelin had crossed their path. Nettie followed its path back to the Irish Sea and placed a large question mark at the end. There was an entire coastline they could have come from. She'd bet the Welsh coastline except that if they came from there and had been aiming for London, they wouldn't have crossed Homer's ship as far north as they did.

"So that is where the war zeppelin attacked you?" Lisselle tapped the large X Nettie had drawn.

"I don't think they were looking for us, but ended up crossing our path by happenstance," Nettie said. "If their plan was to ram the ship into the ship yard in London, going after us would have been stupid."

"True," Lisselle said. "But what if your friend went this way." She took a string, anchored one end where London was on the map. Then pulled it toward the Great Ormes. "They crossed paths if the timing was right."

Homer shook his head. "The paths might have crossed, but I think the timing was off." He moved a small glass napkin ring over where the zeppelin was, then a silver salt shaker a bit past it. "They would have had to have been here to have seen us when they did. But that would have put them at the wrong time to cross Bethlyn's ship. Without knowing where the zeppelin was when it was taken over, there's no way to know if they could have crossed their path. Not to mention, her disappearance might have nothing to do with the merpeople."

"There still could have been some chance they did overlap though," Reaves stepped up now with a new pair of napkin holder and salt shaker. "If they were going at an increased speed, she is faster than you and was carrying less load, then—"

A sharp rap from the front door cut him off. "Now that's rude, we might not be eating, but we could have been." Lisselle was almost to the door when she looked down at her clothing. "Okay, this won't do. Rebecca, can you do the honors?"

Rebecca opened the door as Lisselle stepped out of view. The lights from the street combined with the bright light from inside the house and made it impossible to see who was there beyond an outline of a man-like shape. There was also a nasty stench.

Nettie got to the door before the others, shoved Rebecca out of the way, and slammed the door shut. "Whatever it is, there's sea kelp hanging off of it, and it smells very fishy."

Everyone in the room brought out weapons as whatever Nettie had slammed the door on started trying to break in. Or was just knocking.

"I might have been hasty, does anyone in this town wander around covered in kelp?"

Lisselle's eyes were round and she looked ready to laugh even though she was still holding her sword cane up. "Not that I know of. And you are the only person I know who is concerned she might have upset a monster."

"It really sounds like knocking. I'd think monsters would bash more, knock less?" Nettie waited, she wasn't going to open the door until there was an agreement.

Lisselle looked to Homer. "Think we can handle it?"

He grinned and held up his own blade. "Just like old times. Nettie, let it in."

Rebecca stepped back. She had a small gear pistol, but in close quarters that might not work well.

Caden and Reaves were both armed as well, and Caden nodded.

Nettie swung open the door.

She'd been right on her first assessment, it was a mer-person. Of some kelp sort. The size of a tall man, he was completely covered in kelp. He muttered and floundered forward as the door he'd been knocking on opened and he lost his balance.

Nettie's reaction was automatic and she grabbed him before he fell.

"Homer." The creature's eyes rolled back in his head and his now dead weight brought him and Nettie to the floor.

"Did that thing say my name?" Homer stepped forward.

Nettie pushed back the kelp around his face and upper body, it wasn't part of him but a covering. It was Thomas, one of Bethlyn's crew. And he had sucker marks all over his neck.

CHAPTER TWELVE

———◆———

"THOMAS! WHAT IN THE HELL happened to him?" Caden came forward as well and dropped down on his other side. He pulled off some more of the kelp. "Is it okay to remove this? They didn't turn him into one of them, did they?"

Nettie bent down, he was still breathing, but so shallow she could barely notice it. "Yes, I think we should remove this kelp and find a secure place to dump it, far from the house. No, I don't think he's become a merperson."

Lisselle and Homer nodded, and both went out the door. "Lock it behind us." Homer nodded to Reaves before they closed the door. No one had put away their weapons.

"What can I do?" Rebecca wasn't a fighter, but she was trained and could do what was needed. Right now Nettie had enough fighters. "Can you get a room ready, down on this floor? And ready all the medical supplies you have, he's not doing well."

Caden had been removing the kelp from Thomas and pulled back swearing. "They tortured him. There are knife wounds all along his side. Damn them."

Nettie glanced over, she couldn't see them all, but the ones she could weren't from a knife fight, there were many but they looked shallow, as if he'd been lashed by something. The kelp was all off of him now and his clothes were tattered and torn.

Rebecca came back into the front area and used a blanket to grab the kelp and tossed the bundle outside then relocked the front door. "I figure we don't want it in here given the situation with things coming out of the sea." She looked to Nettie and Caden. "Probably not a good idea to touch it if we can help it. We can take it further away later."

"Thank you, can you stay with Reaves and watch the door while we move Thomas?" Nettie knew she could carry him herself, but he was injured and jarring him more could kill him. Hopefully, two people would keep him steadier. Looking at his wounds, Nettie was surprised he had stayed alive this long. The crew couldn't have been taken more than a day ago, but he looked like he'd been lost at sea for a week.

At Rebecca's nod, Caden and Nettie did the gentlest carry they could and brought Thomas into a small guest room. Rebecca had pulled back the blankets, and hot water, rags, and two full medical kits sat on the dresser.

A knock at the front door made both Nettie and Caden start.

"Stay with him, I'll check," Caden said. "Hopefully, it's just Lisselle and Homer."

Nettie stood next to Thomas but faced the door. Unlike the others, she hadn't pulled out a weapon. She was trained in them, all Society agents were, but between her half-vampire strength and her fangs, she *was* a weapon.

The low murmuring of voices as the door opened told her it was their people. She turned to Thomas. The suction wounds were worse than the knife work. She cleaned them, then, thinking of her own arm, darted out for some salt from the dining room, added it to the pot of water, and then dabbed it on the tentacle markings. They immediately looked less red.

A full examination revealed that the tentacle markings were limited to his neck and arms, and the knife work, or whatever had caused those lash marks, while it looked bad was mostly to cause pain, not to kill. Some of the wounds were decidedly not recent.

She came out to the others still in the foyer after she dosed him so he could sleep. Shutting the door to the room he was in behind her, she motioned for the others to go into the parlor.

"We didn't see anyone else, and by his footprints, he seems to have come from the bay." Homer looked furious. Too many people were dying or missing, and he had no one to fight.

"We have some other issues," Nettie said. "It appears that Thomas was recently tortured, by knife and by tentacle. But he's been somewhere exposed, somewhere without much shelter, for days, possibly longer. His skin indicates a period of extreme exposure and dehydration."

"How can that be?" Reaves had sat to face the front door, but he was listening. "We saw him in London."

"Or you saw someone who looked like him," Lisselle said. "There are ways to mimic others, myths really, of ancient times and old dead powers. But they were myths of the sea hags and spells they used, and that fits right in with our nautical situation."

Caden shook his head. "So, someone kidnapped the real Thomas, held him on what, a deserted island? For a few days. Sent a perfect duplicate to London to impersonate him with Bethlyn, then just now started torturing him? And how did he get free? He was barely able to move, I don't think he could have escaped from anyone."

"There could have been more of the crew replaced, someone else might have gotten him out," Lisselle said softly.

Homer and Bethlyn weren't close, but they definitely had a family fondness for each other. "I don't think she was replaced, I would have known. I only knew her crew in passing, and the rest of you didn't know them at all. But I know her, and the person we said goodbye to in London was Bethlyn."

"We have to tell Edinburgh and warn Gaston to be more paranoid than usual on his trip up here," Nettie said.

"He should be on his way already, shouldn't he?" Rebecca asked. Of course, she hadn't had near as much exposure to Gaston as Nettie.

"Not if I know him. He'll keep stalling until Ramsey threatens to go down there and bring him up himself." Homer was thinking the same way Nettie was.

"I do have a Mudger, Edinburgh sent it down a few days ago." Lisselle got up and headed up the stairs. "I wanted to keep it away from the public areas of the house. Actually, I was figuring on moving it to Gaston's place once he got here, when I thought he would be taking up residence next to us." Lisselle stopped in front of a door. "I'll be keeping it now."

The room she opened was small, made even more so by the amount of gadgets and technology. The Mudger sat in one corner and was newer than Gaston's version.

"Gaston first? With our luck, he'll get on the first train in the morning and not check things." Lisselle warmed up the Mudger.

Nettie knew that was extremely doubtful, Gaston would be checking that Mudger for signs of someone trying to reach him up until Damon dragged him out the door. The Mudgers couldn't store messages, not yet anyway, but they could show an attempted call. Nettie knew that Lisselle knew that as well and was far more concerned about Gaston than she was letting on.

The Mudger finally came to life and Lisselle quickly entered the codes for the connection to Gaston's machine. There was a moment of fear when it kept ringing. There was a click, then a pop, and Gaston appeared. It wasn't that late, but he looked like he'd just woken up—of course the image was never very clear on a Mudger.

"Yes? Lisselle. And the rest of you. I have a perfectly good explanation as to why I haven't taken the train yet."

"Good to see you, old friend, but that's not the only thing we're calling you for. Bethlyn's airship is missing and it looks like some or all of her crew had been replaced before they even got to London."

Gaston pulled closer to the screen. "What? Tell me everything."

Homer had been hovering over Lisselle, so, with a smirk, she got up from the seat. "I think Homer is jumping at the bit to tell you."

With a nod, Homer took the offered seat and told Gaston what happened. Lisselle's version would have been more interesting probably, but Homer's was quick.

"So is Thomas going to survive?"

Homer motioned for Nettie to take his place. "I don't know to be honest. He'd been left somewhere with little water, food, or shelter for at least a few days. When they tortured him there wouldn't have been much resistance left. I've treated what I could and gave him something to sleep. He needs a hospital." She knew they couldn't risk him in the public hospitals and the connections they had in London were useless here.

"We're calling Edinburgh right after you, so we can tell them we need to bring him in," Homer said over Nettie's shoulder.

"Good to know I was more urgent than our leaders," Gaston said.

"And we needed to make sure that you knew to get on the first train in the morning, and both you and Damon need to be on watch the entire trip," Homer added again from over her shoulder. But when Nettie started to rise to let him take the seat, Homer waved her off.

"There were things—"

Lisselle leaned over Nettie's shoulder as well. "That are

not surpassing the fact we have at least one doppelganger, possibly more. I may need to call in my northern sisters, this could be driven by a form of witchcraft."

"I can't help you on that magic work you do," Gaston said. He was again looking for a way out.

"No, you can't. But worrying about you two will make it hard to cast any major spells. And I will be worried about you and Damon unless you are where I can keep an eye on you."

They closed out with more assurances from Gaston that he'd be on the morning train, and from Nettie and crew to not get into any more trouble until he got up there.

Rebecca and Reaves had stayed downstairs to watch both Thomas and the door. The rest were starting to go back downstairs when the shouting started.

Lisselle was the first down the stairs and she ran into the foyer. Reaves was holding the door shut against something that had managed to break the locks without a sound. He buckled a bit as the door pushed open and three long strands of kelp slapped at him. Rebecca was standing a few steps back, but the steady look in her eye said she'd have no trouble shooting whatever came through that door.

Caden and Nettie ran forward and slammed the door shut again. Rebecca might have had her eye and her gear gun on the door, but she was standing in front of the open door of the guest room they'd put Thomas in. She turned at a sound, then turned back. "Help! He's having an attack!"

Lisselle ran in and Homer followed.

Nettie felt the pressure on the door increase, as if every single strand of kelp they'd removed off of Thomas had become sentient, ambulatory, and multiplied. They also really wanted to get in this house.

"We have to fight them off, they keep pushing harder, and we're going to run out of energy." Nettie refrained from pointing out that there were other doors and windows they could attack from as well. The kelp might be moving on its own, it didn't seem to be smart.

Homer came out of the guest room. "He's calmer now, but they're having to sit on him. Nettie, you and I should go out the back. Caden and Reaves, keep this door shut."

Nettie looked to Caden, she was in a better position than him to keep the door shut. He nodded and they quickly swapped places. The door popped open a bit, but not even a strand got through.

Nettie and Homer ran through the kitchen, then out the back and around to the front. The creature trying to get in at first looked like another victim like Thomas, man shaped.

But the discarded blanket lying at its feet said the truth— it was the kelp itself. It turned toward them, even though it didn't have eyes nor ears, and flung itself at them.

Homer had a sword now and sliced through the strands. The parts he cut off stopped moving but what remained continued.

Nettie grabbed her skirts, tore off the outer layer, and wrapped her hands in the fabric. The kelp monster was on her in moments. She used her natural speed and flung it over her head.

A few strands slapped her in the face as it flew over and she fought not to scream. It was as if someone had heated a steel wire and hit her with it. "Don't let the strands touch you, these have some stingers in them." They'd been dormant when they'd pulled them off Thomas, they were fighting back now. They had to take care of this quickly.

Homer started slicing more as the thing gathered itself back up and made another run. Caden came out the front door and ran past both Homer and Nettie with an even larger blanket than the original one spread in his arms. He got as close as he dared, then jumped and engulfed the kelp monster in the blanket. They rolled and he kept hanging on even though Nettie could see some strands were whipping around and striking him in the face and arms.

Lisselle came running out as well, magic driven sparks arching off her fingertips as she slowed down. Caden was still rolling, fighting to hold onto the blanket engulfed creature.

Nettie stepped forward, but they were moving too much for her to have a clear shot, and she didn't want to make things worse.

"We've got this thing." Lisselle stepped closer. "Now!" Caden released the monster and rolled free, strands chased after him. Lisselle whispered a spell and the sparks flew from her fingers and hit the blanket.

Nettie wasn't sure how spells worked, but in a normal situation the kelp probably wouldn't have caught fire, as it and now the blanket were soaking wet. But something worked, the blanket smoked, then burst into flame, engulfing the fabric and the kelp inside of it. The strands couldn't out run the magical flame.

In less than a minute nothing but ash remained. Nettie glanced to Lisselle. She knew her friend was a witch, but aside from a few simple spells, she hadn't seen her use magic much. This definitely made up for it.

"Is everyone all right?" Homer looked at them. Lisselle still looked like she wanted to fry something else; that level of power must be hard to rein in.

"Caden and I both got hit by that thing, but aside from the welts, I'm fine."

"I'm not seriously hurt either, although these marks really hurt."

Lisselle shook off her anger and ran to both of them. "I need to get you both inside and looked at. We've no idea what that stuff will do." She turned to Homer. "Can you sweep up the mess? We should keep it for research, but store it in one of the secured metal bins in the back." She led Caden and Nettie inside. She nodded to Nettie. "I do like your quick thinking of the skirts for your hands, hate to say it, but I couldn't have done it with my pants."

Nettie laughed and looked at her destroyed skirt. "You wouldn't have had to, that was an impressive trick you two pulled off."

"Not as much as it looked, Caden thought of covering the underside of the blanket with rum. Burns nicely once the right fire source is provided. Or in this case, the right spell."

Rebecca shut the door to the guest room. "He's resting again. I think that kelp thing must have caused the spasms. I don't know that he'll live through the night though." She noticed Nettie first. "Your dress! Your face! Caden's hands and face." She shook her head in what looked like embarrassment at her reaction. "Sorry, we've been up here for too long with nothing really happening, let me get the second med kit." She darted back into the guest room.

Lisselle still had both Caden and Nettie in her grasp and she wasn't letting go as she led them into the parlor. Some parlors were fine rooms, for relaxing gatherings—this one was obviously becoming their base of operations.

"I should have come to help," Reaves said as he looked over the wounded.

"I needed you to stay here," Lisselle shot him a stern look. "What if there had been a second creature? Or something else had happened to Thomas? You can't always do what you want if you join the Society. You have to do what is needed, even if it's watching others fight."

Reaves nodded. "Shall I go see about helping Homer? It sounded like you put him on clean up duty." If he was upset at her mild chastisement, he didn't show it.

"Yes, if you would. He can draw things out. Just get the mess off the lawn and into a secured bin in the back. Thank you." She gave him a smile and went back to her patients.

"This doesn't look good at all," she dabbed around the two welts on Nettie's cheek. "Although, they should heal quickly for you at least. That vampiric blood and all." She dabbed something cool and numbing. "This will block the pain until they heal."

Caden's were worse as he had been hanging onto the creature. But none looked deep from what Nettie could tell.

"Ah, at least your looks are safe, just nicked your jawline. Your hands took a hit though." She applied the same medicine she'd put on Nettie.

Caden looked at his hands. "They feel better, but they itch a bit."

Nettie looked closer. One of his hands had tiny tentacle marks, no larger than the end of a drawing stick. "Do those look like small octopus markings?" She turned his hand so Lisselle could see it better. Then held up a magnifying glass.

"They do. So this kelp monster had baby octopi in it?"

Nettie released Caden's hand when he started smiling at her over it. "No. Well, maybe. They could be smaller versions of the creatures who attacked us. I would like to think baby anything's wouldn't be out attacking people."

"Whatever it is, it's itching."

Nettie got to her feet and looked around. "We'll need salt and a bucket."

Rebecca got the supplies and Caden's sigh of relief as he put his hand in the water said the marks on his hand were similar to the ones Nettie had, just smaller.

Homer and Reaves came in from the kitchen. Reaves went to double check the locks on the front door, it appeared the kelp monster had actually used the thin crack between the door and frame to pop the locks

Reaves found some putty of a sort and started shoring up that as well.

"Monster dust stored, front door being secured, and see here, what happened to your hand?" Homer asked as he spotted Caden and his bucket.

Caden lifted his hand out of the water briefly. "The current fashion trend, I got some tentacle bites from our kelp monster."

Homer admired the wounds then nodded. "I noticed there was a slow cooking stew in the kitchen? Not sure about our fierce fighters, but I'm starving and tired."

They settled down to eat, no one coming out of their thoughts long enough for much conversation. A guard rotation was set for the ground level since the only bedroom down there was the one with Thomas in it. Finding out there were attackers all over the ground floor when you were stuck on the one above it wasn't a good thing.

Nettie's shift was mid-way, so she had time to take a bath and change into her night clothes. Her bedroom was adjacent to Rebecca's and connected through a narrow door.

Rebecca stuck her head in after a brief knock. "I am just checking, dear friend. I want to ask you about everything, Caden, everything in London. But you look, quite honestly, done for." She came into the room and lifted up Nettie's chin. "That does not look good you know."

Nettie was looking at the marks in the mirror and completely agreed. "It doesn't feel bad. Well, not now that Lisselle put that numbing compound on it. However, giving my rapid healing, I would have expected it to settle down by now." She put down the mirror and smiled at her friend. "Damon is excited to see you, you know."

Rebecca blushed and sat on the edge of the bed. "He is? Oh my. I feel…well…I was attracted to him, but then I sort of went all vampire minion on everyone. I wasn't sure how he'd felt about me and, thanks to Gaston, I didn't have time to find out in London." The look on her face didn't bode well for Gaston whenever he got to Wales.

"Everyone knows you had no choice in what happened, even I hadn't been able to fight that Master vampire off at first." Nettie shuddered. It was going to be a long time before that incident could be set to rest in her mind. "But I thought it was orders from Edinburgh that moved you both here? Hadn't there already been sightings up here?"

"As I heard from Lisselle, who was not happy by the way, Edinburgh had mentioned the sightings in Northern Wales in a weekly update not long after the aliens were vanquished. Gaston jumped on it and started sending agents all over. I'd expected him to send you somewhere."

Now it was Nettie's turn to think murderous thoughts about Gaston. He'd deliberately sent away everyone except her. There were a few other agents living in the London mansion, but they were often on foreign duties and she rarely saw any of them. "He sent you all away and then watched me. He simply didn't trust me." She was furious, but she was also exhausted. This had been a trying day even for one with her constitution.

"Now, you don't know that…okay, you're probably right. I don't think it is that he didn't trust you, but you have to admit, you are unique. I've looked—there are no records of any other half-vampire. You're the only one known of to be born with vampiric genes. Maybe he simply wanted to study you more."

Nettie laughed. She knew Rebecca was trying to help, but thinking one had been a lab rat for the past two months wasn't much better than not being trusted. "On that note, I am exhausted." She gave Rebecca a hug. "I am terribly glad to be back with you and Lisselle again, but right now I feel like I am going to fall asleep where I sit."

Rebecca patted her head. "As I said, you do look awful. I will wait until tomorrow to continue my questioning… and don't think I'm not going to soundly question you about Caden. I saw how he looked at you when you weren't looking." With a wicked grin, she bounced to her feet and was at the door before Nettie could respond.

"What do you mean?"

"Ah, ah, ah—tomorrow." Rebecca shut the door.

CHAPTER THIRTEEN

CONTRARY TO WHAT SHE WOULD have believed, given Rebecca's parting salvo, Nettie slept like the dead. However, once she realized how that applied to her unique situation, she wasn't certain that was a good thing. Shaking off that dreary thought and her vague annoyance that Caden had been looking at her some way and she hadn't noticed, yet Rebecca had, Nettie dressed, and went down for breakfast.

The smells were wonderful as she came into the dining room. Homer and Reaves were chatting quietly over tea and toast. Nettie joined them. She had no idea whether their cook had returned or it was someone else cooking, but most people didn't like observers while preparing food.

"Good morning, Nettie. Sleep well?" Reaves looked groggy and it took Nettie a few moments to realize she hadn't been called for her watch time. Or she had and they couldn't wake her?

"Oh dear, you couldn't wake me last night for my watch? And how is Thomas?"

"He's still unconscious, I don't know if we can get him to Edinburgh before he passes. They are sending a medical team down, but it will still be a few hours before they arrive. But we didn't try to wake you. Lisselle said you needed sleep, and we agreed." Homer reached for another piece of toast. "You still look a bit peaked if you don't mind my saying. Worn through."

"I do?" Nettie had dressed so quickly that she hadn't

given her looks much thought beyond making sure her hair wasn't a muddle. She stood and looked at herself in the dining room mirror. She did look a bit drawn. And those marks from the kelp creature were still there. "That can't be good."

"What can't?" Lisselle came bustling in from the kitchen with piles of food. She placed the first two dishes, a standard fry of eggs, bangers, tomatoes, and mushrooms, in front of Reaves and Homer. Then she came back out with what had to be an actual serving platter filled with about five times the amount presented to the men and placed it in front of Nettie. Most of it bangers and rashers. A lot of bangers and rashers.

"It can't be good that I still look pale, you made them let me sleep while the rest of you stood guard, and you have now given me enough meat to feed ten grown men. None of that can be good." Nettie forced herself to resume her seat with decorum and not start grabbing the food with her hands. She was suddenly starving.

"Would you tuck in please? I refuse to talk to you until you get something in your stomach; you're getting paler as we sit here." Lisselle added a scowl to her words. Then darted into the kitchen for plates of food for the rest of the seats.

Nettie nodded and dug in. Out of the corner of her eye, she noticed Caden, Rebecca, and Lisselle all join the table and start eating. She didn't care. She'd never been like this. Half of the mountain of eggs, bangers, and rashers were gone before she looked up. "Sorry." She dabbed her mouth.

"That is some serious eating there, lass." Homer looked extremely impressed.

"I have no idea what's wrong, but I am still starving." She went after the second half.

"Better?" Caden asked as she pushed back from the table.

"I think so. Is my color any better?"

Lisselle shook her head. Then she reached over and tilted Nettie's chin. "And those marks look almost worse than last night. Can you drop your fangs for me?"

Nettie didn't like using fangs as parlor tricks, but she sensed there was something more behind this. She dropped them, or tried to. They seemed stuck for a moment before sliding down.

"Okay, they work, you're still half-vampire, but why aren't you recovering?"

Rebecca had been seated further away, but got up and moved closer. "Her pupils look off too. I think that kelp monster did something to change her."

"She also was attacked by the merman we fought in the pub," Caden added. "The one with the tentacles. And she didn't react to the marks until we were coming here. Could two attacks of whatever they carry have done something to her vampire status?" Caden had enough scientific inquiry under his belt that his mind made inquisitive connections—especially when there wasn't anything to sneak up on, spy on, or fight.

Nettie didn't like the direction they were going with this, but she couldn't deny they might be right.

"I still have the notes on your blood from after your prior recovery. After we get a wee bit more food in you, I'll take some more samples."

Not only was Lisselle her superior agent, she was also a good friend—and right. Nettie nodded and accepted another, more normal sized, plate. "Until the people from Edinburgh get here, what is on the agenda?" It was shocking how quickly the second plate disappeared.

"Moving you all in for now, and the duchess. She needs to be here, I simply can't keep going out in that horrible stodgy get up." Lisselle shuddered as the men cleared away the plates.

"The duchess?" As far as Nettie knew there were no other people coming up aside from the delayed Gaston and Damon.

"One of her personalities, lass," Homer said when he came back after clearing the table. "By the way, I offered to help clean and your cook in there chased us out."

Lisselle smiled. "She's an old fashioned girl, doesn't like men in her kitchen." She turned to Nettie. "Yes, the duchess, as I call her, is a unique character. She's flamboyant, extravagant, and wild. I wouldn't have wanted to play her here with only Rebecca and me, but she's safe in a crowd. She's the wild sister to the widow, come to stay when the widow takes to her bed."

"Oh dear, I'm thinking there will be eyebrows raised?" Nettie added some jam to a few pieces of toast.

"If there aren't, I'm not doing it right. Oft times hiding in a loud and garish way works better than decorum. The people of Llandudno won't dare look at me twice."

"She wants a chance to play dress up," Homer said.

Lisselle smiled as everyone got up and reconvened in the parlor.

They were sitting down when a crash came from the guest room.

Lisselle and Nettie got there first. Thomas was thrashing about and foaming from the mouth. Nettie pinned him down, but she was unnaturally weak, and he was exceptionally strong for a dying man.

"I can't hold him!"

Caden came and sat on his legs, and Homer helped pin his shoulders. Lisselle was trying to get a scope on Thomas but she couldn't because he was bucking so much.

"Stand back! There's something coming from his body!" Rebecca yelled as she tried to pull the others away. Reaves took one look and helped her move the others by force.

Thomas twisted and convulsed as dark green water

seemed to come from everywhere in his body. Or it was his body. Nettie swore that his clothes were deflating as the water increased.

"He's dissolving, everyone out." Lisselle forced them out of the room.

"We can't burn him like the kelp monster, we'd burn the entire house." Caden said as he looked around the front room for a weapon against a growing puddle of unhealthy-looking liquid.

"Alcohol?" Nettie ran to the liquor cabinet and grabbed some bottles. "It's not fire, but it could burn another way?" She had no idea if it would work, but that stuff was going to keep spreading if they didn't stop it.

Lisselle nodded and moved aside. "I might be able to help it as well, and keep the house intact. Give me a moment to call in the spell, then when I say, throw those bottles at the floor." She closed her eyes and took a deep breath. When she opened them again their hue was lighter and sparks jumped from her fingers again. "Now!"

The bottles went sailing into the room, their contents spreading over everything. Lisselle muttered a few soft words and the sparks from her fingers leapt to the liquid.

Nettie grabbed Lisselle and pulled her out as a wall of blue flame burst out.

The flame pulled back on itself, then a muffled explosion took place and the blue flame was replaced by sickly black-green smoke.

Nettie and Lisselle were the only ones on the ground since Nettie had to throw them hard to get them clear of the explosion. Homer and Caden helped them up. Rebecca ran and opened the front door to try and let some of the smoke escape.

"We'll need something to fan the smoke out, and try not to breathe it," Lisselle said as she picked up a tray and started fanning toward the door. "Hopefully it will disburse enough to not cause trouble, but it will cause trouble if it stays here."

A few more trays were brought out, the cook started to help, but Rebecca asked her to stay in the kitchen.

"Better she not know." Nettie nodded and kept fanning.

"Actually, she's a retired agent of the Society. I just think since she hasn't been exposed to the smoke yet, it's probably better she isn't."

The smoke dissipated enough to appease Lisselle and people walking by were starting to stare.

Rebecca sat down her tray and went out to the front lawn, partially closing the door behind her. "Sorry, we had a bit of a goof smoking some fish. You know us Londoners." She gave a shrug, raised her hands in the air, then turn and came back inside and shut the door behind her.

She shook her head. "They already think we're quite mad, now it will just get worse. You might need to have the widow make another appearance to scare them a bit."

"Londoners? Didn't you grow up in northern Wales?" Caden asked.

"Aye, born and raised not fifty miles from here. But they don't know that, and my persona is definitely a Londoner. Trust me, I know how small town people act, and I make sure I behave as far from that as possible."

Nettie went to join Lisselle where she peered into the guest room. There were singe marks all around the door frame and the door itself. But the room and house were still standing. The room itself wasn't in good shape though. The bed was burnt to the frame and the floor where the water had been was cinders. Nettie wasn't certain anyone would be able to walk upon it without falling through.

"There won't be anything to study, beyond what little we had before he…oozed." Nettie felt bad for Thomas but he'd looked to be dying when the kelp monster dragged him here. Or he dragged it here.

Homer turned toward the front door. "We need to start a search for Bethlyn's ship. Lisselle, can you see if Edinburgh has gotten their two airships up? I don't want us to cover the same areas. I'm going to go see about any that are here. There were two supposedly coming in this morning."

"I was going to see about the room," Lisselle said. "But we can close it off and let things set until the medical agents get here. There is nothing for them to take, but I want to make sure they agree. Besides, it is even more disturbing that your cousin is missing given the circumstances." She gave a nod toward the guest room.

"I'm going to go see about the docks. Our kelp friend came up somewhere, maybe someone saw him last night." Caden grabbed his jacket.

"Where do you want me, boss?" Reaves was in an odd position, he was still technically part of Homer's crew, but he was also a potential agent.

"Go with Caden, see what you can tell as well. You grew up in a coastal town, see if anything seems out of place. And Caden? I've heard you do a pretty fair British accent, you might want to keep that up here. Americans are rare enough in smaller towns, you'll stand out less if you don't sound like one."

"Aye, that I can do." His accent was light, but working class British.

Nettie smiled. When she'd first met him, and thought he had been the attacker of the real Caden Smith, he'd done the same accent. "Perhaps Rebecca and I should go to market? I assume there is a social hub of some sort?" She winked at Rebecca. If there were any places with social activity, her friend would know where they were. Sometimes being an agent involved sleuthing—but it was often good to start with getting the easiest information first. Much of common gossip was useless and wrong, but there were grains of truth in there as well.

Rebecca smiled. "Oh yes, indeed, there are two and both worthy. If anything odd was spotted last night, we'll hear it."

Lisselle looked at them. "Don't think all this activity is going to get you out of helping me with that room. But for now, since I am the senior agent officially," she paused and gave Homer a look, "I say proceed. I'll see about waiting until the team from Edinburgh comes down and show them what we have."

The men all left and Nettie and Rebecca went upstairs to change into walking clothes. Neither were clotheshorses, and while it was still far slower than men would be able to change, they were both motivated and moved quickly.

They said farewell to Lisselle and headed out.

"I'm worried about the fact that the Thomas you saw in London wasn't a person at all. Or at least not what he appeared to be." Rebecca kept her voice down even though no one was near them. "How will we know if there are others?"

"The same thought went through my mind," Nettie said. "There must be something we can do to be able to tell who has been changed. We don't know if it's something easy for them to do, or this was a one-time event. We need to find that airship, and hopefully the doppelganger."

Rebecca nodded, then smiled. "Now, what has happened with you and Caden? I know you only had a short time together before having to come up here, but I saw sparks."

"I'd like to know where you saw them. Trust me, nothing has happened between us." Nettie was planning on telling Rebecca all about the bit she heard, but would rather do it when they were inside.

Rebecca walked alongside her grinning like a madwoman; clearly she felt that Nettie was holding back.

Nettie rubbed her forehead. "I did hear something, I wasn't trying to eavesdrop, it simply happened."

"And?" Rebecca was still grinning.

Nettie sighed and gave in. So much for not discussing the situation outside. "I overheard Caden talking to Reaves about me. He isn't sure what to do about me, but he did seem interested." Saying it out aloud sounded daft.

"That explains it. As your airship was landing, and the two of you fell over each other, he had a certain look. The speculative gaze of a smitten male as they would say in those romance novels by Miss Pelock."

"He's not smitten." Nettie gasped as it came out much louder than intended. She dropped her voice; she was not having herself or Caden compared to one of those characters—even if she knew Reaves was behind the Miss Pelock books. "He's not. He finds me attractive for some reason." She really didn't want to continue this on a public walkway.

"You really do like him, don't you?" Rebecca wasn't grinning like a mad woman anymore, but now she had a softer smile. It was almost worse.

"I do. He's crass and boastful. And handsome. And very smart. But he likes to show off. He's got a good heart though." Nettie put her hand to her mouth to shut up. "I have it bad, don't I?"

"Horribly bad. But to be fair, he is good looking and quite charming." Rebecca's face grew serious. "And I will have Lisselle put a horrible spell on him if he hurts you in anyway. I've read his files. Lady's man indeed."

First she was pushing them together, now Rebecca looked ready to go find him and punch him, even though he'd done nothing.

"I think I'll be fine, once we finish this case at any rate." She looked up the walkway where a small crowd was gathering.

Nettie was far taller than Rebecca, so she could see a better. What there was to see at any rate. The crowd was at least five people deep, and judging by the work smocks, many had run out of offices and shops. They were gathered at the base of a small pier that had one good sized fishing boat attached to it. A group of fishermen were in the center of the crowd.

"Stand back! We don't know what brought it here." Although the man was yelling for people to stand back, everyone moved forward a few steps. The fisherman doing the yelling didn't notice as he was busy poking at a pile of kelp with a pole.

"Isn't kelp fairly common near the sea?" Nettie kept her voice down. Maybe there was something she was missing since this wasn't her normal environment.

Rebecca tried to see but she couldn't get a good look. "Regular kelp? Yes." The emphasis on regular brought to point the non-regular nature of the stuff last night.

"It's just seaweed. Ya daft." A man near the center yelled out then fought his way out of the crowd. "Some of us have things to do."

Many in the crowd grumbled in agreement, but they didn't leave.

"It moved, I tell ya! I saw it with my own eyes." This came from a battered looking fisherman standing next to the one with the pole.

CHAPTER FOURTEEN

WHEN NOTHING EXCITING HAPPENED, SUCH as the kelp coming to life and attacking people, the crowd dispersed. Except for Nettie and Rebecca and the three fishermen still standing around it.

"It moved." The recent speaker didn't yell this time, but he also wasn't standing down.

Nettie stepped forward. "I believe you. Where did it move from?"

The fishermen looked her up and down, prim clothes, worse, *fancy* prim clothes. She could tell they discounted her immediately.

"Lass, go about your shopping." The one with the pole kept poking at it.

"I can tell you there have been other odd things in the sea. Bath has had its share." She was taking a risk, but including them could get her more information. Besides, she wasn't going to say what had been seen.

"Ye from Bath?" The second fisherman scowled.

"No. London. However, we frequent Bath." She added a bit of high end snobbery to her attitude.

"What's been seen?"

"Oh, they don't tell anyone anything," she dropped her voice, "they don't want anyone to know. But there are things moving about that shouldn't be. Something is wrong with the water."

The first one shook his head and went back to poking the kelp. "This ain't no myth, Miss. It crawled down the wharf like a two year old."

Rebecca had been standing back, but stepped forward. "When did it stop moving?"

"Right as dawn broke," as the second man spoke, the man with the pole nodded. "Aye, the moment dawn hit, it collapsed." He looked at Nettie and Rebecca with interest. "You two think that's the key? Them things we've been seeing and hearing about are all at night."

Nettie really would have liked to have run up and kissed him for that breakthrough. They probably would have made the connection once things settled down, but yes, everything had happened at night.

"I do believe you could be correct, Master?"

He bobbed his head. "Master Davies."

"I am pleased to meet you, Master Davies. I am Miss Nettie Jones and my companion is Miss Rebecca Rhys."

"I was thinking we should toss this thing back in the sea, but I don't want it coming back to life."

An idea struck her. "My brother is a bit of a scientist, he would probably like to see it." It galled her to have to hide behind a man, but here it might work better. For now. "I could send him down when he returns? I agree that letting it back into the water might not be the best idea."

Davies nodded. "Aye, that would work. We'll leave it in this barrel for now. But we need to go back out in a bit, he'll be along soon?"

Nettie smiled. "Oh yes, very soon, I'm sure. Thank you."

The fishermen scooped it into the barrel and dropped a lid on. Nettie waited until they'd gone back into the boat before she lifted the barrel lid. "Oh yes, my brother will be here soon." She spun and took Rebecca's arm. "Come, we must find him and his dear friend."

Rebecca struggled to keep up as they went back to the house. "What brother are you talking about?"

Nettie stopped a few feet before the house. "Me. Us.

We can move about easier and get more answers if we're not dressed like this." She'd never had to worry about it in London, people there were far more forward thinking, even if there was still a balk on trousers for women. But if she needed to be male for a while to get this resolved, she could do it.

Lisselle was working on some papers in the front parlor when they came back in. "Found the answers already?"

"Just found a possible bit of that seaweed," Nettie said. "It appears that the events are always at night, I knew most of them were, but everything has been." She told her about the fishermen and the crawling seaweed. "It appears there was nothing else within the seaweed when it was up and about, but once we change we'll know better."

"Change into what?"

"Men," Rebecca said. "Although I do wonder about our clothing. You are close in height to Caden. I'm a bit shorter."

Lisselle folded her arms and lifted an eyebrow.

Nettie shrugged. "It makes sense, none of us are here really as ourselves, and I refuse to be hindered by potential bias against women in my research here. I agree that I hadn't thought the clothing issue through."

"I'm kicking myself for not thinking of it before you did." Lisselle turned to a closet under the stair and started pulling out boxes. "I always travel with many costumes, and yes, I have gone in disguise as a male before. I think between this collection and pilfering the men's lot, we should be able to make three passable men."

Nettie wasn't going to argue about having Lisselle along. She was senior agent after all. There was also an added level of intrigue now, and Lisselle was a mistress of that.

An hour later Fred Jones, Luke Evans, and Charles Wilding were ready for public consumption.

Nettie, now Fred, patted her chest. "I hope this works."

They'd all bound their chests tightly to keep them flat, but Nettie was a bit curvier than the other two. It wouldn't be good form if *Fred* grew cleavage suddenly.

Lisselle looked her up and down and scowled. "I think you'll be fine, but a looser jacket might be in order. Just in case anything untoward happens." She rummaged around the clothing strewn across her bedroom and finally found one of Caden's jackets. He was much broader in the shoulder than Nettie, but it did give more space for hiding other body parts. "Let me do some tucks."

Nettie wasn't completely certain if Lisselle had a secret mad skill with a sewing needle or she was using magic, but the adjustments she'd been making to the clothes were amazing.

Some theater hair glued onto the face for all three along with strategic make-up and there were three passable men reflected in the hall mirror.

Rebecca seemed most pleased with her new self. "This is wonderful! I've always wanted to see what things looked like from the other side. I think I make quite the handsome bloke." She smiled and adjusted her hat. "As long as we come back before a restroom is needed. That is where I draw the line."

Nettie nodded. "Agreed."

Lisselle looked at them both and frowned. "You look good, as do I, but don't smile. There is still too much prettiness in both of your faces when you smile. We can practice for further adventures, but right now, don't smile if you can." She handed them small men's gloves and donned a pair herself. "Just better to keep the hands covered when going as a man. Trust me."

Nettie and Rebecca shrugged and nodded.

The morning was still early, but the town was bustling. Most everyone had cleared away from the pier. The fishermen were finishing up stocking their boat, but the leader came back as the three approached.

He nodded to Nettie. "You being Master Jones?"

Nettie bit her cheeks to stop the automatic smile and nodded instead. She kept her voice low. "Aye. Master Davies? My sister told me of your find. These are my partners Master Evans and Master Wilding." She shook his hand and was glad for the gloves. She was strong enough to give any man a powerful handshake, but her hands were a bit too delicate to have supported that ruse.

"Here it is, you're welcome to it. Get the barrel back later if you would. We'll be out late, this is an odd run, so just leave it here on the dock." He nodded to the others and marched back to his boat.

"That went well," Rebecca said with a smile, that she immediately swallowed. "That's hard not to do."

"Our first brief encounter went well, but I'm afraid we need to work on training to get you two more man-like if we're going to keep these disguises up for any length of time. Men slouch more than you two for one." She waved her hands as both Nettie and Rebecca started adjusting their posture. "Not now, you're fine from a distance. Let's get this barrel back to the house," she paused as something hit her. "Actually, I think we'll take over the house next door. Homer could have stayed there, but he usually gets a location closer to the bars for centralized gossip. Yes, this will work nicely. I will develop a cover story for us, but at the least Fred and Luke are house mates next door." With that decided, at least to herself, she started marching back.

It was easier for one person to roll the barrel, so Nettie rolled and Rebecca kept an eye on it.

Nettie thought they would first go to the main house, since nothing was in the second one in terms of lab equipment. But that didn't slow down Lisselle as she strode to the house next door. Nettie did have to admit, she being the tallest might look the most manlike, but Lisselle duplicated a man's posture and stride with ease.

Lisselle had the key for the house in her pocket with a number of others and had the door propped open by the time they got the barrel there. Nettie paused when they hit the steps. Only three steps, but it would be hard to get the barrel up them if anyone was watching and she couldn't hoist it up herself. Granted, as a man it would raise less talk than her doing it as a woman, but still.

"Do you want me to help?" Rebecca leaned forward. The barrel was half her size, she wouldn't be able to budge it.

Nettie glanced up and down the lane, it looked clear, but that could change. "Could you keep an eye out? I can move it faster on my own."

Rebecca nodded and Nettie picked it up. Or tried to, she couldn't get it to budge. She tried again; sooner or later someone would be coming down the lane. Throwing herself into it, she bent down to lift it and flung herself a foot backwards.

"Nettie!" Rebecca yelled then covered her mouth.

Lisselle came down the stairs and helped Nettie to her feet. "What happened?"

A tingling overtook Nettie and the world went spinning. "I'm not sure. I feel very strange…" The last thing she saw was the sky as she fell back to the ground.

CHAPTER FIFTEEN

"NETTIE? NETTIE?" THE VOICE WAS familiar but she couldn't work up the energy to open her eyes. Everything hurt. Everything was tired. She tried to raise a hand to make the insistent voice go away, but that didn't want to work either.

"Let me alone."

"What did she say?" the second voice was further away, but also familiar.

"She's refusing to come back. Her pulse is too slow. Do you have more smelling salts, Lisselle?" The voice nearest to her spoke.

"I think we've gone through…wait, yes, one more vial. If this doesn't work, we do something drastic."

Nettie mentally told the voices to go away. Speaking hadn't worked and had taken too much effort. Sleep was what she needed. So much sleep.

A blast of scent slammed into her face and her eyes flew open. She pushed the hand away, but still had no energy. "Rebecca? Lisselle? What's happened?" At least now she knew where she was; the smelling salts had pushed that through her fogged brain, but she could barely sit up.

"Stay down." Lisselle took the small vial of salts from Rebecca. "This is our final vial, and while I'm not sure what's taken you down, I do not believe sleep is the best option."

"Final vial…what happened to the rest?" Nettie found focusing on small things like the vial was better than trying to figure out what was going on.

"You smashed them," Rebecca said. She had stepped back when Lisselle took the vial but hovered in again. "This is the third time you've woken up. But you seem more aware this time."

Rebecca was a disturbing mixture of herself and a man. So was Lisselle. Nettie looked down and saw the same for herself, minus shoes. Slowly events fluttered back. "I promise not to smash that one. I recall the barrel, weakness, and then here."

"You tried to move the barrel, collapsed, and have been most stubborn about coming back to us," Lisselle said. She sat down the vial and frowned. "I was extremely close to using a spell on you. And under that make up, you still don't look well."

Rebecca came forward with a glass of water. "Drink this, then we'll see about getting you upright."

"I'm not—" Just as she was about to protest that she didn't need water, her stomach cramped up and she felt horribly thirsty. She finished the glass in one gulp and held the empty glass out. "Please?"

Rebecca shared a concerned glance with Lisselle, then vanished out of sight.

"What's wrong with me?" She got out before Rebecca came back with more water. That too was a single gulp. "How long was I unconscious?"

"A number of hours, it's dark outside now. You wouldn't wake up at all at first, then woke up, flung about, and collapsed twice." Lisselle took a hold of Nettie's hand and pushed back the sleeve. The marks from the merman in London were red. "Your skin is almost cracking it's so dry. Rebecca, draw a bath, we need to get her in water immediately."

Nettie fought the urge to itch, but it didn't work. The itchiness started where the welts were, then flowed over her body. Rebecca had brought out a pitcher of water before she went to draw the bath and Nettie finished it as fast as she'd done the glassfuls. "I don't understand what's going on." Normally, even her own afflictions would be a source of interest and study. Right now she was in too much pain and discomfort for that.

"I have no idea, but it must be related to the attack on you in London. Something triggered this response. Possibly that thing you fought on the lawn last night."

Rebecca stuck her head into the room. "The bath is drawn. And I dropped a tablecloth over the barrel so it looks a bit less noticeable out there."

"The barrel." Lisselle helped Nettie to her feet. "The exposure from last night, combined with the proximity of the sea kelp in the barrel must have done something to you. That merman's attack in London must have been more than simply on the skin, it embedded something underneath that lies dormant. Come along now."

Nettie got to her feet, but she needed a lot of help. The physical and mental weakness was almost worse than the pain and itching.

They got her to the bathroom and took off the borrowed jacket. Nettie couldn't wait for the rest of the clothes to come off and crawled into the bathtub. The water felt soothing to her skin and even brought back some energy.

"I added salt to it as well," Rebecca said.

Nettie could tell. The salt was calling to her as much as the water. She leaned back and submerged herself as much as she could. "Thank you. I don't know what's wrong, but this feels much better."

Lisselle pulled up a stool next to the tub and peered into Nettie's eyes. "Your pupils look better, and I think your color is coming back." She took a cloth and rubbed off the make-up. "Let me check your pulse."

Nettie started to hold up her hand, then froze and turned

it over. "What's happened?" Thin webbing appeared between her fingers.

Lisselle grabbed her hand before she could drop it back in the water. "Rebecca, get me my kit from the other house."

The look on Rebecca's face said she wasn't happy about leaving her friend, but she did so.

Lisselle turned Nettie's hand slowly. "Does this hurt?" She touched the webbing between Nettie's thumb and forefinger.

"No. It feels very odd, but it doesn't hurt." She patted her neck and face with her free hand but didn't feel anything else. "Does it look like anything else has changed?"

Lisselle peered closely, lifting Nettie's hair to get a closer look at her neck. "Not that I can see, but whatever this contagion is, might go in stages. You are remarkably calm."

"I think the water, both inside and out, has helped my mind recover. I'm so happy at being aware of what's going on that I'm not upset right now." She glared at the webbing. "A bit annoyed perhaps. Quite annoyed to be honest. Do you think this is happening to everyone that merman struck? What about the attacker last night?" A thought hit her. "What if the creatures that have been reported to be wandering about are actually victims of these things from the sea?" While she was glad that she could think again, and that she didn't feel on the verge of collapse, she really didn't relish the idea of turning into a creature with tentacles.

Lisselle shook her head, but was focusing on Nettie's hand. "I honestly have no answers. I am concerned as to what would have happened to a person with normal constitution in this case. Your unique nature gives you far more strength and resiliency than an average human."

Nettie shuddered. "It could have killed someone else, you need to check Caden as soon as they come back. Even more of a reason to find out what has caused it. And find out why my vampiric side didn't fight it off. I feel better, but still weak."

"I think he's fine, his wounds didn't react as yours did. But I agree, he'll need to be watched carefully," Lisselle said.

Rebecca came running back in with a large black bag. It looked like the type used by medical doctors on house calls, but Nettie knew Lisselle had a tiny research station in there. At least the important supplies.

"Thank you, Rebecca," Lisselle said as she released Nettie's hand to look through the bag. "I wish now that we'd taken you to our house instead of this one. We will need to find a way to get you over there soon however."

"I feel much better now, aside from the soggy clothing, I am more than able to walk." She said it, but truth was Nettie really didn't want to leave the water.

Lisselle gave her a calculating look. "Really? Try to stand."

Rebecca stepped forward to help, but Lisselle waved her off.

Nettie put her hands on the sides of the tub, pushed up, got to her feet, and buckled a second later.

"Nettie!" Rebecca did rush up that time, but Nettie had already recovered and sat upright in the tub. "Are you all right?"

"I don't know what happened. As soon as I rose, my entire body turned to jelly." She really wanted to slide back under the water, but it was a matter of principle now. She was not letting whatever was attacking her win completely.

Lisselle shook her head. "Can you lean back and lift out a foot?"

Nettie complied. She wasn't surprised to see webbing between her toes as well. Lisselle pushed the soggy trouser leg up and brought out her magnifying glass. "Your skin might be changing as well. I can't tell for sure, but there might be scales appearing."

She was so calm and quiet that Nettie wasn't sure she heard her correctly. "You said scales?"

"Yes, but very faint, just outlines. A lovely color though." Lisselle looked up with a small grin.

Nettie shook her head. She was getting upset now, but Lisselle was calm, which helped. "What color?"

"Greenish blue." She tilted her head. "This bathing tub is smaller than the one next door, I do think we should move you."

"You want to run a bunch of tests and need my blood over there," Nettie said as she pulled back her shirt sleeve and squinted at the skin. Either the scales hadn't migrated this far yet, or they were too faint to be seen by the naked eye.

"We could bring that odd tank in the backyard into the backroom," Rebecca said. "That thing that looks like it's from an old mine, and does nothing but trap water when it rains? If we cleared everything else, we could have a large place for water." Rebecca was looking at Nettie's hands.

Nettie held one up to her. It was bad enough to have something completely unheard of such as this happen to one, it was worse when yourself, and everyone you associated with were consummate scientists of one type or another. "I've not seen this tank, but a much larger tub of water does sound wonderful. I would offer to help set it up, but standing seems to be a problem."

A knock came from the front room and Rebecca waved for Lisselle to sit down. "I'll get it." She paused at the mirror, most of her male costuming was off, but some of the facial hair still stuck.

"Here," Lisselle handed her a rag with an astringent on it.

"Thank you." Still looking oddly dressed for a woman, but no longer like a male, Rebecca darted out the door.

A moment later Caden, Reaves, and Rebecca appeared in the door way. "The cook told us you'd had some sort of emergency—" Caden glanced over to the tub then covered his eyes and hit Reaves to do the same. "What is she doing in the water with no clothes?"

"Most people do enter a bath tub without clothing," Lisselle said. "However, in this case, she is clothed. Her feet are bare and her arm. But she is fully clothed. We did remove your jacket before she got in there though."

Caden dropped his hand at that. "My jacket? And why are you all dressed that way?" He peered over at Nettie then smiled when he saw the clothes.

Nettie waved back.

"What has happened?" Reaves had been silent up until then, but the webbing on her hand was noticeable even at the other end of the bathroom. His expression was an odd combination of anger and confusion.

"That is a question for the ages, I assure you." Lisselle stood. "But to find that out I need get her relocated to the other house. Rebecca, run the same water and salt combination you did for here, and you two chaps need to help us get her over there. She can't walk right now."

Caden looked at the clothing and Nettie's hand and finally shook his head. "You can all explain everything later, it might make more sense then. Come on Reaves, I think we can put something together. Besides, Homer might have come back, and he has good ideas."

They left and Nettie dropped the smile she'd forced. "Now what do you really think is happening to me?" She'd been watching Lisselle's face as she'd examined her skin. She had an opinion and Nettie was fairly sure she wasn't going to like it.

"Now, there's no way to be sure, I hardly have any equipment here, not to mention there's never been a case of this happening."

Nettie folded her arms and glared, not terribly impressive when lying back in a tub of salt water, fully dressed in men's clothing with a bare foot dangling out of the tub. But it got her point across. "And I know you. You suspect something. Virus?" That would make the most sense, really.

"Possibly, but it could be some odd allergic reaction. You were not normal before the merman attack, this could be something we have never seen, in terms of vampiric science."

"Vampires don't like sea life? No, whatever this is, it is fully systemic. My strength is gone, when I collapsed, you mentioned that my pulse was too slow. I honestly felt like I was in a cocoon and wanted to hibernate."

There was a clatter down the hall, then Homer stuck his head in. "Hello, lass, you got into some trouble?" He stepped in, pulling a sled loaded with blankets behind him. "It's not fancy but we can get you moved over on this."

"You're going to drag her along on a sled down the main lane? Are you daft, man? Even in the twilight you'd both raise too many questions." Lisselle had been packing her things but stopped to shake her head at him.

"No, I'm not. I had the boys take out a few pieces of fencing between the two houses, we take her out the back. Besides, if we're going to be living in both houses, it might be nice to have a way back and forth unseen."

It took some doing, but they managed to get her on the sled and wrapped in the blankets. They were halfway through the back yard when Nettie remembered the kelp. "We should find a place for the seaweed. The fisherman wants the barrel back."

Homer was pulling the sled but stopped. "The which what now?"

"They found some animated kelp, it's in that barrel out front," Lisselle said and patted Nettie's shoulder. "Never you worry, once we get you tucked in we'll look at moving it into something safe and far from you. And get the barrel back to the dock." She waved off Homer's look. "We'll explain it to you later."

The back of the larger house opened to what was possibly originally designed to be a conservatory of some sort. But unlike the wide windows that would be found normally, the sides had wood blocking them until about five feet up.

"Take her to the drawn bath, we can bring her back down here once the tank is set up," Lisselle said.

"I don't really care where you put me as long as I get back into the water." The trip hadn't been long at all and since she was wrapped in blankets around soaking wet clothing, she still was touching water. But she was starting to get that odd itching feeling again.

"You are looking a bit greenish," Lisselle said as they reached the stairs.

"Scales?" Nettie's hand flew to her face.

"No dear, just as if you're ill." She stepped back and Homer scooped Nettie and the blankets up.

"Sorry, lass, but there's no way we are getting that sled up the stairs with you on it."

Rebecca stuck her head out of the bathroom door. "As ready as can be. And I found my swimming outfit. It won't fit you properly, but it will be more comfortable than those clothes." She winked. "And keep you more or less descent."

Homer set Nettie down on a bench next the tub. This bathroom and bath tub were much larger than in the other house, which was nice at least.

"I'll be off checking the lads with the seaweed, the barrel, and getting that tank ready." He nodded and took off.

"He thinks I'm a monster," Nettie said as Lisselle and Rebecca closed the door to help her change clothes. It wasn't lost on her that she'd already been one as a half-vampire.

"Pish, he's just thrown off a bit, he'll be fine." Lisselle helped her change, and it was very noticeable that this suit was barely decent on her and never would be so in public. Nettie was significantly taller and curvier than Rebecca. But she admitted as she slid into the water, it felt much better than the clothing and binding she'd been wearing.

"Leave a towel nearby, if someone has to speak to me, I can drag that in to cover the unseemly parts." She grinned then sobered. "How quickly can you run the blood tests? I'm grateful for this and the tank they are building, but I really don't plan on becoming some sort of fish person."

"A mermaid?" Rebecca laughed.

"I wasn't going to phrase it as such, but yes. I am not going to become one of those."

"I believe you are stubborn enough to not let that happen." Lisselle brought out some vials and started taking samples for her tests. Nettie even suggested a few and they kept working until Caden came to tell them the tank was ready and filled. They bundled Nettie up in a number of towels, and her extra menswear shirt, and Homer came to carry her down again. He did seem more relaxed this round.

"I brought in a hammock from my airship, we don't use them much, and it's not fancy, but it should let you get some sleep and keep you in the water."

"That was kind of you, thank you. I did wonder if I was going to be able to sleep under water, but so far no gills."

The tank itself was an odd conglomeration about four feet high and six or so feet long. A lot of work had clearly gone into getting it together, and it had no leaks. Also, no way to get in.

"I am tall, but even in good condition I would have to scramble a bit to get in there."

"Sorry about that," Homer was still holding her but motioned toward the corner. "Caden and Reaves, can you two set up the ladder?"

The men pulled forward an odd contraption, tall and with mismatched parts, but when they turned it she could see it was a ladder with a small bracing platform up top. They moved it over, Reaves climbed up and locked it in place, and then they stood there looking far too pleased with themselves.

Homer adjusted his hold on her, then carefully went up the ladder. The going was slow, but they made it. She sighed as she slid out of his arms and into the soothing water. They'd connected the hammock to each end, and it was low enough that she would be submerged once she added her weight to it, except for her head.

"Thank you all." She could stand in the tank, her body supported by the buoyancy of the water. Out of the water, she'd almost felt like she was being squished.

"Sleep well," Lisselle said. "There's a bell if you need anything."

Nettie nodded and crawled onto her water hammock.

CHAPTER SIXTEEN

SLEEPING IN THE HAMMOCK IN the tank of water was a bit surreal, but in a way quite soothing. When she woke, she could see the light from the unblocked upper portion of the windows which indicated it was still extremely early, but surprisingly the skies were clear. She stretched and wondered how long this confinement would have to go on. She gave a startled gasp as she looked at her hands. The webbing was completely gone.

She stood and hung on to the top of the tank and tentatively pushed herself out of the water and onto the small platform on the ladder. She still felt weak, but she could lift herself.

Going down the ladder was slow moving, and she held on to the edge of the tank as she stepped off, but her legs held. She also wasn't thirsty, but monstrously hungry. Considering the questionable appearance of her borrowed swimming wear, she put her borrowed men's shirt back on and added a towel around her waist. She didn't look great, but at least if she saw anyone as she made her way back to her room she wouldn't embarrass them.

The house was quiet as she went to the stairs. She was at the door of her room when Caden came into the hall from his own room down at the end. He looked sleepy and disheveled, but luckily was clothed in sleeping wear. She wouldn't admit it to anyone at this point, but a sleepy, vulnerable look suited him.

"Should you be up?" He padded forward but kept his

voice low. Per the hall clock it was just after 6 am.

"I feel better," Nettie said, then waved her free hand at him. "No more webbing. I thought changing into some real clothes and eating breakfast would be nice."

Caden nodded. "That is a fascinating outfit. Lisselle and Rebecca explained the menswear, but even with my shirt, there is no way you'd be mistaken for a man right now." He tilted his head. "You know, up until yesterday I don't think I've ever seen your hair down. It's very nice." He looked awkward the moment the words came out.

It was hard to believe that someone with his skill in wooing women was looking embarrassed about a simple compliment.

"Thank you." Nettie smiled and patted the damp ends. To be honest, she wasn't that fond of having her hair up all of the time, and wasn't sure why she'd started wearing it that way. Leaving it down more often might be something to think about.

"Yes, well, I'll be off then, probably a bit early, so see you at breakfast." He stubbed his toe as he turned, caught himself before he fell, and went back into his room without further comment. It would probably be better for both of them if they were able to move him and Reaves over to the other house. Although, Nettie and Rebecca would be visiting as their male selves once they resolved her little fishy issue, they wouldn't be sleeping over there.

Nettie went into her room, took a proper bath to get the salt off, and then changed into regular clothes. She lifted a strand of hair and gave it a good look. If she was going to leave her hair down, she needed to have a bit of a trim. Satisfied that she looked significantly better than she had coming up the stairs, and in dire need of food, she descended again.

Rebecca and Reaves were setting breakfast places and both froze as she came into the dining room.

"Why are you up? You couldn't even get out of the tank last night." Rebecca rushed forward but stopped when Nettie held up her hand.

"Whatever happened is gone." She frowned. "Although if my condition is related to the merpeople and we are correct about them only coming on land at night, then this could be a temporary reprieve. I might be tied to the same cycle, but in reverse since my natural state is to be on land."

Rebecca hugged her tightly. "I'd rather you were fine for good, but I'll accept this for now." She pulled back and peered into Nettie's face. "You still look pale though. I do love your hair, why don't you wear it down more often?"

"I hadn't really thought of it before, it's more common to have it up or out of the way."

"For old spinsters' maybe," Lisselle said as she entered the room. "That's why I keep mine short, resolves the issue. And I've found having my hair like this disturbs many people." She grinned. "I am glad to see you up and web free, but I think you should sit down and get some food. Water?"

Nettie took her seat and shook her head. "No water please, I think I'm all right on that for a while, but I am starving and in desperate need of tea."

Reaves had the tea pot out and her cup poured before she finished her sentence.

"Thank you, Reaves. Are all of Homer's crew this gallant?"

"I can't speak for the others, but politeness is valued everywhere." He gave her a wink. "I am glad to see you up as well."

"Where are the others?" She knew by the smirk on her face that Rebecca was thinking of Caden. Nettie ignored her.

"They are bringing in some samples from the back. There was an incident last night."

Nettie had already gotten a few bites of toast in, but tilted her head in question. That should have been brought up immediately.

"Nothing was harmed. There were some sea kelp strands left at the back door. It wasn't the pile you got from the fisherman, they have that mess still secured, and there's no sign that it escaped. But something tried to get in last night."

Nettie picked up on the unsaid, 'into the room you were in'. Now to be fair, it could have just been an attempt on any door available, but coming on the same night as her change, she doubted it was random. She started to get up, but Lisselle pushed her back into her seat.

"Not you, at least not until I say so." She went into the kitchen and brought out a plate for her. Reaves got up and brought out the rest of the food for the others.

Nettie was ravenous, but stopped mid bite. "This must have been growing yesterday, whatever it is that is attacking me. I was equally as hungry then, very unnatural for me. Whatever this thing is, it appears to be modifying my already odd metabolism." Then she ate as quickly as she could without being rude.

Lisselle pulled out a notepad and jotted it down. "I'm afraid I still haven't been able to discover much, but it does appear to be an odd virus of sorts."

"So something we can cure?" Rebecca was mostly playing with her food and she kept watching Nettie.

"I'm not going to grow gills in front of you, you know." Nettie took some more tea.

"Yes, I do think it is something that we can cure." Lisselle's words sounded optimistic but the scowl on her face wasn't.

"And? I know that look."

"And I have a feeling that last night might have only been the start. This might go away in the light of day, but

I fear it could get much worse before we can find a cure."

Nettie was strangely optimistic at the news. But it almost felt that it was happening to someone else. "Has there been any word on Gaston? Or Bethlyn and her crew?" There were too many things going on to only focus on what might or might not be happening to her.

"Gaston and Damon are finally getting on the train today, with a few agents as escorts. But they will be going up to Edinburgh first, and are not expected to be down here for a few days at the least," Homer said as he and Caden came in and took their places. "Nothing on Bethlyn though. Edinburgh's two airships got called away and we saw nothing on our jaunt yesterday, but we couldn't go far."

"I think we have to go out looking for them again, take another angle," Caden said. "There are only so many places that an airship could have gone down completely unnoticed. The air station here telegraphed the others anywhere near their initial path, they weren't seen at all after crossing into southern Wales."

Homer shot Nettie a concerned glance. "There are a number of things we have to worry about."

She put down her teacup. "I am first and foremost a scientist of the SEU. I am also a half-vampire, and I might currently be fighting an infection of a sort, one that does tie directly to the reason we are up here." She looked each person at the table in the eye. "We do our job. If I become a liability to the mission, we will deal with that when it occurs. Bethlyn and her crew could be injured, prisoners, or lost; we owe it to them to find them."

Homer looked embarrassed and Lisselle looked proud. "Well put. To be on the side of caution, I believe we should keep your tank ready, secure the back doors, and make sure wherever you go, you are back before twilight."

Nettie nodded. Although that did mean she would be

unable to go on the search for the missing airship, at least until they figured out what was wrong with her and could control it.

"Please forgive me, I should have remembered who I was dealing with." Homer settled in. "I believe we can get a good search done before we must turn back. Now the question, what to tell Edinburgh?"

"Nothing about me yet."

"Everything."

Nettie and Lisselle spoke at the same time, with very different views.

"Please, Lisselle? At least until we have a better idea what is going on with me? You know they will take me back up there for study, and I can't let that happen. Not yet." There was a terror in her heart at that thought. Even now, knowing the sea was just a short distance away was calming. Being trapped in the SEU headquarters was a chilling thought.

"I agree with Nettie," Rebecca had been quiet during the exchange but looked determined now. "You know they will take her. They might not if it had been one of us, but Nettie?" She shook her head. "She's too unique."

Caden nodded. "I'm with them."

Lisselle shrugged. "Part of me still thinks they could help, but the other part doesn't trust them to play nice with this. And Homer and I do have reputations as rebels within the Society to uphold." She waggled her finger at Nettie. "But if I fear your life is in danger, and beyond what we can do for you here, I will commandeer an airship and take you up there myself."

"And I will let you," Nettie said. "I don't have a death wish, but I do feel I'm far more valuable out here than as a test subject in Scotland."

The rest of the morning was spent assorting who would be going after what, although the three men weren't completely in agreement with the women disguising themselves as men and going about town, they finally caved in.

"I don't know why you have to have your male counterparts stay in our house though," Caden said.

"Ease of association." Rebecca shrugged. "Having a large and eccentric mansion with a group of unrelated men and women in London was odd enough, out here it is noticeable. We can still keep the ruse of the connections between us, but separate houses for the men and women will raise less issues. And now that we have that passageway in the back it won't be that noticeable when we go back and forth."

After the breakfast dishes were put away, Homer, Reaves, and Caden went to meet with the rest of Homer's crew and set up the best course to find the missing airship.

Edinburgh believed that Bethlyn's airship might have been targeted because Gaston was supposed to be aboard. His last minute change thwarted them. The attack they'd faced by the war zeppelin was being marked down as wrong place and wrong time. If the zeppelin was planning on attacking the London airship field they wouldn't have planned to attack another ship along the way.

Nettie would feel much better when Gaston and Damon joined them. Lisselle was a solid scientist, but Gaston was on an entirely different level than any of them. She was sure that with him involved they'd be able to solve her problem.

Lisselle was going to take more blood from Nettie and run another battery of tests. The standard tests hadn't been helpful, so she was planning on pulling in some odd ones and perhaps even a little witchcraft if need be. Nettie and Rebecca were going to go back out and finish what they'd started yesterday in terms of examining the locations of the prior appearances of the merpeople. There was no immediate need for them to go as men, but Nettie felt there would be fewer eyes on them that way.

Caden shook his head at their decision, but handed her a shirt and jacket. "These are both a bit tight in the shoulders, so they'll be easier to fit to you. Just don't get cocky," he looked to Rebecca too, "either of you. You're granted more protection as women than as men in much of society. And scruff up your faces more, from what I saw last night you were still too pretty to be men."

He, Homer, and Reaves left.

"He does have a point. A few actually." Lisselle lifted Nettie's chin. "I think some good shading can make you look manlier. Probably better than the facial hair. And, I know you, Nettie, I'm more worried about you thinking your vampiric strength will get you out of things. I know you're feeling better now, but need I remind you how weak you were? Don't count on your supernatural abilities right now. Keep your heads down, gather information, but don't get involved."

Nettie almost argued, then sighed. Lisselle had her to rights. She'd become too accustomed to being able to get out of most situations, first with her brain, secondly with her strength. Taking that for granted could be fatal for an agent. Last night had been a scary time for many reasons.

Once they'd changed Rebecca and Nettie into passable men, Lisselle shook her head.

"I don't like to use glamours lightly, they are taxing and can be misused. But since neither of you have had full training in undercover, I am afraid your voices and mannerisms might give you away." She walked around them slowly. "I want you to speak in your best manly voice. The trick is not to go any lower than your normal voice than you need, it will keep it from sounding fake. Nettie, you first."

"Hello, my name is Fred Jones." She tried to do what Lisselle said, but it was hard not to want to go as deep as possible.

Lisselle nodded then turned to Rebecca. "My name is Luke Evans." She did the same thing Nettie had done.

"Okay, when I say, I want you to start repeating the alphabet. This is more a support spell than real glamour, and if you try hard enough you can still sound like yourselves."

Nettie heard the change in their voices by the letter H. They sounded like themselves, but there was a timbre that wasn't there before. By the time they got to Z neither sounded like themselves.

"Now I don't want to put a glamour on your movements as well, at least not a full one." Lisselle walked around them again. "Too many glamours can increase risk of exposure, not to mention you should learn how to do this without magic. For now, try to slouch a bit more, unless you come across other men, then pull your shoulders back a bit. As you go about, watch how men walk. Men of different stations move differently. Homer, Reaves, and Caden all have different walks. Homer plows through things, Reaves always stays steady and slow, and Caden walks like he's trying to sell someone something. When we're all together I'll have them walk for you." She finally nodded. "Okay, this is as good as we will get for now. Don't stay out more than a few hours, and do not take risks."

With that admonishment, and with them focusing on trying to slouch more, Nettie and Rebecca left the house. They went the way they'd begun yesterday, but avoided the dock.

"Was it really only yesterday?" Nettie kept her volume down but it was still disturbing hearing something other than her voice coming out.

Rebecca nodded. Then looked around and dropped her voice to a whisper. "I know, it seems days ago." She pulled back and patted her throat. "This is disturbing. Now I am afraid to say anything."

Nettie smiled, then quickly ran her hand over her mouth to hide it. It wasn't that men didn't smile, it was that their smiles were different, and until they got it down to a fine art, they needed to show less of them.

The bulk of sightings had taken place near a pub at the edge of the market section of town. It would be better to have done a recon during the evening, but given Nettie's current condition, that was out. One of the people who had reported seeing a creature was the daytime bartender who'd been chased by one on his way home. It had been early in the evening, but the sun had set, so it was plausible that he saw something.

The pub was dark, but there were half a dozen patrons inside. Even though she'd eaten a monstrous amount less than two hours before, the smells coming from the patrons' meals were making Nettie's mouth water.

"He's at the bar now, let me do the talking, we probably want to order something to eat. It's too early for a drink."

Rebecca gave her a side-eye look. "Since when? You order food, I'll get an ale. Less suspicious that way, and I heard your stomach as soon as we walked in."

They approached the bar and Nettie debated taking a table. But this way they could chat with the bartender with ease.

"What'll ya have?" He was an unassuming sort, matched the description, and didn't appear the type to be telling tales.

"I'll have an ale." Rebecca kept her words clipped and nodded in emphasis.

He turned to Nettie. "I'll have the fry, and hot tea."

The barkeep grunted, then put down the ale and a pot of tea and went to get the food.

Nettie waited until he was coming back before starting her argument. She started it in the middle, as if she and Rebecca had been debating something. Fortunately for her, Rebecca was a quick study, and after a moment's pause, she jumped in after Nettie's lead.

"I'm telling ya, that's what I saw. Clear as you sitting there, up at the Castle."

"I'm saying you're daft." Rebecca took a long sip of her ale.

The barkeep put down Nettie's food but didn't leave. He nodded to Nettie with a scowl. "You two aren't from here, are ya?"

Nettie didn't have to fake her interest in the food, she looked up mid-bite. She swallowed quickly. "Naw, here from London. Sister is here with people on a retreat."

"You've been to Conwy?" He looked at the glass he was polishing. The question was simple, but the meaning behind it was more complex. He'd definitely heard them and knew what they were talking about.

"Went there a few days ago," Nettie dropped her voice and looked around as if to make sure no one was close enough to hear them. "Saw something up at the castle on our way back that night. It was leaving the castle and heading into the water near the fishing boats." She snorted and tilted her head toward Rebecca. "This one wasn't paying attention. Now he's calling me a liar. But I know what I saw." She went back to her food as if that was the end of it. But she watched him out of the corner of her eye.

The barkeep was quiet, but he'd been cleaning the same glass for two minutes. Finally he coughed. "What'd ya see?" His voice was low.

Nettie sat down her food and watched the barkeep as if weighing his intent. "I saw a creature. Covered in vines or seaweed. Tall like a man, but oddly shaped. It looked like it had too many arms. But it was too dark to see much more." She leaned forward. This was complete embellishment, the reports had only mentioned sightings at the castle itself. But it would make sense a sea creature had to go back—and if it was like the tentacled fishman they'd seen in London, he would look misshapen.

The barkeep studied her long enough that Nettie began to fear some of her disguise had come off. Finally, he spoke. "It's true. There are creatures, sea creatures mind you, coming out and walking about. Here and Conwy, maybe others, but for sure here. I saw one." The pause he gave as he watched their faces was weighing their reaction.

"I believe you." Rebecca took another sip. "Fred here is sometimes daft, but you seem solid. What did you see?"

"A creature like what your friend saw, but mine definitely had extra arms, or something. About my height. It was stumbling like it was injured somehow. Kept looking in the store fronts, then wandered back to the beach, and kept walking. Chased me a bit, but didn't seem to actually be trying to catch me."

"It didn't do anything?"

He scratched his head. "Seemed like it was looking for something. Unlike that one that attacked Old Man Jeeves." He shook his head, picked up a new glass, and started polishing.

Nettie and Rebecca shared a glance. There hadn't been a mention of an attack. Other sightings yes, but no attacks.

"What attack? If these things are dangerous, we need to know," Nettie said as she sat down her fork.

"Happened a few weeks ago, full moon. Jeeves lives out at the edge of town, has a farmstead of sorts. Anyway, he came into town that next morning all covered with cuts and bruises. Weird red marks too. Said he had to fight for his life on account a sea monster tried to eat him."

"Eat?" Nettie wasn't sure she'd heard right. They might have confirmed the barman's sighting, but he could be making this one up.

"That's what he said. Held up his arm all covered in

sucker marks as proof. Pretty much got himself laughed out of town. That was before more folks saw strange things."

Nettie finished her food and pushed the plate away. "Where might we find him? I'm curious about someone who had an encounter with one."

"We don't know. He went back home after getting laughed out of every pub in town. Didn't come to town the next week, so a few folks went to check on him. His place was tossed a bit and abandoned. A few great puddles of some liquid and mounds of seaweed, but no Jeeves. Now with what folks have seen, some of us anyways, we're thinking the sea monster came back and got him."

A chill went down Nettie's spine. This farmer would have been the first known contact and beat the other reports by a few weeks. No word had gotten out of Llandudno about it though. Most likely when they first found his place, they'd not worried about it, thinking he'd come back. Unfortunately, a month was too long for there to be biological evidence left now. But the description of his injuries fit Thomas'. Jeeves had been there when the townspeople came out to his place—but all that was left was the goo.

They put down money to pay for the food and drink, then left. Part of Nettie wanted to stay and ask more questions, but she could tell the barkeep was starting to get twitchy about talking. More people had seen strange things since Jeeves first came to town with his wild story, but they still weren't talking about it publicly.

They tried a cheese shop where a morning clerk had reportedly seen a strange shape coming out of the water. But the clerk in question was home with a cold. Three more attempts were also met with the person being off that day, home ill, or visiting relatives.

"Either this is a massive coincidence, or they were warned." Rebecca sat down on a bench. It took a few adjustments to get comfortable and not look lady like but she did it.

"I don't know about warning them. The barkeep wasn't comfortable, but he didn't seem threatened. Unless there was someone else in the bar." Nettie flung herself onto the bench with a sigh. "I should have been watching them as well as him."

"I didn't think of it either. What do we do now?" Rebecca looked down at her pants leg. "I believe I might join you and Lisselle in favoring pants, these are quite freeing."

"Why is he staring at his pants like he's never seen 'em before?" The man's voice came from behind Nettie.

"He's just so pleased with the quality, not his usual type." Nettie said then turned and favored the speaker with a nod. "And you'd be?"

"Mathlin, Richard Mathlin. Or crazy Mathlin works too. You the two gents who were asking about the sea mon-sters, eh?" Mathlin was short and round, almost similar in shape, age, and bearing to Gaston, only far more scraggily and pale.

"We were asking about sightings," Rebecca said. "My friend here saw something over in Conwy."

"Aye, ya did. Jeeves got taken by them too. No one wants to talk about it. Afraid they'll be next." He seemed to be waiting for something.

"But you know the truth of things." Nettie didn't put it as a question, it was a statement. Mathlin was the town eccentric, most people probably didn't even notice him. But in Nettie's experience, the odd ones were often the most observant because they were discounted by the rest of society.

His deep blue eyes were suddenly sharp. "Aye, that I do. Of many things. You're looking on the wrong side of the water though. *They* like the other side better."

"The other side of water?"

"Aye. This beach is the North, but there's more people on this side. The other side is the West side beach. Less people."

"Less people means more of the creatures come out?" Nettie watched as his eyes faded a bit. He was far sharper than he wanted to let on.

"Can't hurt to check now, can it? And ye'd been right about them warning the others. MacGregor was in the pub, he heard you and warned the others."

MacGregor was the train master who'd been rumored to have seen a sea creature while checking a line. He'd also been drinking at the time and steadfastly denied everything once he sobered up. They'd spent hours wandering and looking into areas of sightings even if no one else would talk to them. Nettie estimated they had about three hours before twilight.

She got to her feet and crossed her arms. She was easily a head taller than Mathlin. "You can show us this place?"

"You sure, Fred? We still have some things to do." Rebecca stayed seated but didn't look happy about Nettie's direction. They could take care of themselves, but Nettie knew it was related more to her curfew than anything else.

"We have time. Our good friend here is going to show us where these creatures have been."

He smiled. "That I can do. Been saying for a while we needed to get some proper folks out here." He started walking briskly without waiting for them.

They quickly caught up. He stayed silent as he led them out of the market area, past some more homes, then finally mostly open land. The walk was farther than Nettie had thought, but she could see the other beach in the distance. The road was a ways away, he was taking them down a path that ran parallel but was obviously for foot traffic.

The sounds of the waves crashing could be heard when Mathlin stopped and turned on them. "Now, where is Gaston and why are you two ladies dressing like men?"

CHAPTER SEVENTEEN

—◆—

NETTIE TOOK A STEP BACK, pushing Rebecca back as well. "I don't know what you're talking about. Was this a trick to rob us?"

Mathlin's laugh was a rusty sounding cackle. "You're agents for SEU, you normally wear women's clothing, and are scientists rather than fighters. Although "Fred" here is thinking of ways to disable me as we stand here. You're from London, which means you work with Gaston, who is noticeably not here."

Rebecca looked to Nettie with a shrug, one Nettie echoed. Whoever Mathlin really was, he knew too much to let go without getting answers. Had he been someone working against the Society, he could have attacked them already.

"You have us," Nettie said. "I am Agent Jones and this is Agent Rhys. Yes, we work with Gaston, he is on other business. The Society is quite concerned with the recent issues in the area. Now, who are you really and how do you know of the Society?"

"Agent Jones, eh? *The* Nettie Jones? The one who saved the free world from vampires and aliens? Nice to meet you. And you as well, Agent Rhys. I told you the right name, but my affiliation is a bit more muddled than what I implied. I was an agent, years ago. Mostly stationed in the stews in London. Then had one too many cases that tore at my soul and left." He looked up into the sky as if adding something in his head. "Been fifteen years ago. Moving around since, but I usually come back here. I wasn't lying about waiting for the proper people to arrive, I was about ready to send Edinburgh an anonymous note about the events down here."

"Do you really have any leads, or was that just a ruse to get us away from town?"

"A bit of both. I took samples of what was left of Jeeves, have them in my storage. There is definitely something bad going on, there are some other hermits like me out here, the sea and peace and quiet calls to us, but at least five are missing." He paused. "And I caught a fish person yesterday. It's in water, in a cave."

"What? Take us there! We've been loitering about when you have a merman captured? Take us to him and tell me everything about how you caught him." Nettie started walking the way they had been going but stopped when he hadn't moved.

"Sorry, you are very much as described. I still have friends in Edinburgh and they keep me up on things. I was shocked that a single agent had done all that you'd been reported to have done during the Queen's event. They assured me it was more than believable given the agent. They were right about your determination for certain."

Rebecca passed him and joined Nettie. "We do have some obligations back in town, if we could get moving?" She still looked and sounded male. But her stance was all pissed off woman.

"Aye, we can get there quickly this way." He crossed the road and went up over a hill. A small house was hidden by the hill and sat on a beautiful strip of beach. A rise at the end of the beach was rocky and looked to be indented by caves.

"The merman first, if you please." Nettie headed him off as he started going toward the house. "You do realize that we will need to bring in the rest of our agents on this."

"Yes, yes, yes. Trust me, I weighed my options well before approaching you. But why isn't Gaston here? There is no way I'd miss him if he were in town."

"He's been delayed, but will be here shortly." Nettie believed Mathlin in that he was formerly involved with the Society, but she was going to censor what information she gave him until she spoke to Lisselle.

Mathlin nodded, then headed toward the caves. Only one was a large cave, and even that only had a mouth about as tall as Rebecca. Roughly crafted steel bars blocked the entrance.

"How did you capture him?"

"He actually captured himself," Mathlin said as they walked closer. "He got stuck in the cave two mornings ago and couldn't get out before sunrise. I found him asleep here and put these grates in before nightfall. Luckily he's not one of the ones with tentacles." There were two grates. One blocked an entrance to the water and let the waves go through, the second faced the land. They stopped at the land one, and it was high enough that right now no water came through.

Nettie looked closer at the bars. One of the octopi merpeople could have ripped the grating off. She shielded her eyes with her hands. The cave wasn't that deep, but it was dark. The man lying there looked like a man. Just a man. He was asleep, lying up against the rocks and didn't seem to be disturbed when the waves crashed against his face.

A tip of what looked like a giant tail flipper appeared across from him as the water went down.

"Is he still alive? Are they diurnal? And if that's his tail, how are they walking on land?" Rebecca pushed her face against the bars to see better.

"He's alive, I threw in some fish late last night, and he ate them. I don't know that they are truly day sleepers, but the sunlight definitely hurts them, it makes sense they'd sleep if caught on land when the sun came up. As for the rest, I was hoping some scientists might be able to figure it out."

Nettie shook her head. "There must be a number of different types and abilities to these merpeople. In London, we believe a group of them tried to blow up Gaston's mansion. We were accosted by a bunch of them at a pub in the evening. But at least one of them had been spotted earlier, when the sun was still out."

"Maybe they are adapting? Coming back onto land?"

The sleeping merman twitched but didn't open his eyes.

"I think we want to move this discussion away from our friend. He's not going anywhere." Mathlin turned and led them up the hill to his house.

It was small, probably not much larger than Gaston's parlor, but it looked well-tended.

"I can put on some tea," Mathlin smiled. "I play the eccentric in town to keep people at a distance, I forget how nice it is to actually talk to people. Especially SEU agents. Please have a seat, I'll be right back."

They sat and Nettie looked around the small but neat front room. The people from town might believe his ruse, but no one would if they saw his collection of books. Treatises on mythological creatures, spells, higher level physics and calculus. Many of the books were ones she or Gaston had, and were also probably from the Society. Whatever had chased him away from SEU had not dimmed his love of knowledge.

"Here we go, even some biscuits." Mathlin sat out a full tea service and two plates of biscuits.

"How long have you been out here, again?" Nettie took the cup of tea he offered. She was disturbed by his duplicity at first, but there was a sincerity that came through in his home.

"Almost fifteen years. It seems like another lifetime."

Rebecca took her tea and leaned forward. "Do you miss

it?"

He started to shake her off, then sighed. "I think I do. It wasn't until Jeeves and all the sightings, but I miss trying to do something for good, instead of just surviving."

"When Gaston gets to town, you can talk to him about it." Nettie nodded to the collection of books. "They look well read."

"Aye, that they are. We'll see. Now about my theories. I don't know that the—what did you call them? Merpeople? I don't know that they are changing to come on land. I believe they are fighting back against us for one reason or another; and I think they were human long ago." He got up and pulled out a slim book. "I borrowed this from Edinburgh when I was still an agent and never gave it back. Looking at odd cases helped when I was trapped dealing with the ugliness of humanity." He handed it to Nettie and Rebecca.

"An Explanation of the Stranded People of the Archipelago of Atlantis?" Nettie opened the book so both she and Rebecca could read it. "I've never seen anything that indicated Atlantis was real."

"This from a half-vampire who helped fight off alien invaders?" He tilted his head and smiled. "The Society has access to more information and technology than the rest of humanity, but there are still many things that even we don't know."

Nettie looked at the front cover. "Elfthrith Allsmythe, is that the same one who is in charge of the Bath station?" She and Caden had briefly met her when they were trying to find the vampire hive in Bath. Charming, but saw far more than normal people. A clairvoyant of odd powers. Rebecca had discovered she had clairvoyant tendencies, but they hadn't assigned her to work with Elfthrith yet.

"She's still down there?" Mathlin grinned. "She always liked being able to go to the water. An old spirit that one."

Rebecca flipped the book back to the front page. "Not just old spirit. This book is seventy years old."

"Eh, old spirit, old body. Some people don't age the same as the rest. Thing is, she has evidence in there that Atlantis did exist, and when it fell, some of its people were trapped. They changed or died. There's a few theories that the Atlantians were mystics and spell users. After all, they were the ones the Runners were looking for when they crashed. They'd been in communication."

"Interesting. Then why, after all of these years, are they coming to land?"

"That I have no theory on. Could be a long time grudge. Could be we're venturing too far into their world. Could just be nasty merpeople."

Rebecca had turned to the window and pulled on Nettie's arm. "It's getting late, we need to get back, or Lisselle will be worried."

Mathlin laughed. "That's who you are! You're the little Welsh girl who's been playing at traveling companion to Agent Lisselle. I almost approached her a few times, but lost my nerve. She still married to Homer?"

"Married?" Nettie and Rebecca said at the same time. She was sure she looked as shocked as Rebecca did.

"I take it from your reaction they aren't. I'd seen an airship lift off this morning, thought it might be him."

"It was. I don't believe they're married at this point, but they seem to get along fine." Nettie was stunned. She felt there had been a relationship in their history, but marriage? That was extremely surprising.

"They're good people, just a bit too fiery for marriage."

Rebecca had rankled a bit at the little Welsh girl comment, but recovered quickly when there was gossip to be had. "So the Society doesn't frown on marriage between agents?" She shot Nettie a knowing look.

Luckily, Mathlin was watching Rebecca, Nettie was certain her own face had gone red.

"Aye, they're accepting of it. Not happy mind you. Marriage can lead to many complications whether it succeeds or not. Ideally, they'd like to keep a married couple as a team for jobs, but if their skills are too different it makes it tricky."

They chatted a bit more, mostly about living out here. Nettie wasn't sure how much he could be told about their situation and he seemed unsure as to how much he really wanted to know.

Nettie looked up. The day was quite late at this point. "I do hate to leave so abruptly, but we need to get back before nightfall. I've an experiment I'm working on." That wasn't far from the truth, he didn't need to know the experiment was herself.

Mathlin rose. "Might I ask if you could pass along my greetings to the others? Lisselle, Homer, and Gaston once he gets here? I have enjoyed talking to you and I believe this case is one I can help with."

"Not to mention you have one of them in a cage," Rebecca said as she rose.

"I will tell them. How long will you hold the merman?" Nettie headed for the door. They really had dawdled too long.

"As long as I can. I don't want to hurt him, and I do think we need to study him. Good evening ladies."

They quickly made their way up the hill and toward town. Nettie's legs were far longer than Rebecca's, so Rebecca jogged to keep up.

They were almost back to the house when Nettie started to shake. "This is completely unfair, I believe we have at least fifteen minutes before sunset."

Rebecca stopped and grabbed her arm. "Are you changing?" She looked around even though she'd kept her voice low.

"Something is happening. I'm feeling very thirsty and shaky."

"Can you make it, or do we need to rest?"

"Resting will make things worse, let's get there as soon as we can." The weakness flowed through her body and an overwhelming urge to run and dive into the ocean hit her hard.

Rebecca grabbed her arm again. "I don't know what you're thinking but you're drifting the wrong direction. We are only a few houses away."

Nettie stumbled and let Rebecca guide her to a bench. "This is bad. I don't know that I can walk at all right now."

Rebecca looked around. A worker was coming back from the quay with an empty wheelbarrow.

"Might I borrow that? My friend doesn't drink usually, and he had a bit too much." She pulled out some coins as the man narrowed his eyes at them. "I'll bring it right back and pay you."

"Aye. Bring it to this house here." He picked up the coins in her hand, grunted, and handed off the wheelbarrow.

"I'm not going back in that."

"Do you want to stay here until you go fishy?" Rebecca's voice was low but she got the point across.

The fact that Nettie had to be helped into the wheelbarrow reinforced that she needed to use it.

Rebecca was small, but stronger than she looked. Even so, a sick grandmother could have covered the distance faster. They were turning up the walk to their house when the door flung open and Caden came running out.

"What happened to her?" Even though Nettie was clearly conscious he turned to Rebecca. Nettie scowled. Just because one was in a wheelbarrow did not mean they were incomprehensible.

"What are you doing here? I thought you were going

to be gone a few days?" Nettie wanted to push him and Rebecca away from her, to show them she could get out on her own. Unfortunately, that wasn't the case.

"News for when we're inside," Caden said but his eyes darkened. He scooped her up then set her on her feet and let Rebecca roll away the wheelbarrow. "Put your arm around me, I have you."

Nettie did so and he started moving toward the door. She was leaning heavily on him but was glad that he didn't try to carry her. She didn't want to have to explain to anyone more than she might already if this Fred persona needed to go out again.

Rebecca came running back as the rest of the household came out.

"What happened? We were in the kitchen and didn't know you were out here." Homer stepped forward. "Do you want me to help?"

"She's going fishy," Rebecca said.

"I've got her." Caden tightened his arm around Nettie's waist as they hobbled up the stairs. "We need to get her into the tank immediately." He held up one of her hands. He'd noticed the webbing before she had.

The others all stayed out of the way as Caden half-carried Nettie toward the back of the house. Nettie could smell the water of her tank and was ready to crawl there herself.

The rickety ladder from before was replaced with a wider, sturdier staircase. Clearly someone had been busy. The stairs were able to accommodate two people side by side, going up together, and had a nice wide platform at the top.

Nettie slipped off her shoes and jacket before Caden helped her up the steps.

"Thank you." She stepped into the water from the top and swam a bit to work out the shakes. Then she came up to the edge, folded her arms over it, and nodded to them all. "Now that that's settled, Rebecca and I have news, but I fear yours is bad, so you go first," Nettie said to Caden and Homer. "Why did you come back so soon?" Her clothes weren't comfortable soggy like this, but she could change after they'd learned what happened and they could clear the men out.

"We found the airship about a hundred miles south east of here. Crashed, but salvageable. In fact, Bethlyn should have been able to recover enough power to limp to a town. The balloon is intact, it's been deliberately deflated." Homer paused. "After the crash landing." That wasn't good. Someone didn't want it getting back up easily, nor being easily spotted.

"But no sign of the crew? What caused it to crash?" Nettie continued to hang onto the side of the tank. It was an informal way to have such a conversation, but she was starting to feel her strength come back.

Caden darted out and came back with chairs from the dining room. Then brought more until everyone was seated around the tank. Nettie almost felt like she should be doing flips or leap through a hoop.

"Nothing beyond a trail that led through a field and was completely obscured after a few hundred feet. I didn't see blood or any sign of injuries. As for what brought it down? Until we get it back here and I can take it apart, I'm not sure." Homer's scowl looked to be etched into his face.

"It did look like someone sabotaged it though," Caden said and Reaves nodded in agreement.

The look on Homer's face said this had been an ongoing debate, but he finally ran his hand through his thick gray hair. "Aye, that it did. But we still can't tell what their aim was. Almost everything on the ship was still there. We loaded the cargo onto mine and brought it back. We've set all of it in the front room."

"How can we get the airship back here though?" Nettie asked.

"Edinburgh is taking care of that. I'd wanted us to be involved, but Ramsey is making my ship and me stay here. He's afraid there will be more activity."

"Now what of your news? Aside from the two of you staying out far longer than I told you to and Nettie almost changing out there on the walkway?" Lisselle seemed calm but there would be fallout from this for certain.

Rebecca deferred to Nettie who quickly filled them in on Mathlin. Both Lisselle and Homer seemed glad to hear that name, but they refrained from asking questions until Nettie finished.

"Oh, and he has a merman captured." She hadn't meant to leave that to the end but somehow it got pushed back. There seemed to be some brain fog when she changed.

"What now?" Homer leapt to his feet with Caden and Reaves right behind him.

Lisselle scowled at them. "You can't think you're going out there right now? Although I do wonder why the other merpeople haven't tried to rescue him."

"I hadn't even thought of that, changing back and forth is slowing my cognitive processes." Nettie sunk a bit more into the water. The soggy clothing actually worked to keep her skin damp longer, but it was still sensitive to drying out.

"Mathlin has had him for two days; wouldn't they have tried to save it by now if they were going to?" Rebecca scowled as she realized that she hadn't thought about that either.

"They could have been waiting, or unsure where he was. If none of his people knew he was there?" Nettie couldn't believe that hadn't even crossed her mind before now.

"The longer he stays there the more likely it is they will find him. Mathlin was a good agent once, but he's not young, they could easily overpower him." Homer was already heading for the door. "We fortified the back door, and will lock the front, but we need to get out there."

Rebecca rose. She was still in her men's clothing and was looking quite fierce. "You'll never find it without help. Even with me along we might not find it in the dark. But obviously we have to try."

"If you are going, you're going armed." Lisselle rose. "I can protect Nettie and myself here, but you should all take gear guns." She left the back room and came back with two boxes of gear guns. The small, almost pistol looking weapons were strictly SEU issued. Unlike a standard pistol, the gears and wheels allowed for a variety of settings and could emit an electrical charge to stun someone instead of killing them. For the most part, however, agents only went about fully armed when in dangerous situations.

"You're going to need more than weapons though," Nettie said. "There is nothing out there, and his home is on the other side of a hill, hiding any light."

"Sparksticks? Those are still not fully tested."

"No, but I take it we have some?" Nettie smiled. The sparksticks, as they were so poorly named, were dry cell and miniature incandescent electric lamps that were portable. They'd been invented a few months ago by the Society, but they were still not common.

"Aye, we do. I wasn't sure we should be using them being as they are still under study, but I have them on my ship. We can get them on the way."

The rest gathered the needed supplies. Everyone was concerned Mathlin might need rescuing should the merpeople try to take their friend back. Lisselle started to hand them empty sample gathering containers, but Rebecca and Caden beat her to it and held up the ones they'd already packed.

"Good then, there's some chance for you young ones

after all." She escorted them all out, then came back with a glass of water and a plate of food for Nettie. "I assume you are still eating regular food? No other changes?"

"It smells good, and I'm hungry, so we can assume that hasn't changed." Nettie pulled up her pants leg, but the scales hadn't started yet. "Just the webbing and weakness. Which does go away once I'm in the salt water. But it started before sunset, and hit extremely hard."

Lisselle had out a pad of paper and jotted down some notes. "Anything that came before? Or just the fatigue?"

"Not really. Thirsty, shakes, then I couldn't walk and almost ran into the ocean. Have you found anything?"

"Your blood is definitely changing, but doesn't match anything we have on file, at least not here. We need some more samples. If they can't bring back anything from Mathlin's capture, we might need to contact Edinburgh."

"Not yet, please." Nettie splashed water as she smacked herself in the head as a thought hit her. "Mathlin had some of the remains of that farmer, Jeeves. He gave us a vial. It should still be in the jacket." She shook her head. "I am sorry, I'm not thinking well right now."

Lisselle fished the vial out. "You are going through some massive changes, that's bound to play with your mind. I'm going to go run this through a few tests and see what I can find. Do you need anything else?" She sat down an extra pad and pencil near the food.

Nettie started to shake her head, then looked down at her clothing. "Could I get that bathing suit back? It was too small, but better than this."

"Oh! Now I'm the one forgetting things. I went out and found a shop near that hotel, they were still setting up, but I managed to get them to sell me two bathing suits for you. Let me get them."

She returned with two packages and unwrapped one. "This one is a two piece, top and bottom. The other is a longer skirt type one. I would have bought two of the two piece, but they only had one in your size." She put it at the top of the ladder along with some more food and a full pitcher of water. "And don't forget to use the bell if you need me."

Nettie made sure she could reach everything, her strength was returning but best if things were close by. "You'll come back down once you find something?" That was possibly one of the worst things of this situation, here there were major scientific events happening, and she couldn't run any tests. Most vexing when she was the test subject.

"Of course. I do wish we could give you something to do, but I haven't figured out how to make the equipment waterproof."

"That's okay, I'm feeling better so I should be able to run through some tests on my own. Notes on reactions, changes, that sort of thing."

Lisselle was almost out the door when she stopped and turned back. "Are you certain you're all right? Not just right now, but about all of this. It is dramatic, even for you."

"It is. But I am a half-vampire, so my constitution is stronger than most. And I came back from being forced into becoming a full vampire. I can come back from this." Her smile wavered a bit. "And if I don't, I have the best people in the world to take care of me."

"We will fix you, one way or another. I promise." Lisselle smiled. "If you need anything, just ring."

Nettie finished eating, changed out of her men's clothes into the bathing suit, then settled in her hammock. It was a bit early for bed, yet she was limited in her options. Small blue green scales, still mostly outlines of them, had appeared on her legs since the first time she looked. They were also appearing on her hands, but so faint she first thought she was imagining them.

Her skin felt the same as it always did, although she did

wonder if the scales came in completely if she would get that slimy feel fish had. That was a disagreeable thought and she shoved it aside. She simply wouldn't let the change go that far.

She rolled out of her hammock. There were no gills that she could feel on her neck; she'd have to ask Lisselle for a mirror next time. But still, testing her ability to breathe underwater should be done. She took a breath, then pushed herself to the floor of the tank. Human bodies tended to float, particularly in salty water, so she'd expected to have to fight more. She braced herself against the two narrowest walls of the tank, but it wasn't as hard as she'd thought to stay down. With the amount of salt in the water, she should have been popping to the top.

That was an interesting thing she'd need to report to Lisselle as well. And then they would have to see if that held true when she changed back to herself in the daytime. Was she changed all of the time and it only manifested during the evening, or was she only changed during the evening?

She'd been pondering that thought when she realized she was no longer holding her breath. That brought a choking sensation and she pulled her legs under her and pushed to the surface. "That was interesting." Until she thought about not breathing, her body was doing fine on its own. She would have to add that to her notes for Lisselle. She dried her hands on the towel draped on the tank, and wrote everything down. More things to study.

She tried going back down to the bottom a few more times. While she still went down far faster and easier than seemed reasonable, she couldn't duplicate the breathing under water and had to come back up for air. Her time for holding her breath seemed to be increasing however.

She'd finished her studies and notes, the only other notable change, was that her eyesight under water did seem superior, and the salt didn't sting at all. With a sigh, she sat aside her notes to be clear of any water should she need to leave the tank quickly, and returned to her hammock.

Dreams of being out in the open ocean were drifting around her head when yelling broke her out of her sleep.

"We need a doctor!" Homer was yelling from the front room. Pounding down the stairs indicated Lisselle had come down. She and Nettie were the closet they had to doctors. Nettie had a medical license, even though it was to work on the dead. She could still have helped…if she hadn't been trapped in a tank of salt water.

"Bring him in here, there's more room," Caden yelled as he came into the back room where Nettie was.

Homer and Reaves came in carrying Mathlin. He was bleeding from at least two injuries in his torso and looked horribly pale.

"What happened?"

They all looked up as if they'd forgotten she was there. Then Caden shook his head. "The man is a damn fool, that's what happened. We'd managed to get the merman close enough to the bars to get some samples. He might have been surviving, but he appeared weak, the water inside the cave was too shallow for him to submerge completely is my guess. Then more of them came swarming out of the water. We all jumped back, but Mathlin defended his cage. I told him to let them rescue him. But he attacked them with a spear, they retaliated, and we hauled him out of there."

"Where's Rebecca?"

"She's grabbing towels and padding. Lisselle's moved a lot of her equipment down to the parlor and the bedroom down here is still destroyed," Homer said. "This is going to have to be our hospital area."

Lisselle came in with Rebecca with enough towels and bedding to cover a hospital. In moments they had a table up, covered in bedding, and Mathlin laying upon it. His eyes fluttered as they gently put him down.

"Mathlin? Are you conscious?" Nettie called down to him from her tank. His being unconscious would help when they were ready to operate to close his wounds, but it would be better if he started out awake and Lisselle could knock him out. Less chance of him waking up when he shouldn't.

"Agent Jones? Where am I?" He tried to move and blood seeped through his clothing.

"Keep him still!" Lisselle had donned a smock and gloves. "Nettie, keep him talking until I can get him under. Mathlin, don't you dare die on me."

He still wasn't opening his eyes, but a small smile crossed his face. "I know that voice. You brought me back to town. My merman, I wanted him to be under study."

Rebecca had put together a concoction, drew it into a needle, and held it up. Lisselle nodded and Rebecca gently injected Mathlin. Far stronger than the ether used in hospitals, the chemical was created and used by the Society. Mathlin's jaw went slack as he was put under.

Lisselle quickly cut away his clothing and examined his torso. "Rebecca, I'll need you and Homer to help with this. Reaves and Caden, he shouldn't be able to move under this, but stranger things have happened. Hold him still no matter what. I need to make certain the wounds are clean before I close him up."

Nettie felt useless as everyone did their part, but there was no way that she could get out of the tank, and even if she did, there'd be nothing she could do if she collapsed on the floor.

Both wounds were thoroughly cleaned of any residue from the weapon used, and Lisselle closed them both up quickly and neatly. Rebecca knew exactly what to hand her, and even Homer seemed to have his role down.

She'd closed him up and covered him with more towels

and blankets when the back door rattled sharply as something slammed into it.

CHAPTER EIGHTEEN

"IS HE OKAY?" CADEN CLEARLY wanted to check the door, but he didn't want to endanger Mathlin.

"Yes, I've closed him up and he should recover. Go and see what that is, but since it's possibly one of the seaweed creatures, or a merperson, do not let whatever is out there touch you." Lisselle peeled off her gloves and smock.

"Take torches, not the electrical kind," Nettie said as they ran for the front. "They hate fire." She really had no idea where that thought came from, but even as she yelled for them to get fire a coldness settled in her gut.

Caden nodded and he, Homer, and Reaves ran toward the front of the house.

The back door crashed again. Rebecca calmly held up her gear gun and Lisselle held one up as well. If the things outside got in, they'd not take them easily.

"Is there one more? I might be stuck in water, but I'm not useless." Nettie wasn't sure how effective even a gear gun would be on a pile of mobile and possibly sentient seaweed, but it was better than nothing. Unless it broke in and decided to join her in the tank, she couldn't really do anything else.

Rebecca was closer to the tank, so she handed Nettie her gun then ran and got another from the box.

The door shook again. This time it sounded like it was going to be rattled off its hinges.

A reflection of flames bounced across the glass in the high windows as the others got to the backyard; the pounding on the doors stopped, and a high-pitched keening sound was heard.

"Don't lower your weapons, there could be more than one creature out there." Lisselle was stationed nearest the door, the first line of defense between it and her patient.

Nettie wasn't sure if whatever was out there was after her, Mathlin, or something else entirely. They'd already drawn unhealthy interest from the sea creatures before she changed and they'd found Mathlin.

The reflection of flames burst up higher and the keening got louder. A charge from at least one gear gun went off, a stun setting by the crackling sound it emitted, and then there was silence. Even when fighting for their lives, SEU agents would try and keep the general populace from knowing what went on around them. The flames died, then more silence and darkness.

"I'm going to go check," Lisselle said and headed for the doorway into the rest of the house.

"I should go, if they didn't stop it and are injured, you need to be here to save them," Rebecca was asking permission, but it didn't look like she was going to listen if the answer wasn't what she wanted.

Lisselle looked from Mathlin to Nettie to the door, then finally nodded. "But you only go to the edge of the backyard. If you don't see them, you come back immediately, do you hear?"

Rebecca nodded and flashed a smile to Nettie, disturbingly coquettish in her men's clothing. "I've come a ways, eh?" With that, she ran through the house.

"I hate that I'm trapped here. I should have been out there with them," Nettie said.

"In your current condition? What would you do, fall on the evil doers? Understand your skills and abilities, and understand how they can change. I taught you that your first month with the Society." Lisselle watched the door, but Nettie heard the grin in her voice.

"You never covered turning into a fish, however."

"I didn't know you were going to try that option." They dropped into silence as they waited, no sounds coming from the yard beyond the door should be good.

The front door unlocked and voices could be heard. Lisselle was looking between the back door and the rest of the house, but Nettie waved her on.

"Go see what they caught. I doubt they'd leave anything alive out there, but if so, I do know how to use this gear gun."

Lisselle nodded and ran into the house. Nettie didn't have to wait long, as they soon came trooping to the back. All looked a bit disheveled, but no wounds she could see.

"Another seaweed creature." Caden put his gear gun down and handed a bag to Lisselle. "I don't know that they are sentient, they appear to be single minded and keep on their target even when they are being hacked apart. We burned most of this one, as it wouldn't stop. But we saved this piece for study after stunning it repeatedly."

Lisselle took the bag. "Excellent. I'll have to be careful not to expose any of it to liquids." She held the bag open so Nettie could look inside.

It looked like a few strands of burnt and dried rope, but Nettie was grateful there was something more tangible to study than ashes. "There weren't any merpeople?"

Caden blushed. "There was a pair, a merman and a mermaid. She distracted me and they got over the fence before I could shoot them."

Caden was a good enough fighter that he wouldn't have been embarrassed about missing an enemy. Unless there was another reason.

"She wasn't dressed?"

"Not completely. A few strands of sea kelp covered most of her, but Caden got an eyeful." Homer laughed. "Perhaps that should be a tactic we teach, how to stay calm when your enemy forgets their clothes."

"The others we've seen were dressed, but the one Mathlin caught was bare chested. They must change into clothes when they know they are coming on land, and these didn't get a chance to," Nettie said. "I assume the male was mostly nude as well?"

Rebecca didn't blush, but she did nod enthusiastically. "Yes, he was. And they are in very good shape. Maybe they're all just extremely fit."

"The ones in the pub in London weren't in good shape. But they might have been a different type. I still think there are different kinds of sea people." They weren't behaving like a cohesive species, at least not from what she'd seen so far. She wished she could pull samples from them to test her hypothesis, but doubted that would happen anytime soon.

"There are many things we don't know about them," Lisselle said as she finished putting away her medical supplies. "I believe we have done what we can to discourage them from coming back tonight; beyond that, we must wait and see." She did a final check on Mathlin. "I want to leave him here for now, we can relocate him to the other house in the morning."

Homer and Reaves headed back in the house.

"We've already moved our things, so we'll be off. Caden still has his stuff here, so he'll get first watch. We'll come back for our shifts," Homer said.

"I assume you aren't trying to say the poor women folk can't defend themselves?" Nettie folded her arms. Yes, she was temporarily stuck in a tank, but there was no room for sexism in the Society.

Homer held up his hands. "Never. Especially not with you three. I have Rebecca and Lisselle in the watch rotation. You are excused since you're a bit trapped at the moment."

With that, they all left. Nettie climbed back into her hammock and fell asleep this time.

She'd been dreaming of the sea, and waves crashing overhead, so waking up completely under water wasn't too shocking. A hand holding her down was.

She pushed up, shoving her attacker back and off the ladder. Mathlin cried out as he fell, but for a man who'd been sewed up following serious injuries, he rolled to his feet quickly. Nettie grabbed the bell and the gear gun and rang as she used the stun setting on him.

Mathlin took two direct hits, his eyes opening wide right before he crumbled.

Caden was the first into the room, he held his gear gun up as he scanned for the attackers. "What happened?" He started to go to Mathlin, but Nettie called him off.

"Mathlin tried to drown me. I woke up to him pushing me under."

"What?" Caden's question was echoed by the others as everyone came crowding in. Lisselle must have been able to call over Homer, he and Reaves arrived looking winded but got there quickly. Most likely they had been off planning something and not sleeping.

"Did he say anything?" Lisselle went to Mathlin but only after she made sure Caden was covering them both with his gear gun.

Mathlin's face hadn't relaxed and he still looked in pain.

"His eyes originally were a weird ice blue, far lighter than normal, but that vanished when I shot him the second time." Satisfied that enough of the others had gear guns, she put hers down. "He was far stronger than someone with his injuries should be."

Lisselle pulled away his bandages, then sat back so the others could see. There wasn't even a scar. "Okay, that's new. Where can we lock him up? I don't think he's a merman, but he's not only human. I'll need time to figure it out, but the middle of the night isn't it."

"Had he been just human when he was in the Society?" Nettie knew she wasn't the only non-human in SEU, but most of that information was on a need to know basis.

"He used to be," Homer said. He and Reaves stepped forward and they lifted Mathlin back onto the table. "Can you spell a small room? There is a room next door, one door, no windows, a basic restroom, not much more than a bed in it. If you can spell it to reinforce things, we can lock him in there."

"If you lock it, I can make it break proof." Lisselle looked down at Mathlin and shook her head. "He was a good man. I can't believe he's turned evil. And if he wanted to hurt Nettie or Rebecca, he could have tried when they went out there." She held up her hand. "Yes, I know he knew about Nettie, but he still could have hurt you. So why not then, but now?"

Nettie watched as they carried him out the back and then as Lisselle locked everything back up. "I don't think he's evil. I've nothing to base it on beyond intuition, but I don't. His face changed when he was pushing me down. More than just the eyes."

"Since you're awake now, could you write down everything you noticed? If we're dealing with something other than the merfolk, we need to know, and notify Edinburgh." Lisselle paused on her way out the door. "You said he stated he was in contact with some agents in Edinburgh? Then we definitely need to notify them."

She left to go spell the room they'd locked him up in, leaving a now wide-awake Nettie and a sleepy Rebecca.

"You can go back to sleep, you know. I'll be fine, and Caden and Lisselle will be back soon." Nettie went through drying her hands and quickly jotting down everything she could recall. She'd been so asleep that it was already fading like a dream would have.

"I shouldn't, we were keeping watch, and right now I'm the only one left." She yawned. "Except for you. He didn't hurt you, did he?"

"Not really. It was odd. He looked furious, but also trapped, like there was something he had to do."

"Kill you?"

"No. Well, possibly. I haven't told anyone yet, but I was able to breathe under water earlier. Until I thought about it, and my mind pointed out how impossible it was, but I did it. I have no idea how long I'd been under the water when I woke up with Mathlin holding me down."

Rebecca pulled up one of the chairs and dropped into it, but she kept a gear gun nearby. "You can breathe under the water? Can you do it now?"

"Probably not. My rational brain seems to shut it down. But what if I was doing that, and he was trying to pull me up? There is obviously something more about him, even I would be hard pressed to heal as quickly as he did. Perhaps he wasn't trying to kill me."

"But…he…hmmm. You could be correct. It's still extremely odd. I will say, he was doing badly when the merpeople attacked him. I'd wrapped him as best I could so we could bring him here, but he lost a lot of blood. I don't think he's friends with the merpeople, whatever he is."

The front door opened and Rebecca got to her feet, her gear gun steady in her hand.

"It's us," Caden came in first, followed by Lisselle. "Mathlin is secured, he's delirious, talking in an odd language, but he's secured. Homer and Reaves will stay there to make sure nothing else happens."

"Odd language?" Nettie knew many languages and Lisselle was fluent in even more.

"Very odd," Lisselle said. "And not one I've heard. In the

morning I'll call for a Runner. They have every known language in their databanks. Mathlin stopped talking and passed out again or I'd send for one now." She yawned, which was echoed by everyone, even Nettie.

"What time is it?" Nettie had lost all sense of time, but it still wasn't light outside.

"Just after two am." Caden stretched. "I, for one, am exhausted, I assume you all are as well."

Lisselle nodded. "I'm taxing my magic levels; didn't use it much for years and now I'm flinging spells all over the place. I can cast a trigger spell on the house until morning. It's not strong, and is tied to the four of us, but it will warn us if anyone comes in."

That settled, they checked the locks once more and went to their beds.

Nettie drifted off quickly and the ocean was soon calling her in a dream. Something was wrong and she needed to help it. She was jerked out of her dream when she flailed in her sleep and fell out of her hammock. Wiping her face off, she noticed her hands weren't webbed anymore and the light from the sunrise, dimmed by cloud cover, but still there, was shining through the high windows.

Her new bathing suit covered her much better than the borrowed one did, but she still wrapped a towel around herself once she got out of her tank and then headed up stairs.

There was no one up and about as she went to her room. She took a bath to rinse off the salt water, dressed, and went downstairs. She almost put her hair up in a bun, but changed her mind and left it down.

The cook, Colleen, was rummaging around by this time, so Nettie stuck her head in to say hello. Although she kept to herself, she'd been polite each time they'd met, and she smiled and nodded when Nettie stuck her head in. Then the smile dropped. "I am sorry, things will be a bit delayed this morning. I was at my sister's place and just got Lisselle's note. Is Mathlin really here?" She turned back to Nettie. The look on her face was a combination of exasperation, hope, and fear.

Nettie wasn't sure which answer Colleen was hoping for. "Yes, he's next door. Do you know him well?" They did live in the same small town, it would make sense they at least knew of each other. But there seemed to be something else going on.

"I did," Colleen said and dropped into the kitchen chair with a sigh. "Back when we were both agents. But Lisselle's note was brief, why did he come to Llandudno?"

"What do you mean? He lives here. You've never seen him?"

"I thought he died to be honest. Vanished after he left the Society. He's been here this entire time?" Her fists clenched. "I need to talk to him."

"Right now there are a lot of questions about him, so that might take a bit. Were you close?" That was an inane question, obviously there was something between them. Mathlin had spent years avoiding Colleen and she looked ready to break his neck for it. But it was polite to ask.

"Yes. But I'm not up to talking about it to others until I get some answers from him." She pushed herself to her feet. At least she no longer looked hurt and unsure, now she was mad. "I work through anger by cooking, so you had all better be extremely hungry." She nodded to a cart. "There's some tea and toast, I'll bring the rest out when it's done."

Nettie nodded and pushed the cart out. Mathlin might or might not be an enemy of the Society, but he had Colleen seriously upset.

Lisselle was coming into the dining room when Nettie came out of the kitchen. "Ah, good, you've recovered again. No webbing, I presume?"

Nettie held up her web free hands and gestured toward the kitchen door. "Can I show you something in the parlor?" It wasn't that she thought Colleen would be eavesdropping, but the walls were thin.

Lisselle led the way and Nettie shut the dining room door behind them. "Did you know Colleen and Mathlin knew each other? And not from here? He's been living in the same town as her for years and managed to avoid her ever seeing him."

"What? No, I didn't. Colleen technically lives in Conwy, but she does spend a lot of time here. Did she say why he would be avoiding her?"

"No. She wants to wait until she's spoken to him first. But she is extremely angry."

"That's odd. There is far more going on here than we originally believed. And possibly has been for years. After breakfast I'm calling a Runner and we can start getting answers as to what Mathlin was speaking last night. I wasn't able to run much in the way of studies last night, but there is an interesting component in Mathlin's blood. A defensive one. No matter what I do to it, it heals and recovers."

"But why didn't he heal when he was first attacked? Rebecca said he was in bad shape, and he looked awful by the time he got here."

Lisselle shook her head. "There must have been something in the wounds that inhibited whatever healed him. Something too small for me to see, but that was removed when I cleaned them." She started pacing.

"You've been around Gaston too much."

Lisselle looked confused until she realized what she was doing. "True. It does seem to be helpful however." More noises came from the dining room. "Sounds like everyone is here. And even if not, Colleen is going to want us to eat."

"She gets angry a lot?"

"Not a lot, I would say, but enough that Rebecca and I

have had to eat our weight in food a few times."

Caden and Rebecca were talking quietly and drinking tea when Nettie and Lisselle joined them. No sign of mounds of food, but there was a lot of noise coming from the kitchen.

Homer and Reaves came in and sat down.

"I hope everyone is hungry." Lisselle shot Rebecca a glance.

"Oh dear, what happened this time? Yes, everyone, eat lots of food. Lots."

"I'll explain later." Lisselle nodded to Homer.

Colleen came out with her arms full. "I might need some help." She started putting down her dishes and Caden and Reaves darted to the kitchen to grab the rest.

The amount of food would have fed half of the town. It was a good thing that Nettie's metabolism kept going odd, she was currently ravenous.

They kept the conversation light after the first attempts to bring up Mathlin by Homer were cut off quickly by Lisselle and echoed by Nettie.

Reaves excused himself and stuck his head into the kitchen. "Miss Colleen, this food has been so wonderful, I was wondering if I could share it with the rest of Homer's crew? They are trapped with little more than pub food for their repast."

Nettie shook her head and hid her laugh. If Reaves did decide to become an agent, he was going to be one of the smooth talking ones, or maybe he'd been hanging around Caden too much.

The response wasn't loud enough to carry into the dining room, but Reaves' laugh was clear. "Thank you. They do not deserve such wonderful food, but they will be happy for it." He stepped back into the living room. "Problem solved. We have too much food and the crew could use it."

"*My* crew?" Homer crossed his arms and studied Reaves.

One thing with that beard, it made it difficult to figure out his expression. "Aren't you still part of it?"

Reaves nodded to Caden. "I've been talking with Caden and Rebecca, she being a new agent and all. I was going to wait until Gaston arrived, but yes, I am going to petition to become an agent."

Colleen came out with a whoop. "Then we will really celebrate this evening! You will love it young man, action, adventure, it is the life." She beamed, then her smile dropped a bit. "And I see in the faces of the ones without gray hair the question of why did I leave then? After all, I'm not much older than Homer there. But you're too polite to ask." She shook her head and shared a smile with Lisselle. "Polite agents. What a change. I'll tell you any way. I got tired. My heart was tired, my spirit was tired, and my body was tired. I came here for some rest, found a connection with the sea in my heart, and stayed. But never you fear, if you need an extra defender, I still maintain my gear guns, and practice every Sunday afternoon." She nodded to them and went back to the kitchen. "I'll call you forth, oh young agent-to-be, when I have the food boxed for travel." She waved to them all and shut the door.

Lisselle clasped Reaves shoulder. "This is great news, Reaves, welcome. But I fear we can't celebrate too much at this point. There are studies to run, a Runner to summon, and we need to sort out all the supplies and belongings. There is no longer a living room in this house."

Technically, there was. But Homer had brought everything from Bethlyn's downed airship in, and Lisselle wanted to sort it. Most of it was Gaston's and she wanted to pull out the scientific equipment he'd brought.

"How is Mathlin?" Nettie felt bad about him being locked up. The more she thought about it, the more she believed he hadn't being trying to kill her. But there was something wrong with him.

"You can check for yourself," Colleen came out with a covered plate and a pot of tea. "I've made him food. Nothing fancy, he doesn't deserve fancy. I'll go over there when I've settled and am no longer likely to strangle him with my bare hands."

Nettie took the tray and leaned forward to whisper to Colleen. "You didn't poison him, did you?" She smiled to show she was joking. She hoped.

Colleen laughed. "No. But he deserves a bit of discomfort. Mention the food is from me, though, will you? Might make him a bit nervous." She nodded and stalked back to her kitchen. A moment later she yelled for Reaves to come get the food for the crew.

Rebecca looked to the tray. "I'll join you, if you don't mind. I might need to give him a piece of my mind."

They went out the front since the back was still heavily locked. Not to mention two women bringing food to a sick neighbor wasn't questionable.

The room they'd put Mathlin in did resemble a small cell. It was as if whoever designed the house built a conservatory in the back, then annexed a separate room with a bathroom.

Nettie knocked. The key was on a hook next to the door but she wanted to give fair warning before they went in.

"Mathlin? Rebecca and I would like to bring you some food to break your fast."

Silence greeted them at first, then a rustling. "You can come in."

Nettie put her ear to the door, then sighed and pulled back. "And you can step back to the far wall if you please. Might I remind you that I am half-vampire? Along with my superior strength, I have exceptional hearing. And Rebecca has a gear gun." She didn't have a gun, but he didn't know it.

Nettie handed the tray to Rebecca and pressed her ear

against the door again. He was making enough sounds that it did sound like he'd moved. If he hadn't, he could face her. She opened the door and peeked in, he was where he was supposed to be in the back. The room was too small to have much of a back, or much of an anything. But it had the essentials.

She took the tray from Rebecca. "Very good. We are coming in. Rebecca has put away her gear gun but is not afraid to use it. And you do not want to see how I managed to dispatch both aliens and full vampires on my own." He already believed she had done far more than she had during the crisis, might as well use it to her advantage.

"I will behave. I really am quite hungry. You have tea as well?"

"Of course, we're not savages." Nettie placed the covered tray and tea pot on the small table near the bed. He would either need to sit on his bed or stand to eat. "Even though you did try to kill me. Which is rude, you know."

He'd been starting toward the table but stopped with a frown. "I do apologize. The young American told me that if I ever harmed you again he would find ways to keep me alive as he took my insides apart. He seemed quite upset."

"Caden?" The comments didn't sound like him at all. He'd been keeping to his British accent for the most part, but he was the youngest male there.

"Aye. Seems extremely defensive of you. But as I told them, I don't recall anything after the fight with the merman. I woke up in this room. I don't know why I'm not dead."

"That's what we'd like to know as well." Nettie waited until he'd gotten some tea and food in him, then filled him in on everything that had happened once he'd been brought to town. Rebecca stood near the door looking fierce, with one hand near her pocket as if she did have a gun. Gun or not, it was difficult for a small, cute woman to look tough. She was managing however. Perhaps she'd been practicing with Lisselle these past months.

Mathlin kept eating and nodding. "I don't recall any of that. My eyes are clearly not ice blue and I don't know any language other than English. This food is wonderful, by the way. Compliments to the cook." His encompassing smile showed that he assumed it was one of them.

"Yes, Colleen sends her regards. She'll be by to talk to you later. She hopes you enjoy her cooking."

The look on Mathlin's face was worth waiting for the story of the two of them. Shock, terror, and a bit of longing all marched across his face at varying speeds.

"Colleen, you say? She made this for me?"

"Yes," Rebecca cut in, clearly enjoying his discomfort. "She was most curious as to how you have managed to avoid her for years. You don't appear shocked that she is here, and it's a small town. The assumption is that the avoidance was thought out."

He looked to the food and tea, started to set down his utensils, then picked them up with a shrug. "If she's poisoned me, then it's already too late, eh? Since she'd here, I am assuming that Lisselle is investigating as well? She was always a crafty one." He smiled to make sure they got the witch joke, then went back to his food.

"Yes, we are all looking into it. There is something odd about your blood."

"Speaking of odd, I don't understand what you were doing in a tank of water in the middle of the night to begin with. As I said, I don't even recall being in such a room, but why were you there?"

"More experiments. None of which you need to know about." She got to her feet and nodded to Rebecca. "We'll leave you now to finish your food."

He nodded but was focused on another cup of tea.

"I'll have someone bring over more tea if you wish."

"Thank you, that would be lovely. Do you know if they locked up my place? That's really all I have left."

"I can check," Nettie said, then shut the door.

"You were far too nice to someone who might have drowned you," Rebecca waited until they were away from the house to speak.

"I don't know that he did. His face…there was something *other* about it. And I know his eyes were completely different."

"Ghost possession? Oh, I would dearly love to see one of those. I read about them, but one hasn't been sighted in fifty years."

Nettie nodded but instead of going back to the house they were staying at, she walked out to the ocean walk. "If it is, I'm sure Edinburgh will step in quickly. Do you mind if we walk a bit out here? The fresh air helps clear my mind."

"I'm fine with it. Do you really think that Caden threatened to tear Mathlin apart? That is extremely romantic you know."

Nettie looked at her friend and shook her head. "Savage bloody mayhem is romantic?" She tried to look serious, but couldn't hold it. "It actually is, isn't it? I mean, logically, I am stronger than him, so if someone defeated me, I don't know that he would win. But it is nice to know he would try." They strolled along the walk, and Nettie felt herself relax as they spent more time near the water. That probably wasn't a good thing, unless there were some water based vampires she'd never heard of before.

"Should we go back out and look for clues? Maybe go over to Conwy? The castle ruins are quite exciting."

Nettie nodded vaguely as she stared at the sea.

"If you start eating raw fish, I will have to take steps," Rebecca said, shocking Nettie out of her thoughts. She'd been drifting off far too much as of late, never a good idea, especially bad in her situation.

"Where did that come from?" Nettie turned away from the ocean. She *had* been thinking about the sea, but she seriously doubted that she had been muttering about eating fish—raw or cooked.

"You were looking toward the sea and had a wild gleam in your eye. I don't know what—" Rebecca stopped mid-sentence and pointed out over the water. "Isn't that the fishing boat we saw? What's it doing?"

Rebecca's eyes were extremely good. Nettie had to focus on it for a bit before she could determine it was the same boat. It was being pulled in by the tide and showed no signs of life on its decks. Nettie seriously doubted that the captain she'd met would let that happen to his boat if he were still alive.

"Go get Homer and everyone," Nettie said. "I'm going to see what I can do." She took off her shoes and handed them to Rebecca. "Do take these for me as well?"

"You cannot mean to go in there?" Rebecca tried to block Nettie. But considering there was open beach on either side of her, and, if needed, Nettie could pick up Rebecca and physically move her, the action was for show more than substance.

"I have to try and stop it from crashing. Someone could be on there and unconscious." She glared down at her skirts. "That is it, I am switching to women's trousers after this, and this small town can simply be shocked. Bring help!" She stepped around Rebecca and ran into the water. A thought struck her as she got waist high—skirts could be tied up; she'd seen it in a Society fighting manual once. She pulled the bottom through her legs and tied it around in the front. Not attractive, not proper, but it left her legs free to swim.

She reached the boat, but even listing as it was, or because of it, it took far longer to get on board than she'd expected.

They were almost to the dock.

Nettie finally pulled herself on board, but there were still no signs of life. She didn't have time to search, as the boat was still moving. She turned the wheel and heard what she thought were the engines, they weren't off as she'd thought, but left in a low idle. She got them back up and managed to turn the ship back out to sea. With the full engines behind it the boat had no trouble going past the waves.

She kept the throttle low enough that it wouldn't go too fast, but strong enough to get through the waves. The fuel gauge seemed to be dropping quickly, which would leave the boat back at the mercy of the ocean.

And there was a smell of petrol.

She looked out over the deck and realized that what she'd taken to be water, had been fuel, and there were a few barrels of it tied to the deck at the far end as well.

The engine started sputtering and sparks were filling the lower deck. Nettie swore and dove into the water just as the ship exploded.

CHAPTER NINETEEN

GRANTED, SHE'D GOTTEN THE BOAT away from the beach and the dock, where it could have caused far more damage, but it did mean she was out fairly far when the boat blew up.

"Too bad this didn't happen at night, swimming back would be no problem." She glanced at the flaming boat, if there had been anyone on it unconscious, there was nothing she could do for them now.

Swimming back was slow, in a major part because of the weight of her clothing. Dumping the skirt completely would have helped, but even though she'd now committed to investing in numerous pairs of women's trousers, she wasn't quite ready to appear in public in naught but her underclothes.

A crowd was growing on the beach, but no other boats had come out. Since the boats here were almost all owned by fishermen, most were still out to sea at this time. She was surprised to see a quickly moving rowboat heading for her, however.

Reaves and Caden were heading toward the boat first, then Reaves waved and they changed direction toward her. Getting her in the boat without tipping it was a bit of a comedy of errors and, once accomplished, Nettie quickly undid her skirts to cover her legs.

"Thank you for coming. Not being fishy in the day time was a problem today." She looked over to the flaming boat. "I wasn't able to see if any of the crew were still onboard.

If they were, they were unconscious or dead. But there was far more petrol outside of the engines than should have been. Barrels of it. Someone was trying to crash it into the dock."

Caden had been silent but lunged forward to hug Nettie. "Don't you ever scare me—us like that again." He squeezed her, then dropped back.

Reaves was carefully looking out over the beach, then looked back when Caden returned to rowing. "I do agree, we thought we'd lost you."

"Not yet," Nettie said as she watched Caden. But after his burst of emotional reaction he was focusing on getting them back to shore quickly. "I do wonder if that vessel was targeted because of the captain's interaction with one of the sea kelp creatures. I would venture that none of us should be on the water any longer than absolutely necessary."

Both men took that as a hint to row faster, which wasn't intended, but not a bad idea.

Homer, Lisselle, and a very put out Rebecca waited on the beach as they rowed up. There were many others as well, but all stayed a bit clear. They did appear more to be watching the boat burn than the people coming out of the rowboat, but Nettie did see a few longer glances cast their direction.

"I am afraid we are no longer subtle. Might need to have Gaston pull out some sort of Yard investigation ID and come out as those kind of investigators," Lisselle said as she helped Nettie into some large and ungainly water boots. "I figured you needed something unless we were going to sit here while you dried off, thought it might be best to give you something you can at least walk in."

Nettie put them on and turned to face the water. The boat fire was almost extinguished and two more rowboats had headed out toward it. Neither appeared to be getting too close, just keeping a safe distance and making sure it didn't drift forward while the remains still burned.

Caden and Reaves went to speak to a man, most likely the person they took the rowboat from. He seemed upset at first, then smiled when Caden handed over money.

They all went back to the main house, they really couldn't investigate what happened with the entire town watching. Not to mention at the rate it had been burning there would be little left when it finally came ashore.

Nettie excused herself to go upstairs and dry off and change into fresh clothing. She was spending enough time in her life right now being soggy, she didn't need to increase it.

They'd gathered in the dining room, since the living room and parlor were still crowded with boxes and cases. Nettie shook her head as she sat down and took the cup of tea that Rebecca offered. "Someone turned that boat into an explosive device. It was supposed to crash into the dock; I think we have to assume the merpeople are stepping up their battle plans."

Homer nodded. "The first reports we had were them scouting, now they're trying to remove the problem. We didn't have a choice but to send people up here, but I can't help but notice the incidences are increasing since we've been here. And they have focused on this house." He turned to Lisselle. "You never had a problem before we got here?"

"Not a one. Neither of us even saw anything that was reported by the townsfolk."

"It's us, something about us is bringing them out." Nettie looked to Homer, Reaves, and Caden. "All of us were involved in the fight at the pub in London."

"And one of you was seriously marked by it," Lisselle said as she looked to Nettie.

"You think they are after her?" Caden shook his head.

"Then we get her out of here on the first train and keep her safe."

"I do have some say, and I won't be going anywhere right now. Yes, they have increased their attention. Yes, I might be part of it." Nettie leaned forward and glared at Caden. "But my connection can also help us. This is a chance to discover a brand new life form. No one is keeping me from it."

There was always a chance that her unique situation could compromise the mission—the debacle of the battle against the aliens and the vampires was seared into her mind. But Caden wasn't coming from that. He was coming from the same reaction he had when he threatened Mathlin. His feelings for her.

"I have to agree with Nettie," Homer said as he shared an odd look with Caden. "She could be essential to this investigation and she is the most powerful among us, even if she is turning fishy at night."

Lisselle nodded. "Not to mention, even though he's not here yet, Gaston is the agent in charge and if anyone is being removed, he'd be the one to do it."

Rebecca and Reaves were silent but Rebecca was giving Caden a narrow eyed look and Reaves was looking at him in sympathy.

"On that note, I believe we should go next-door, get a Runner, and see if he can speak to Mathlin in whatever language he was using before." Lisselle got to her feet and Nettie and Rebecca joined her.

"We'll go see about the fishermen, but I have to check something with the airship station first, we'll leave in a half hour." Homer nodded to Caden and Reaves, then picked up a satchel near the door and headed out.

Lisselle started to lead them out, but a beeping came from upstairs. "Oh dear, I'm afraid calling the Runner will need to wait a few. That's a direct call from Edinburgh on the Mudger. It might be a little while, I'll come find you when I'm finished."

Reaves grinned. "I'd like a chance to ask more new agent questions then." He held out his arm for Rebecca. "Parlor next door?"

"Quite. These agents don't tell you everything." Rebecca waved her hand to encompass Nettie and Caden as they left.

This was the time to confront Caden about his over protective ways. And she couldn't do it. "I need to go check something in my room." That was the stupidest thing to say, it wasn't as if she had a lab up there. But when she'd met his eyes, she knew nothing logical was going to come out of a confrontation, so she ran.

His response was an odd nod and shrug, there might have been more, but she was already up the stairs.

This was stupid. She was avoiding him, he was trying to wrap her up in a protective shell—all because of emotions that may or may not be real. She paced around her room. They'd had an interaction—a kiss—after saving Britain, and possibly the world, from aliens. Yes, she'd felt something, but one shouldn't discount an adrenaline response as an explanation.

She started sorting random thoughts. He'd never once tried to contact her while he was in Bath. But then, she hadn't contacted him, either. He was a known charmer, wooing female enemy spies was his trademark in his old position in America as an agent. However, he'd been acting a bit awkward around her at times. Yet since he'd been back they had been bouncing from one stress filled event to another—again—adrenaline could be the culprit for their feelings.

She happened to look out her window as Caden skulked around the side way and headed toward the back of the house. The situation was becoming ridiculous—she needed to end this once and for all.

Before she could change her mind, she bounded down the stairs and into the backyard.

To find no Caden. He couldn't have gone far, she'd been moving quickly, and a quick peek into the yard next door showed no signs of him there.

The far corner of the yard held an old gate embedded in a wall. She hadn't noticed it before, but aside from chasing seaweed creatures, she hadn't been out there. Caden had clearly gone outside somewhere and she wanted to talk to him about their situation. She appreciated his concern, but it couldn't interfere with the case—or their jobs as agents. She steeled herself to resolve this and let them continue with their lives unencumbered.

The gate looked rusted, but closer examination revealed that the handle was not and the gate itself was open an inch. Curiosity overwhelmed any brief spark of caution at who might be on the other side if it weren't Caden, and she quietly opened the gate.

She attempted to be quiet at any rate. The door might have been in more use than originally assessed, but it was still a rusty hundred-year-old door, and the noise was terribly loud to her ears.

She wasn't sure what she'd been expecting, but seeing Caden sitting amongst a variety of well-tended plants was not it. She felt guilty about startling him.

She immediately thought of when she found Gaston in his garden back in London. "Do you have high blood pressure too?" Was this a trend among agents? Gardening?

"What?" He shook his head and rose to his feet. "No. I thought I heard something out here…" His voice trailed off and he raised his hands. "Never mind, you caught me, and if I don't confess you will find out the answer regardless. I like plants. Specifically, I enjoy spending time in small, hidden gardens. It relaxes me, and things have been a bit stressful lately if you hadn't noticed." He crossed his arms and looked braced for an onslaught of mockery.

She certainly wasn't going to challenge such an endeavor. Nettie spent enough time alone that she rarely had to go forth and seek solitude, but Caden was far more gregarious. It never dawned on her that someone like him might need some time away from things. She felt her cheeks go warm; she shouldn't have disrupted him. The conversation she had planned could wait.

"I am extremely sorry that I interrupted your rest. Please go about what you were doing." She had her hand on the gate handle when he reached her.

"Actually, I'd like you to stay," he said as he studied her face. "You are a most perplexing woman, Agent Jones, did you know that? You are focused on your job with such a tight beam that you often don't see the world around you. You can be abrupt and condescending, yet innocently charming beyond belief." He reached up to brush a leaf off her shoulder and left his hand there. "I don't know what to think of you."

A dozen sharp retorts evaporated from her mind. *Damn the man.* "You shouldn't think of me then." That wasn't what she'd thought to say, nor what she meant. His soft brown eyes were becoming far too appealing. And the way his deep brown hair fell over his forehead…it was far too long to be conventional. She had to fight the urge to touch it. There was only one way to resolve this.

Using her vampire speed, she placed her hands on each side of his head and kissed him. She'd meant it to be a retaliatory test for the kiss he'd given her in the airship all those months ago. A chance to verify that what she'd felt when he had done it then had simply been adrenaline at the resolution of their prior adventure. Maybe if he noted it as well, he'd stop trying to protect her. Not her original plan when she came out looking for him, but it might work.

The warmth spreading through her body indicated she might have made a serious misjudgment. Caden froze with his arms down at his sides at first, then quickly pulled her closer. His increased participation in the kiss was enough to scramble her brain completely.

When they finally broke free, Nettie found herself swaying a bit. Caden still had his hands around her waist so he steadied her.

"Are you okay? You were the one who started it you know." A worry line crept between his brows and Nettie found herself noting it, but then drifting down to his mouth.

"I'm not sure," she said then moved for another kiss. Slower this time and Caden responded immediately.

She'd been kissed before, ones which had little depth or meaning. But she suddenly found she didn't want to stop touching Caden. They broke free again and this time both were unsteady.

"There is an old table and chairs over there, maybe we should sit."

Caden's eyes were a bit wide and Nettie had a bad feeling hers were as well. She tried to school her face as he led her to the sitting area, but found she really didn't want to. This was not going to make things easier to work around each other.

"That's not a good face. I'll ask again—are you okay? And you did start it. Twice."

"I was simply testing a theory." Nettie sighed. Brushing it off at this point wasn't an option. At least if she was true to herself. "Very well. I wanted to tell you that you don't need to protect me. I am perfectly able to protect myself." She found her gaze had travelled to his mouth again and she jerked it back. That was going to have to stop. At least in public where it could be awkward and embarrassing. "I might have also been thinking about that kiss you gave me on that airship after we'd turned back the aliens. It's only scientifically prudent to validate reactions that are the outcome of certain actions."

"The kiss from over two months ago?" The corner of his lips went up the smallest of margins. "And what was your conclusion, Doctor Jones?"

She was well and truly trapped. Keeping him at arm's length wasn't possible now and she really wanted to kiss him again. "Inconclusive, I'm afraid."

He leaned closer. "Your experiment was invalidated because it wasn't replicated exactly. In the sample, I had kissed you." The last was barely whispered before he pulled her over toward his chair and kissed her.

He was right; not that initiator seemed to make a difference in the outcome, at least not based on her current reactions to him.

She pulled away. "I do believe we have ruined my adrenaline theory."

He traced her cheek with the tip of his finger. "You don't seem upset."

"That would not be the word I'd use for it, no." They might have declared a truce with each other, but there could be other repercussions. "But what will this do to our working situation? You are already risking yourself to protect me, and, while sweet, it is misguided. Now that this has happened?" She started sorting scenarios in her head. There was no going back now, and she knew neither of them were willing to back down on working this case.

"Rebecca warned me about that," he said with a sorrowful tone that shook her out of her thoughts. "She called it your thinking of tea in India look."

Nettie shook herself and rapped him on the chest with her knuckle. "I was thinking about our situation."

The half-opened gate swung completely open and

Homer stuck his head in. "Everyone has been thinking of it, lass. Took you two long enough."

Nettie felt her face grow warm, but Caden had a broad grin. "The lady wants what the lady wants." He looked so cocksure that Nettie almost had second thoughts.

Homer's laugh shook the small garden. "Oh, now that she's chosen, you were sure all along? Nettie, my girl, the long-winded gnashing of teeth this lad has had over you for the past few months has been painful. It was a trying time for many of us."

Nettie smiled and turned to Caden as he looked to be trying to shut Homer up with his eyes alone. "You were afraid you couldn't woo me?" She leaned forward and kissed his cheek. "Then it's a good thing that I wooed you." She didn't give either man a chance to respond, but used her increased, half-vampire, speed to race out of the garden and back into the house.

CHAPTER TWENTY

H ER HEART WAS RACING WITH far more than just her speed when she got into her room and flopped on her bed. Kissing Caden those three times was something magical. He was insufferable, cocky, stubborn, and possibly had the best kissing ability in the western world.

"I have truly made a muddle of things." She'd have to talk things out with Rebecca and Lisselle, but this had made the prior issue with Caden worse.

A light knock on her door brought her out of her musings. She stopped by the mirror to straighten herself out. Not that Caden had mussed her much, but she felt thoroughly rattled and was quite afraid that it showed.

Lisselle was on the other side of the door. "Shall we go call our Runner now?" She paused, tilted her head, then stepped into the room and shut the door. "Something has happened."

"But the Runner—"

"Can wait a few minutes more." She took Nettie's hands. "What's happened?"

"I confronted Caden about his over protectiveness. Well, one thing lead to another and I was curious about that kiss we'd had before, and in the interest of scientific inquiry, I kissed him. It was a perfectly rational solution to an uncertain situation. The result was less helpful than I had hoped."

Lisselle's smile was wide. "Now I know you've got it bad. I don't believe I have ever heard you babble before. I take it by your reaction and current blushing that he kissed you back."

"Yes. But this can't be good. How will we work together? And we can't work apart either, that would be horrible. Wondering all of the time if the other was all right? Awful. But what if we're together and it's a risk to others?" She paused. "I'm babbling again."

"Completely. Couples within the Society have been known to work, you know."

"You and Homer."

"Found out, did you? Yes, he and I were briefly married. I still adore him, and I think he feels the same. But we're both too independent, marriage didn't work for us. But friendship has."

"I am extremely independent. This will not work."

"You are a kind and loving soul who was passed around as a child and learned to rely on yourself. I've noticed a change in you, you're relaxing more. You are you, and he will have to accept the fact that you are stronger and faster than he is and always will be. But he knows that. This could work."

"You already knew about this?"

"I'd gathered from watching the two of you since before we defeated the aliens. You light up a bit when he's near, even when you're annoyed at him. He seems awkward and unsure, at least for him, when you're around. When two people impact each other that way, there is something there." She tilted her head and gave a warm smile. "I believe you two will fight and love fiercely. But you'll be one of the couples that makes it."

"That sounded final. I do like him, very much it would appear, but "making it" sounds all thought out. And final." Nettie had to calm her racing thoughts. They just had their first serious kissing, this could go nice and slow.

"Easy there," Lisselle said. "I meant I think you two are a good match. Now, are you ready to find out what odd and mystical language Mathlin has been speaking?"

Nettie nodded and peeked over to the mirror for one more quick check. "He is insistent that he recalls nothing of what happened after he was attacked by the merman, also claims to only speak English." They left her room and started down the stairs. "I believe him. I don't think there was malice in him either time we've spoken. Rebecca is hoping it's a possession."

Rebecca waited for them at the door. "That would be extremely interesting. We could be famous if it's an interesting ghost." She gave Nettie an inquiring look and Nettie wondered if her entire recent history was plastered on her face.

"You two can discuss things later," Lisselle said. She led them out to the front. "Let it be said that Nettie has had an interesting time on many levels and any ghost would probably make us famous. But aren't the merpeople enough?"

"Yes, they are exciting, but ghosts—I grew up with ghost stories." The tone in Rebecca's voice said that made them far more valuable. Nettie was walking behind them and Rebecca kept trying to turn back to her.

Nettie was grateful that she'd talked to Lisselle, she was like the mother she'd wished she'd had instead of a vampire mother who abandoned her with her father as soon as Nettie was born. But her conversation with Rebecca about Caden would need to be much more…silly. She couldn't think of a better word for it.

"Isn't that so, Nettie?" Lisselle spoke with a tone that indicated that might have been the second time she asked. She was pointing to the door to Mathlin's room.

"I am sorry, I was thinking, what did you say?"

"Thinking like babbling?" Lisselle smiled. "I said, I think we should replace this door with grating if we have to keep Mathlin here. Better for him and us and it will give Homer's men something to do. They did a nice job on your new stairs."

Nettie fought the warmth that crawled up her checks at the mention of babbling. "I agree completely on all counts. Yes. Grating." She sounded stupid even in her head and Rebecca turned around with narrowed eyes.

Lisselle stopped them by holding up a Summoner for a Runner.

Nettie counted two seconds after Lisselle tore the envelope before the Runner appeared. Their time varied, but never more than ten seconds by Nettie's counting.

"What is your need?"

Lisselle stepped closer and then motioned to the door where Mathlin's room was. "There is a prisoner behind that door, he possibly attempted to harm one of our agents and is acting and speaking oddly. Specifically, he spoke a language that I do not recognize. We need you to identify and translate."

"Understood." The Runner stood at attention outside of the door.

"One problem, how are we going to get whatever is inside him to talk? He didn't recall any of it, so I don't know that he can speak it on demand," Nettie said.

"Maybe if whatever is inside him hears it, it will respond through him?" Lisselle gave a shrug and nodded to the Runner.

"I can endeavor to communicate in all languages." The Runner moved a step closer to the door.

"Should we open it or leave it shut?" Rebecca was staying back but she didn't look frightened. It looked more as if she didn't want to miss anything.

"Runner," Lisselle said as she put her hand on the door handle. "The person might become extremely aggressive once you trigger the language and he changes. I will need you to restrain him but not hurt him."

"Affirmative."

Lisselle nodded to Nettie and Rebecca and opened the door.

Mathlin had been resting, but he sat up slowly. "A bit early for lunch?"

"Mathlin, I'd like to speak to whatever being is inside of you. Rather, I would like the Runner to speak to it." Lisselle stepped aside and the Runner stepped forward.

They didn't even have to wait to run through any languages to trigger the thing inside him. Mathlin took one look at the Runner and his eyes lost all color and he started speaking quickly—and totally in an unknown language.

The Runner tilted his head, then nodded. He grabbed Mathlin as he ran forward and held him.

"There is another being, but it is old and confused. It called me a Rhaildian. I believe we may have a spirit of one of the Atlantians."

Nettie stepped forward. "An Atlantian? As in someone from Atlantis? How do you know?" She watched Mathlin, aside from his eyes and an odd twitching as if a bee were buzzing around his head, he looked the same.

"Rhaildian is the name of my people. From long ago, before we journeyed here." There was a sorrow in its voice that Nettie had never heard before from one of them. The Runners had come seeking help from the Atlantians centuries ago, not realizing their friends were long gone under the sea.

"Why is he here? How did he get to be in Mathlin?" Nettie blushed and stepped back to give the lead to Lisselle. "I am sorry, it's just so exciting."

Lisselle laughed and shook her head. "Not to worry, and those are valid questions."

The Runner continued to hold Mathlin as he spoke. Mathlin relaxed a bit and responded.

Nettie was linguistically gifted and could speak French, Spanish, German, and read a bit of Russian, but the fluid sounding words that flew around them sounded nothing like any of those languages.

"He does not know how he came to where he is. There is much confusion in him."

Mathlin rattled some more off, then slumped forward.

"He said he cannot stay active in this body long, and cannot speak any more now. But he was glad to see me." The Runner gently laid Mathlin back onto the small bed. "I believe he does not realize that his people are gone." Again, that bit of sorrow that Nettie had noted earlier in his voice.

The Runner stepped back out and they all left the room. "Is there anything else you need?"

Lisselle shook her head and the Runner vanished.

"That is exciting, it will be more so when the ghost stays around longer and we can get more information." Nettie shook her head. "The Runners still report everything to Agent Zero, don't they?"

They walked back to their house.

Lisselle didn't look happy. "Yes, so we can expect some visitors soon, most likely when Gaston's train arrives. But an Atlantian? I'm having trouble with that. They've been gone so long their entire culture is nothing more than myths and whispers to everyone except the Runners. Yet one has now just appeared? Why, after so long?"

"The mermen. They've never been seen before either, yet clearly they have been around for a long time," Rebecca said from behind them. She'd not been as excited as the other two as she'd been hoping for a more traditional haunting, but she did have a valid point.

They moved things around in the parlor and settled in. Nettie started the discussion. "Do you think the mermen *are* the Atlantians? Maybe some survived and became what they are now? Most theories supported the belief that, even with their advancement, they wouldn't have been able to get their people to a safe place in time when the disaster struck, and they were in the middle of the Atlantic Ocean."

"I have no idea," Lisselle said. "But I believe we will need tea." She got up and went toward the dining room and kitchen.

"Okay, now what happened?" Rebecca leaned forward. "Mathlin spoke Atlantian?"

Rebecca scrunched up her face and waved her hand at Nettie. "I know that. What happened before that? Something has changed about you, I can tell. I am just not sure what it is. Is it about Caden?" The smirk she was throwing Nettie's way said she might have said she had no idea, but she had a good guess.

Nettie looked over her shoulder. Lisselle already knew, but the rest of the household didn't need to discuss it. Besides, there were more important things afoot. "Not now. I promise we will discuss it all tonight. My tank room if I change, my bedroom if I don't."

"As long as you promise. I am your best friend, you know. I need to know these things." Rebecca sat back and straightened her skirts as Lisselle wheeled in the tea cart.

With a nod from Lisselle, Nettie took up serving tea. "I feel as if there are clues around us, but vital parts are missing."

"I agree. And while you were off trying to get blown up, although you did save people who might have been struck had that boat made it to shore, I ran some more tests. Rather, the ones that had been running finally came back with results. Whatever you are turning into, or being affected by, is different than the samples of the merpeople, the humans who turned to goo, and the living seaweed." Lisselle shook her head. "You appear to have similarities to them, but enough differences to make me pause."

"But wouldn't she be different? She's not fully changing. And are the merpeople, the goo humans, and the seaweed all the same? That seems a bit odd." Rebecca said as she settled in with her cup of tea.

"They aren't, and yes, that would be odd. But they are all more similar to each other than to Nettie. And it's not the human/vampire parts of her that are causing the difference. She has a very exotic component in her blood, which I've never seen before, but that is not like our other sea folk."

"We need better equipment," Nettie said. "That Master vampire we destroyed had said my blood was exotic, but no tests have revealed anything. I'd still like to wait as long as we can, but I agree that we might need to take me to Edinburgh." The thought was horrific. Being on the scientific end of things most times, made being on this end frightening.

"We need to keep Nettie here as long as possible," Rebecca said. "But if we think they'll be sending people down here once the Runner tells them what happened with Mathlin, and who might be haunting him, how are we going to keep Nettie's tank and the reason for it a secret?"

Concern flashed across Lisselle's face at that, even though she was trying to not show it. "I believe Gaston will force them to give him some lead time, he can be pushy when needed, and he carries some weight with Agent Ramsey and Agent Zero. But we won't have much time."

Nettie got to her feet. "Then we'd better cure me before they get down here. Since the investigation into the boat and the fishermen is being handled, shall we run some more tests?" She tipped her head toward the stairs.

Lisselle and Rebecca both got to their feet as well. "Let's see what we can get before she goes fishy," Rebecca said as she went up the stairs.

"That's not scientific you know. Calling me fishy."

"It's your fault for turning fishy. I think it's appropriate."

Rebecca waited until Nettie got to the top of the stairs then flung her arms around her. "You need to recover. Quickly. I couldn't bear it if you turned into a fish." Her voice was muffled.

"She will be okay. There is no way, with all of us, and Gaston, that she won't be all right." Lisselle hugged them both and then moved to her study. "I asked Gaston to bring down the results of the bomb components from London, and a small sample of the weaponized sea urchin. I'd like to see how they compare."

"I'd like to know why, when at least some of the sea life weapons from London started up here, we haven't seen anything like them being used here. That boat was destroyed by a large amount of petrol and fire. If they have the ability to build the advanced explosive device that attacked us in London, why didn't they use it here?" Nettie took a seat at the desk.

"That is a good question," Lisselle said as she started turning on equipment.

"Could there be two groups? I know the report said that the Runner identified water from the Irish Sea as the source of the location of the water from the missile, but this group so far hasn't shown any of the technology abilities that you saw down in London," Rebecca said. "If there were two groups, and one is far more advanced, that could explain some of it."

Nettie nodded. "Three, if whatever is haunting Mathlin is to be believed. But how could these people, whether they are separate groups or not, have been around for so long without being noticed?"

"No idea…" A series of alarms went off from two of the machines in front of Lisselle. She peered closer at them, then looked at Nettie. "Nettie? Have you ever been to Egypt?"

CHAPTER TWENTY-ONE

LISSELLE HAD BEEN LOOKING AT something on the transgoling, a Society machine that could separate components better than the strongest centrifuge. And she looked more than a little disturbed.

"No. That's an odd thing to ask."

Lisselle waved at the screen. "Not really, it will make sense if you look at this. I am reminded that I need to train you both on the newer machines, but this has separated out what is mitigating the effect of the merpeople in your blood. It's a unique component of the Egyptian pharaohs. Part of what made them so powerful was that most of the lineage had some magic. Over centuries, the lines diluted too much to have any power, which was why they fell." She turned and looked Nettie in the eye. "But you have that component. I've never heard of a living person with this element in their blood."

"My father was a blond haired, blue eyed Englishman, I doubt he had any ancestors from anywhere beyond the British Isles."

Lisselle nodded enthusiastically. "But your mother was a vampire. As far as we can tell, she is the only vampire to ever give birth. Your dark hair came from her."

"You think my mother was a few thousand-year-old daughter of Pharaohs? I have a hard time believing that." As a child, Nettie had made up many different things that her mother had been, she didn't find out that she'd been a vampire until long after her father had passed away. A long-lost princess had been one of her favorite thoughts. But this was a bit too much even for a child to believe.

"There is something here that connects to the element isolated in Cairo. I've no idea about your mother, even now, no one has ever found a trace of her. But somehow, that element is fighting the mermaid's genetic influence."

"Now I'm even more unique."

"It's not a bad thing, and both of those gifts from your mother are possibly why you're not a vial of goo right now."

"Blunt, but true. It's difficult when you'd like to be normal once in a while." Nettie stood up and peered at the results. Lisselle was correct, they didn't mean much. "Is there anything else I need to know?"

"Sadly, I can tell you nothing beyond the fact it is there, and it is helping you. Gaston should be able to establish more of how this will impact you. To be honest, it is probably why you were able to survive as a half-vampire and survive the transition back from a full vampire."

"Will this help us figure out the merpeople?" Rebecca asked.

"It might, but it will take time. They are part human, but mutated long ago. I need one alive to know more."

"So, they could be Atlantians."

"Possibly, I don't know how air breathers could have changed that quickly though."

"We need help!" Homer's voice came from below.

All three ran down the stairs to find Homer holding up a bloody, and rapidly passing out, Caden. Reaves was also bloody, but upright.

Nettie got to Caden first, took him from Homer, and laid him on the sofa in the parlor. "What happened?" A quick assessment indicated that most of his injuries were superficial. Aside from a bloody one in his side. She ripped open his shirt and wiped the blood away. "He's been stabbed."

"Yes, we were ambushed," Homer said as he forced Reaves to sit. "Caden had been in the lead, so they got him first. They were merpeople."

"In daylight? Yes, it's late afternoon, and overcast, but that sun is still high enough in the sky. There go our theories." Lisselle had rushed upstairs to get her medical kit and came back. "How do you know they were merpeople?"

Homer pushed back his sleeve. Telltale red marks were there from his wrist to his elbow. "They started changing before we were able to overcome them." He looked down at Caden. "He kept fighting even though they got him in that initial attack."

Nettie moved over so Lisselle could come closer. "Would it be better to move him to the tank room? That table is still there, we'll just need new towels and sheets."

Rebecca jumped to her feet. "Let me set it up."

"We're losing this battle and we're not sure what we're up against or what the rules are." Homer shook his head. "That attack wasn't accidental, or just because we were in the wrong place at the wrong time—they were looking for us."

Rebecca came back and Nettie moved Caden into the tank room. Reaves tried to get up to help, but while he was conscious and mobile, he looked pale.

Lisselle sent him back to his chair with a glare. "Unless you want to join him being unconscious, you will stay right there. We will fix you after we get Caden stabilized, and I will not have you making your injuries worse."

Reaves opened his mouth, then shut it without a word and nodded instead.

Nettie got Caden into the tank room before the others. She leaned close to his ear as she put him down. "There is a good chance that I might be falling in love with you; dying right now would make me extremely vexed. Please do not do such a thing." She thought he twitched, but his eyes stayed closed.

Lisselle came in and the two of them finished pulling off the ruins of Caden's shirt. His torso was bruised, but the only dangerous wound was the stabbing. Red tentacle marks, like the ones on Homer, were on both of his forearms.

"He will be okay, won't he?" Nettie hated the fear and terror she heard in her voice, but it wouldn't be fair to find him and lose him this quickly.

"I believe so, yes. No vital organs were hit."

"Then why is he unconscious?" Rebecca was hovering around the edges, close enough to jump in if need be.

Nettie looked at his arm. In addition to the tentacle marks, there was also a pair of thorn type objects. "These. They look an awful lot like the sea urchin barbs." She fought down the wave of terror that hit her. The ones she'd examined in London were different than these but had enough poison to kill large animals. However, if they were the same, Caden would already be dead. Not a normally comforting thought, but it was reassuring in this case.

Lisselle darted upstairs and brought her smaller microscope lens down and adjusted a number of gears. "Very much like. Perhaps we spoke too soon about not seeing them here. There are some differences though. These seem crude compared to the reports I saw on the London barbs. I can get them out, but it is going to hurt. Hold him down."

Nettie, Homer, and Rebecca all held on to Caden as Lisselle carefully removed the first barb. Caden's eyes flew open and his yell tore at Nettie's heart. He strained but they managed to keep him held down.

His eyes dropped closed until Lisselle pulled out the second one. He almost broke free, and this time his eyes stayed open once he settled back down.

"Caden? Can you hear me?" Nettie hadn't let go in case he tried to move again.

"Yes," his voice was raspy from yelling but the look in his eyes was clear. "And I hurt like hell." He winced. "Sorry, ladies."

Lisselle smiled. "I'm sure we've all heard worse. I believe that the barbs were causing the bulk of your problems. Stabbing aside. Rebecca, can you put them in one of the glass cases? We will need to examine them closely, after I clean and close up this stab wound."

Nettie stopped holding his shoulders and took his hand. Caden smiled and squeezed it.

Once he'd been stitched up, and given a special healing salve that Lisselle had created, they pulled up chairs around him and brought Reaves in. His injuries were mild and just needed some cleaning.

Sadly, there wasn't much more to add to their situation, it happened too fast to get many details. Four men attacked them as they went to meet a friend of the missing boat captain. They'd not realized they were merpeople until first one, then a second, released tentacles. Reaves was the only one not struck by any tentacles, although he was attacked, his opponent didn't show to have that ability.

"So, what will this do to us? Turn is into merpeople?" Homer looked from his arm to Nettie.

Lisselle made a show of looking at both his arms and Caden's but Nettie could tell she was stalling. The recent news of how Nettie was surviving sat hard in her stomach. Neither man had her odd blood history. She squeezed Caden's hand harder.

"I think it's probably worse than that, given the way Nettie is trying to squeeze off my hand," Caden said.

Lisselle looked at the men then shook her head. "There's no way to know for certain. Keep in mind, Nettie didn't start changing until after the second attack with that sea kelp monster."

"Now *I'm* worried. Lisselle is stalling," Homer said.

Nettie lessened her grip on Caden's hand but didn't let go. "There's something in my blood, not the vampiric status, but probably also from my mother, that seems to be mitigating the effects of the merpeople element. I'm not one of them, but I am changed."

"And not a pile of goo." Caden struggled to sit up but a glare from Lisselle got him to lay back down. Her herbs and magic would help him heal quickly, but not that quickly.

"It doesn't mean that will happen to either of you." Nettie was a horrible liar and her fear made that extremely clear even to her own ears. "There must be a way?" She looked at Lisselle.

"I think there will be, but I will need Gaston to help. We need to replicate the Egyptian component of your blood and see if it can be introduced into Caden and Homer's blood. And any other victims we have."

"Egyptian? Just what did we miss?" Reaves' wounds had been dressed by Rebecca and verified that he didn't have any tentacle marks, but he still looked worried for his friends.

"There is an extra component in my blood, an additional donation by my vampire mother. Lisselle believes it has ties to the ancient Egyptians. It was probably the mysterious element that the Master vampire was drawn to in my blood." Nettie was proud that she only gave a slight shudder at mentioning that incident.

"It appears this is what is making her change instead of break down. I have hope that once Gaston gets here, we can isolate it and find a cure."

"So we might turn into fish, like Nettie?"

"Possibly, but perhaps not," Lisselle said. "I believe we can make it so there are no changes to either of you."

Noises came from the front of the house, but before anyone could get more than a few steps in, Gaston and Damon appeared in the doorway.

Gaston shook his head as he surveyed the room. "I leave you all for a few days on your own and look at what you've done? I presume the extra house you mentioned is next door?" At Lisselle's nod, he turned to Damon. "Damon, store our bags next door if you would, the rest of you, debrief me."

Nettie couldn't help it, she let go of Caden's hand, ran over, and hugged Gaston. He froze for a moment, emotional demonstration was not something he normally did, but then returned the hug.

He patted her arm as they broke apart. "There, there. I'm sure whatever the problem is we can all figure it out." He looked at the large tank. "Whatever is that?"

"That, my friend, is part of our problem." Homer brought out two chairs from the dining room and nodded to Gaston. "Might as well sit, this will take a while."

An hour later and Gaston and Damon were caught up.

"Not to be crass, but you say you change at dusk? How close to that time?" Gaston practically demanded she change the moment Lisselle explained that part and was disappointed when they told him of the night issue.

"Probably soon," Nettie said as she looked up at the sky through the high windows. "If you don't mind, I would like to take the time to actually change into my swimming clothes before I have to go into the tank. I've already damaged too many articles of clothing by wearing them in salt water."

"That is a good idea." Lisselle got to her feet. "And we should probably return these chairs to the dining room before Colleen comes out looking for them."

Nettie was almost out the door when Caden called to her. She came back against the tide of chairs being moved, but he stayed silent until everyone left.

"I wanted to tell you that I heard you when you brought me in here. I feel the same." He was too pale by far, but he looked better than when he came in.

Nettie felt her cheeks go warm. "I was concerned."

"And your words brought me back." He gave a little laugh. "Sorry, I didn't mean that to sound cheesy. But I was fading out and your words *did* bring me back. Thank you. If we can both stay alive long enough, we can see where this leads."

Nettie kissed him on the forehead. "If you die on me, I will find a way to haunt your spirit forever."

"Don't spirits do the haunting?"

"Not in this case." She turned and went to go change. She would have rather waited until after dinner, but she was really getting tired of soggy heavy clothing.

CHAPTER TWENTY-TWO

NETTIE HAD GOTTEN CHANGED AND downstairs before the first wave of fatigue hit her. She was grateful that she hadn't died after being attacked, the others who had turned to goo were prevalent in her mind. However, this changing each night was becoming extremely bothersome.

She almost went into the dining room, but someone could bring her food and it would be nice to not struggle to get into her tank. Caden had been moved from the tank room already by the time she came in. Part of her had hoped he'd still be there, but Lisselle's medicines and magics must have started helping. Most likely he was a prisoner in his room with orders not to get up.

The sigh that escaped her as she slid into the water was startling. The other times she'd changed, she'd already been feeling like she was drying out by the time she'd gotten into the tank. This time she got in there before that happened, but the sense of relaxation as she slid into the water was real. "That can't be good."

"What can't be good?" Gaston had come in silently behind her. He smiled but there was a sadness in his eyes as he approached the tank.

"There are, as you know, a number of things about this that aren't good. But the most recent is that I am feeling like the water is home. I haven't changed yet, but it felt right to get into the water."

Gaston came up the stairs and sat on the top ledge. "I

am so sorry this has happened. I would say had I been here I could have protected you, but I fear I couldn't have stopped this."

"Thank you." She looked down, the webbing on her hands came in faster this time. "Want to see the fish girl?" She held up her hand for him to examine.

He peered at it in a scientific manner, then met her eyes. "We will get you back from this."

"Dinner is being called," Reaves said as he stuck his head into the room. "Nettie, Colleen is bringing yours directly."

Gaston looked awkward as he climbed down off the stairs but nodded again to Nettie. "We will beat this." Then he and Reaves left.

Colleen brought in a huge meal with another pitcher of water. Nettie's thirst hadn't been as bad as that first night, mostly due to getting herself into the water sooner. But she figured the thought was well meant and probably couldn't hurt.

"Have you talked to Mathlin yet?" Nettie asked after she swallowed her first bite. Colleen liked knowing that her food was enjoyed.

"No, I'm still working up what I want to say to him." A pair of chairs remained in the room and she pulled up one and sat. Although still obviously upset, she wasn't as bad as she'd been when Nettie had first told her of him.

"How did you think he'd died?"

"Word got back to me in Conwy that he'd gone out on a fishing ship, right after stepping down from being an agent, and the entire vessel and all on board had been lost at sea," she paused. "We were going to be married." The sorrow in her voice was more for the pain that her distant self had faced than now. At least she no longer seemed like she was going to go over and strangle him.

"I'm sorry. He must have had a reason."

Colleen's laugh had no humor in it. "Aye, and then he

stayed here and managed to avoid me for fifteen years? He had a reason all right—he didn't want to marry me. Which is good in a way—my life has been simple, but fulfilling." She got up and turned to go. "Eat everything, I can't imagine these changes are good for your body. Need to keep your strength up."

Nettie wanted to say something comforting concerning Mathlin, but couldn't think of anything before Colleen was gone. It was an odd situation to be sure, but if he truly wanted to avoid her, why stay so close? There must be something they were missing behind Mathlin's actions. Maybe it was related to the Atlantian who had taken up residence in him. She reached over the lip of the tank to her pad of paper and jotted down a few notes—they needed to find out when this spirit took up residence in Mathlin; if an entire crew was believed lost, there could be more like him. The food vanished quickly while she was debating things with herself, and then Rebecca came in.

The discussion about Caden was silly, goofy, and exactly what Nettie needed.

"Tell me again about the kiss," Rebecca had brought in a pile of biscuits and tea and they'd worked their way through them as they chatted.

"Which one?" The laughter that followed was comforting. Nettie had never had many friends growing up, having them now was precious.

Nettie sobered as darker thoughts crept in. "You'll still come see me if I change completely, right?"

"That won't happen. Gaston and Damon are here now. With all of them, they will find a way to fix you." The set to her jaw was impressive, but fear showed in her bright blue eyes.

"But what if they can't?" Nettie held up her hand, spreading it to show the webbing. "This came on faster tonight."

Rebecca looked at Nettie's hand, then at her face. "I don't care what you become, Nettie Jones. I will always be your frie—"

Her word cut off as she screamed, and her eyes rolled back in her head. Nettie half leapt out of the water and grabbed her before she could fall off the stairs.

Reaves came running in. "What's happened?" He was looking everywhere at once trying to assess where the threat had come from.

"I don't know. She was fine, and then yelled."

Rebecca shook herself and let out a long slow breath. "That was a bad one. I need to tell Lisselle it's wearing off." She pulled back and looked from Nettie to Reaves. "Sorry to have startled you, just had a bad clairvoyant attack. Lisselle has been helping me control them with herbs." She wiped away tears. "That one was wretched."

Nettie peered into her friend's eyes. "You seem in focus now, but your eyes rolled back. What did you see?"

"Fire, destruction, disaster. I know that sounds bad, but it didn't feel bad. It was old, very old."

"Isn't clairvoyance supposed to be in the future?" Reaves had stepped forward, but seemed at a loss as to how to help if there wasn't a threat he could fight.

"It is," Rebecca said. "Somehow the threat of the future is connected to the threat of the past. And the connection is deadly."

CHAPTER TWENTY-THREE

"THAT'S NOT AS ODD AS you having a vision about the past. And why didn't I see it as well?" Nettie settled back into the water, but stayed close to the stairs in case Rebecca needed help again. When Rebecca had her visions before, she took Nettie along for the ride. It had been a future that never came to pass, but had been all too real in the moments they flashed through it.

The second time, Nettie had used Rebecca's projection ability to show the invading aliens what their vampire allies were really doing with their blood. That did not make them happy at all and didn't end well for the vampires.

"Ah, the time you both were involved in alien situation, I read up about that one." Reaves came further into the room. There might not be a threat at the moment, but curiosity was a hallmark of all agents whether they be brand new or in the Society fifty years.

Rebecca took a long drink of her tea, poured another, and finished half of that before answering Nettie. "I think no one else being able to go through it with me might be part of the herbs Lisselle gave me. She didn't want to stop my ability, but as we were working through my learning to control it, she felt the fact that I pulled people along was a dangerous issue. Thanks to the herbs, I haven't had a vision in a few months."

"What did you see of the past? Could you see people or how far in the past it was?" Reaves pulled up a chair, flipped it around, and settled in.

"No people, but it was as if they were just out of range. The fact it was the past was a feeling more than a seeing." She gave a shrug. "Not sure if this makes sense, but there was an oldness in the vision."

"Should I go get Lisselle? They all went next door after dinner. Caden's been relocated there because there's a room downstairs for him and he's not supposed to move much." He gave Nettie a grin. "He's not happy, on many levels."

"I'm glad he's alive." Nettie sobered. "The barbs we looked at in London had a lot of poison in them, it appears these are different, but they are still dangerous. I know Lisselle has extra abilities in healing, but I don't like to think what the residue from them could be doing to him."

"It's killing you that you can't go run the tests yourself, isn't it?" Rebecca asked.

Nettie shook her head and dipped a bit lower in her tank. "We have more than enough excellent scientists here, yourself included." She paused. "Well, maybe. It's not that I doubt anyone else can do the job, it's more a matter of me needing to do something. Being trapped here like this is most vexing."

"I'm sure Gaston will find a way to get you working on things during your swim time." Rebecca smiled.

Most likely she was right. Gaston would view her situation as prime time to get work done once he adjusted for the water issue.

Nettie turned back to Reaves. "You never told us if you found anything out about the boat? Or if it was discussed, I wasn't there." Nettie was trying not to feel excluded, but she was aware there were things she was missing being in the tank.

"Aye, briefly talked about it at dinner, but I can give you the full story." Reaves nodded. "We found out that the boat had actually been out since you saw it—they'd not come back. There was some concern it sounds like, but it wasn't that uncommon for a boat to stay out if they needed to."

"So no one was looking for them? Where would they have gone?"

"Ah, there are small islands, islets really. Not on any maps outside of ones kept in secret by the fishermen themselves. If we can get one of those maps, I think we might be able to gain some clues as to what's truly going on here." Reaves nodded a bit to himself, then continued. "The captain and his crew are all upstanding members of the community, no enemies known of. Aside from the sea kelp creature as they were leaving that day, nothing else was unusual. Which means that it was probably related to the sea kelp creature and the merpeople. Or something from one of those islands. The man we were going to meet when we were attacked in the alley might have had more information on the fishermen and the islands."

"These secret islands might be some place the merpeople guard, or at least feel protective about. Since we can assume that *something* is bringing them to land, we should assume they have areas they are protecting." This could be a lead for this case, one that Nettie should be able to participate in once they got a hold of one of those maps.

"Like an invasion?" Rebecca didn't look happy as she rubbed her arms. The last invasion had ended up with her being kidnapped by aliens and turned into a vampire drone.

"This is very much an invasion," Nettie said. "Part of the problem is that our enemy can retreat to a place that we can't go."

"Maybe we can," Reaves said cautiously. "Think of it, we have some of the brightest minds in Britannia here. Gaston should have the reports from Edinburgh of the vessel that fired the missile from under the Thames. Even though they can breathe in water, they were in a protected vessel to fire the weapon."

"That's a good point. There was no need to protect them from the water," Rebecca said.

"Unless they were counting on how much easier it would be to not be seen in that contraption," Nettie said as she shook her head. "We should make note of that observation, but not put much energy into it. They didn't need air under the water, but we do. You saw the vessel, how hard would it be to make something larger, that we could use?"

Reaves let out a loud sigh. "It would take time. There have been attempts, but they have limited application. And if we're going against armed and dangerous water breathers? We wouldn't stand a chance."

Nettie sat in her hammock. "True. It's one thing to be going under water to fight other humans, the merpeople would still have us at a disadvantage." She tilted her head and looked to Reaves. He was shooting it down before it got out of the room and yet he'd brought it up. "So why did you bring it up?"

"Because, maybe there is a way to use that technology, to go beyond it, and to make individual suits for us air breathers."

"How would we keep them with air? If they are using tubes and hoses the merpeople would still win." Nettie was all for new inventions, but they needed to level things between the groups if they were going to take the fight to the merpeople in their domain.

"I think we can get around that." He actually blushed. "I have a fair amount of time and freedom on Homer's ship, lots of time for theories, tests, that sort of thing. I'll get my notebooks over here tomorrow, but I believe we can make it work." He walked around the tank. "I led them on the build for this, and it's holding well. We might need to borrow it for tests. Or see about building a second one."

He started muttering to himself and was almost to the door when he shook his head and turned back to them. "I do apologize, ladies, but I've got some ideas floating around. Excuse the pun."

Nettie waved him on. "By all means, go get them down before they vanish."

Rebecca nodded. Reaves gave a distracted wave and left the room. They heard the front door open and close as he left the house.

"The entire reason they opened that hole in the back fence between the houses was so people weren't going back and forth at all hours of the night," Nettie said. "Yet no one goes out this door." She pointed to the extremely chained and locked back door.

"Indeed, but they weren't counting on multiple attacks from sea creatures coming from that direction. I think the consensus is to leave this door locked unless absolutely necessary."

"Have you had any more visions?"

"No." Rebecca yawned. "But I might start dreaming out here if I don't go to sleep soon. I am very glad for you and Caden. Now if you two can just stop getting hurt and turning fishy long enough to become a proper couple, I will be most pleased. Good night. I will see you in the morning."

Nettie said her good nights, then went back to the edge of the tank near the stairs, dried off her hands, and started planning. Reaves might have a head start, but Nettie wanted a project. She had a photographic memory and quickly sketched the vessel from the Thames.

"Now, how to make this work for a human."

Nettie woke the next day twisted in her hammock. She turned herself upright and had a brief panic about her notes before she recalled finally giving up and putting the writing supplies safely on the top of the stairs. A quick check of her hands and legs told her she'd returned to normal.

"I might have to get them to find a way to create a bedroom suite down here if this goes on much longer." She lifted herself up and out of the tank, dried off, and went through to the upstairs. She glanced longingly at her unused bed. That was going to be another issue. That hammock was handy, and quick thinking on Homer's part, but it was becoming a bit wearisome.

Once she was cleaned and dressed, she made her way downstairs. A soft rapping at the front door stopped her from going into the dining room.

She cracked open the door. "May I help you?"

A short woman stood on the stoop, clearly less than five feet tall, older, but one of those faces that it was hard to read true age. She looked up and down the street before turning back to Nettie. "I need to come in, you're all in danger."

"Can you clarify that, please? It is rather early to be receiving visitors." Nettie didn't want to be impolite, but she didn't know who or what this woman was. It was clear that too many people in this small town were aware that the group living here were not what they seemed.

"You must be Agent Jones," the tone was rough, but the smile softened it. "Yes, check everyone; but I've been followed and I need inside *now*."

The tiny lady moved so quickly that even Nettie couldn't grab her and she was inside the front room before Nettie could turn. Considering Nettie's status, and her half-vampire speed, that alone could raise a few flags.

"If you know who I am, then you know what I am. I don't want to hurt you, but I will restrain you if I need to."

The woman looked like any laugh that came out of her

would be a cackle. Nettie definitely wasn't expecting the big booming laugh that would have better fit Homer after he'd had too much to drink.

"Do you want to try? I'm still testing out my land legs, but I bet I could give you a run." She looked around the front room, peered into the still burnt and mostly closed off guest room, then turned back with a frown. "That is a sorrow. I am sorry so many of your people have been lost. We'd hoped things would settle down, but nothing is going to plan."

"I really do need you to explain yourself before you go any further."

The older woman was at her side before Nettie could blink. "Oh no, they got you too. This has simply gone too far. Agents or not, you need my advice." She held up her hand, which looked normal. "Watch." Suddenly full webbing appeared along with delicate scales that vanished into her sleeve. She shook her hand and it all returned to normal.

"You're a merperson?"

"That's as good a name for us as anything. Aye, I'm one of the proper ones. We hadn't realized the others had made their move until our own enclave near that place you call Bath was attacked. Where is Reaves?" She was peering around the empty rooms as if nothing she'd said was startling in the least.

Nettie wasn't sure which revelation was more startling. What she appeared to be or that she was asking for Reaves, of all people. "He's out…but he's not an agent yet."

"*Yet*?! Oh, that boy. I told him he wasn't to join…never mind. I believe I need to talk to your people." She marched into the dining room and took a seat at the head of the table. "Could you gather them? Some of that tea beverage would be lovely as well. So exotic."

Nettie was rarely speechless, but she was now. With a

nod she went into the kitchen to find Colleen working on breakfast. "Might we have the tea now? We have a visitor."

Colleen narrowed her eyes. "Do you need me to run for help?"

"No, I don't think so. We do need to get everyone into the dining room though."

"I can watch our guest while you gather everyone." She nodded to Nettie. "The tea cart is ready to go. If you need help, just yell."

Nettie took the cart out, then started to pour. "I am sorry, I didn't catch your name? It would be best to have something to call you."

"I didn't give it. Names can have power you know. But you may call me Frilin. Yes, I like that. And Reaves will know who is here. Best to get your friends who are in this house first though." She sipped her tea with a sigh. "This is almost worth coming to shore for."

Nettie left Frilin and darted upstairs. Both Lisselle and Rebecca were getting ready to come down, but Nettie convinced them to move faster.

"I can go next door," Rebecca said. "You go downstairs and entertain." She darted down the stairs and out the door.

Lisselle brushed off her trousers and nodded. "Let's go meet this interesting woman."

Colleen was standing in the kitchen doorway, her eyes narrowed as she watched Frilin. Frilin, however, was ignoring her and completely focused on her tea.

She looked up as they entered the room. "Ah! The leader. Agent Wilding" Frilin smiled and nodded to the table. "Would you enjoy some tea?"

"I would, thank you so much, Frilin." Lisselle didn't even pause as she took the seat next to the older woman.

Nettie sat down across from her and Frilin poured for her as well. She could almost see the women silently gathering information on the other. Then she realized that she was seeing something else. Almost invisible sparks were coming off their hands. Lisselle was a witch, could Frilin be one as well? Maybe she wasn't a merperson at all.

"You are strong, and fear not, I don't mean you or your people harm." Frilin's hands stopped crackling and she returned to her tea with a sigh. "Quite the contrary, I'm hoping we can help each other."

"Who are you and what are your people? Are they all magic users?" Lisselle's hands stopped crackling as well, but only after Frilin's had.

"I'd rather wait until everyone is gathered, if you don't mind."

The front door barged open and Rebecca lead the men into the dining room. Not surprisingly, Reaves was right behind her. Caden was being wheeled forward in a chair pushed by Damon, but he looked much better than last night and was clearly not happy about the chair.

"Mother? What are you doing here?"

Everyone froze at that, especially Nettie and Lisselle, who knew what Frilin was.

"My boy! Well, I was going to wait until I explained a bit more to these nice friends of yours before telling them of our familial connection, but you've let the fish out of the trap. Yes, all, I am Reaves' mother, among other things." She looked up and nodded toward the kitchen door. "I believe that former agent Colleen would like to bring out that wonderful food I am smelling."

Colleen looked to Lisselle first, but relaxed at her nod. "It would help if you would all sit." She went back into the kitchen.

The others sat down, with Gaston taking up the seat at the other end of the table. That he hadn't said anything was shocking. And it didn't last.

"Very nice to meet you, I am Gaston, but you apparently

know us."

"It's very nice to meet you as well. I am going by the name Frilin right now, and I didn't realize you were who came arrived last night. Yes, I know you all, at least who you are. And no, my son hasn't been talking out of turn. He came to the land all on his own, I have other resources that brought me up to speed."

"You're a merperson, so that means Reaves is as well?" Nettie wasn't sure how she felt about that revelation at all. Reaves was one of the people who was causing this change in her? "Is that why you weren't given the same tentacle treatment as Homer and Caden when they were attacked? Which side are you on?"

"I am on your side," Reaves said. "So is my mother and our people. We aren't the ones behind your change or any of the attacks. But, the attackers might have sensed what I was." He looked to Frilin.

Her smile dropped quickly. "And who you were, as my son. This is disturbing news. My spies tell me the ones in the local waters here are unaware of our increasing presence, but that has changed."

"I do hate to rush a lady, but maybe you should begin from the start? Just who are you?" Gaston hadn't touched his food yet, but a glare from Colleen as she brought out more made him pick up a piece of toast.

"You are right, I apologize. Very simple to get things on track. I am the queen of the sea, Reaves is one of my children. We are Gleniars, that's our name for ourselves in our language, but merpeople is far more descriptive in your language. We are an old race, very old. And mostly live deep in the ocean. We have places we can come to the surface, places guarded from human eyes by magic. And some of us, my line is one, can come onshore as humans and move on land and breathe only air."

Nettie was fascinated. This could explain the discrepancy

in the technology between the merpeople. "The others can't seem to be out on land in the daytime, except for three that ambushed our people yesterday and at least one in London. And my changing is only happening at night."

"The others shouldn't be able to come on land at all. We are a separate species from human, not mutated humans, nor fish. The others, the Dagths, are mutated humans. Their genetic material doesn't allow them to go out in the sunlight for any length of time. Most of our people can't either. But somehow they are changing that. That they were able to come on land during the day is a bad sign. They are greedy and violent and want a war."

"With who?" Caden had kept to his wheeled chair but had pushed it forward to the table.

Frilin paused to get a few bites in. "Everyone. Dagths want our power and technology. They want to destroy humans because they want your power and technology, and to stop you from going into the sea. One of your agents, McGrady was the name, worked with them for a while. He filled them with ideas before he vanished."

"How does Reaves play into this?" Homer had been silent, but there was a lot of tension in that question. Reaves had been a trusted member of his crew for years—and a good friend.

"I am sorry that I couldn't tell you, Homer." Reaves started, but Homer shook him off.

"I would like to hear it from your ruler."

"He's said many good words of you over the years, Homer. You would have been a fine ruler under the waves. There are only ten percent of our population who can be air-walkers. Since my line, as I said, is one, family members go on land, usually in their youth, to see how things are here. They do report what they see, but most are not spies, and they return to a life under the waves. Reaves never came back to live in the water. But he is not a spy."

She leaned forward at that point, clearly she knew what Homer was thinking.

"I fit better here, and in the sky, than I do under the waves. I gave up my place in the line of succession years ago to stay here. I visit from time to time. But it's no longer home."

Homer still looked upset, but Reaves looked so miserable that Nettie believed him.

"So how am I turning into whatever I'm turning into?" She left off the rest of the sentence, and how do I stop it, but it was lurking in her mind.

"I don't know. I have brief information about the current situation up here, and I'm not a scientist. They did something to you, but I'd warrant you aren't turning into one of them."

"She's not," Lisselle said. "I'm running tests, and have been since this started. She's not the same as the other merpeople, the walking sea kelp, or the humans who dissolved."

"There were people who dissolved? Reaves, I know you're not a spy, but this should have been reported," Frilin said.

"I did. I told Rockpore, he said he'd get the information to you."

A shadow crossed Frilin's face. "This is not good. I haven't heard from him in almost a week."

"He said he would be contacting you that night. I should have gone myself, but I can't use the chutes the way he can."

"Chutes?" Nettie was still processing everything.

Reaves nodded. "Aye, our people are mostly to the south, the waters outside of Bath, Cardiff, those areas. But there are chutes that we use, portals through the water that can get us back and forth quickly. After so long on land, it has become difficult for me."

"Either Rockpore has been replaced, kidnapped, or killed. I am going to have to check on my other spies here." Frilin got to her feet quickly. "I am sorry, but this must be done. We cannot help your people if ours are under threat."

"Can I get a sample from you? To compare with Nettie's." Lisselle had also gotten to her feet.

Frilin looked to the front of the house, then back to Reaves, then gave Lisselle a nod. "Quickly though."

The two women went upstairs to Lisselle's lab. A few minutes later, Frilin had quickly left out the front door and Lisselle was thoughtfully making her way downstairs.

"I have everything running on every sample I have. Reaves, I'll let you finish eating, then I'll need samples from you too. Caden and Homer, you'll be next. I need to see what is going on with your exposure. I do hope she comes back, I have so many things to ask her."

Gaston had kept eating but watching everything. Nettie narrowed her eyes. He was usually in the thick of things, yet he stayed quiet? "Are you okay?"

He looked startled as he was still in whatever thoughts he'd been wrapped up in. "Yes. I was admiring how far you have come as agents. Even our newest one. You don't need me anymore." There was a melancholy there that Nettie had never heard before. Judging from the looks on Lisselle and Homer's faces, they hadn't either.

"Now where is that coming from?" Lisselle scowled.

"He's feeling his age. Yup, went through it myself, long ago." Colleen had come out of the kitchen and took up a seat near him. "You're tired and wonder if retirement is the best option." She paused, but before he could respond, smacked him in the shoulder. "Stop it. We all go through that at different points, sometimes we go out too early for the wrong reasons. You still have too much to do."

"That was succinctly put, and I agree." Lisselle folded her

arms. "Yes, we can survive without you, many of us have been for years. But that doesn't mean you're not needed."

Homer stayed silent, but Nettie gathered from the look on his face that he was going to have a long private conversation with Gaston. One that may or may not involve drinking.

Gaston shook his head. "You're right, just feeling old. I'm not here and everything falls apart."

The words were there, but Nettie didn't believe them. Something was rattling him and he wasn't going to share. She'd give him his space for now. But if the discussion with Homer didn't shake him out of it, she'd have to work on him. This behavior of his started with his doctor telling him to relax, which appeared to be having a negative impact on him. She'd sort him out if need be. She still needed him, and would for many years.

"I was thinking Rebecca and I should go to Conwy today. Investigate the castle and where the sightings were along there. There's most likely a pattern to the sightings prior to our arriving and muddling things—I'd like to find it. I do think I'd prefer to go as men, to allow for more freedom of movement. Besides, I still need to order some women's trousers."

"You could stay here and run tests?" The hopeful look on Caden's face faded under her glare. "Sorry. This is new."

"What's new? What else have I missed?" Gaston still had a bit of a sadness, or maybe it was just fatigue, but he was rallying and trying to hide it.

"Nettie and Caden have finally admitted their feelings for each other," Homer said with a shrug. "Caden's gone protective on her."

Caden glared at Homer.

Gaston burst into the first real smile Nettie had seen since he'd gotten to town. "Finally! That took far longer than one would think. Unfortunately, I might have muddled things by moving them apart, but you'd think they would have overcome that. Amour!"

Nettie shook her head. Everyone knew, it seemed, except for her and Caden. "Regardless, while I appreciate the concern, as long as we get back well before dusk, we shall be fine." After collapsing twice, she would need to make sure it didn't happen again, or they would put her on house duty.

"Damon, I'd like you to go with them." Gaston turned to his houseman.

Damon wasn't serving here, but he seemed to feel awkward sitting at the table. He quickly pushed his chair out and got to his feet. "Gladly. Is there anything I should know about your condition? Things I should take?" His questions were directed to Nettie but his glance kept darting to Rebecca.

"Nothing really, if things get bad we might need a cart. I'd rather travel in that than a wheelbarrow." At his look of confusion, Nettie waved him off. "Nothing to worry about. Rebecca and I need to go change. If that is acceptable to you?" She had a feeling part of Gaston's issue was with Lisselle being in charge up here. Technically, he was still the senior agent, but it would feel odd stepping in where someone else had been doing it with them still there.

Gaston looked to Lisselle, they both nodded.

"You could visit the house I've rented. I still have the lease on it, though it appears things are moving fast enough that I should stay here. Just make certain nothing untoward has happened to it."

"I'll see about finding one of those fisherman's maps." Homer got to his feet and headed for the front door.

"And Gaston and I will have a nice interview with Reaves," Lisselle said as Reaves started to follow him. "And a few tests, it will be a lovely day."

Reaves hung his head and followed Gaston and Lis-selle up the stairs. "I guess my application to the Society is through now."

Nettie heard Gaston laugh as they got to the top of the stairs. "Oh, never you mind that. You said you wanted to join, and you will go through the process. We're not letting you out that easily." Clearly, his being non-human was less of a problem and more added to his benefit for the Society.

Nettie thought that Frilin might have another thought about that; she hadn't seemed happy about the agent issue. But that would be a battle for later.

"It might take me a bit longer to get my man clothes together without Lisselle, let me go get a head start. Damon, perhaps you could go ready the carriage?" Rebecca said with a smile.

Damon's eyes darted to Caden and Nettie, then he grinned. "Gladly. I will see the two gentlemen outside."

Rebecca darted up the stairs before anyone else could say a word.

"That wasn't obvious at all," Nettie said as she dropped down into the empty chair next to Caden.

"Not a bit. But I think they are trying to give us some space in the middle of things." He took her hand. "I won't nag, but be careful? You're not invincible."

"I am quite aware of that. Well, at least now I am. There is nothing like having everything you take for granted removed from you to have a wake up. I will be careful, but you have to trust me. I'm not the one who came back stabbed and with barbs in him. You need to be careful as well."

"No, you are just becoming a fish, but not injured," He laughed, then his face sobered. "I will be careful, you be careful, and we can each worry about the other silently." He leaned forward and kissed her.

"Be well," Nettie whispered as they finally broke away.

Then she ran upstairs to change.

Nettie shoved aside her thoughts of Caden and quickly changed into her man garb. The make-up took a little bit longer, but she looked reasonably male once she was finished. No one was downstairs when she came down. Considering that Caden wasn't supposed to move himself, Damon must have come back to help. Rebecca came down shortly after her.

"How do I look?" She spun. She was still too short and cute for a really great disguise as a man, but it was enough to keep most people from guessing she was a woman unless they really watched her.

"Not bad, but I might suggest that you not spin like that."

Rebecca laughed and spun once more, stopping when a sound came from the door.

Damon came in the front door and nodded to them. "I believe you two gentlemen asked for a carriage?" He might have smiled a bit more at Rebecca than Nettie, but he did try to include both.

"Excellent, I think we'll start at the castle." Nettie marched out and boarded the carriage. Rebecca and Damon were right behind her. He started to try and help Rebecca into the carriage but he caught himself in time. They would have to be careful.

Damon started the carriage down the road and Nettie sat back to take in the view. She hadn't seen much of Llandudno since they'd been there, but mostly it looked as expected; a quiet, sleepy seaside town which was becoming a nice retreat for weary British citizens. The trip to Conwy was short, and soon Damon was pulling up to the castle ruins. This was one of the castles built to control the Welsh in the thirteenth century, but little remained of the grandeur now. Actually, it was doubtful that most modern buildings would be around in almost six hundred years, so it held up better than expected.

The sighting that had been reported had been on one of the guard towers. From the description it was one of the two closest to the waterway. How they were to get there was another issue. Nettie was glad they'd changed into men's clothing. There were some rather rickety ladders leading up to the walkways that didn't look terribly trusty, although there were two men up there that she could see. Judging by their supplies and easels they were artists. Three more people were in the center where the great hall would have been.

"We should have brought art supplies and blended in." Nettie muttered to herself.

"I could go get some?"

Nettie turned to Damon. He was far more awkward around them than he should be, and Nettie had a feeling it was more than just his attraction to Rebecca. As when they were having breakfast, he seemed like a man without a purpose.

"Damon, you are more than your station. Gaston believes so, and so do we. You are here as our companion, not as a servant."

Rebecca had been taking in the majesty of the castle ruins, but turned at Nettie's words. "Oh dear, Fred is right, my friend. You are a valued asset to the scheme." She smiled, then dropped it.

"Thank you, Fred and Luke. I was feeling a bit—" His words were swallowed as a rumble jolted through the foundation of the castle ruins.

One of the artists tumbled and slid down the wall, and the second tried to grab him. Nettie looked around for any signs of what caused the explosion, then ran to help.

Rebecca and Damon were right behind her when a second jolt hit and almost knocked them all to the ground.

"Get the tourists out of here," Nettie yelled before picking up speed. The second jolt had knocked the second artist off the side as well, and they were high enough that the consequences would be serious if they lost their grip.

The ladder they had been using wasn't far away, but it looked even worse up close than it had from a distance. She looked around, Rebecca and Damon had cleared everyone out. She could try and do what she needed to do with, hopefully, no one really noticing. The two artists would only notice that they didn't fall to the deaths. Hopefully.

Propping the sad ladder up, she ran up it and leapt to the walkway. A snap as her foot left the final step told her that wasn't going to be an option going down. They were near the tower she'd come to investigate, but as tempted as she was, lives needed to be saved first.

She darted over to the first man, the original victim, and grabbed him just as he let go. She sat him against the tower wall, then reached the second. They looked confused, but grateful not to have fallen. She needed to get them down before they started wondering how she was doing this. She picked up the first man, and half dragged him to the tower stairs.

"You need to climb down, there could be another jolt." She peered down the tower, not in great shape and probably why they kept using the ladders, but there wasn't a choice. The ladder was a pile of broken wood at the bottom.

"We can't, it's haunted." Although he'd been painting, usually a hobby of the visiting idle rich, the Welsh accent told her he was local.

"You have to, unless you want to be the one haunting the place." She gave her best impersonation of one of Gaston's scowls to reinforce her words.

"Fine, but if I get kilt by that spirit, I'm coming after you." He made his way down the twisted tower stair.

The second man was on his feet but looking down at

the ladder.

Nettie waved to him. "Come this way, only way to get down."

He started to come toward her, when a third jolt hit. At the same time a scream unlike any she'd heard before came from the tower. "Stay there, hold on!" She yelled to the man on the walk and tore back to the tower stairs. The first artist was already at the bottom, he hadn't screamed.

The wail came again. This time she could tell it was coming from the top of the tower. A shape moved into view, man shaped and covered in seaweed. In the day light.

"Mine." The word was garbled, but the thing seemed to be facing her. The creature made her blood boil—literally—and her fangs dropped into place as she felt her control leave. Her body was reacting to whatever it was and calling forth the vampire blood.

A shuffling sound made her turn back. The second artist was terrified and walking backwards without looking.

Nettie ran to him but couldn't catch him before he went over the edge. She moved faster than she thought possible and leapt after him, cradling him as they fell. The air slammed out of her lungs and the world went red. The artist took one look at her, and collapsed.

"Ne—Fred!" Rebecca came running back into the ruins with Damon right behind. The artist that had come down through the tower was running to them as well.

"I'm fine," Nettie said as she got to her feet slowly. "Okay, not completely fine, but I will be." She spun Rebecca around so that only she could see Nettie's face. "What color are my eyes?" The red film was gone, but she needed to make sure. The odd burst of wild strength seemed to be gone, hopefully the rest was as well.

"They look fine," Rebecca said. Then she looked back up to the walkway. "I know you're strong, but even for you that jump should have broken a few things." She kept her voice low.

Nettie turned to find Damon helping the artist she'd grabbed to his feet while his friend ran toward them from the tower. The creature they'd seen had vanished.

"I don't understand any of this. How did you save me?" The second artist looked to Nettie.

"I was going to ask the same. I tried to save you but we both fell off the walkway. I have no idea why we weren't both busted up." She made a show of checking herself for broken bones, then shrugged when she didn't find any. Even with Lisselle's spell on their voices, Nettie knew she had to be conscious of word choices.

"What caused the earthquake? And what was that thing at the tower?" The first artist looked to his friend. "You okay?"

"No idea on any of it," Nettie said. "We came to see the ruins." She didn't want the artists to stay, none of the other tourists and artists had come back after Damon chased them out and things would be much easier if they could get these two out as well.

"Think I can go get my supplies?" The second artist looked ready to head for the tower.

The first artist looked at the walls and shook his head. "The ladder is busted and you're not catching me going up there again. Not with whatever that thing was up there and the ground shaking. No one's going to climb up there and take our supplies. I'm going to the pub." He waved one hand to his friend and started walking.

His friend looked at the walkway, then turned to Nettie. "Not sure how you did it, but thanks for saving us. We'll be across the way calming our nerves if ye all want to join." He shivered. "That creature was almost worse than falling off the walkway." He followed his friend out of the ruins.

Nettie and the others watched them leave, then she shook her head. "No idea if more people will come in for a stroll, but we need to see if we can find out what happened. Were those quakes only at the castle, or the whole area? What was that thing, and how was it out during the day?"

Damon looked around. "I can go check the surrounding shops, see how far out people felt the quakes." There was still a tiny bit of a question to his voice, but Nettie was glad he was acting as one of them, not as their houseman.

"Excellent. I am going to investigate up the tower itself. The stairs still look as stable as they were before, so that's reassuring," Nettie said, ignoring the fact it hadn't looked terribly stable to begin with. It was the one from the initial report, the same one where she had seen the creature.

Rebecca put her hands on her hips. "I think I'm going to go out by the water, see where that thing could have come in from that no one saw it in broad daylight."

A flash of concern crossed Damon's face, but then he noticed Nettie watching him and took a deep breath. "If either of you need me, just yell. What time should we reconvene?"

Another proud moment for Nettie concerning Damon. She might need to have him give pointers to Caden. "I'd say one hour. I am concerned about that thing being out in the day time, and we should get back to report it to Lisselle and Gaston."

Damon went out the same way the artists had gone. Rebecca waited a moment then leaned into Nettie. "We will be talking about what happened when you jumped later."

"I had every intention of sharing what happened with you," Nettie said with a grin. "Thank you for not saying anything in front of Damon. This was new and I'm still sorting it out myself."

"Very well. And do be careful." Rebecca headed to the waterway behind the castle ruins.

Nettie shoved her concern at her own actions aside; even for her, a jump like that wouldn't have normally left her unscathed. That creature had been out during the day, and that was a serious issue. Was it an aberration or were they changing that quickly? The tower stairs were tight and steep, well designed to keep attackers out, Nettie hoped they weren't going to cause her problems if that creature was still up on the walkway.

She made it to the walkway, grateful for the pants she wore. It appeared empty, but there was more to the tower above her. She crept up the stairs slowly. The top had a small rim around it, if anything or anyone were up here, they would have to be crouched down, and most likely had ill intent.

The stone was in remarkable shape for being as old as it was, but there were crumbled edges. She held her breath as she misstepped slightly. No sound came from above, so she continued on her way.

To find an empty tower. Walking around it took less than a minute, still nothing.

"At least the view is lovely." She could see across the water on one side, the rest of the ruins on the other. She almost missed the odd darker sections of the wall as she turned to go down. They were damp with something heavier than water. Peering over the side it was clear that strands went all the way down and to the outside of the castle. She reached down and pulled out strands. Seaweed, but she'd already seen that covering the creature. But there was more. There were no odd octopi in this bit of kelp, but there were tubes. Many gathered together in one section.

She pulled out her specimen bags and put as many pieces in as she could. Climbing down was less precarious and she made better time. The creature had a rounded head, too rounded and too large at least in comparison to the rest of the torso. Had they started using water breathers and some sort of helmets on land when they were still trapped in their fish form by sunlight? She walked along where the artists had been, but there were no clues to be found. Aside from the fact that the artists she'd rescued weren't terribly good. At least not to judge by the works they'd left.

She went out into the main ruins, they'd said an hour, and she still had at least half of that left. Maybe she could go out the back of the ruins and see if there were any more odd tubes, or even seaweed, although they really did have enough of that.

This side of the castle was less travelled with a small trail that went through the trees and grasses and lead to the water. Three small holes, with debris such as a small explosion might make, were next to the walls, about two feet apart. Possibly enough to cause the quakes. She gathered some samples, then moved on. There appeared to be more seaweed down the way a bit, so she walked in that direction. The body she almost stumbled upon couldn't be seen until she was falling over it. Swearing was not the best form for a woman, but Fred swore—a lot.

The beaten body before her was Damon.

CHAPTER TWENTY-FOUR

NETTIE RUSHED TO HIM AND pushed aside the plants. Whoever dumped him here had counted on no one coming this way for a while. There was no blood that she could see, but he was unconscious and had bruises on his face; but he was breathing, and a further check revealed no other visible injuries.

She tried to guess how long he'd been there. Had he been replaced and the one she'd sent off a while ago was a merperson? The only replacement they'd seen so far, that they knew of, had been out at night, but then the recent kelp creature had been out in daylight this time.

A groan from Damon brought her back, speculation could wait. Alas, the groaning stopped and he still was unconscious. She needed to get him back to the carriage and find Rebecca.

It was dangerous moving someone with unknown injuries, but leaving him there to find a better way to move him could prove deadly if his attacker came back. She gently picked him up and slowly made her way around to the front where they had the carriage. Again, she was grateful they went out as men, it would be odd enough having a man carry another man as easily as she was—a woman doing the same would have caused too much talk.

She was almost to the carriage when Rebecca came around the corner from the ruins. "Net—Fred? What happened?" She ran forward and tried to help, but Nettie was losing strength.

"Get the carriage open, I need to get him inside."

Rebecca quickly opened the door as wide as it could go and stood aside, but it was clear she wanted to grab Damon.

Nettie's strength failed as she got him onto the seat. Not so much a complete failure, but more like what she felt a normal human might feel like.

Rebecca climbed in as well and fussed about Damon to make him comfortable.

"What's happened? Is Rebecca all right?"

The last thing Nettie expected was to hear Damon's voice coming from behind her. "Keep an eye on that one, sit on him if you have to." She could tell Rebecca was confused, but she knew she'd do it. Nettie spun.

Yes, a second Damon, dressed like the other, and looking hale and hardy. "Where have you been?" She stepped in front of the open carriage so that he couldn't see inside.

"I was waiting back in the ruins as we'd said. When neither of you showed up, I came out to look. Is she okay?"

His voice sounded right, he looked exactly like Damon, but there was no way to know which the real one was. She was going to have to handle this carefully.

A loud thunk and a yelp from inside the carriage moved things along.

"He's awake and fighting," Rebecca's yell ended up in an ooof, and the formerly unconscious Damon came flying out of the carriage with Rebecca tumbling out after. Although unexpected, Nettie was glad to see the small gear gun in her friend's hand.

"Two?" Rebecca stepped back but still had to keep shifting from one to the other with her gun.

Nettie looked around. No one else was close enough that they would be able to tell what was happening. But that probably wouldn't last long.

"Who are you?" The Damon who came up recently

got it out a moment before the carriage one, but he still echoed it.

"Both of you stand down. Rebecca is an excellent shot and can easily hit both of you in non-fatal but disabling areas while we sort this out." Nettie glared at them and let her fangs drop into place. "I need you to each get in the carriage slowly. We're taking you back to let Gaston and Lisselle sort you out."

She felt bad about having to treat the real Damon that way, but it was necessary.

Neither looked like they were going to move, then Rebecca coughed and motioned toward the carriage. "Now. I might need to shoot you. And the real Damon would understand why."

They climbed in, the one Nettie found unconscious was moving a bit slower, but they both got in.

"It'd be best if I stayed in back with them and your gun. I'm faster." Nettie didn't take her eyes off either Damon as they settled into their seats. Rebecca handed her the gear pistol, and then climbed into the driver's seat.

They started out fine, but as they began to cross the bridge that lead away from Conwy, the Damon she'd found unconscious started twitching and his features began to blur. He lunged forward, but the second one, clearly the real one since his features didn't blur, grabbed him and they scuffled. Blood was drawn on both. The blurred one's blood was non-human greenish, the real one's was red. Faster than even Nettie could move, the blurred one slammed the real Damon's head into the roof of the carriage, broke the door, ran out of the carriage, and dove into the water below them.

The carriage swerved, but Rebecca recovered quickly.

"Keep going! Damon is injured. We need to get him help." The sea creature had been armed, and a wicked looking blade stuck out of Damon's side as he crumbled over. "We need to get him under care immediately." He was pale and bleeding from his side and his head.

Rebecca didn't say anything, but the horse picked up speed.

"Hang on, Damon. I'm sorry I couldn't tell which one was you. That creature had collapsed and I believed you'd been attacked." Nettie kept talking to him as she tried to make him comfortable without moving him too much. She was a strong believer that unconscious people were aware of who was around them, even if they might not recall it upon awakening. It made her feel better as well.

Rebecca slowed the carriage down and a quick glance showed they were on their street. Rebecca stopped in front of their house, and Nettie ran inside. Yes, she could possibly carry him herself, but she didn't want to dislodge the knife by jostling him if she didn't need to.

"Damon's been attacked!" She yelled as she ran toward the back of the house. They'd left the gurney in her tank room.

Pounding down the stairs indicated someone was home.

"What? Are they targeting us one at a time?" Gaston and Lisselle had come down together, Reaves was not far behind.

Nettie was glad to see Reaves, he would be better able to help her carry Damon inside than Rebecca.

"There was someone who looked like him injured and unconscious outside the castle, I brought him to the carriage thinking it was him. Then we couldn't tell the difference when the real one showed up, so I tried to bring them both back." She grabbed the stretcher and ran back outside.

Rebecca was inside the carriage with the door open. She helped Nettie move Damon to the gurney.

Gaston peered inside the carriage. "Did the other one dissolve?"

"No, he started to lose shape a bit though. Then he and Damon fought and he dove off the bridge into the water."

"He started losing shape? And you couldn't tell them apart at first?" Reaves looked worried as he picked up the other end of the stretcher. But it wasn't at Damon's wounds. "They shouldn't have that ability." He shook his head, but it was more about something going on in his head.

Colleen came out and took the horse and carriage from Rebecca. "I've taken care of enough of these, go make sure your young man is safe."

The others might not have heard her, but Nettie did. Rebecca blushed and followed them inside.

"Get him to the table. I see the knife, what else is wrong?" Lisselle had her medical kit out as she watched them approach.

"Head injury," Nettie said as she and Reaves gently placed Damon on the table. "The fake one slammed him fairly hard trying to get out."

Reaves looked at the knife and his scowl deepened. "That's even worse. It's a ritual blade from my people, but I know none of my people would have done this. It's going to be tricky to get it out as well, they have barbs."

"I don't know that I can do it here." Lisselle studied the wound and shook her head. "We need to get him to a hospital."

Gaston was also peering at the blade. "Agreed, but the Yard will need to step in. Get him ready to move, I need to get some things."

They were moving Damon back outside after asking Colleen to swing the horse and carriage around again, when Gaston came out. "Caden is not happy about being left behind, but we can't use a wounded Yard agent." Gaston handed folded ID's to Nettie and Lisselle. "Nettie you'll use Caden's. Reaves, I need you to stay here. You and Colleen guard the houses and Caden and Mathlin. I doubt we'll have an attack in broad daylight, but they are changing their abilities and tactics."

Lisselle climbed in the carriage with Rebecca and Damon, and Nettie and Gaston took the driver's bench.

"I'll drive, I memorized the map of this town. Besides, I do recall seeing you drive your steam bike." Gaston rolled his eyes and clicked to the horse.

Nettie sighed. "I do wish I could have brought her up here."

"No." That was the end of it, and he returned to driving. Gaston was a careful driver, but he quickly got to the hospital. He marched inside and came out a moment later with who had to be a hospital administrator. "You understand the need for secrecy, and the fact that the weapon used must be released to my agents once it is safely removed. We have it on a good source this blade has teeth."

"I do understand, we will make no mention that the patient is a…person of importance." He was going to most likely mention Scotland Yard, but caught himself.

A pair of large orderlies came out and took Damon inside. Rebecca started to follow, then stopped and looked to Gaston and Lisselle.

Gaston nodded. "Agent Evans will be waiting with him. Evans is one of our best *men*."

Nettie caught the slight emphasis on men, and saw that Rebecca did as well. She'd been looking a bit too female in her stance and behavior.

"Thank you, Gaston." Rebecca lowed her voice and looked stern. "I'll report if there are complications."

"Excellent. We'll send relief in a bit." Gaston turned and went back to the carriage.

"Will he be all right?" Even with her medical school background, Nettie couldn't tell. She really hadn't gotten a chance to examine him.

Lisselle looked back toward the hospital as she climbed into the carriage. "I think he will be. If we'd been in London with the full resources of Gaston's Dungeon, I might have tried to help him. But a tricky blade is dangerous."

They reconvened in the second house. Caden was recovering extremely quickly and was antsy to get back in the game. He and Reaves were playing cards when they came in, but he gladly set them aside. Homer had been at the larger house, chatting with Colleen but saw the carriage and joined them.

"Well? Will he recover?" Homer looked concerned but distracted.

"I believe so," Lisselle said. "I also believe that we have a way to discern the merpeople from humans, the greenish blood. But how are they able to mimic us? And why isn't Reaves' or his mother's blood green?"

"They shouldn't be able to mimic anyone. If I had to guess I'd say that one of our scientists who went missing and was presumed dead a year ago defected to their side." Reaves turned to Nettie. "You said when you first found the copy that it was unconscious and unresponsive? That would go with the problems we had. We were not trying to mimic people though. A scientist was trying to clone cells for healing. But he got frustrated at the pace my mother made him go. The copied cells couldn't hold cohesion."

"But the one that copied Thomas held it for at least a few days," Homer said. "Even if he'd switched with the real one right before they got to London, Bethlyn's crew were there for two days."

"If the scientist in question is behind this, that was probably him. He had some genetic abnormality which gave him mimicking abilities. It was what started as a party trick and became his research. Then his obsession."

"Why is their blood green, yet yours isn't?" Nettie hadn't had a chance to test his blood, but both Gaston and Lisselle had. They would have noticed green blood.

"We are different species," Reaves said and shrugged. "Even though we have fins and tails and most of my people can't come onto land at all any more, we're closer to humans, genetically, than they are—now." He took a breath and looked around the room. "My mother wouldn't have wanted this brought up yet. They were part of what destroyed Atlantis. Our people are the descendants of the Atlantians, but, in a way, so are they. The true Atlantians had knowledge, skills, and abilities that no one currently can come close to. But a civil war destroyed them. Some were already acclimated to the sea, many still died, but the survivors became my people. The merpeople were experiments, scientists were trying to uplift sea creatures to a higher level of sentience."

"It's been a few thousand years," Nettie said. "Did the other merpeople finish their uplift on their own?"

"My mother would be better at answering that," Reaves said. His normally long gaunt face looked almost skeletal now. "For years many of our people have wanted contact with the humans. My mother fought it. She felt that the humans, no offense, would corrupt and possibly capture our people."

"She also forbade you from joining the Society?" Nettie recalled Frilin's reaction when she'd mentioned it.

Reaves gave a sideways smile. "She strongly suggested against it. She also initially hadn't been happy about my joining Homer's crew. Then she watched him, and heard my stories, and decided that it was all right."

"The Society would be the best place to start making contact with humanity," Gaston said. "Maybe she didn't want you to get ideas if she felt your people weren't ready."

"There's little choice of that now," Caden said. "These attacks are going to make your people reveal themselves, if just to prove they aren't the same species."

Lisselle shook her head. "This still makes no sense. Reaves' people are in the south, near Bath. Recent underwater attacks brought our interest there, then the attack in London, yet the other merpeople have been staging some incursions up here for what, almost a year? What are they doing?"

"I think they were trying to draw attention to us down south, to expose us, or at least make you and other authorities focus down there. Those weapons you found were stolen from one of our deep base labs, one with connections to here. Including the missile they fired, based on how you described it. The boat was so modified, I didn't recognize it. The incidents up here are them testing their new abilities. This is a far less populated area, lots of water access, and fewer humans."

"If it weren't for Nettie thinking of the Runner being able to tell where the water came from in the attack, we would be tearing apart the waters around Bath right now," Gaston said.

Everyone dropped into their own thoughts for a few moments.

"On another note, I did get some of the secret fishing maps." Homer held up a collection of papers. "I was able to get six, there are apparently more, but I couldn't narrow down who had them."

"How far away are they? Do they all have islands, or just fishing locations?" Reaves didn't hold out a hand for them, but he looked like he wanted to.

Homer handed most of them over. "Might make more sense to someone familiar with the waters, even if these aren't your home. Good guess though, only three have actual islands, but they're so small and hidden they don't appear on any other map. I also got this one, shows Ireland as well. Look what's right in the middle." He unfolded the map he'd hung on to. A few locations were circled, but one had an island. It was circled in red.

"That's where the war zeppelin must have been boarded. But why would they have gone there? Not to mention without an airship dock, those monsters can't land, can they?" Caden took a look at the map, then shrugged and passed it around. He wasn't in his rolling chair and he was still moving stiffly.

Homer shook his head. "No, we can't land at all without a docking station. Not even on an unmarked island."

"Unless there is a secret dock there," Gaston said. "I'd say someone in the royal air army is up to something, with or without the Queen's knowledge. I'll notify Edinburgh and see what they know. Someone will need to notify the Queen directly." Gaston didn't look up as he studied the map.

Lisselle scowled at him. "There are other agents currently in London who can do that. You need to stay here."

"Mais, I didn't say anything." The look of feigned innocence was as planned as his heavier French accent.

A marching of booted feet came right before a sharp rap on the front door.

"Are we expecting anyone?" Gaston rose to answer, at this point maintaining Lisselle and Rebecca's ruse was pointless.

When everyone shook their heads, he opened the door a crack. "Oui?"

Three police constables stood on the stoop. "We're looking for Homer Tremain, he's been called in as a character reference for a recent prisoner."

Homer pulled the door open wider and stepped forward. He was almost a foot taller than Gaston, so didn't need to step in front of him. "I be him, why are you looking for me?"

The front officer nodded. "One Bethlyn Ragthin was picked up and is suspected of murder. She has said you can vouch for her. Said she was working with the Yard." The look on his face said he doubted it, but was here to officially log that he tried.

Homer nodded. "Aye, she's my cousin. Who is she charged with murdering?"

Nettie was impressed at how calm he was being, especially given the circumstances of her disappearance. But his jaw twitched through his beard.

"She was found burying the remains of two men and a woman. She admitted to killing them, said it was self-defense. The records we found were that they were her crew."

Gaston stepped forward with a billfold held up, if he breathed hard his belly would hit the front officer. "Do you see this badge, officer?" His French accent was gone completely. "I am a recognized agent of the Yard and I am under special authority of the Queen. I will be taking Captain Ragthin into my protection. She was working under the Queen's direction."

The officer stepped back. "That is highly unusual—"

"Do you or do you not recognize these seals?" Gaston had also unfolded a small piece of paper that Nettie had never seen and shoved it into the constable's face. "This is issued by the Queen herself. My actions cannot be questioned."

Nettie had never seen such a document and she couldn't get a good look at it now. She would ask to see it later.

The officer paused, looked at the seal and signature, swallowed heavily, and finally nodded. "Understood. What would you have us do?"

"Very good. My men will follow you to retrieve Captain Ragthin, and you will turn over everything you have concerning her case to them."

The constable stepped back and moved toward the walkway. "If you would come this way, gentlemen."

Nettie looked to Gaston, but he lifted his chin for her to

follow Homer. Caden and Reaves followed as well.

The leader was a few steps ahead of them, but one of the others dropped back near Homer and Nettie. "So she's your cousin, eh? Strong woman. She put up a serious fight when we went to take her in. Didn't really think she was a criminal, most don't admit to their deeds."

"She is my cousin, and a damn fine airship captain." Homer got the words out but he was looking ready to hurt someone.

Nettie leaned forward to face the nosy officer and gave a stern shake of her head. He nodded and backed off.

"Where did you find her?" Nettie asked. Homer was staring straight ahead but she knew he was listening.

"That's the odd bit. She was off in the middle of nowhere, about ten miles south of town. We got a tip from someone that there was a lady stranded. Didn't expect to see her burying bodies."

"Who tipped you?" She doubted these men normally ranged that far away from town.

"We don't know. A note was left."

"We'll need that note." Homer was still looking at the back of the lead constable's head.

"Now I—"

"Do you want us to go back and get Gaston? We all work for the Queen, and report to her regularly." Nettie didn't want Homer to get too upset. He was keeping his temper in check so far, but it would be hard to get Bethlyn out if they locked up Homer as well.

"You may have everything." He picked up speed and soon they were in front of the police station.

He walked them through, nodding to the appropriate people to let them know it was okay.

Bethlyn was a sad change from when they'd separated in London. Her hair was wild, her clothing filthy, and she sat there with her head in her hands.

"Get her out," Homer said as he watched his cousin.

"I'll need to have papers filled out."

Nettie stepped forward. "I'll take care of the papers, let her out now, if you please."

Caden and Reaves stayed behind everyone as silent enforcers, but they glared around and kept their arms folded. Nettie was certain no one besides her noticed Caden was favoring his injured side.

The lead constable nodded to one of the men behind them, who then waved to Nettie.

"If you'll come this way, sir, we can get these processed."

Caden followed Nettie over to the desk, Reaves stayed with Homer.

"Thank the gods you came," Bethlyn's voice had more fight than she looked, and Nettie was glad to hear it. Homer's voice was low in response and Nettie couldn't pick out more of the conversation.

The constable who had waved them over pointed to a small pile of papers on a desk. "If one of you could read, comment, and sign these, we can turn her over to your custody."

Caden stepped forward. "I'll take care of this, Fred," Caden said as he patted her on the shoulder. "Your writing has been horrible ever since that accident stopping those train robbers."

Nettie had already taken the seat and looked up in confusion for a moment. Her writing was impeccable. And extremely feminine. Trying to write less womanly in a spur of the moment tense situation like this wasn't the best option.

She got to her feet and handed the pen to Caden. "Thanks for that, forgot they might want to read this."

Caden went to work on the documents, and she walked back to Reaves, Homer, and Bethlyn. No one was saying much, but Bethlyn was still on the wrong side of the bars.

"Why isn't she out? Or do you really believe that four men working for the Queen are going to break her out of here before the proper papers are done?" Nettie was proud of the manly growl she added.

"It's not procedure."

Homer and Reaves turned to echo Nettie's stance.

"Fine, but please don't leave with her until the paperwork is done. We are still gathering the evidence." He added that bit quickly as if that were the real reason he didn't want them to leave.

Nettie moved closer to the bars and flashed a smile to Bethlyn. Her eyes went wide at first then she tilted her head in question.

Homer patted Nettie on the back. "I don't think you met Fred before you left, he's working with us on this case."

The constable opened the cell and Bethlyn came out and shook Nettie's hand. "Very nice to meet you, Fred. Thank you for helping me with this situation." The wink she gave said she'd figured out it was Nettie. "I assume Gaston and Damon made it up here?"

"Aye, he's who is getting you out. You'll be dealing with him and Edinburgh." Homer raised his voice a bit. "And the Yard, but they and the Queen are behind you."

Bethlyn gave him a sideways look, but shrugged.

"Here are all your papers, signed. Rather rude that many of them are duplicates." Caden rose from the desk. "Perhaps you think people aren't reading them? Very fast readers in our bunch."

The constable took the papers, then handed over a large box, a second one sat behind him. "These two boxes are all we had."

Nettie glanced through the first box. "The note that told you where our agent was?"

"Ah, yes." He reddened and reached into another desk,

retrieving a scrap of paper. "Sorry. Again, this is not normal procedure."

Nettie gave him a nod as she took it from his hand and tucked it inside her jacket. "Thank you. I'll make sure this gets handed directly to Gaston."

Homer was already leading Bethlyn out toward the doors. Caden started to grab one of the boxes but Nettie stepped in and grabbed it first. Reaves grabbed the second one. "Don't want to tear open that wound from London, mate." She figured by not implying he'd been hurt in town there would be no questions. She knew Caden wanted to get back into full form, but the box was heavy.

He wasn't happy, but he stepped back.

"You really are living the life; fighting, spies, whatnot." One of the constables said. "It must be terribly exciting."

"And dangerous," Nettie said as she followed the others out the door.

Caden waited until they were a block away before speaking. "I could have handled that box."

"You were already favoring your side. The muscles that run along your torso are going to take time to heal, just picking this up could have set you back. You most likely will have to endanger them soon; but risking that for no reason didn't seem prudent." Nettie tried to keep her tone from scolding, but from the look on Caden's face, she hadn't succeed.

He stayed silent the rest of the way home. But he didn't look mad, just thoughtful.

"Which house?" Homer paused as he approached Lisselle's place.

"There is more stuff still in this one, so more room in the other," Nettie said. She was beginning to miss Gaston's large mansion.

"I'll tell whoever is home that we're going next door." Caden turned up the walk for Lisselle's place and the rest made their way next door.

At first it appeared that no one was there. The door was unlocked, but no one came forth when they entered. Then Nettie heard voices in the back. Including some familiar French swearing.

Homer led Bethlyn toward the back, Nettie and Reaves followed.

"Ah, I figured that was you all. Any trouble?" Gaston looked up as they entered.

"Not really, particularly after Fred here made a few good points." Homer pulled out a chair for Bethlyn, but she shook him off.

"Thank you, but I've been sitting for two days. That's how long it took them to go get you."

Gaston and Mathlin had been chatting over a full tea cart through the grating of his cell, so Nettie poured for Bethlyn. She might not want to sit right now since she was clearly furious but she could use some comfort.

"We might want to move this to the parlor," Homer said. "No offense Mathlin, but you're no longer an agent, and we're not sure what's going on with you."

Mathlin shrugged. "Understood. Not sure I'd be trusting me in your case either." He sat back down on his bed.

They moved to the front parlor and Nettie took off her jacket and hat. "This is not a comfortable ensemble." What she really wanted to do was remove the binding from her chest, but that would be going a bit far. Once they'd debriefed Bethlyn, she'd see about changing clothes.

Lisselle and Caden arrived from the main house, and Bethlyn looked to Homer. "Now?"

"Aye, tell us your story," Homer said. "She whispered part when we were still in that station."

"It's short and not good. Apparently my crew had been replaced right before we headed down to London. Since this was our last stop, I assume they were swapped here."

She held up her hand. "I know it sounds unbelievable, but my crew was replaced by fish people—like the ones you spoke of fighting in London."

"We believe you," Lisselle said. "Your man Thomas, the real one, we believe, came to us a few nights ago. I am sorry, he passed away before we could learn much." She leaned forward with a small knife. "I hate to do this, but we've found that the shape changers have different blood than we do."

Bethlyn held out her hand. "Whatever you need." She winced a bit at the cut, but the blood was red. "Thank you for verifying. After what happened with my crew, I was wondering if I was me myself."

"At what point did you crash?"

Bethlyn sat down once Lisselle wrapped her cut hand. "Within a few hours of separating from you. The thing pretending to be Thomas was furious that we left without Gaston. He tried to say he had separate orders from Edinburgh that Gaston had to be brought to Wales no matter what the cost. I knew damn well that no such orders would have been given. They tried to turn Bessie around, three against one were not good odds in my favor, so I crashed her."

"Then you deflated the balloon," Homer said with an approving nod. "Good work."

"Aye. It stopped them from getting back to London, but they over powered me at that point. We marched in circles, they were trying to find water. At the time I thought someone had bought my crew. I didn't realize the truth for a full day. By then they were lost and starting to fall ill. Then they started showing signs of fishiness and I was able to overpower all three. Just finished burying them when our friendly Welsh constables showed up."

"You got there two days ago?" Lisselle asked.

"Aye, and told them to come get Homer. They didn't

do anything except feed me from time to time. Until this morning. Not sure what changed, but the Captain sent his men out to get you, and he took off."

"Do you know where to?" Caden had been looking through the box of evidence, but hadn't appeared to have found anything important.

"No. I was pretending to sleep, but he kept his voice low. Something agitated him." She looked over to where Caden had things out alongside the boxes. "That blue book isn't mine, nor any of my crew. Well, not any of my real crew." She pointed to a large faded blue notebook.

Gaston reached over and Caden handed it to him. "Smells like salt water." He flipped through the pages. "But the ink on here is undamaged." He was flipping quickly enough that it was clear he wasn't reading anything.

"What's it about?" Nettie could see lines of text and drawings, but short of standing and taking it from him she couldn't see anything else.

"That is a good question, want to try and read it?" He closed it and handed it to her.

Gaston was right, there was a saltiness to it, but it wasn't water stained. The words were clear and undamaged. They also made no sense. "Is this a code?"

Reaves looked over. "Might I?" Nettie handed it to him. "Not a code. Well, not only a code. Some is just an old language."

"The other merpeople?" Caden picked through everything he'd set aside already, looking for anything else written.

"Sort of. They developed their language from ours. This is an old version of our language. One hardly used in a few hundred years."

Caden gave up his search of box one and headed over to box two. "That book is old, but not that old."

"Exactly." Reaves was grim as he struggled to read a bit

more. "I'm not well enough trained in the old languages to translate this."

"How can you reach your mother?" Gaston asked as the book passed to Lisselle after Homer and Bethlyn shrugged it off.

"I'd have to go to Bath. She left word that at least two of our long time contacts here are missing and she was going back home for reinforcements and to call the council to see if we are going to war."

"I hate to say it, and technically you're still Homer's man, so he has the call, but I think you need to go to Bath. If your people are going to war, so are ours. These attacks have been on land," Gaston said.

Bethlyn was looking more and more confused as the discussion went on. "Maybe it's because I've been having a horrific few days, and I really think I need a bath and change of clothes, but *who* are Reaves' people?"

Nettie didn't want to speak out of turn, there were a number of agents there who outranked her. Bethlyn was an agent of the Society, but she was one who had been compromised.

There was a pause, one that Bethlyn noticed judging by the downturn of her mouth, but Gaston finally briefly explained Reaves' unique status.

"You're one of the fish people? I'm sorry if I killed anyone you knew."

Reaves scowled. "Those are not my people. My people were once the Atlantians, but we evolved when Atlantis was destroyed. Part of the destruction was brought on by the ancestors of the ones who replaced your crew members. They have been silently growing in strength over the centuries."

"I agree with Gaston," Homer said. "You need to get this information to your mother and her people. I think she also needs to see the maps I obtained for the secret fishing spots and islands, maybe she will recognize something about them." He unfolded the papers he'd brought in before they went to get Bethlyn.

Lisselle held up her hand. "I agree, but I think anything sent with Reaves needs to be copied. We can't send the book though."

"I won't move through them quickly, but I will be safe in the chutes, only my people can use them," Reaves said.

Caden shook his head. "And what about the spy you gave information to about the attacks who has now vanished? Could he have given the information as to how to use the chutes to the other merpeople?"

"No." Reaves rubbed the back of his neck. "Maybe. It's more than just the ability, but it wouldn't be hard for them to start using them if they knew how. We were so certain that they weren't a threat. We've been lying to ourselves." He sighed. "I can help copy the maps. And bring back someone who can translate the book if my mother can't leave quickly enough."

Gaston pulled out a pile of papers and pens. "Four of us can get through it quicker."

Lisselle rose to her feet. "And I am going to take Bethlyn and get her situated in a room at home. I believe all the things from your ship are in the parlor, possibly even your personal items."

Homer looked up from his work. "I brought everything, including your personal items and those of your crew. Which might also give us some information about the ones who replaced your crew."

Bethlyn nodded as she and Lisselle went toward the door. "Honestly, I don't care what I wear, as long as it's not this. But thank you. And thank you for believing me."

Nettie looked around, it appeared the four men were doing an excellent job making copies. "I believe I will be returning next door as well." She stuffed her hair under her hat and put her borrowed jacket back on. "I have had enough of being male for the day."

Various grunts and nods echoed in the room before she left. She was turning onto the front walk when a messenger boy came up. "Does Nettie Jones live here?"

"She does, but is out right now. I'm her brother, Fred Jones, can I help you?" Nettie really wanted out of her disguise, but that might have to wait a bit longer.

"I need to give this note to her. Came from the telegraph office. How long will she be out?" The boy clearly wanted to drop his missive, get a tip, and go off to something else.

"I can take it, brothers can do that for sisters, you know." Nettie tried to make her voice sound trustworthy.

"Yer right. Here you go. Give it to your sister." He shoved the envelope into Nettie's hands and left his hand out.

Nettie smiled tightly. Not subtle this one. She fished a few coins out of her pocket, grossly over tipped him, and then went to the house. The boy was gone before she even opened the door.

Once inside she examined the envelope, but there were no clues. Her name was hand written on it. Then she opened it. It wasn't a telegraph no matter where it came from. But it was hand written on telegraph paper.

"Dr. Jones,

We must meet. Utmost urgency. Today, at four pm, behind the cheese shop. Come alone." It was signed only by a pair of initials, JC. The man who'd not been available to speak to them, but who had reported seeing a sea creature near the cheese shop was named James Clearwell. This could be him reaching out.

Four o'clock was a half hour away, but the cheese shop was very close. She would have time to change and get down there. She was going up to her room, still re-reading the note for missed clues, when she almost smacked into Lisselle coming down.

"I've Bethlyn settled, whatever is so interesting?"

"A boy brought this for Nettie Jones, her brother paid him for it." Nettie handed Lisselle the note and continued up the stairs.

"And with all the attacks of late, do you really think this is a good idea? And four o'clock? What if it's someone who knows of your issue and is trying to trap you out after dark?"

"It's not a great idea, but you've said before what we do involves risks. We need more clues for this case—a lot more." Nettie sighed as her binding male clothes came off and she put on her dress. "I never thought I'd appreciate women's clothing."

Lisselle helped her remove the make-up and resume looking like herself again. "You'll clear it through Gaston. I'm sure he's going to want you to have some backup. There, Nettie Jones is back to her glorious self." Lisselle stood back and admired her work.

"Fine, we'll see what he says." Nettie went down the stairs, Lisselle didn't follow her to the door.

"I have some things to discuss with Colleen. Just make sure you're back before the tiredness hits, and that he has a backup for you."

Nettie nodded and left. She refrained from pointing out that Lisselle went on all sorts of dangerous missions alone, without back-up. Of course, one of those times she was kidnapped by vampires and Nettie and Caden had to rescue her, so that wasn't a great example.

Nettie nodded to Homer and Caden, who were in the front room looking over the items from the constables. Gaston and Reaves were missing.

"Where did Gaston go? I need to ask him something." One of them would most likely be her back-up, but she wanted to tell Gaston first. "And where's Reaves?"

"Gaston is chatting with Mathlin again, they served

together long ago and have old tales to recall," Homer said. "Reaves has taken the copies and gone to the chutes. He'll come back after he talks to Frilin."

"Thank you," she said and went toward the back.

She was almost to the back room when she heard a grunt and a heavy thud. Mathlin shouldn't have been able to reach Gaston through the bars, but they were the only two in the back.

Mathlin was trying to reach Gaston's prone body when she ran in. "What did you do?" She moved so quickly that she got her hand through the bars and was holding him a foot in the air before he could pull back. He didn't fight back aside from trying to pull away her hand.

"Not. Me. Grabbed his chest."

Nettie flung Mathlin to the floor of his cell and spun to Gaston. She flipped him over to confirm what Mathlin said. He was holding his arm and his chest and wasn't moving.

"I need someone to get Lisselle! Medical emergency!" She pulled Gaston out so that he was lying flat. He'd had a heart attack for certain, but it hadn't killed him. Yet. It felt like it took forever before she heard footsteps and a door slam.

Homer came running in. "Caden went to get her, what happened?"

"He had a heart attack." Nettie said as she bent over him.

Lisselle and Caden came running into the room with Bethlyn behind them.

Lisselle paused then spun to Caden. "Get those two big black boxes from the living room, bring me the slightly smaller one first. Damn it, I told him to be careful." She swore under her breath. "I need that first box now!"

Caden came back hauling the box. Nettie swore; she should have helped him, but she didn't want to leave Gaston. Lisselle hadn't said what the boxes were, nor why they were over here instead of with everything else at the other house. Nettie hadn't even noticed them until now.

"This goes no further than us, it's still in its trial studies, but we have no choice. It's a mobile sonic defibrillator actuator that will send a current to restart his heart. I hope." She connected a dozen or more wires to Gaston's bare chest then sent a current through. His body jerked but he wasn't coming back. She did it twice more. "This has to be the last, we might have lost him." The fourth time was the charm. Gaston's breathing steadied.

"We have to get him to Edinburgh," Nettie had read up on this invention, it was extremely experimental. Gaston might be breathing now, but he needed more help than either she or Lisselle could give him.

"Agreed. Homer, you need to get your airship—" Caden was standing back with the second black box.

"There are smaller ships in the airbase, I can get him there faster." Bethlyn still looked pale as she cut him off, but she looked Homer in the eye. "You know I'm faster with the currents and a small airship. You can all come with us and keep gear guns on me the entire time if you don't trust me."

"Nothing that dramatic yet," Lisselle said as she motioned for Caden to bring the second box forward.

The large black box became a huge geared contraption as it unfolded at Lisselle's touch on a series of buttons. The first part had restarted Gaston's heart—Nettie wasn't sure what the rest was going to do.

Lisselle finished un-folding, checked a few gears and screens, and then waved Nettie back over. "This is how we keep him alive. I need you to move this over Gaston, then I'll need Homer and Caden to lift him on the board and hold him until the back support expands."

The machine looked like a giant mechanical spider made of gleaming gears, wires, and spikes. A board was off to one side of it, but looked far too small to support anyone, let alone Gaston.

Nettie moved it over Gaston, using her strength and Lisselle's guidance. It snapped into place around him, and as Caden and Homer supported him the board expanded underneath and soon he was completely incased, including a mask. A soft beeping came from the machine and color began to flow back into Gaston's face.

"Is he going to be okay?" Nettie removed her hands from the machine, but didn't step back.

"He has an artificial heart, your machine should show that." Mathlin's voice came from behind them. He was rubbing his throat where Nettie's hand had been, but he looked okay. Although very sad.

"I don't see anything…" Lisselle swore and stepped close to the bars covering the doorway. "How come none of us knew about it? He's right, the response is close to human, but the mechanics show if you look closely enough."

"He's a spy who doesn't want anyone to know something, and he's pretty good at it." Mathlin said, then held up his hand to keep her back. "I've known him longer than any of you. It was when we were new agents and had gone to investigate a sighting of a naga in India. A real one. And it was real, and had a small village worshiping it. It had already destroyed two other villages, so we didn't have a choice but to go after it ourselves."

"The naga struck him in the heart?" Nettie's hand clenched. Naga's were rare giant snakes that hid deep in jungles. They were fast, deadly, and extremely smart.

"It tried. I cut off its head as it lunged forward. But one of the villagers who was still under its influence stabbed Gaston as I battled the naga. Even back then the Society had ways to stabilize injured bodies, but a stab through the heart would have been too much. A shaman of the village, the first to break free of the naga's spell, had enough magic to keep Gaston alive long enough to get him back to Calcutta. There was a larger Society headquarters there than now, they saved him, but his heart is all gears and coils. They told him to replace the mechanical heart every ten years." He shook his head. "Knowing him that's the original in his chest and it is over thirty years old."

"Damn you, Gaston, you should have told us." Homer looked ready to take apart the contraption he was in and rattle him until he answered.

"I can still take him," Bethlyn said quietly.

"No. Not because we don't trust you, we do; those things you defended yourself against were not your crew. But he needs to get to Edinburgh immediately." Lisselle pulled out a summoning envelop.

"I thought the space that the Runners go through isn't safe for people?" Nettie had believed it would be greatly exciting to travel that way when she first joined SEU. She'd been disappointed when told it wasn't possible.

"It's not, however the cradle will keep him protected. His systems are completely powered by it right now." Lisselle ripped open the envelope and a Runner appeared.

"Cor, haven't seen one of those gents in far too long. Good to see they're still on our side." Mathlin let out a whistle.

Lisselle tipped her head back to look at the tall form. "I need you to take him to Agent Ramsey, his fake heart has given out."

Nettie stepped back as the Runner stepped forward and turned the cradle so he was holding it. With a nod, the Runner and Gaston vanished.

"I've said I'm sorry, and I don't know why I might have attacked you, but can't I please be let out now? That's what Gaston and I were discussing before he collapsed."

Nettie looked closely at Mathlin's eyes, she'd noticed they changed when he spoke his Atlantian language and stayed that way when the Atlantian spirit was still in charge, even if he spoke English. They hadn't changed yet.

"You saw a Runner a few days ago. Right before Gaston and Damon arrived. It spoke to you." She knew Lisselle had wanted to take things slow with Mathlin and whatever it was that was sharing his body, but they didn't have that option anymore. Either they could win over the thing inside him to their side to help with the coming battle, or Mathlin would be spending the rest of his life in a dark cell in Edinburgh.

"What are you talking about?" The confusion was honest as he looked to each of them.

"We need to call another Runner." Nettie continued to watch him.

"Are you certain?" Lisselle was packing up the contents of the first black box.

"Yes, they need to speak to it. We need the information both of them have."

"Both?" Mathlin looked around his cell. "I'm the only one in here."

"What is your need?"

Nettie turned to the Runner. "I need you to speak Atlantian to him. Ask him to talk to us. And translate his responses."

The Runner spoke a few words.

The words were as strange and liquid as before and Nettie felt a chill of almost recognition. Too bad neither Reaves nor Frilin were around, it would be interesting to know if they could understand the language.

Mathlin frowned and shook his head. Then his chin dropped to his chest. When he pulled it back up his eyes were that clear ice blue. He said words to the Runner and the Runner turned to Nettie. "The name of the being is Thiliantic, they demand to know why you are disturbing their rest."

That was something, they at least got a name this time. The last time had been extremely disappointing in her opinion. This time the voice had sounded far surer of itself.

"Why are they in the body of the man? What is their purpose here?"

Again the language, but far faster and stronger. This was a major difference from the disjointed mumbling of before. The Runner nodded before turning to Nettie and the others.

"They say they were forced here long ago by those who are trying to bring Atlantis back to the land. It does not belong of the land, only of the deep. Thiliantic wanted to rest, to guard their people as needed. But then the Flinking came. They want power. They trapped Thiliantic in this vessel years ago."

Nettie looked to the others at the odd term, but everyone shrugged. "What does Flinking mean?"

"There is no translation I can find into your language. It refers to failed ones. Atlantis collapsed. Some went to land. Some went deep into the sea to rebuild. Some refused to choose and are now destroying everything. Flinking."

That sounded like the merpeople they were fighting with now. At least from Reaves' comments of them. Nettie thought she heard emotion in the Runner's voice and was gratified that her campaign to integrate the Runners with society was working.

"Your people couldn't go deep enough to find the Atlantians, could you?" The Runners had crashed their space vessel looking for help from the most advanced society on Earth. One that had already gone deep into the oceans by the time they got here.

"No. We cannot survive deep water. The Flinkings were still trying to survive and didn't recognize us. The others had already moved deeper. They could not help."

Nettie knew most of the Runners who had come to

Earth all those years ago had not survived.

Mathlin's body shook and the voice started again.

The Runner translated for them but stayed facing Mathlin. "Thiliantic cannot stay in contact long, the form being inhabited is weaker than an Atlantian body. The form wasn't trying to kill you. It was Thiliantic, mistaking you for a Flinking. Think of better questions for next time."

Mathlin stumbled back and fell onto his bed.

"I felt something that time," he said as he rubbed the side of his head and got to his feet. "It was me, but it wasn't me. That voice inside of me is a person?"

The Runner tilted its head. "The voice inside of you is a trapped spirit that belongs to an Atlantian."

Mathlin's eyes went wide. "Never knew they could speak like that."

"Spirits rarely do." The Runner turned back to Lisselle. "Do you have further need?"

Lisselle looked to Nettie who shrugged then shook her head. "No. Thank you for coming."

The Runner vanished a moment later.

"So the Runners carry on conversations now? And what was it nattering on about? Or was I imagining that too?" He looked to all of them. "Have I gone crazy?"

"The Runners are becoming more socialized, so yes, they do talk more," Nettie said. "It was speaking the truth, you have been host to a spirit from a departed member of the Atlantian race. That's what caused you to try and drown me a few nights ago. The spirit inside of you thought I was a bad person." Simplified, but she didn't think he needed the details right now. He was looking a bit overwhelmed.

Mathlin looked from one to another, then dropped down to sit at the foot of his bed. "How did this happen? When did it happen?"

Homer leaned forward to speak to Lisselle. "Not that this isn't fascinating, because it is. But I need to run Bethlyn up to Edinburgh. Reaves will meet me and the rest of the crew there once he gets back from Bath. He should have communication from his mother on their status."

Lisselle turned to Bethlyn. "I think you were as much a victim as Thomas, and the rest of your crew. Don't blame yourself. They can help you recover in Edinburgh."

Bethlyn's smile returned to its normal brightness for a moment. "Thank you. Hopefully, we'll all meet again once this is over."

As they left, Caden turned to Lisselle. "I'd better go see what Colleen is up to, we had a project going earlier." He gave a nod and a quick smile to Nettie, then left.

"Colleen is working on cases again? Good for her. Never did sit right that she left the Society just because I was done."

"She left because of you? Why did you lie to her? She said she was told that you and a crew died at sea. You knew she was living in Conwy, and often worked here, yet you avoided her for years. Why?" Nettie knew it was none of her business. But Colleen was a friend now, and she wanted answers from the man who'd hurt her.

Mathlin looked uncomfortable but also confused. "I…I can't explain it. I did love her. But then I went on that boat." He stopped and looked down at his feet, shaking his head as if trying to find something. "I remember coming back here. I wanted a place by the sea. I knew Colleen, but I didn't *know* her. It was odd." He looked up. "You think that trip was when I got my Atlantian traveler? Maybe he doesn't like women?"

"Or your traveler is a woman. Thiliantic could be either male or female and we only hear them through your vocal cords." Lissette pulled up a pair of chairs for her and Nettie. "That could be why you were still drawn to stay here, but avoided Colleen because of your past connection that Thiliantic had no interest in."

"We really need Frilin here. If her people are in fact the descendants of the Atlantians, they might know who Thiliantic was." Nettie knew they were closing in on the secret of what really happened to the Atlantians, and what had created the Flinkings but they needed to close in faster if it was to help them fight the Flinkings off.

"There are more people from Atlantis?" Mathlin rubbed his face. "Forget about letting me out of here, I need to stay here where it's safe until this gets sorted out."

Lisselle put the black box in the corner of the room. "We need Reaves to contact Frilin, and he's going to Edinburgh. I don't think we can sort things just yet." She turned to Mathlin. "We can let you out, Mathlin. Thiliantic doesn't seem to mean any of us harm, nor are they working with the ones attacking us. We can safely presume that the ones we have been fighting are the Flinkings."

Mathlin was silent for a few moments, and Nettie thought he might have been serious about not wanting out. Finally he got to his feet. "It's time for me to face things, I've been hiding from Colleen and pretty much any aspect of my old life for too long. If you let me out, I'll clear things with her. Then go check on my place. But I will help you in this fight, me and … Thiliantic? Interesting name. But male or female, they and I are together for now. So we need to come to terms."

Lisselle unlocked his door. "Colleen and Caden are working on a project, see if you can help, then talk to her."

Mathlin smiled. "Aye, sneak up on her so she won't start hitting me before I can say my piece. Good plan."

"I should probably go over as well, they might think you escaped otherwise." It was already almost five, whoever sent her that note would need to reach out again. It was far too late to risk being away from her tank.

"I'll go as well, we can do some more lab work on those bits you found in Conwy," Lisselle said.

"Did you know that Gaston was having problems? That's a very advanced and specific item to have along for no reason." Not that Nettie wasn't extremely grateful, but it did raise questions.

"Obviously, I wasn't informed enough," Lisselle said grimly. "Edinburgh said that Gaston was having some health issues and sent the equipment down when they decided you were all coming up. But they never mentioned him having a mechanical heart that was far overdue for a change out."

"I'm glad they sent something along, but I agree, warning would have been less stressful," Nettie said.

Mathlin was silent during the walk over but his hands kept clenching and unclenching as they walked up to the front door.

"Are you going to be all right, Mathlin?" Nettie asked as she came next to him. He'd been a few steps ahead of them but paused on the top step.

"I will be. Might be nice for that Atlantian person to come out now and explain things to her."

Lisselle laughed. "We'd have to get a Runner to translate as no one else understands your internal friend. And no, we won't be doing that." Mathlin had looked hopeful for a moment. "You have to face this."

He took a deep breath and went inside.

Lisselle held up her hand. "Let's give him a minute."

"Do you think Gaston will be all right?" Nettie had wanted to ask it since the Runner took him, but was afraid to hear the answer. "We need to get word to Rebecca and Damon."

Lisselle turned to face her. "Yes, I do think he will be fine. With everything that he's been through, there's no way this will take him away from us. And yes, we need to tell Damon. But carefully. I received a missive from a connection at the hospital, that Damon has been stabilized.

The knife was removed, and turned over to Agent Evans. Damon is awake and resting and Agent Evans is staying with him. We might have to pry her away at some point."

"Is Rebecca staying the night there?"

"I would assume so, but it might be better if she came home first and changed. Being in disguise is going to get more difficult the longer she keeps it up. I'm not sure how clearly she's thinking yet."

They were walking into the front room when Caden came out of the dining area.

"Mathlin is in the kitchen getting an earful from Colleen," Caden said. "You'll be glad to know that once they got some ground rules set, she will not hold any of his past actions against him until after the current crisis has been resolved."

"I've not heard any shouting so that's good. It's in his favor that she's a former agent as well," Nettie said.

Caden shook his head. "I would not want to get on her bad side. He's turning shades of white I've never seen on a living person. And did you know she has an extensive background in explosives? She does."

Their conversation was cut short when Mathlin came bustling out from the kitchen. "I'll be back in a day or so, once I've settled affairs at my home." He all but ran out the door.

Colleen came out as well. "I am sorry I wasn't there for Gaston, will he be all right?"

Mathlin had looked bad when he came out, Colleen looked better than she had in a few days.

"He will be fine, Edinburgh will fix him up so we can give him some words about his actions," Lisselle said. "We need to tell Rebecca and Damon. Actually, I do wonder if he knew of the fake heart."

"Do you think that you can carry on without me?" Colleen turned to Caden, then back to Lisselle at his nod. "I'd like to get out for a bit, and I could check in on Rebecca and Damon."

"If Nettie will step in, I believe we can carry on without you," Caden said with a sideways smile.

Nettie had never noticed how mischievous his eyes could look. It must be due to their current budding relationship. Or maybe he'd always been that way and she'd been too busy trying to hide her feelings to notice.

"I'll go with Colleen, there are things I'd like to check as well." Lisselle looked down at her trousers. "Let me change first. But I am going as me in a dress, not as the widow. Our covers are ruined now anyway." She vanished upstairs.

She came back with a bundle. "A change of clothing for Rebecca. We'll be back in a bit."

Nettie turned to Caden as they left. "I believe that leaves me to work on your project? You won't give me a hint?" There were a number of things going on right now, but she wasn't sure which this one was.

"Nope." Caden smiled and lead the way to the kitchen.

They were crossing the dining room when a sudden weakness slammed into Nettie. She tried to catch herself on the nearest chair but tumbled to the ground.

Caden ran back to her. "What happened? Are you hurt?"

Panic flooded Nettie's mind and she froze. "I can't breathe."

He dropped down beside her. "Your pulse is too fast, Take deep breaths." He lifted her up onto a chair.

The deep breathing worked, but she tried to hit his arm away. "You're going to pull out something."

"Hush, I'm fine. You're not. Do you need to get into your tank?"

"Yes, but I can't walk. This is worse than it's ever been." She held up her hand and the webbing was in full form. The scales on her hand and arm were almost fully outlined.

Caden slid his arm under hers and lifted up. "I'm getting

you there. Do you need me to carry you?"

"No, I'm fine." She buckled as soon as she tried standing.

"That would be a yes." He grunted a bit as he picked her up but he stayed steady. "Lisselle gave me special, state of the art bandages. I'm fine."

"I hadn't said anything." Nettie dropped her head to his shoulder, she was just so tired.

"You flinched like you were trying to climb out of my arms." He carried her to the tank room. At the base of the stairs he gently swung her down, keeping his arm around her. "Not really safe to carry you up the steps. Sorry about ruining more clothes, but you're looking worse, we need you in the water now." He started working them both up the stairs.

"Agreed." Like the other times she'd waited too long, the smell of the salt water in her tank was calling to her. But she was too weak to get there on her own.

They made it to the top platform and Caden held her while she slid into the water. She dropped down to get fully submerged, then came back to the top.

Caden was sitting on the platform. "Better?"

"Yes, still weak though." Her dress was extremely uncomfortable in the water. "Could you get my swimwear? It's lying on my bed."

"Anything else?" Caden was already at the bottom of the stairs.

"Water." Being in the water was helping, but, like the first attack, she was incredibly thirsty.

"Be right back." Caden ran out of the tank room.

Nettie swam a bit to work out the shakes. Being alone with Caden would have been romantic, if she wasn't in the process of turning into some sort of sea life.

Caden came back with the swim dress and a pitcher of water. He sat them both on the platform and started to sit down, then caught himself and turned red.

"I'm sorry, you probably want to change clothes. Ring your bell when you're done." He quickly left the room.

Nettie quickly changed and left her wet clothing on the edge of the tank. The swim dress was not as comfortable as the swim suit with a separate bottom, but it felt much better than her water soaked dress had. She made sure she was presentable, finished the water, and then rang the bell.

"Better now?" Caden stuck his head in. "Do you need more water?"

"I'm fine for now, thank you. We need to talk about this though." She held up her hand. "I'm not sure what there is between us, but it's not going to work if this gets worse." She gasped as she recalled he and Homer had been attacked as well. There had been so many things going on. "How are your injuries? Where the suckers got you? Let me see your arms." Her situation was extremely unfortunate, but it could kill Caden and Homer.

Caden rolled back his sleeve to show smooth skin with no marks at all from the suckers. "Lisselle made a solution out of something in your blood. They have vanished, and the last blood test I had this morning showed that I'm fine. So is Homer. Lisselle can't clear it out of your blood yet, but she can help others thanks to you."

"But I'm not able to heal myself. This is who I am now," Nettie said. "How can you be involved with a woman who has to spend her nights in a tank of water? And once Edinburgh finds out, they'll take me away, and no one will see me. I'll just be a subject to study." Nettie was a logical and steady person, she didn't feel either right now.

"Are you crying?" Caden leaned as close as he could without falling in the tank.

"No." Nettie turned away at first, then moved closer to him. She felt so alone right now. This was not like her at all. "Yes. It seems so hopeless. I've overcome much, but I don't know the way out of this." Caden took her in his arms and she sobbed into his shoulder. "This is very unprofessional."

"It's very human," he said. "No matter what you are, you are still human."

"But look!" Nettie was full sobbing now as she held up her webbed and scaled hand. She hadn't cried this hard since her father died when she was five. But it was too much.

Caden took her hand, inspecting the webbing and the scales, then kissed it. "It is a lovely color, you know. And the webbing and scales are still part of you. I will stand by you no matter what you become. And you know we will all fight to keep you from being locked up. Besides, now that we know there are sentient species of human off chutes who are roaming the water, what's better than being the first underwater agent?"

Nettie smiled and wiped her tears. Then she kissed Caden slowly. If she were going to have a break down, at least this was a nice way to recover. "Thank you, but technically Reaves might be the first. He had already started the process of becoming an agent before I was transformed. But I agree, having agents who can go under water will be handy in building a relationship with the merpeople."

"And I will be the liaison to the sea agents." He held her face. "You are an amazing woman, no matter what you become."

"I believe you said that already, or something of the sort. But I don't mind hearing it."

The front door and the sound of voices brought an end to their solitude. Not a romantic time per se, but his support meant more to her than anything else that he could have said or done. To completely breakdown, both emotionally and physically, in front of someone, and have them lift you up and still respect you was value beyond any time spent murmuring sweet nothings.

"You changed early?" Lisselle asked as she came in with

Colleen right behind. "Or you had no choice." She added and nodded to the clothes draped over the rim of the tank.

"She collapsed right after you left," Caden said. "Sorry, I should have let you tell them." The tone of his voice said he was going to make certain they knew.

"I wouldn't say collapsed…fine, yes, I did collapse. Pretty much folded to the ground in the dining room." She'd changed her story at the look in Caden's eyes. He would support her and protect her, but not if it was something that could endanger her. "I went fishy extremely suddenly and very thoroughly." She held up her hand to show the webbing and the tiny scales. "My condition seems to be getting worse."

"You don't know that," Caden said. "Maybe exposure to the merperson, the Flinking, who was pretending to be Damon increased your reaction tonight. You did touch him?"

Lisselle laughed. "Sometimes I forget that you are more than just a handsome face and brute force, Caden. He has a good point. I read your brief, you carried the merperson to your carriage. There could have been something that your physiology responded to."

Colleen nodded. "Don't give up yet, you'll be right as rain soon. Now if you will excuse me, I have dinner to prepare." She gave a smile and whistled as she left.

"I will hope you are correct, and I won't give up yet. Colleen seems happy."

"She is still tickled about Mathlin," Lisselle said. "I don't know what will become of them once this is over, or if his Atlantian friend can be removed. But after all these years, having that mystery solved is a blessing. Is there anything else? Nettie looks upset."

Caden shook his head. "You know stubborn people, they don't like their body messing with them. She was annoyed at her body for collapsing before she was ready for it. Everything is fine."

Nettie squeezed his arm in thanks. He would tell others about any physical issues she had in order to save her, but her emotional breakdown didn't need to be shared.

"As long as you are certain. Since it's only the four of us, maybe Colleen won't mind joining us for dinner in here. I will see if that is acceptable and then go change."

"How is Damon? How did he take Gaston's collapse?"

"He's recovering well. The injury to his head was not as bad as we thought, and although the knife caused some damage it was far less than we feared. Rebecca quickly swapped out Agent Evans the male for Agent Rhys the female and she will be staying the night. Although, had she stayed male, I wouldn't have had to commandeer the room next to Damon's in the name of the Queen. They were not about to allow an unmarried woman, agent or no, to share a room with a man."

"How much did he already know about Gaston's fake heart?" Nettie wasn't happy that he'd kept such a secret for so long.

"He knew, but Gaston never told him it needed to be replaced. I believe Mathlin, in this case, over Gaston. Of course Damon immediately wanted to go chasing after Gaston in Edinburgh. Rebecca and I convinced him otherwise. He wasn't happy about Gaston's duplicity either." She nodded to them and went to change back into her trousers.

"Thank you for not letting on about my breakdown," Nettie said once they were alone again.

"I'm here for you, never forget that. I'd better go see to the set up if we're dining in here." He gave her a quick kiss on the head, then went down the stairs and left.

Normally Nettie enjoyed being alone with her thoughts, but these recent ones were disturbing enough that she'd prefer being in a room full of strangers. The tank wasn't long enough for any sort of a real swim, but she found herself swim-pacing as she tried to work through her thoughts.

It was more than her sudden collapse, although that was vexing enough in its own right. She'd have to work with Lisselle in the morning to see what had changed and if there were a way to use whatever she helped Caden and Homer with on her.

There was something else that was throwing her off mentally. She'd never been one for introspection into her own feelings, but she was having an issue with her mindset. She felt odd, like she didn't belong.

She didn't get too far in her mental discussion with herself when the front door slammed open. No gear guns were around, but she still had her bell if she needed to contact someone.

The running feet paused at the dining room, then kept coming.

"Nettie!" Rebecca looked wild as she ran into the tank room, as if she'd run through people's hedges the entire way from the hospital. "Thank goodness, you're okay." She charged up the stairs and pulled Nettie's hand. "You are all right, yes?" She sat down at the edge of the platform, still holding Nettie's hand.

"I'm fine, why are you here?" Nettie wanted her hand back, but Rebecca was extremely upset.

"I had another vision. You were there, you'd gone even fishier. I am sorry to say you were dying. Out in the open water, you were dying. And I couldn't help you because I couldn't get there." She pulled harder on Nettie's hand as tears ran down her face. "I could see you, as clearly as now, you were being killed by the other merpeople. *I couldn't save you.* You must promise me, you will not go into the ocean until this fish issue has been reversed."

"I have no intention of going into the ocean," Nettie

said, but she felt the lie behind her words. Each time she changed, the call of the ocean tugged harder. But she certainly wasn't going to admit that to Rebecca right now. "Not all of your visions have come true, most have not. We never died in a fireball during a snow storm outside of the morgue, did we?" She smiled but Rebecca wouldn't share it.

"No, but that doesn't mean that other visions I have won't happen. A few have come true. And that one didn't because we changed the actions and we were not working there during winter when it snowed."

Nettie could tell Rebecca just came up with that idea, but she looked proud of the reasoning, so she wasn't going to argue. "I will stay away from the ocean whenever possible." Nettie squeezed Rebecca's hand. "But I do want you to realize that even Lisselle doesn't understand completely how your visions work. Your last one was of the past, which is wildly unheard of for clairvoyants. There might be more at work in your psyche than you know."

"I know what I felt, Nettie Jones. I felt you losing a battle you were not meant to fight. You need to stay out of the ocean." She stared at Nettie intently.

"I will do my best. What type of battle was it? The more details you give me the better chance of me avoiding it." Rebecca's fear was practically rolling off of her, and Nettie felt she had to do something to calm her down.

"You were in the water, I couldn't see you closely, but you were there. A large underwater building was behind you. You were surrounded by merpeople and a merman with jet black hair ran you through with a long pike." She started shaking again. "He watched you die." Rebecca pulled her hand free from Nettie's to grab her head as pain appeared on her face. Then she reached over again and pulled Nettie closer. "It was this."

Wild images hit Nettie's mind and at first she couldn't

sort them. Then she realized they were how the world would look under water. There were merpeople around her, chanting something, they'd been keeping her from escaping, and she was weak. A dark haired merman came forward with a hand extended, as if to help her. Even as her mind screamed a warning, his other hand stabbed forward and a horrible pain cut through her stomach. Blood drifted around her and she felt herself dying.

"No! Nettie! Snap out of it!" Rebecca yelled as she shook Nettie out of the vision. "Breathe!"

Nettie's eyes popped open and she gasped for air. The way her heart was pounding, she wondered how long she'd been holding her breath.

"I wanted you to understand the danger, not go into it, and die!"

"See here now, what's going on, and who's dying?" Lisselle had changed and come back in with Caden directly behind her. "And when did you get here?"

Rebecca wiped her eyes. "I had a vision while at the hospital, I had to come back here." Then she recounted the entire thing while Nettie tried to get her heart rate back to normal.

Caden came up the stairs and took one of Nettie's hands. "Are you okay?"

"I will be," Nettie said. "I know that Rebecca didn't plan on pulling me along quite that strongly, but that is as close to dying as I want to get for a very long time."

"Well, we now know Nettie has to stay out of the ocean. When Reaves comes back, we can see what he's planned for ways to get the fight down to the merpeople without her." Caden didn't look comfortable sitting on the edge of the platform as he was, it really wasn't a lot of room for two people to sit, and he also didn't look like he was moving.

"It would be better if we *all* stay out of the ocean," Lisselle said. "Even before this, Nettie wouldn't have fared well, and the rest of us definitely wouldn't, regardless of what Reaves has invented. We can't count on his people in this, we need to keep it out of the water."

"Might I have a say? Let me rephrase that, I will be having a say," Nettie lifted herself as far out of the water as was comfortable. "I believe Rebecca, I felt that vision just as real as I feel being here right now. But I also know that risks will be needed to stop this. We need to know what the merpeople's plans are, and if that means I have to go into the ocean, I will go. But, I know what I felt, and I also know that I can't breathe under water enough to get me that deep."

Rebecca looked hopeful. "Then it might be far in the future." She grabbed Nettie in a hug. "I am so sorry I dragged you into such a deep vision, but now we know what to look for. It could be weeks before it happens, we can change it."

Nettie looked to Lisselle over Rebecca's shoulder. Yes, she couldn't hold her breath long enough to have dived that far—yet. But Nettie's changes were picking up speed. Lisselle gave a slight frown, but Caden looked ready to believe the same way Rebecca did. Sometimes not knowing the truth was easier. Not to mention, there was a chance they could be right.

"What's all this, are we eating in here?" Colleen looked into the room. "I've got plenty of food."

Caden got down the stairs first. "Sorry, I was going to set things up. Rebecca, can you help me move things around?"

They quickly got a small dining area set up and soon everyone was eating. Nettie kept nudging the conversation to lighter subjects, history of the area, the castle in Conwy, anything but the merpeople. Lisselle looked like she noticed what Nettie was doing and started adding to it.

Rebecca's vision was still haunting Nettie's thoughts,

and she needed to gain her bearings before she faced it. Between that and her meltdown over the change, she was having a most unusually emotional day.

Lisselle had projects for everyone, although Rebecca quickly went back to the hospital with promises of meeting Nettie for a nice long talk after breakfast the next day.

Nettie jotted down any tiny details she could about elements of the day that could have led to her quicker decline into fishdom this evening. And more specifics about Rebecca's vision and her own view of it than she had been comfortable speaking out loud. The lights in the house were out, except for the two in her room, when Nettie finally put down her pen and paper and crawled into her hammock. She was able to control the larger light from her tank, but always left the smaller one on in case she had to leave the tank at night. Things secured, she drifted off to sleep.

Rebecca's vision incorporated itself into her nightmares, but it couldn't go beyond the snippet she'd experienced with Rebecca. She couldn't see what led to the attack, nor much about the merpeople around her. After numerous times being stabbed, she finally fought to awaken.

Her hands were shaking. And fully covered in scales. She tried taking a deep breath, but the air felt thin. She sank to the bottom of her tank…and breathed. Like breathing air, but also odd and thin. Panic hit for a moment as the vision came back. But knowing what would happen meant she could change it. Hopefully. A wave of pain hit her muscles. She needed to be out of this tank, but not on land.

She went back to the surface, again the air felt thin and now it seemed tinged with metal. There was no time to explain to anyone, she needed to get into the ocean, into true salt water, now. It was literally as strong of a need as breathing.

Climbing out of the tank was painful and slow. But the

time in the salt water had strengthened her and the need for the ocean kept her going. Hobbling, she quietly left the house, there was enough of the moon showing through the clouds to see the water, but her heightened instincts would have led her there without sight.

She stumbled into the water, relief and strength spreading through her muscles the deeper she went. She started swimming out further.

"Nettie! What are you doing? Come back!" Caden had followed her to beach, he ran directly into the water.

Nettie's heart broke but she knew she couldn't go back. The urge to be in the water, to be fully a part of it, was too strong.

She turned away from him and kept swimming, diving deeper as she went. There was such a glorious sense of freedom in the water. She could move with ease, even breathe without the awkward feeling from inside the tank. She gasped and put her hands to her neck, Small gills were now there. She swam to the surface to tell Caden to go back.

He was a strong swimmer, but something was pulling him under. He was quite a bit behind her, and he went under twice. He kept coming toward her though.

Nettie swam back to him. She couldn't be on land anymore, but he shouldn't die because he didn't understand that.

As she got closer, tentacles swarmed out of the water and engulfed Caden. Strong swimmer or not, he wasn't coming back up this time. She dove deep, seeing an octopus-like merman pulling Caden to his death.

Her blood went hot and her fangs dropped into place as she charged forward and attacked the merman. "Let him go!" Talking underwater was odd, but felt natural. The octopus man hung on tighter to Caden but stopped his decent. Nettie was on him and held her fangs over his throat.

"I will rip your throat out and let the crabs and sharks feed on you!"

"You're one of us." The merman snarled, he didn't release Caden.

"I am *me*. Let. Him. Go."

Caden was released but he was already unconscious. Nettie punched the octopus man, grabbed Caden, and tore to the surface.

She stayed in the water as she worked on squeezing the water out of Caden's lungs. He finally coughed and spat more out, then tried fighting his way free of her.

"It's me." Nettie spun him around to see her.

"You have to come back to shore. Rebecca's vision could happen. You can't be in the ocean." There was a terror in his eyes that she'd never seen before.

Nettie looked into his eyes and gave him a gentle kiss. "I can't leave." She pulled away and lifted her lower body. Where she'd had legs, she now had a tail. It was quite lovely actually, with frills and a light blue-green color. The transition must have happened while she was trying to free Caden, she honestly hadn't felt it. "I don't think I can come back from this." She flapped her tail in and out of the water. It was an odd sensation, but it also felt right.

"You have to. We need you. If that vision comes true, you'll die." He paused, "I need you."

"I can change the future. I have to. I don't have a choice. How can I come back to land? I don't have legs anymore, Caden. Are you going to keep me like a giant pet fish? Live in that tank? Then what, send me and my tank back to London?" She flicked her tail. "I'll take you back as far as I can, you need to go back to land. Tell the others that I will miss them. Make sure Rebecca knows that I will respect the vision and will make sure it doesn't happen."

"You might have accepted this, but I haven't. I will find

a way to get you back, I'm not letting you go." He looked ready to say more, then turned and slowly swam toward shore.

She stayed a bit behind him, she didn't think any of the merpeople would be up to fighting her right now, she was probably the only vampiric mermaid in the ocean, but better to not take chances. Part of her heart broke when Caden climbed out of the water and slowly turned.

She waved, he didn't. Caden shook his head and walked away from the beach.

She watched until he was out of sight, then turned and dove as deep as she could. Somehow she knew that even when the sun rose, she would still be the mermaid she was.

CHAPTER TWENTY-FIVE

NETTIE FOUND A NICE ROCK at the bottom of the water to sit on. The tail was going to take some getting used to, but after a few attempts she was comfortable.

Two merpeople swam her way, one was the tentacled one who tried to kill Caden. He pointed her out to a male with a tail like hers. They started swimming closer so she snarled and bared her fangs. This situation might or might not be their fault, but it wasn't making her happy, nor had the attempt on Caden's life. She'd left everything she knew, a man she very likely was falling in love with, and was heading toward a possible vision in which she died. She was *not* in a good mood.

The mermen backed off and gave her a wide berth as they went out into the open ocean.

She needed to think, everything had happened so fast. She had to assume this was her life now, and she needed to figure out what to do about it.

All indications were that the Flinkings held no love for humans. And now she was in a position to find out why. She couldn't go back on land, but she knew that her friends wouldn't abandon her. And she believed Caden, he was a stubborn man. But the evidence was all in place that there was going to be fight one way or another—those on land would be involved whether they wanted to or not. Had emotions not been so rampant, she would have told Caden to send someone back to the beach tomorrow so she could establish a meeting routine. She might not be able to go on land anymore, but she could still work for the Society.

She needed to find a spot where the Flinkings wouldn't notice and that would be safe for Lisselle or someone to meet with her. Drat, she doubted they had invented underwater paper and writing implements. Then again, look at all that the Atlantians had invented, paper that would work under water wouldn't be that hard at all. She'd need to reach out to the Atlantians as well. Meeting with Reaves in the waters here with the Flinkings would be risky, but he could be extremely helpful.

Nettie pondered her options. Although the test hadn't been completely validated, it did appear that she was turning into an Atlantian, as opposed to a Flinking; even in the vision, her blood had been red not green. Unfortunately, judging by her current situation, she was one of the sea-only ones. She would still hold on to hope that her condition could be reversed at some point. Gaston might be in Edinburgh, but he was still one of their best minds, and once he recovered, she knew he'd do anything he could to solve this.

Until then, she had to do what she could to prevent all-out war.

The local merpeople had to know who she was, even though the ones here hadn't infected her, they were clearly of the same group. But they had been exposed to traitor agents before. The evidence Frilin provided indicated to Lisselle and Gaston that Agent McGrady had either been converted by them or went willingly to their side. Lisselle had gotten more information that it appeared he had been trying to build a connection between the vampires and the merpeople. One that fell apart when the vampire-alien alliance crumbled and McGrady died.

She needed to pass herself off as a traitor to the Society and an asset for their side. Her tail swayed as she thought.

An interesting feeling and phenomenon. It wasn't deliberate, and once she noticed it she stopped.

"Did they abandon you?" The voice behind her was soft and female. And Nettie hadn't heard her swim up at all. She was going to have to work on developing more awareness of her surroundings down here.

Nettie turned with a sad look. She needed a way in and this might be it. The woman before her was a mermaid, one with a tail more like a shark than Nettie's frilly thing, but still very becoming. Her long deep black hair was caught up in a number of braids and twists.

"Yes. They promised to help me, but once the change set in, they betrayed me. They were going to use me for study."

The mermaid's dark eyes narrowed. "I thought you rescued one of them?"

"He was the only one who cared. But even he couldn't protect me against the others. I will protect those who protect me." Nettie let her fangs drop into place and the mermaid swam backwards a bit.

"So, you really are a vam-pire? That is the term, yes?" The odd manner in which she said vampire and her wanting clarification confirmed that while the Atlantians have been watching humans for decades, the Flinkings had not.

"Yes. I suppose I am the first one of your people with fangs. Actually, your people are now my people."

"My name is Lshia, what is yours?" The tone was friendly and conversational, but there was a calculating look in her eyes. Nettie might be of value, and Lshia was determining how much.

"I am Nettie."

Lshia swam closer and dropped her voice. "I heard you threatened to rip out Jashion's throat? Is that true? Could you do that?"

"If he was the one trying to drown my human friend, then yes on both counts. I can, and I would have, had he not let him go. Nothing against your friend personally, but as I said, I protect those who are on my side." It was a balancing act, being fierce enough to make others fear her, but make sure they believed that she would be on their side if they supported her.

The smile the other woman gave her confirmed Nettie's thoughts that there was no offer of friendship in her reaching out to Nettie. She was looking for an ally and she believed she'd found one. "Oh, he is not my friend, I would have been happy had you followed through with your threat. But he is the right fin to my brother, and killing him would have cost you a place to live. The ocean can be a scary place without friends. The Atlantians will kill you on sight once they know what you are. We can protect you."

Nettie retracted her fangs and gave a small smile. "I believe I will like being around your people, Lshia."

"Come this way, I will introduce you to my brother," she paused. "He is the second in line to rule, and always looking for new alliances."

Nettie paused at that, but kept her face smiling and neutral.

They swam in silence for a while, which gave Nettie time to adjust to the swimming process, it was far easier than she'd believed, most likely due to the strong tail she now had. She also had a chance to study the ocean. The colors and types of plants and fish were amazing.

Lshia's hair did give her pause. The color was very much like that of the merman who killed her in Rebecca's vision. Was her brother the one who did it? She would have to be prepared for him if he were.

After about ten minutes, Lshia stopped by a cave. Closer examination showed it was more made than natural. "This is my home, I prefer living a bit further out from the center of our village. While your clothing is unique, it will stand out even more than your fangs." She waved her hand to encompass Nettie's swim dress. "I can give you proper clothing so you blend in better. Follow me."

The cave was far roomier than the outside would imply. Little touches like shells and carvings made it almost homey. Nettie studied what had been done. If she was destined to a life under the waves, she was going to make it as pleasant as possible.

Lshia's garment was tighter than Nettie's swim dress, it covered everything but also allowed for freedom of movement. The fabric was far more vibrant than the current land fashions, and had small stones and shells woven into it. Lshia tilted her head as she studied Nettie for a few moments, then flicked her tail and vanished down the hallway. She came back a moment later with a lovely swath of green and gold fabric.

Nettie accepted it, but couldn't figure out where to start. The garment on Lshia looked to be a shirt with a long trailing bit that went half-way down her tail, but obviously, it was like this long piece of fabric in her hands. "I hate to sound ungrateful, but how does this work?"

Lshia's laugh was clear, like sea bells. "I will show you over your human outfit, then you can go back to my room and change."

It took a few tries before Nettie felt comfortable enough to go to the bedroom and try it herself without her swim dress. The room was clearly a bedroom, but there wasn't a bed as she would know it, but rather a long canoe type thing filled with soft fabrics. Interesting. She quickly changed, tugging a few times to make certain the shirt wrap would hold, it folded down to half way down her tail and looked stable, then she swam back to the front room.

"You look wonderful," Lshia said as she swam around Nettie. "But let's see what we can do to control this wild hair." A few minutes later and Nettie's hair was pulled into a long and twisted braid that hit past her shoulder blades.

"Thank you, I feel far more comfortable now."

"You look like you belong. Now don't worry, my brother holds power, but he isn't a tyrant like the Atlantian rulers."

Nettie swam alongside her as they continued the way they'd been going before the detour.

"It is truly lovely here, how long have your people been in these waters?"

Lshia came out of her thoughts with a start. "We've had an outpost here for generations. But most of us relocated here a year ago. We used to be further south, but the Atlantians chased us out. This is a better location for our plans actually, far fewer of those dratted humans up here." She paused and looked over her shoulder. "I do hope that doesn't offend you, but humans are not liked by our people."

"I was never just a human, they judged me because of my vampire status. I was never really one of them." Nettie put as much resentment as she could into her voice. For this to work, she needed to make sure they believed she disliked the land dwellers as much as they did.

"I wondered about that. Do you really drink the blood of your victims?" Most humans would have been too embarrassed to ask that, but if the merpeople were all like Lshia they had no such social quandaries.

"I do not," Nettie said as they approached a ship that had recently sunk. She recognized it almost immediately, the fisherman's boat that exploded. "I could, of course, if I needed to. But I find the concept off-putting. I am also stronger and faster than humans, another thing they dislike." She paused after they passed the boat. "I saw this boat, the humans tried to get me on it to save someone, but I almost died because of their actions."

"That was us, Sorry that the humans put you in harm's way. The ones on that boat were already dead and gone by the time you went onboard. I know you wouldn't have meant to, but you changed its direction while trying to get off. It was supposed to crash into their dock. Now that I know you, I will explain the mistake to my brother."

"Had those humans hurt your people?" Nettie really wanted to ask many questions about the boat and the three men who'd died. But too many questions could imply she was more concerned about the people in the boat than what threat they were to the Flinkings.

"They had destroyed a sacred fishing ground. We might not have been back here for long, but our ancestors lived here long ago. We sent one of the seaweres to warn them, but they destroyed it, then kept returning to our grounds. It was my brother's idea to load the boat with stolen fuel and crash it." She gave another one of her shark-like smiles, then returned to swimming.

Nettie was definitely going to have to warn the others. The maps that Homer had found quite possibly lead to the same sacred spots that cost the fishermen their lives. From what she'd seen of Lshia so far, she doubted if the locations were actually sacred—most likely they had worth of some kind.

Nettie spotted signs of many cave homes as they continued their swim. Once she knew what to look for they were easy to spot, but had she been swimming through on her own she probably wouldn't have guessed what they were. Just ahead of them was a huge pile of stones, the type used to build the cave homes, and obviously gathered elsewhere. Directly beyond that was a massive building, one that showed that as they'd been swimming out they'd also been swimming deeper. It looked to be at least three stories high and the sun playing on the water above them was quite a ways up. And there was no way she would not recognize it—that was the building that was in the background of Rebecca's vision. This was definitely the place.

On some base level, she didn't feel that this was the right time, but nevertheless, she would be aware of her surroundings. Especially when she met Lshia's brother. Nettie had a brief moment of panic as her mind caught up with how deep they were—then logic kicked in and reminded her that this was her domain now. Her body was built for this. It had forced her into this. She could handle herself and survive down here.

The huge structure became more palace like as they swam closer and more Flinkings were in the area. Nettie had seen some in the distance on their way here, but there were dozens of them going about daily business in the area outside the palace.

"It is overwhelming, isn't it? It's not as grand as the Atlantians, but we did ours without slave labor."

CHAPTER TWENTY-SIX

"THE ATLANTIANS HAVE SLAVES?" REAVES hadn't said anything of the sort, and his mother didn't seem the type to maintain slaves, but she knew little of any of the sea people really.

"They *had* slaves. You'll learn more from our teachers as we welcome you into our society. But we were slaves of the Atlantians for centuries. We fought our way to independence and that is why they are fighting us."

That definitely didn't go with what Nettie understood of the Atlantians, but she nodded sadly and kept her thoughts to herself. Lshia was telling her important things, and would stop if she realized how crucial they were to Nettie, and why.

"I am glad your—our—people fought free. I wouldn't have liked to have been a slave."

"I am glad you have joined us, however you came. Now let's go find my brother."

They swam past a dozen or so merpeople, Lshia nodding to only a few. Nettie noticed that the ones she nodded too seemed more prosperous than the ones she ignored. Obviously, a type of class system existed down here as well.

Most of the men had bare chests, and while a few were in good shape, most were not. Or her judgement was clouded by Caden. She let out a long breath as the tension at the thought of him and what they could have had flowed through her. She would grieve that relationship later, right now surviving, and stopping a war, was more important.

The palace looked like something from the land from a distance, but up close it was clear the builders were not human and it was designed for beings of various sizes who swam. The Flinkings were definitely multi subspecies, all vaguely humanistic, but a few were almost as round as Nettie was tall.

There were no doors or windows to the palace, just open portals to swim through, although there were two guards standing with wicked looking pikes outside of the main entrance. They briefly nodded to Lshia.

"This is an honored guest who my brother will be pleased to meet."

The guards turned back to watching the rest of the area in front of the palace and Lshia lead them through.

"Is it truly that dangerous here? I had hoped I was free of the fear I had on the surface." She didn't have to fake her discomfort much. The weapons used by the black-haired merman looked like a shorter version of the large pikes they'd just passed. A quick glance revealed that none of the other entrances had guards.

"It's not dangerous really, at least not for us. But we are at war with much of the world around us. And once the humans realize what we've been doing, they will try to fight back." She led them down a narrow corridor. "We need to be ready, and if the Atlantians decide to come up here—they will be in for some rude surprises." She paused in front of a large door and turned to Nettie and adjusted her shirt wrap and made tiny touches to her hair. "There now, pretty as a picture. I'd recommend going in strong, show your teeth. He will be the one to decide what your position within our community will be. Once the battle is won and the new power is in place, there will be changes." Her grin was supposed to be friendly. It wasn't. Nettie was a chip to ensure Lshia was in this new world and part of the power behind it.

Nettie steadied herself. Granted, where they were right now wasn't the same place the vision showed her being attacked in. But that didn't mean that it had to start there. Nettie wanted to ask more about proper decorum, but Lshia had already pushed open the heavy door.

The room would have looked at home in any well-established mansion in London. The furniture was designed to look like high-end parlors there as well. Considering Nettie's incident with trying to get comfortable sitting on a rock with her tail, she knew that few of the merpeople in that room would be happy sitting in those chairs. Clearly, there was some standard used to impress people.

A small group of merpeople were in the middle of the room, but they didn't turn around until a young man near the door officially, and very loudly, introduced them.

The merpeople turned, one had long dark hair, but didn't look like the one from her vision.

"Might I present my brother, Lord Aither. Brother, Doctor Nettie Jones. She's finally changed, as you foretold."

Nettie's shoulders relaxed as she realized it wasn't the man from the vision. She also let out a breath she hadn't realized she'd been holding. The merman that Lshia nodded to was a heavyset blond. His tail was also slightly shark-like, almost more like a combination of multiple sea beasts. Aside from that he had little in common with his sister.

"I am pleased to make your acquaintance." Nettie dropped her fangs briefly and gave a slight bow, she'd not figured out the political arrangement for the merpeople, but if he was second in charge, he must have some rank.

An object behind Aither caught Nettie's attention more than he did. Once she'd established that he definitely wasn't the person from Rebecca's vision, and none of his hangers-on were, she'd glanced around the room. A small, lightly glowing blue orb in a clear glass case against the back wall was definitely out of the ordinary.

Aither extended his hand to her, blocking her view of the object. "I am so pleased to meet you. We'd heard there was one of us coming forth from those on the land. There hasn't been a transition for years."

Nettie shook his hand, keeping enough pressure to remind him she wasn't a normal human. "Have there been others?"

"Yes, we get people who long to be with the sea, who don't want the normal life. We try to change them, but it doesn't usually work. Although, one of your people almost made it when we were still in the south. McGrady, he said his name was. Said he had vampires who would be on our side. Then he abandoned us." The glare in his eyes didn't bode well for McGrady if he'd still been alive.

Nettie wasn't too surprised to have confirmation of McGrady's betrayal. And this might be another way for her to get inside of what they were doing. "He was working against everyone, and he died. Many vampires also died because of his actions." Direct lies were difficult because maintaining them in stressful situations was almost always impossible. This wasn't a lie.

"I wondered if that had been the case." Aither nodded. "He had a sneaky way about him. Did you kill him? I heard you threatened Jashion."

Nettie held herself higher, not easy to do when one was holding a position while swimming. "I did not. McGrady died at other hands. And yes, I threatened Jashion. He was killing someone who had been supportive of me. As I told your sister, I defend those who help me."

"I like that. Tough, but fair. Will you have a problem fighting against the rest of your former companions?"

"No," she spat it out quickly. "They saw me as nothing but scientific fodder. As a scientist myself, I can understand it to a point. But they would have locked me up for the rest of my life."

Aither's eyes lit up. "You are a scientist? Perhaps we need you more than we knew." He turned and swam back to the orb against the wall. "We need to gather more of this material and make it work for us." He unlocked the case, then pulled out the orb.

It reminded Nettie of a fancier version of the crystal ball that charlatan fortune tellers used. But she was pretty sure none of them glowed like that.

Aither held the globe out to Nettie. "No one handles this but me, but I want you to be able to help us gather more. Hold out both of your hands."

Nettie did as she was told, noticing that the conversations around them had stopped. The globe felt heavier than she would have expected, and quite a bit cooler than the water around them. It wasn't a solid color but looked to be mottled—it almost looked like there was something moving inside of it. She'd need to study it more, but how she was going to without equipment she had no idea.

"What does it do?" She reluctantly handed it back to Aither. The fact he let her hold it was visibly shocking to the merpeople around them, she didn't wish to cause ill feelings.

Aither locked the orb back up and then turned back to her. "It gives us power. Our leader is back in the southern waters, trying to bring the last of our people here without the Atlantians stopping him. That orb allows us to tap into the old powers our ancestors left us. The ones who call themselves Atlantians are liars and thieves. We are the true descendants of the lost people from Atlantis. The orb allowed us to build quickly here, call to life the seaweres, and even copy human form."

Nettie nodded, hoping it looked like it was done in appreciation. In reality there were a lot of questions flying through her head. She needed to stay calm and not react to anything that could give her away. "Seaweres?"

"The beings who look covered in seaweed," Lshia said. "They are my specialty and move under our command. Neither they or the creatures that live in their fronds have much sentience, but they have a lot of anger." She looked far too pleased with herself.

"Those seaweres came from the people of Atlantis?"

"Not directly, but controlling things such as them was common a thousand years ago. The orb's powers let me do it."

Nettie fought down her reaction. This was the cause of a lot of deaths. She didn't think that kind of power in Lshia's hands was a good idea. Or in any of their hands. Once she was able to figure out what it was, and how they found it, she would have to find a way to destroy it.

Lshia continued, "We know there were once hundreds of them. If we can find more of them and learn better how to use them, we can defend ourselves against the humans and the Atlantians."

"That is really all we want, freedom to live as we wish," Aither said. "And *where* we wish." He acted as if his people were the victims, but the look on his face was as calculating as his sister's.

"You have that right. We all do. How long have your people been working on this? I've never seen or heard of anything like that orb." Now that she knew what it did, she wished she hadn't handed it over so quickly. In fact, she wanted nothing more than to grab it and flee. Whatever that thing was, it had far too much power if it was doing what they claimed.

"Our leader, Biethan, has known of them for a long while. He was the one who brought us out of our servitude to the Atlantians. He had our brightest people up here working on finding the orbs over fifteen years ago. They found a power of some sort, but a ship of humans got in their way." He shrugged. "They destroyed the humans, but in the fight, the scientists died as well. We found the orb and the remains. It doesn't do all that Biethan believed, some part of it is missing, but it's doing enough to get us where we need to be."

"No disrespect," the dark haired merman who'd been next to Aither the entire time said as he gave Nettie a sideways look. "But even though she looks like us, it was the orb that changed her. She is still human. Should she know our secrets and plans?"

Aither shook his head. "That is why you will always be below me. Nettie is an ally; no one can change her back, her people have betrayed her, and she is a scientist, which we need. Who else would be better to help us claim our rights both below and above?"

The dark merman nodded and tipped his head as he swam backwards a bit.

"Now that that is settled, does anyone else want to question my judgement? No? Very good. We need to get things moving here so when Biethan gets here we are ready for the next phase."

The hangers-on all disbursed, leaving Aither, Lshia, and Nettie alone in the large chamber. If Aither was the second in command, she wondered what Biethan's chambers looked like. Relics from dozens of land cultures adorned the walls, most small, many broken, but they all worked together to give a feeling of grandness.

Aither flittered his fingers after the departed merpeople. "It's so wearying having them hanging around all of the time, no wonder Biethan keeps going off on his own." He rubbed his hands together. "Now, I believe we have an empty home nearby, which Lshia can move you into. It's next to the laboratory. We do have some younger scientists who are working on the mystery of the orb. I believe that you will be able to show them the way in which studies are done."

He'd implied at first that he hadn't known that she was a scientist, but the more he spoke, the more Nettie believed that he had full knowledge of who she was.

Something outside grabbed his attention and he swam to a portal, then turned back with a frown. "Get settled, then we'll get you working on the orb." He dismissed them as he went back to his portal.

Nettie wanted to ask more questions, but Lshia shook her head. The mermaid looked concerned about something as she led them out.

"What's wrong?"

"Let's go inspect the house my brother gave you," Lshia lifted her voice loud enough that Nettie looked around to see who she was aiming it at. There were less merpeople around than when they went inside, but they all seemed focused on whatever task they were doing.

The black haired merman and a group of at least six others swam away quickly. Nettie noticed the long pikes they carried but turned and followed Lshia in silence.

The house they went into was a smaller version of Lshia's. But it would work as a place to live. It wasn't lost on Nettie that it was in the grouping of homes nearest the center of their community. Where she could be easily watched.

Lshia looked out the door before she shut it. "There is something going on, something that my brother has not seen fit to share with me." Her tail lashed as she scowled toward the direction of the palace.

"Do you know where they were going? The ones with the pikes?"

"Not specifically, but that was a fighting pod. They only go out like that on a big hunt, or to attack something." She turned back to Nettie. "There are no large schools coming through right now, so it is not a hunt."

"What could they be after?"

"Something to help my brother. I think he knows where to find more of the orbs, but not how to get them. He's up to something, something beyond declaring war on the humans and the Atlantians."

In Nettie's mind those were both huge things. "Is he trying to make a power grab? Those things happen with the humans regularly."

The violent tail twitch gave her the answer before Lshia responded. "I am just tired." She turned to Nettie and flashed a smile. "I am sure everything is fine. Biethan will be back soon, and things will settle down." The smile as she said their leader's name was the first real one Nettie had seen from her.

"Where did he go? Since my acceptance to your community only goes so far if your leader doesn't approve, I'm anxious to meet him." Aither had seemed too comfortable in his power, although he spoke of Biethan, Nettie wouldn't doubt some sort of political move was happening.

A slight frown crossed Lshia's face before it was chased down by another real smile. "He often goes off to find new things for us. He's been gone long this time, but it's hard work he's doing. Went down with ten of our bravest fighters, but they hope not to have to fight down there. Aither keeps in touch with him."

Nettie hadn't seen anything that looked like a Mudger, and while she wouldn't doubt if the Atlantians had something similar, she did doubt the Flinkings did. But Lshia seemed content that her brother had been in communication with their leader, and Nettie didn't want to upset her. Her own feelings were that Aither was either planning, or had planned, a coup.

"I look forward to meeting him." She made a show of inspecting the small house. Sufficient and furnished. She had a feeling most of the merpeople spent their time out swimming about.

"You will love him," Lshia's voice went up a bit. "He is brave and powerful."

Nettie didn't know if the feeling was mutual, but Lshia definitely had her eyes on Biethan.

Shouting from outside broke up their discussion. Lshia opened the door, slightly at first, then flung it completely open.

The shouting was coming from people as they swam into the open center area. The mermen who had taken off minutes before came back with a body in tow. Nettie's heart slammed into her throat when the face and hair came into view, it looked like Caden.

CHAPTER TWENTY-SEVEN

NETTIE ALMOST SWAM OUT THERE but then the ones surrounding him pulled back and she saw that the man was blond. And he wasn't a human, but a merman.

"Oh no! Warlan! Biethan will be upset at this, they were as close as brothers. Come with me, and stay close." Lshia swam to the center where everyone had gathered. Aither was there, and aside from not seeing the one who killed her in the vision, Nettie had a horrific feeling of déjà vu. The tension felt as Rebecca's vision had.

The group of hunters lay down the dead merman and Nettie got a good look at his face. It was the one Mathlin had trapped in his cave. The one who'd been freed by his people a few days ago. At first Nettie thought perhaps there had been damage done while he was in low water and he died after they freed him. That was until they turned him over and the bloody wounds became visible. Ones that would have only been caused by bullets.

Aither looked down at the body and slowly shook his head and lifted his voice so all gathered around could hear him. "Our kind are nothing but sport to the humans. They captured Warlan when he was doing nothing but gathering food. They kept him trapped, starving, exposed to the elements of their world. Then they killed him rather than let him come back to us."

Nettie couldn't figure out how that could have happened, he'd been alive when the merpeople took him back. Those wounds looked too fresh to have happened a few days ago either. And yes, guns were human, but the merpeople had demonstrated that at least some could go on land. They could have stolen a gun. A chill went down her spine as the yelling grew uglier. Aither or his people killed Warlan to blame his death on the humans.

And take down another one of Biethan's supporters. Nettie knew enough of strategy to know how bad this was. But there was no way she could tell anyone here.

"We need to destroy the humans now. Clear the land that surrounds us." The dark haired man from the meeting room yelled. He kept looking at Nettie and Lshia came forward to block his view.

"She is not human. She is one of us, and a powerful ally in our fight. Who saw Warlan's murder?" Lshia swam to the dead merman and passed her hand reverently across his face. "Might his eyes follow his killer forever," she said it in a singsong voice, and it was echoed by many of the merpeople around them.

But not by the ones who had brought him in, and not by a growing group behind them.

"No one saw it, the humans tortured him and left him to drift," the dark haired one said, then turned to Aither. "You feared this would happen. There have been others who have gone missing. The humans are slaughtering our people. We don't have time to wait for Biethan to return. Decide now."

Nettie didn't like the looks on the faces around them, but they weren't looking at her anymore.

"I do not want to take action in his stead, but it is true I have had no communications through the orb from Biethan in many days. We may have to take action without him."

Lshia shook her head. "We have to wait, you need more orbs."

"I failed to tell you, sister, that I have found a way to

extend the orb's power. And we have ways of cutting off the local humans from their fellows—thanks to a shipment of exploding missiles I had stolen from the Atlantians. And some friends who have been changed to explode rather than poison." He held up a glass box filled with sea urchins. "We can take this town and hold them until our vampire mermaid finds the rest of the orbs." His smile wasn't nice, and Nettie realized that while he might not think she was on the human's side, he also didn't think she was on their side.

She'd seen maps, cutting this part of the land off from the rest of Wales wouldn't be impossible with enough explosives on the roads and the train tracks, and more planted in the countryside—particularly if they were similar to the one they used against the mansion. And they could easily block any aid from the sea.

Merpeople were breaking up into muttering groups, but far more seemed in agreement than disagreement. Lshia was silent, but watched her brother carefully.

Nettie had to find a way to get this information back to Lisselle and the others, but she couldn't risk being caught. Her gathering of information might be the only thing to slow the Flinkings down. That and getting her hands on that orb again.

More shouting coming from behind the palace broke her out of her thoughts.

This time a group of ten mermen were bringing in a pair of alive and fighting fellow mermen.

"We found these two Atlantian spies."

They brought them both to Aither and dropped them.

Nettie choked as first one face then the other was turned out to the crowd. One was Reaves. He looked beaten, but not seriously injured. The second one, supposedly an Atlantian like Reaves, was the dark-haired merman from Rebecca's vision.

Nettie slowed her breathing and kept the anger and fear from calling up her vampire blood. How could the person who killed her in the vision be one of Reaves' people? Reaves scanned the crowd, keeping his glance upon her as short as he'd done with the rest of the crowd. Even if they knew Reaves was part of her group, there was no need to remind them.

"Kill them!" The chant started small, but grew quickly.

Aither held up one hand. "That is not our way. The humans kill without reason. The Atlantians as well. We have always had the Challenge. Three days locked up. Then a fight for each to determine if they are worthy of judgement." He scowled as a few started up the chant again. "It is our way. I speak in Biethan's absence. Take them both to the Rocks."

Nettie watched as they secured both Atlantians in tiny stone and metal cages. There would be little room to sit, let alone lie down.

"Come back into your house, there are too many people looking our way." Lshia swam past her into the home.

"They will fight without a court? Yes, they may be Atlantians, but there was no call as to what they were doing." Nettie was already mentally working on a way to get them free. Or at least Reaves. The other might be a companion of Reaves', but Nettie couldn't discount Rebecca's vision.

"If they survive their fights after three days of no food and no rest, then they get to state their case. We haven't had any actual court cases in years. Just being an Atlantian is enough for the Challenge."

"Or human," Nettie said.

"They will not go after you as long as you are on my brother's good side. He will show them your value." She swam toward the door. "I will have someone bring you food. I recommend that you stay inside your house this evening. I must have words with my brother." She was gone before Nettie could respond.

Nettie opened the door slightly and watched her swim toward the palace. There was also a small covered window in the house, and it had a better angle to see the Rocks so she shut the door and took over the window. Reaves went into the first one without a fight. The other fought back and was thrown in roughly. The metal gates slammed shut.

It was an awkward angle to study from, but Nettie studied the Rocks and, more importantly, the gates, until a knock came at her door. She opened it to find a thin merman with a metal covered bucket and plate. "Aither said to bring you food. Hope it doesn't shock your human sensibilities." He didn't snarl, but he also didn't wait to see if Nettie was ready for the food before he tossed it and swam off.

Nettie grabbed it and sat it on the table, then went back to her window. Reaves was in the cage closest to her, so she couldn't see the far end of the other one. An arm slid a wrapped parcel of something into the dark-haired merman's cage. Yet nothing into Reaves' cage. Since they weren't supposed to have food, that alone would have raised suspicion of the other merman.

The cage looked to be assembled crudely out of found parts, including standard hinges. Pinned hinges could be removed. Lift the door up, pull the pins and it opens on the hinge side.

Right in front of a guarded palace. Even waiting until nightfall wouldn't clear the area. She needed a distraction. Caden had always said explosions made the best distractions, but she couldn't see herself finding anything of that sort.

She studied the area around the palace and the cages for anything that might work. The shadow of the massive pile of rocks came into view. Moving a few of the larger ones near the bottom would bring down enough to cause a distraction. As long as she removed them from the side away from the front of the palace.

There was a little time before night, she noticed the darkness growing, but it was still an hour or so. She swam to the food and lifted the metal cage keeping the food inside. Raw fish and sea plants would not be her food of choice, but her transformed body felt otherwise and her stomach grumbled. "Well, I'm going to need all my strength to move those rocks, so we'll give it a try." It wasn't nearly as bad as she'd expected, or she was really that hungry, the food was gone in minutes.

A few hours later, the open area in front of the palace was empty. Nettie swam out her door and behind other houses so the guards wouldn't see her. She swam around the pile of rocks for a few minutes trying to gauge the best place to pull from. The bottom ones were almost as tall as her, they would cause the most destruction if removed.

She picked the biggest one and pulled. It rocked a bit, but nothing more. Taking a deep breath, she tried again. More shuffling, but not enough. Then she thought of when Caden had almost been killed. How she felt for that brief second when the murdered merman looked like him. The hot vampire blood was called forth and a red film covered her eyes. They would kill all she loved if she didn't move this rock.

Grabbing it again, she pulled back, rolling the boulder with her. It almost worked too well as the precariously balanced pile immediately started crashing. Nettie swam back behind the house closest to Reaves' cage and waited as the crashing caused people to come swimming out of their homes. Even the guards swam to the rocks as the pile grew lower as more crashed away.

Nettie darted to Reaves cage, lifted the grating with one hand, and pulled free the hinge pins. Luckily both were in poor shape as her muscles were starting to give out.

"What's happening?" Reaves swam forward.

"Jail break, come on, they'll be back."

Instead of following her, Reaves turned to the other cage. "Klyn too. I can't leave him to die." He started lifting up the grate as Nettie had but he needed two hands so he couldn't pull the pins.

Nettie shook her head, but swam over and pulled the pins. She'd didn't trust Klyn at all, but if they argued none of them were getting out.

Klyn nodded to her and Reaves lead the way out. They'd swam far enough from the compound that the yelling was distant, but still had a way to go before they reached shore.

"Wait up, they really did a number on my head." Klyn had been dropping further back as they swam.

Nettie tried to drop back as well, but the urge to get Reaves to shore pushed her on.

Klyn's injuries were clearly fake as he darted forward in a burst of speed, a small knife clutched in his hand as he swung for Reaves. Nettie grabbed his tail as he passed and slowed him down.

Reaves spun and blocked the blade and knocked it out of his hand. "Klyn! What are you doing? You're one of my mother's trusted advisors." Reaves grabbed the blade and sliced him to keep him back.

"I've been working for the true sea people, not the Atlantian dogs." A drift of green seeped out from the wound.

"A spy?" Reaves was stunned and lost the advantage he'd had of the blade. Nettie was still holding Klyn's tail, but he gave one sharp flick and she was flung into some rocks. Klyn darted forward and he and Reaves fought over the knife. Reaves took a slice to the ribs before Nettie could recover and swim back. Klyn was moving forward when she grabbed his tail again, this time bracing herself as she swung him as hard as she could. Both she and Reaves heard the crack as Klyn smacked into the rocks and crumbled to the sea floor.

Reaves started to swim to him, but Nettie blocked him. "No. The others will come and you're bleeding." She pulled on his arm and forced him back toward shore. The water was getting shallower when she let him go. "Tell the others what happened. I will find a way to leave messages for you."

"What? Come back to land with me, you can't stay here." Reaves pulled on her arm. His tail had already changed to legs.

"I can't change," Nettie said. "I can't."

"Try." He kept pulling her along, but she had to crawl on her hands with her tail behind her. No matter how hard she thought of it, her legs would not come back.

"I can't. Maybe it's my vampire blood, maybe the Egyptian, or maybe I'm the wrong type of mermaid. But you have to go. Now." She pulled free of his hand and swam away as fast as she could. There was no going back. Her legs were just not there anymore.

She heard shouting from the direction they'd left Klyn in, so she went around it and out into deeper water. If she swam far enough, she could get to the side where Mathlin had his cottage.

But she was too tired. The vampire strength was gone and she found herself swimming slower. Finding a secluded spot, she folded to the sea floor. A nap wasn't a good idea, but she couldn't go any further.

CHAPTER TWENTY-EIGHT

ROUGH BANDS CIRCLED HER AND pulled her out of her sleep.

"She's waking up!"

"Get the bag over her, her eyes went red before and she might have powers."

Fabric was roughly thrown over her head. Nettie hadn't recognized the first voice, but the second was Klyn. She hadn't killed him.

The ropes dragged her along, but she couldn't see anything because of the bag. A clanging sound came then she was thrown against a rock wall.

Aither's voice spoke. "We've repaired the gates, thank you for showing us their weakness. You have three days, then stand in Challenge." The gate slammed shut.

The seaweed ropes were to keep her contained as they captured her, and she was able to wiggle free once they'd locked the gate and she removed the bag. To see Klyn staring at her through the bars.

"I have claimed right of Challenge. I will take my time killing you, you will feel unimaginable pain before I let you die." He swam away awkwardly.

His tail seemed bent. She might not have killed him, but she'd injured him. Of course, after three days being locked in this cage with no food, he was probably still going to win their fight.

The days passed slowly. Merpeople would swim by, but once she looked at them they would dart off quickly.

Mocking the condemned wasn't as interesting if they were afraid of them. Nettie found that the lack of space was as bad, if not worse, than the lack of food. There was no way to get comfortable.

By the morning of the third day, she was ready to welcome death. Had she been a full vampire, the lack of food might have been remedied by attacking one of the others. But right now a small child could fight her off. She was weak and exhausted. The only thing that had kept her going was the hope that Reaves was able to get the information to the Society. That when Aither and the others made their attack, it would fail.

And that Caden would be safe.

Aither and another blond merman swam forward. The gate was opened and the second merman pulled her out and into the center of a crowd that had gathered. Good thing, as her tail was stiff from lack of use.

"I, Klyn, Challenge the human, Nettie, for crimes against our people and myself." He waved his arms to accent his words, he held the short pike she'd seen in Rebecca's vision in each hand, but he didn't move much. His tail must still be damaged.

"Do I get a weapon?" She got that out before the guard holding her smacked her hard.

"The Challenged do not speak unless they survive. They also don't get weapons."

Nettie focused on Klyn, trying to draw up any kind of vampire reserve. Some strength flowed, but it wouldn't be enough.

Everyone swam back from her and Klyn, and Aither raised his hand. "Begin."

Lshia was on the edge of the circle, but she swam away when Nettie looked over.

Klyn clearly was waiting for her to charge him, which was stupid even if she had been at full strength. She folded her arms but stayed in place. "Is your tail not working? It looks a bit withered." Maybe if she made him angry enough he'd forget his threat and kill her quickly.

Klyn swam forward but there was definitely a problem with his tail. It didn't offset her exhaustion though. He swung with both blades and she managed to knock one free before it sliced her. Her fangs dropped and she went for his throat.

He got the second blade up and stabbed hard but his unbalanced tail threw him off and he missed. He used his empty hand to grab her throat.

She tried bashing his arm but she was too weak. Her windpipe was being crushed. She felt him swing out with his blade. But then yelling came all around them and he released her throat.

"Rocks! Someone is throwing rocks on us!" Two of the guards had already been hit. But the rocks didn't look that large. They looked familiar though.

Nettie gathered all the energy she had left and swam behind the nearest house just as the rocks exploded. They weren't rocks, they were the depth charges that Homer, Caden, and Reaves had been working on in London. She'd venture to say there was at least one airship above them.

Klyn found her and attacked with his short blade. He didn't care if his people were under attack, he was going to kill her. The blade cut into the building behind her and stuck. Nettie swung out as hard as she could to push him away.

At the same moment a series of explosions took out the palace. A huge piece of debris smashed into Klyn and crushed him to the sea floor. Nettie didn't think he was coming back from that.

She kept away from any other Flinkings she could see and started swimming toward shore.

Lshia appeared before her. "I can't let you leave. You are

under challenge, you betrayed my people."

"Your own people betrayed you. They killed Biethan, you know that, right? Deep in your heart? Your brother and his people planned this take over."

"No." But her face betrayed her words and she crumbled. "Maybe you're right, but you are also betraying my people. Look what your people did to Warlan."

Nettie looked around, she could try to swim away, but in her state Lshia would catch her in seconds. "Human weapons killed him, but I doubt they pulled the trigger. I know that Warlan was freed by pike-carrying merpeople days ago. Would he have gone back to the humans without speaking to your brother?"

"No, he wouldn't have. I don't know what's going on, but if they killed Biethan…I won't stop you." She dropped her head and then moved out of the way.

Nettie started to go then spun back. "Come with me, there's no life for you here."

The shark grin was back. "There's no life for me out there either. This way maybe I can get some revenge for Biethan. Go. They're coming."

Nettie nodded and swam away. There was not really a friendship there, but an understanding. The explosions kept going but they were behind her now. She swam closer to the surface and smiled. A fleet of nine airships, led by Homer's, were using what she had to assume were the final version of the charges he, Reaves, and Caden had made. Judging from the results below they'd been extremely successful in their creations. Now Caden's comment about Colleen being an explosives expert made new sense.

"They worked pretty well, if I dare say so myself." Reaves' voice came from behind her.

Nettie spun. "Why are you here? You need to get out of this water. They will kill you."

"They are a bit busy right now, and you shouldn't be in

the water either, not to mention, someone had to aim the charges away from you. We also thought we had more time, so I had to signal an attack before we were completely in place." Three more Atlantians, very heavily armed, swam into place behind him.

"How did you communicate with airships?"

Reaves smiled and held out a mirror and an annoyed looking electric eel. "As long as I had energy I could send a code to Homer. Now we need to get you out of here."

Nettie shook her head. "You saw, I tried, and I can't change. Your mother said most of your people can't change."

"I know you can, come with me."

Nettie swore softly. "There's another reason, the orb. I have to get that." She couldn't believe she'd almost forgotten it. She'd seen Aither and his people flee the attack, but none of them had come from the palace, that didn't mean they wouldn't go back later on. She couldn't let that stay there.

"The what?"

"They have an Atlantian relic, an orb of power. That's how they advanced so quickly and could change what they looked like and go on land. They can't keep it."

"Come back and we can—"

"Reaves, I am your superior agent." She held up her hand. "Yes, declaring that you wished to join makes you under our ranking. I am ordering you to let me go."

"I am a royal, and you're in my domain. I am ordering you…to let us go with you." He didn't look happy but she'd take it. Truth be told, she might need his strength to get the orb back.

"As long as you understand the goal of this mission is getting that orb."

He took a deep breath, muttered Caden's name, and a few choice words, then nodded. "We follow her."

They swam back with two of the guards in the front. More than once one of the Atlantians would hold up his fist and lead a change of direction as one of the Flinkings came too close. The bombing had moved away from the palace and Nettie led them in through the rubble. It wasn't as bad as she'd expected but it still took more than a few minutes to find the orb. The glass case was shattered so she covered it in ruined material found in the rubble as best she could and tried to hand it to Reaves.

He and the guards looked terrified and kept their hands away from it.

"What? Take it and get it back to land."

"Do you know what that is? That's a spirit sphere. When our ancestors passed, the really powerful ones, hundreds of years old, their essence was placed in one of those to guard our people."

Nettie swallowed. Thiliantic had said he wanted to be left in peace to guard his people. Was he related to this orb? "Okay, we can work this out later. We need to get it out of here." She again tried to hand it to one of the Atlantians.

"Nettie, we can't touch it, not just because of it being sacred, but we can't. Only the owner of the orb, the being behind it can touch them. That you can is another indication of how different you are from us."

"Fine, get us out of here. We'll have to put it in something when we get to shore. I can't go on land."

Reaves looked ready to argue, shook his head, and nodded for his people to lead them out.

They got to the shore unmolested and the airships were widely spread out over the bay, but not dropping explosives anymore.

"Get a boat or something to drop this in."

Reaves nodded for his people to leave and they all walked out of the water, their tails turning to legs before they reached shoulder deep. "Nettie, you can change. I know you can. I can feel it here." He taped his chest. "You aren't like us, you are quite possibly the most unique being on the planet. But I know you can do this. Think of the people who love you. You need to do this." He took her hand and looked into her eyes. "Follow me. Don't look at the water. Just keep moving forward."

Nettie felt a coldness in her stomach. She wanted to believe. She needed to believe. Keeping her eyes on Reaves' face, they moved forward. The air felt warm on her face and shoulders and a gentle warmth came from the orb. And they kept moving. The sand felt rough on her feet. "Feet?!" Nettie almost dropped the orb as she looked down. Her legs and feet were there. She had no idea if the orb did it, or it just gave her the mental strength to make the change herself, but she really hoped it was the later. The clothing she wore didn't cover enough of her legs, but really wasn't that much shorter than her swim dress. Two of Reaves' men came running back in and handed Nettie a longer swim dress.

Reaves smiled. "Lisselle was ready. She knew we'd get you out."

She juggled the orb back and forth, finally letting Reaves drop the swim dress over her head. It looked ridiculous, and felt awkward, but she was covered, and walking.

A group of people were coming toward the shore and Rebecca started running toward her. Followed closely by Lisselle, Colleen, Damon, and Mathlin.

Rebecca hit her first, trying to hug her around the orb. "Oh, do put that down. You're back!"

"She can't put that down. But one of you might be able to hold it." Reaves stood back.

Lisselle came up and looked at the fabric bundle in Nettie hands. "Is it a bomb?"

Nettie watched as Mathlin came closer. It might be better to test her theory slower, but she had a feeling they didn't have enough time. She removed the wrapping.

Mathlin stepped forward, at first just interested. Then his eyes changed, becoming the icy blue when Thiliantic spoke. "You have my shell." It wasn't the authoritative voice from the other encounters, it was almost soft and confused.

"This was yours when you died, wasn't it?"

Mathlin/Thiliantic nodded. "Can I hold it?"

Nettie held it out to him as Reaves and his men looked on in a combination of fear and wonder.

Mathlin/Thiliantic took it and sighed. "I cannot go back inside, not yet. I lack the power right now." He looked up and his eyes stayed icy. "But I will. Thank you for bringing this to me." He held it close and kept looking at it.

"So is it over? Is that all? We won?" Rebecca still had one arm around Nettie.

Lisselle took the other side. "I don't know. Homer was sure of the explosive devices, but I doubt they will give up. You look terrible."

"It's been a difficult few days," Nettie said as she leaned on her friends. She'd have to work with Reaves as to how to control her changing, but she felt they could do it.

Homer's airship was almost directly over them and Caden was waving.

Nettie waved back. "Go land!" He looked ready to find a way off without landing.

Caden's laugh was a wonder to hear. A moment later pikes, shooting out of the water at a force no person would have, slammed into the balloon of Homer's airship and it started crashing.

"They've got launchers firing from the sea! Get the other ships up!" Reaves yelled.

Homer set off a horn as his airship crumbled into the shallow water and the other airships all started lifting higher.

They weren't just aiming at the ships. Arrows came out of the water, striking one of Reaves' men in the chest. Everyone moved back as a line of fifteen Flinkings came out of the water. All were wearing odd round globes over their heads and armed with what almost looked like old fashioned crossbows.

One aimed at Nettie and Rebecca, but Rebecca and Lisselle were armed with gear guns and fired. There was no way to determine who hit him, but the merman fell back into the water.

Nettie dropped to the ground and hid behind a short wall. Weak and unarmed, she was too much of a target. Mathlin dropped down next to her.

"You brought this. Who took it?"

She pointed to the Flinkings as more came out of the water, all armed. Everyone on land had taken cover, but the odds were not in the humans' favor. "They took you from it, they have been using its powers to destroy others."

Mathlin was silent for a moment, then nodded. "I will need you to stand with me. Hold my shell, and hang on to this form's arm."

Her friends were trapped and the other airships couldn't come down to help. More Flinkings were heading to Homer's crashed airship. She nodded.

They both rose quickly, Mathlin pulling her to her feet as he shoved the orb into her arms. She grabbed his shoulder and held on as lightning crackled through him. His eyes flared and an arc of what looked like an electrical charge darted from him to each one of the Flinkings as more came out of the water. A charge went out even further into the water. "Do not think to follow here again." The water exploded in a massive water spout and the Flinkings collapsed.

So did Mathlin.

Nettie went down next to him and shoved the orb back

into his hands. He looked at it and gave a small smile. "I would have liked to go back in there, but I fear I don't have enough energy."

Ten Runners suddenly appeared on the beach and surrounded Nettie and Mathlin. "You need." They all spoke at once and touched Mathlin and the orb as Nettie scurried out of the way.

"Thank you, my friends, he is back in his shell." The voice started as Thiliantic and ended as Mathlin. The Runners vanished.

Caden came running through the shallow water where Homer's airship had gone down.

"Nettie!" He almost bowled her over as he ran to her. "Are you okay? Please say you're okay. And you don't have a tail, and look, no webbing." He grabbed her and kissed her with no concern for decorum or the people around them. There was little she could do but respond in kind.

"Did you hit your head when you crashed?" She finally asked when they broke apart. While she was extremely happy to see him, he seemed almost delirious.

"No," he said. Then rubbed his shoulder. "I might have a little. But you can never do that to me again."

"I will endeavor not to do so." She looked over at Mathlin. He slowly pulled back from the orb and his eyes were normal again.

"That was interesting. Thiliantic let me feel everything this time." He patted the orb gently. "He is thankful to the Runners and the Society for restoring him and asked to be put back where he belongs." He looked up to Reaves. "He said your mother would know where."

"She should be here with our fighting force in a few days. The Flinkings damaged the shoots so our travel will be limited for a while. My people and I will guard the orb until then." Using the fabric Nettie had carried it out in, Reaves scooped up the orb and he and his people left the beach.

Lisselle and the others started heading back, Rebecca lingering a bit until Lisselle shook her head. Rebecca ran back, kissed Nettie on the head, and then ran toward the others. "I'll see you at home soon enough!"

Caden got to his feet and helped Nettie to hers. She was still weak, but feeling stronger. Returning to land must agree with her. They were taking it slow walking back, holding hands, but not really saying much.

Nettie looked around sharply as Caden dropped to the ground. Had they missed one of the attackers?

"Caden! What happened?"

He looked up and shrugged as he stood back up. "I dropped something extremely important, something I've been carrying with me. I wanted to do this somewhere more romantic, but I'd like to get it done now." His eyes were earnest and a small secretive smile appeared and he dropped to one knee on the beach.

"Dr. Agent Nettie Jones, you are the smartest, fiercest, most exasperating woman I have ever met. And I will never be your equal. You make me a better man and challenge me every day. Will you spend all the rest of my days with me?" He held out what he'd dropped, a small black box. He flipped it open to reveal an engagement ring. "I love you and can't imagine a single day without you."

Nettie knew she was in love with him, and he'd indicated that he felt the same…but marriage? She looked into his eyes. Yup, she was lost for sure. "Even if I become a full vampire again? Or a mermaid? Or who knows what?"

"Anything at all. You'll still be you. Will you marry me?"

She looked into his eyes and smiled. "Of course, you obstinate man, I have to marry you; who else will keep you out of trouble?"

THE END

DEAR READER,

Thank you for joining in on the second adventure for Nettie, Caden, and their fellow members of the Society. I really hope you enjoyed it.

If you're also interested in a little bit of space opera, please check out the first book in The Asarlaí Wars trilogy-WARRIOR WENCH.

Magic, mayhem, and drunken faeries run loose in THE GLASS GARGOYLE, the first book in The Lost Ancients fantasy series.

I really appreciate each and every one of you so please keep in touch. You can find me at *www.marieandreas.com*.

And please feel free to email me directly at *Marie@marie-andreas.com* as well, I love to hear from readers!

If you enjoyed this book (or any book for that matter ;)) please spread the word! Positive reviews on Amazon, Goodreads, and blogs are like emotional gold to any writer and mean more than you know.

ABOUT THE AUTHOR

MARIE IS AN AWARD WINING fantasy and science fiction reader with a reading addiction. If she wasn't writing about all of the people in her head, she'd be lurking about coffee shops annoying innocent passer-by with her stories. So really, writing is a way of saving the masses. She lives in Southern California and is currently owned by two very faery-minded cats. And yes, sometimes they race.

When not saving the general populace from coffee shop shenanigans, Marie likes to visit the UK and keeps hoping someone will give her a nice summer home in the Forest of Dean.

More information can be found on her website *www.marieandreas.com*